Prais

# WHER
## THERE IS LIGHT

"Illuminating! *Wherever There Is Light* deftly shines light on the heartbreak of prejudice, the unbreakable ties of family and the enduring power of love. Peter Golden is uniquely qualified to write this sweeping and historically accurate novel."

—Mary Alice Monroe, *New York Times* bestselling author of
*The Summer Wind*

"Like the photographs captured by its heroine, *Wherever There Is Light* is a soul-stirring saga of dualities: joy and sorrow, darkness and a gleam of something bright, things in reach and things just beyond the frame. This impossible, yet inevitable, love story grasps your heart and doesn't let go."

—Julie Kibler, *New York Times*
bestselling author of *Calling Me Home*

"A uniquely American story of two unlikely lovers on disparate paths who struggle against mid-twentieth century racial and religious intolerance. Meticulously researched and beautifully written."

—Amy Hill Hearth, *New York Times* bestselling author of
*Miss Dreamsville and the Collier County Women's Literary Society*

"What color is love? These words break our heart as Julian and Kendall spend decades attempting to reach across chasms of bigotry. Weaving histories of race and slavery in America, the Holocaust in Germany, and Paris after World War II, we hope against all odds for an ending of which we can be proud. Peter Golden has given us a gift of a book."

—Randy Susan Meyers, author of *Accidents of Marriage*

ALSO BY PETER GOLDEN

*Comeback Love*

# WHEREVER
# THERE IS LIGHT

─────────── ✳ ───────────

*A Novel*

## PETER GOLDEN

WASHINGTON SQUARE PRESS

*New York    London    Toronto    Sydney    New Delhi*

WASHINGTON SQUARE PRESS
An Imprint of Simon & Schuster, Inc.
1230 Avenue of the Americas
New York, NY 10020

First Washington Square Press trade paperback edition October 2016

WASHINGTON SQUARE PRESS and colophon are trademarks of Simon & Schuster, Inc.

For information about special discounts for bulk purchases, please contact Simon & Schuster Special Sales at 1-866-506-1949 or business@simonandschuster.com.

The Simon & Schuster Speakers Bureau can bring authors to your live event. For more information, or to book an event, contact the Simon & Schuster Speakers Bureau at 1-866-248-3049 or visit our website at www.simonspeakers.com.

Interior design by Kyoko Watanabe

Manufactured in the United States of America

10 9 8 7 6 5 4 3 2 1

Library of Congress Cataloging-in-Publication Data

Golden, Peter.
  Wherever there is light : a novel / Peter Golden.
    pages; cm
  I. Title.
  PS3607.O4525W48 2015
  813'.6—dc23
                            2015011899

ISBN 978-1-4767-0558-3
ISBN 978-1-5011-0763-4 (pbk)
ISBN 978-1-4767-0561-3 (ebook)

*One more time for Annis and Ben,*

*and*

*For my sister, Frann*

*Wherever there is light, one can photograph.*

ALFRED STIEGLITZ

# PART I

# Chapter 1

Julian Rose was about to have his life upended again, but he didn't know it, not as he hurried through South Orange Village. The Christmas lights strung above the sidewalks and in the store windows transformed the snowflakes into sparks of red, green, yellow, and blue and emblazoned the crowds of shoppers with a pastel glow, which gave Julian the impression, as he walked toward Gruning's Ice Cream Parlor, that the magic of the season had dropped him inside a painting.

Julian rarely missed an afternoon at Gruning's after visiting the cemetery. He ordered a scoop of coffee chip with hot fudge and whipped cream. The bill always came to under two dollars, but he left a five-spot for a tip. Understandably, some waitresses hoped that he would take a different table instead of the one in back facing the doors. He never did. That was because Gruning's was located between Columbia High School and South Orange Junior High, and by three thirty it was loaded with teenagers. Julian loved watching them burst through the doors in bright, noisy packs and imagining that his daughter, Holly, was among them. The kids would walk toward him, then turn up the stairs to a side room, and the blend of their voices, laughter, and the rock and roll they played on the jukebox soothed Julian in a way he found difficult to explain and impossible to give up. All he knew was that while Holly had been deprived of her future, these children would one day start families of their own, and that reality was enough to temper, for a blessed moment, his heartache.

When Julian finished his ice cream, he walked up front and stood in line at the register, which was behind the glass cases of homemade candies. A Negro woman with a maroon kerchief over her head and clutching a black pocketbook to her chest was talking to the cashier. Beside her was a slender brown stalk of a boy holding a battered valise. The Negro woman was speaking too softly for Julian to hear her, but he could hear the older couple ahead of him, a bald man in a Chesterfield topcoat and his blue-haired wife in a mink stole—three dead animals attached head to tail.

The man said, "Darling, do we really need to wait for chocolate cherries?"

"Yes," she replied, turning and nodding back toward the Negro woman and the boy. "Don't blame me. I didn't know the candy stores closed in Newark."

The most generous interpretation of her comment, Julian thought, was that she disliked waiting behind colored people. He wished the minks would spring to life and bite her. Since that was unlikely, he glared at the woman. In his younger days, Julian had been a regular at the Stork Club and other stops on Manhattan's party circuit, and pictures of him, tall, broad-shouldered with dark, wavy hair alongside actresses and high-society girls in pursuit of pleasures unavailable at cotillions, filled the tabloids. More than one gossip columnist had noted that Julian had the rugged good looks and easy grace of a movie star, complete with a strong jawline and cleft chin. But clichés didn't do justice to his presence or explain why people in general and women in particular frequently stared at him when he entered a room. His face seldom registered emotion, and it was his stillness, combined with his steady, blue-eyed gaze, that made him so magnetic and gave him a vaguely menacing air.

The woman didn't seem taken with, or intimidated by, Julian. She glared back at him, obviously believing that she had nothing to fear from this overage Ivy Leaguer in a muddy-patterned tweed sport coat, a hideous pink shirt, and a silly tie dotted with red-and-white dice—the last gift his daughter had given him.

Swiveling around to see the object of his wife's disdain, the bald man had a different reaction. Perhaps it was because someone had once pointed out Julian to him or because he remembered his picture from the newspapers and the stories he'd read about the prince of bootlegger royalty in Newark, the late Longy Zwillman's boy wonder, who unlike Longy had dodged every government investigation and parlayed the lucre that sprouted in those illegal bottles of spirits into a real-estate empire.

"Let's go," the man said to his wife and pulled her toward the doors, the wife walking backward, keeping her angry eyes on Julian.

He ignored her and paid the cashier. The Negro woman and boy were gone, and he didn't see them out on South Orange Avenue, where gas lamps shone in the snow-flecked light. Julian considered walking up a block to his broker's office and saying hello to his money, but that bored him. Better to go home and read the *Newark Evening News* and watch a little TV.

"'Scuse me, suh," a woman said, and Julian looked down and saw the Negro woman shivering next to him in her raincoat. The hair visible under her kerchief was white and her face was as furrowed as a walnut shell. "You Mr. Julian Rose?"

Julian nodded, and the woman said, "I'm Lucinda Watkins. Friend of Kenni-Ann Wakefield. Y'all know Kenni-Ann?"

It was a shock hearing her name. "Kendall, yes. How is she?"

"Sorry to say, suh. She dead."

The wind was blowing the snow against his face, but Julian couldn't feel the cold. He heard himself say, "Dead?"

"Yes, suh. And she make me promise to come find you if somethin' happen. I get change to call yoah house and the cleanin' girl say y'all most likely be heah. A waitress tell me you jist left."

"Where's the boy?"

"He gettin' a ice-cream cone."

"Is he Kendall's son?"

"Yes, suh. Bobby be Kenni-Ann's son and . . ."

"And?" Julian asked.

"And he be yoah son too."

# Chapter 2

Julian lived on a wooded, four-acre lot in Newstead, a tony enclave high above the village, in a long, flat, granite and glass house—the brainchild of an architect from Harvard, who, as his scores of critics had charged, harbored a desire to design spaceships. In fact, when Bobby Wakefield entered the great room with its dark red cement floor and gawked at the hanging bubble lamps and soaring, concrete fireplace, he asked, "Do the Jetsons live here?"

Lucinda said, "Bobby, don't go sassin' nobody."

"Yes, ma'am," he said with a faintly embarrassed smile that made his face the image of Kendall's, and Julian felt such an ache in his chest that he had to turn away.

Lucinda said, "Mr. Rose, I'd like to be catchin' a bus back down to home."

"You're welcome to stay. I could buy you a plane ticket tomorrow."

"No, suh. If'n the Lord meant me to fly, He'd a blessed me with tail feathers."

All Julian had uncovered on the ride from the village was that Lucinda and Bobby had taken a Greyhound from Miami to New York, then had ridden two other buses to South Orange. Julian was anxious to talk to Lucinda, but not in front of Bobby. He took the boy's valise, and they went up a flight of bleached-oak steps to the guest suite.

"How'd you know my mother?" Bobby asked.

"My father taught at Lovewood College."

"He's not there now."

"He passed away."

"Your mother too?"

"Her too." He studied the boy, who resembled his mother with his light-brown complexion, the flawless symmetry of his features, and hazel eyes. "We'll get acquainted later. Make yourself at home while I talk to Miss Watkins."

Lucinda stood with the strap of her pocketbook looped over one arm and her coat folded over the other. "Got me a nine-o'clock bus from New York."

Julian said he'd get her there and persuaded Lucinda to have a cup of tea. He sat across from her on the bench in the breakfast nook.

"Kenni-Ann's heart done quit," she said, stirring her fourth spoonful of sugar in her cup. "Doc Franklin say it was a bad valve. Born with it. I used to look after Bobby, and Kenni-Ann be goin' on 'bout you while we's waitin' on the ambulance. She told me where to find your address and the money to come and said you'd do right by Bobby."

"I will."

Lucinda glowered at him, her eyes hard and black as coal. Julian couldn't blame her for not trusting him. History has a habit of telling everyone's fortune.

※

At the Chicken Nest in South Orange Village, Julian bought Lucinda sliced barbecued chicken on poppy-seed rolls, a quart of potato salad, an apple pie, and a six-pack of ginger ale. They argued about whether she'd accept the food as Julian drove through the Lincoln Tunnel. Bobby sat in the back seat of the Thunderbird without speaking until Julian reached Port Authority. Lucinda turned, instructing Bobby to do like he'd been told, and Bobby put his arms around her neck and said, "I promise."

Julian hopped out of the car and held out the shopping bag to Lucinda.

"Not use to a white man worryin' if'n I got what to eat." She opened her pocketbook, withdrew a manila envelope, and handed it to Julian. "A rich man like you oughtta be smart enough to know he ain't got to go believin' ever-thing he read."

After Lucinda took the bag and disappeared inside the station, Julian got into the Thunderbird and wedged the envelope under the sun visor.

"Come up front," he said to Bobby.

The boy climbed into the bucket seat.

"You hungry?" Julian asked, inching in front of a city bus.

"No, sir."

Julian was wondering why Lucinda had warned him about the contents of the envelope when Bobby said, "My father died in the war."

"I'm sorry."

"Were you in the war?"

"World War Two, yes."

"Not that war," Bobby said. "Mom told me my father was at Pork Chop Hill."

"That was a battle in Korea."

"I know. I saw the movie with my mom."

Bobby rested his head on the back of the seat, saying nothing, and by the time Julian pulled into his garage, Bobby was asleep. His daughter, Holly, had been gone for over a year, and Julian had forgotten the joyousness of carrying a sleeping child, their weight and warmth filling you with wonder at your power to protect and to love. Julian sat Bobby on the bed, helped him off with his shoes and clothes, tucked him under the quilt, and kissed his cheek.

"Are we home?" Bobby murmured.

"We're home."

※

In the great room, Julian sat on the built-in couch and sifted through the papers: report cards, mostly straight As, from schools in Paris and, part of the last two years, in Lovewood; a list on notepaper, in Kendall's precise handwriting, of Bobby's childhood diseases and vaccinations with corresponding dates; his passport, the pages with stamps from every country in Western Europe except East Germany; and a signed letter, notarized a month ago at a bank in Fort Lauderdale, naming Julian as Bobby's legal guardian in the event of her incapacitation or death.

But it was Bobby's birth certificate, issued by the New York State Department of Health, that set off Julian's anger, both old and new, at Kendall. Bobby had been born on November 14, 1953, a date approximately nine months after Julian's last encounter with Kendall. A Dr. Claude Balt had signed the document, certifying that he'd delivered Bobby at Harlem Hospital. That was less than thirty miles from where Julian was living, and he was dumbfounded that Kendall hadn't called him until he'd read the name in the box reserved for Father: Otis M. Larkin.

Lucinda's warning had to be about the birth certificate. She probably thought Julian wouldn't take Bobby in if his paternity was in doubt. Kendall knew better. She knew that Julian loved her and that he, having arrived in America from Germany at the age of fifteen broke and alone, would never refuse to care for her child—regardless of whether he was the father. Did Kendall know about Holly? Julian didn't see how that was possible, but he couldn't think about it anymore because he was crying quietly and his throat was as dry as sand.

# PART II

# Chapter 3

On Sunday morning, thirty men from the Third Ward Gang were eating in the Weequahic Diner and giving the waitress with the big hair a workout, sending her to refill the baskets of Danish so often she said, "I'm not standing on a conveyor belt here." The men broke up like she was Groucho cracking wise, and the waitress joined in because their collective tip would pay her rent and because, despite their kibitzing, these fellas were the salt of the earth, even if some of them had nicknames out of a vaudeville act.

For example, the Goldstein twins. Everybody began calling them Looney and Gooney during Prohibition, when the twins, whose faces brought to mind a matched set of demented owls, specialized in uncovering where shipments of competitors' liquor were going so their colleagues could hijack the trucks. The Goldstein method was to douse a member of a rival gang with gasoline and flick lit matches in his direction until he gave up the routes. Looney was not as gifted with the matches as Gooney, so on occasion they had a bonfire.

Abner Zwillman, leader of the Third Ward boys, owned the most famous nickname—due to the press and a potpourri of US attorneys, FBI agents, and IRS examiners—and he strode into the Weequahic as dapper as a Latin bandleader. He was known as Longy, in Yiddish, *der Langer*, the Long One—a nom de guerre that went back to when fourteen-year-old Abe, already over six feet tall, and his friends used to protect Jewish peddlers from the hooligans who harassed them.

Longy sat at the table behind his men, where Julian Rose was reading the play *Strange Interlude*.

Longy said, "That O'Neill's depressing."

Julian put down the book. "I think that's his point."

"His point's you should leave the theater and go hang yourself?"

"Saves money on dinner."

"Funny," Longy said, except he wasn't smiling. He and Julian were at odds about the diverging paths of their careers. Longy was thirty-four, nine years older than Julian, but he was the closest thing Julian had to a real father. Less than a week off the boat, Julian had gone to the Riviera Hotel to see Longy, who had made millions in liquor and had most of New Jersey in his pocket. First thing Longy said to him: "You're taller than me," and then he put his arm around Julian and added that his friends called him Abe. He gave Julian a job on his trucks, protecting his bottles of liquid capital, and Abe came to respect the kid: give Julian the business, he'd put your lights out before you could blink, and he had a brain like an adding machine. Julian was also the only one who could control Looney and Gooney, and he was smoother than mouse hair when it came to paying off any guy Abe needed on his side.

When Prohibition ended, Julian was halfway rich and wanted to repay Abe, pressing him to be his partner buying the woods and farmland that ringed Newark with an eye toward residential and commercial development. Abe kept saying no, and Julian kept trying. Now he said, "Saw a swell piece of property in Verona."

"C'mon, Newark's what Jews got instead of the Promised Land."

Abe was kidding himself. He had nothing against real estate but preferred nurturing his gambling action, cutting sweetheart deals with union bosses and politicians, and strong-arming the proprietors of any place you could stick one of his jukeboxes and cigarette machines. Why? Because Abe believed being a gangster was his edge when he was hobnobbing with the moneyed cream of the American crop. To them, Abe Zwillman was a kike from the tenements of Newark. Longy, however—Longy was a man they could respect, or fear, and Julian thought that all this game would get Abe was a trip up the river, and Julian wanted to save Abe, the man who had saved him, from dying in jail.

Longy said, "You'll deal with those Nazi jerks in Irvington?"

Irvington was a shot-and-a-beer town just south of Newark with few Jews and lots of Germans who attended the rallies of the Hitler-worshipping Deutsch-Amerikanischer Volksbund. Julian had retired from the intimidation racket, but Nazis were a special case.

"I'll handle it. Eddie O dropped me off and went to hand out some Christmas money to the Irvington cops so they'll go slow when the calls come in."

"Don't let Looney and Gooney croak nobody. I can live without the headlines."

※

Eddie O'Rourke was outside, leaning against his white Chrysler Imperial. "Top of the morning, boys," he said as Julian and the Third Ward Gang filed out of the diner.

Any strangers passing by would conclude that they were beholding a good-natured, freckled-faced fellow in a snazzy tweed coat and cap with some merry Galway music in his voice. They would be partially correct. At other moments, when someone was paying him to collect from recalcitrant debtors or when he was in a less benevolent mood, Eddie O could be unruly enough to make the Goldstein twins appear well-adjusted.

"You're goin' with us?" Looney said. "Since when're you a Jew?"

"Since your sister chewed off my foreskin."

Most of the flesh bulging Looney's plaid sports jacket was muscle. He said, "Say somethin' else about sisters, I'll knock your teeth out."

Gooney said, "We ain't got no sisters," but Looney was not deterred by this technicality, and as he moved toward Eddie, Julian smacked him on top of his head with his book.

"What'd ya do that for?" Looney asked Julian, his feelings more bruised than his scalp.

Eddie replied, "To hear if your head was really hollow."

Looney said, "You wasn't his best pal, guess how long you already woulda been dead."

"Time to go," Julian said, and climbed into the passenger seat of Eddie's Chrysler.

✳

"What's eating ya?" Eddie asked as Julian stared glumly out at the statelier homes of the Weequahic section, where Jews who'd cut themselves a slice of America the Beautiful had relocated from the Third Ward.

"My folks just arrived from Berlin. My father got a job teaching at a college in Lovewood, Florida. I'm going down tomorrow."

"That's good, no? With what's going on in that hellhole?"

Eddie was referring to the mobs rampaging through Berlin, smashing the windows of Jewish shops, setting fires, and beating Jews in the streets. Julian had seen the pictures in the papers—the glass shining on the sidewalks like rime and smoke spiraling up from the cupolas of the Fasanenstrasse Synagogue, built by prosperous Jewish Berliners like Julian's father, the esteemed Herr Professor Theodor Rose, who had proclaimed their Germanic pride by erecting a temple indistinguishable from a Teutonic castle. The mobs had swept across Germany, Austria, and Czechoslovakia, and the rioting already had a name: *Kristallnacht*, the Night of Broken Glass.

"I been trying to get them out for a year," Julian said. "My father claimed he was too busy writing his history of the Enlightenment. *Building a Better Tomorrow*, he's calling it. His argument that science and reason will save us from ourselves."

Eddie laughed. "Don't he read the papers?"

Julian kept looking out the window. Then: "I used to skip school to hang around the nightclubs. It pissed off my father."

"That makes sense," Eddie said.

"I loved those joints. It was like going to the circus."

✳

The German-American Bund held so many rallies at the picnic area on Montgomery Avenue that the locals dubbed it Hitler Park. It was surrounded by a flimsy wooden fence, a challenge that Gooney addressed by throwing his beat-up DeSoto in reverse and smashing through a section of fencing. Eighty or ninety Bundists in storm trooper regalia dashed toward the splintered wood, but over half of them fled when they saw who had invited themselves to their party. Julian and Eddie stood under the bare trees as Longy's men, armed with Louisville Sluggers, began flattening the Bundists who lacked the judgment to flee. Eddie was bored, and Julian was preoccupied thinking about his parents and recalling the day he'd left home—October 9, 1928.

He was holding a suitcase and standing on the stairway of the Roses' four-story stone mansion on Mauerstrasse, his right cheek stinging from his father's slap. His father was up on the landing, screaming at him, and his mother was at the bottom of the stairs, sobbing. Julian had to catch a train to Hamburg and a ship to New York, where he'd been born, toward the end of Theodor's lecture tour, exactly fifteen years before. His mother had paid for the tickets, believing that if Julian stayed in Berlin, the fights with his father would've escalated until one of them murdered the other. Elana Rose had always seemed so fragile to her son, as if she had never recovered from being abandoned on the doorstep of the Hebrew Orphan Asylum in Newark, and Julian hugged her. "I love you, Mama." His mother didn't stop crying, and his father was still screaming that Julian was a lazy bum when he went out the door. Julian didn't return to Berlin until 1935, after the Nazis had dismissed Jewish professors from their posts. To survive, Theodor had sold the house to a gentile colleague from the university, who allowed the Roses to reside on the top floor, though he charged them *Jüdische Miete*—Jewish rent—triple the going rate for Aryans, and made them use the side entrance. Theodor scowled when he saw his son's sleek, double-breasted gabardine, but Julian hadn't come to patch up things with his father. He was there to arrange for Elana to receive a monthly stipend via a Swiss bank in Lucerne. His mother handled the bills, and they both knew that Theodor wouldn't have accepted the assistance even if he and his wife had starved.

"Hey, numbskull!" Eddie shouted. "The SOB can't breathe!"

Looney, having dropped his baseball bat, had a Bundist on the ground, and he was strangling him. Julian went over and tapped Looney on the shoulder. "You gotta let him go."

"Can't I kill him a little?"

"Nope."

Looney stalked off. Gasping for air, the Bundist stood. He had a dopey horse face, and his expression was so laced with fear that Julian felt sorry for him. The wailing of police sirens was growing louder, and Julian turned to walk back to Eddie, whose hands were cupped around his mouth, and as Julian heard Eddie shout, "Behind you!" a baseball bat slammed into his back. Julian lurched forward, fighting against the pain shooting up his spine to remain on his feet and annoyed that his new black fedora was on the ground. He turned as the Bundist cocked the bat. Before he could swing again, Julian kicked the man's knee as if it were a football. The Bundist screamed in agony and fell.

Inside Julian there was a place where he stored a combustible brew of the hurt and fury of his childhood and his feeling that he would be alone for the rest of his life. Julian only saw this place clearly in his nightmares. In the daylight, he avoided descending there by ignoring any provocation and using his head. He couldn't do that now. Perhaps it was recalling his leaving home or his hatred of the Bund, but Julian lost control of himself and kicked the Bundist in the face. A geyser of blood spurted from his nose, and Julian was about to kick him again when Eddie and a police sergeant grabbed him.

The cop said, "O'Rourke, you didn't pay for this shit. The captain'll have me writing reports till Saint Paddy's. You and your Jew buddies get outta here before I lock all of you up."

※

As usual, after he erupted, Julian was overcome by revulsion. He was silent until Eddie drove into the serene reaches of South Orange, where Julian saw families in their Sunday best walking home from Mass at Our Lady of Sorrows and noticed two boys in cowboy hats and fringed buckskin jackets running through the brown-and-gold leaves at the curb.

Eddie said, "So where's this Lovewood?"

"Broward County. Where Abe and the others got those swanky gambling joints."

"Maybe you wanna bring me with you to Florida?"

"Why? You don't gamble, you collect."

"Suppose you start beating on a guy, who's gonna stop ya? I hear the cops ain't too palsy-walsy down there. They'll put you on a chain gang."

The stores in South Orange Village were closed. Julian resided on the top floor of an apartment house he owned at the edge of the village, and he didn't reply until Eddie pulled up to the awning of his building. "Thanks," he said.

# Chapter 4

Garland Kendall Wakefield, a petite Negro woman in her late forties and the president of Lovewood College, didn't hate white people. Yet ever since Halloween, when Orson Welles had narrated an adaption of the novel *The War of the Worlds* on the radio and frightened millions by announcing that Martians had invaded New Jersey, Garland asked herself: if aliens *had* herded every white person into their rocket ships and blasted off into outer space, would she miss them?

No, not a single one.

Now, with guests coming for dinner, Garland finished hot-combing her salt-and-pepper hair into a bob and went downstairs in what amounted to her uniform—a high-necked, ecru silk blouse, an ankle-length, black chiffon skirt, and black laced shoes with low heels. She went into the kitchen, and Derrick Larkin, the young man she hoped her daughter Kendall would have the sense to marry, was standing there in a three-piece suit and tie and holding a noose in his hand.

Garland said, "Jarvis Scales left me another present?"

"I saw it driving in. Tied to the front gate. I wouldn't say it's Mayor Scales."

"Then it was Hurleigh, his brother. Same thing."

"Jarvis doesn't—"

"Doesn't what?" Garland said. "Jarvis doesn't want to buy back his family's land? Jarvis doesn't have the same name as his grandfather who sold my grandmother and broke my father's heart when he was nothing but a child?"

Garland's father, Ezekiel Kendall, had been born a slave in Love-wood. The night after his mother was sold to a plantation in South Carolina, Ezekiel ran off to join her. He never did find her, but he stumbled on a spur of the Underground Railroad that led him north to Philadelphia, where he made a fortune as a caterer to the gilded Main Line. Despite his wealth, Ezekiel regarded a college diploma as the sole guarantee against a life fetching and carrying for white folks, and after Garland became the first Negro to earn a degree from the University of Pennsylvania's School of Education, Ezekiel enlisted her help with founding a liberal arts Negro college on the land where he'd been born. In 1926 a hurricane flattened the region, spreading foreclo-sures like the flu, and Ezekiel purchased just over two thousand acres for pennies on the dollar. It was Jarvis's father who had lost the land, and now Jarvis was intent on buying it back.

"Have you considered a compromise?" Derrick asked, putting the noose on the counter. "The school occupies a hundred acres, and there's another five hundred for fruit groves and crops, and the cows, pigs, and chickens. You could sell Jarvis some acreage, earn a profit, and everyone would be happy."

"Happy? I own three miles of beachfront and the law says Negroes can't step on the sand. And Jarvis won't settle for 'some acreage.' He knows hundreds of new hotels have gone up in Miami Beach. Maybe Jarvis wants to build hotels. Or sell to someone who does. Three hun-dred and eighty-seven students are graduating this year, and half of them couldn't have afforded a degree without us. That was my father's dream. And his dream's not ending in my lifetime."

"Mrs. Wakefield, I didn't mean to offend you. I have to fetch Kenni-Ann and my brother now, but if I can help—"

"Maybe one day, if you keep on with Kendall, I'll have a lawyer in the family, and we'll figure this all out."

When Derrick was gone, Garland dumped the noose in the white enamel garbage bin and said out loud, "Jarvis Scales, you can go shit fire and save a penny on matches."

✳

Thirty-three hours after boarding a train at Penn Station in Newark, Julian and Eddie arrived at Lovewood College. At the Wakefield house, a pinkish-tan stucco palace on a hill overlooking the campus to the south and the ocean to the north, a Negro butler opened a wooden door inlaid with brass medallions of laurel wreaths.

"Gentlemen," he said, "come in and drop your bags."

They had brought a gift—two bottles of Jameson's Irish whiskey and two of Old Grand-Dad bourbon—to thank Mrs. Wakefield for the invitation to dine and to stay at the school's guest cottage. Julian gave the box to the butler, who said, "The ice and glasses are in the parlor."

They went down the front hall, past a large oil painting of a spiky-limbed tree with pink-and-gold blossoms on a plateau above the ocean with waves crashing against the cliffs. The parlor was a brightly lit room with a terra-cotta floor, a wall of windows facing the water, and a beamed ceiling with a whirling fan. A lump rose in Julian's throat when he saw his parents, and he greeted his father first because his mother, with tears steaming down her cheeks, would require more effort to control his emotions.

Julian usually spoke German to his father, though Theodor, who had attended boarding school in Britain and studied at Oxford before completing his doctorate at Freiburg, spoke perfect English. *"Hallo, Vater, Sie gut aussehen,"* Julian said, and it was true—Theodor did look well. He was twenty-one years older than his wife, had met her on a lecture tour in 1912 after speaking at Krueger Auditorium in Newark, and took the shy teenager, with the long blond hair, eyes the color of turquoise, and a heart-shaped face of finely sculpted features, to a Romanian restaurant, where she tasted her first piece of steak; three weeks later they were married an hour before Theodor spoke at a synagogue in Charleston, South Carolina. To Julian, his father still resembled the photographs of the illustrious philosopher who had enthralled audiences with his rich baritone and his prediction that the Zionists would fail to establish a homeland because enlightened nations like America, Germany, and France would remain safe harbors for Jews. Theodor's profile was still noble enough to stamp on a coin; his silver mane of hair had not thinned, nor had his beard gone completely white; and he stood as straight as a sentry in his dark chalk-stripe with the gold watch chain strung across his vest.

Gripping Julian's hand firmly, Theodor said, "*Guten Abend, mein Sohn.*"

That was it—after three years, but Julian supposed that *Good evening, my son*, was an improvement over being slapped across the face and called a lazy bum.

Julian turned to his mother in her moss-green cotton frock and enfolded her in his arms. The only sounds in the parlor were Elana's muffled sobs and Julian repeating, "Don't cry, Mama," and no one watching them would have suspected they were witnessing anything other than an adoring mother reunited with her loving son. Yet the truth was that Julian's relationship with Elana had been more painful to him than the blowups with Theodor. Julian recalled his mother as a hovering angel who was always bleeding from invisible wounds that Julian believed were his responsibility to heal. After supper, while Theodor wrote in his study, Julian would keep her company, drying the dishes, listening to her wonder aloud what deformities of her soul had led her parents to abandon her to the lonely mists of an orphanage. Night after night, Julian waited for her desolation to recede. It never did: even her describing the joys of assisting the doctor who came to take care of the children echoed in his memory like a doleful nocturne. Now, as he let go of his mother, Julian recalled how desperate he'd been to boost her spirits, and how helplessness and guilt had crushed him when he failed.

"This is my friend Eddie," Julian said.

"I'm happy my son has a friend who would travel with him to Florida," Elana said. Theodor grunted a hello and eyed Eddie like a beat cop about to roust a wino from the gutter, but he did introduce them to Garland Wakefield, who was kind enough to point out the side table across the parlor that doubled as a bar.

Eddie was drinking an Irish straight up, and Julian a bourbon on the rocks, when a young woman entered from the front hallway with two men trailing her like courtiers.

"Jesus H. Rockefeller," Eddie mumbled.

In her milk-white dress, the woman was as radiant as a bride among mourners. Her thick, sable hair was brushed back well past her shoulders, and Julian assumed, incorrectly, that she'd studied dance. His assumption was based on her white ballet slippers and her posture, which appeared as rigid and supple as a sapling as she glided over to greet Theodor and Elana. Julian admired the white linen clinging to her curves as she came toward him with Garland and her two-man entourage, but it was her face that transfixed him: the luminous hazel eyes and high cheekbones, the bowed lips above a perfect chin, all of it adding up to a tawny, exotic beauty that he'd only thought possible in a fairy tale.

Garland said, "These are the Larkin brothers, Derrick and Otis," and as the four men shook hands, she added, "and this is my daughter, Kendall."

"Nice to meet y'all," she said.

Julian could never adequately explain to anyone the effect of her voice on him. He'd expected Kendall to sound youthful and dainty, but her voice, despite its faint southern melody, was as cool and piquant as the ocean breeze coming through the parlor windows—a wise voice that somehow, with a perfunctory greeting, communicated to Julian that she was charmed by his interest. Julian was no expert at this game. His most enduring romance had lasted five months.

"You cats get lost on the way to the Cotton Club?" Otis asked as Julian watched Kendall go into the dining room with Derrick. Otis, the shorter Larkin brother, with glistening processed hair and an elfin face, was decked out for the boards at the Savoy Ballroom: a long, black sport coat with a purple-checked pattern that would give an acrobat vertigo; wide-legged, mushroom-colored pants pegged at the ankles; and gleaming two-tone shoes.

"Where you from, jitterbug?" Eddie said.

Aiming what had to be the cockiest grin on either side of the Mason-Dixon Line at Eddie, Otis announced, "Edgecombe Avenue, Harlem, USA."

"Sugar Hill. Julian and me used to go hear Cab Calloway play an after-hours joint up there—but we're from Jersey."

"Close enough. I been cracking books here since September, and away-down south in Dixie ain't nowhere for a rug-cutter from the shiny Apple, you dig?"

Eddie pointed at the fifths of Jameson's and Old Grand-Dad, and Otis said, "You swing, my man! Can I get a taste of that Irish, rocks?"

As Eddie fixed Otis a drink, Julian saw Derrick pull back a chair for Kendall at the table. Derrick was so handsome that if he'd been white, some Madison Avenue sharpie would've stuck him in an Arrow shirt-collar ad. Yet Julian wasn't without hope. You couldn't miss the intelligence in Derrick's face, but it was a face without guile, the face of an orderly man who Julian hoped would be a little too square for Kendall.

Otis said to Julian, "My big bro thinks he's in the clover 'cause he picked himself the high-yellow blossom of Lovewood. But any boy tangle with Kenni-Ann, he gonna wind up feeling like a one-legged man in an ass-kickin' contest."

"They getting hitched?"

"Who knows? Kenni-Ann's a senior, and Derrick copped his sheep-skin last June. He's down from DC to visit. He's at Howard Law. Gonna practice with our daddy's firm."

In the dining room, Derrick was seated across from Theodor. The two men were engaged in an animated discussion, while Kendall's attention wandered until she noticed Julian staring at her. She smiled at him, her expression an enticing blend of curiosity and defiance, but before Julian could respond with a smile of his own, Kendall turned toward Derrick and his father.

※

The seating arrangements were a problem. Garland was at one end of the table and to her left were Julian, Elana, and Theodor; to her right were Kendall, Derrick, Otis, and Eddie. Hence, Julian was across from Kendall and had to force himself not to stare at her. In addition, during the salad course, he had to look right at Derrick and listen to him and

Theodor dissect Hegel. After ten minutes of Hegelian wisdom on the order of "All the rational is real and all the real is rational," Julian excused himself and retrieved a bottle of Old Grand-Dad.

After gulping three fingers of bourbon, Julian was feeling better, but then the butler, bearing a platter of baked chicken, stopped by his chair, and Elana piped up in the most maternal of voices, "My son likes the thighs."

Kendall smiled at his being treated like a five-year-old, and Julian felt embarrassed as the chicken was placed on his plate. Then Elana said to her son, "Doesn't this look delicious?" and dipped a serving spoon into a bowl of string beans and heaped the vegetables beside his chicken. Staring at his food, Julian thought that his on-again off-again pal, gossipmonger Walter Winchell, would have a field day with this one, declaring in his nasal rat-a-tat-tat: *Let's go to press . . . Word has reached me that the big Jersey Rose, man-about-town and ex-giggle-water salesman, is his mommy's baby boy.*

Julian dedicated his energies to emptying the fifth of Old Grand-Dad. He overheard Otis tell Eddie that he was going to take him over to the piano in the music building and show him how "One O'clock Jump" should be played, but Derrick was doing most of the talking. His topic was the national letter-writing campaign that he and other Howard Law students had organized to once again try to convince President Roosevelt to support federal antilynching legislation.

Addressing Elana and Theodor, Derrick explained, "Down South, whites who lynch Negroes aren't prosecuted, and Florida has the most lynchings in America. In Fort Lauderdale, when I was a sophomore here, a Negro man was arrested for asking a white lady for food and—"

"That poor man had a name," Garland cut in, her shoulders back, head high, as if her chair were a throne. "He didn't have a penny in his pocket, but he had a name."

"Yes, ma'am," Derrick answered. "His name was Reuben Stacey. Reuben was arrested and while the deputies were taking him to jail, a white mob took Reuben and lynched him. The police knew the murderers, but nothing was done."

Kendall said, "I'll never forget the photo of Reuben in the papers. It was horrible."

"Yes," Derrick said, touching Kendall's hand. "When I saw that picture, I promised myself that one day I'd try to help and do something."

"You could wait for people to die and better people to be born," Julian said.

"Pardon," Derrick replied, a keen edge to his tone.

Julian glared through a russet haze of bourbon. "Pardon what?"

Derrick had been the captain of Lovewood College's debate team, and he mistook Julian's gelid blue stare for an intellectual challenge. Otis, the hepcat, was more familiar than his older brother with men of Julian's ilk, and he called out, "Be cool, big bro."

Derrick cast a withering glance at Otis, and Garland, who had been studying Julian, stated with an imperiousness that did not invite dissent, "Let's have dessert."

Julian was washing down a bite of key lime pie with Old Grand-Dad when Kendall said, "Mother, we have to talk about the life drawing class."

"We talked about it, and my answer is the same—no."

"Drawing nudes is integral to art. Ask Professor Rose."

Everyone, except Julian, shifted their attention to Theodor. "You are correct, Miss Wakefield—it is an aesthetic tradition with a lengthy history—but I'm a philosophy professor, and your mother is president of the college."

Utterly controlled, Kendall told her mother, "If you don't want to pay someone to pose nude for our class, I'll do it myself."

Julian, numb enough from drinking that a dentist could've extracted his molars without him knowing it, asked, "Can anyone sign up for that class?"

Then he laughed and heard Eddie and Otis join in. Derrick wasn't amused, and Garland was still speechless from Kendall's declaration—let alone Julian's question—and her outrage was apparent in the stern knit of her brow.

Elana, upset that her son had offended Garland, said to Kendall,

"Tomorrow why don't you, Derrick, and Otis take Julian and Eddie for a tour of the campus."

Kendall let her eyes linger on Julian, and Garland glared at her daughter as if to say, *I don't give a damn if that white boy could pass for Cary Grant, don't you dare look at him like that!*

Kendall, glancing at her mother, replied, "What a terrific idea."

# Chapter 5

You did notice Kendall's a colored gal?" Eddie said, stretched out on one of the single beds in the guest cottage.

"I got drunk, not stupid," Julian replied, lying on the other bed. "But you figure the jerks who hate Negroes like Jews any better? Or Catholics? I don't give a shit what color anybody is."

"A lotta people do. I bet her ma does. And you might wanna talk to Kendall about it."

"I have to ask her out first."

"Where you gonna take her? They won't let you in together down here."

"To the Tavern," Julian said, referring to the finest restaurant in Newark, where the owner was a personal friend.

"Shrewd. That's fifteen hundred miles from here. Give you a chance to talk."

"I'm tired of being alone. You've got Fiona. Would Fiona like Kendall?" Fiona was a knockout off the boat from Dublin and employed as a barmaid at McGovern's on the night Eddie met her. The two of them were real lovebirds when they weren't threatening to kill each other.

Eddie chuckled. "Fiona likes everybody but me."

Julian drifted off thinking about Kendall, only to be awakened when Kendall knocked on the screen door, calling, "Ready for your tour?"

"In a minute." Julian changed into a polo shirt, linen pants, and tennis shoes, then scurried into the bathroom to take a leak and spread Pepsodent on his teeth.

"Have you seen Eddie?" he said, going outside.

"He and Derrick are listening to Otis play the piano. We're meeting them at the music building."

Kendall was wearing a white beret, a navy-and-white Breton-striped top, and dungarees rolled up past her sleek calves.

"You're staring," she said, smiling.

Julian followed Kendall across a blacktopped road to the campus. "I wasn't. I was just wondering when you became a French sailor."

Kendall laughed, the faintest note of melancholy underneath the joy. That same melancholy backlit her face, one of the reasons Julian couldn't stop looking at her: she seemed to reflect his own melancholy, which made him feel less alone.

She said, "What gave me away? The beret or the shirt?"

"The shirt. I had one as a kid. The year my father lectured at the Sorbonne."

"How wonderful. A year in Paris."

Wonderful wasn't how Julian would describe it. He was tutored in their apartment and learned how to speak French while his mother learned how to spend sixteen hours a day in bed with the assistance of an inexpensive Bordeaux.

Kendall said, "I'm an art major, but my minor is French. I want to live in Paris." Julian was less than overjoyed by that information but perked up when she added, "First I'm going to New York. To study at the Art Students League."

"That was your painting in the front hall?"

"Yes, it's the mythical lovewood tree. From an Indian legend about a woman trying to return to her true love and how he waits for her under the tree forever."

"I thought it was really something."

"It was really derivative. I was taking a course in Monet."

Past the chapel, with its white bell tower and steeple, was a bronze statue of a bearded Negro man in tails and top hat who stood on an inscribed granite pedestal:

### EZEKIEL KENDALL
### 1847–1934
### "AIM FOR THE HIGHEST"

"My grandfather," Kendall said. "My mother and I lived with him in Philadelphia."

"Your dad?"

"He died when I was a baby." Kendall's tone had a matter-of-fact quality that was misleading. According to her mother, Robert Wakefield was a light-skinned Georgia boy with soft curly hair and chips of jade in his brown eyes who served as Ezekiel's chief assistant. Garland married him to please Ezekiel, who wanted a son-in-law to handle his catering business while he taught Garland the fine points of managing his portfolio of coal mines, oil fields, blue chips, and gold. Five months after Kendall was born, Robert announced that he was leaving and lit out for Los Angeles, where he was promptly run over by a dump truck on Los Feliz Boulevard. As a girl, poring over the brittle photographs of her father, Kendall blamed her mother for his leaving, believing that it must have been insufferable being the husband of such a driven, uncompromising woman: even her grandfather used to tease Garland by saying, "Girl, you done got the happy-go-lucky aura of Queen Victoria." Ezekiel had been a beloved paternal stand-in for Kendall, but the absence of her father pained her. When she was in high school, Kendall resolved that if she ever had a son, his name would be Robert, not just to honor her father but, odd as it sounded, as a way to meet him.

"Ezekiel had a house the size of a castle in Center City," Kendall said, running her fingers over her grandfather's shoes. "He had servants and a chauffeur, but every weekday morning he'd make me waffles or oatmeal and take me to school and kiss my cheek and say he loved me. You could ask him any silly thing, and he'd give you an answer right quick. Otherwise, he rarely spoke. I was intrigued by him, but he always scared me some."

"I can see why."

Ezekiel appeared to gaze out at a land visible only to him, and the single-mindedness on his face was so unassailable that it bordered on cruel.

"Did he have a wife?" Julian asked, and Kendall flinched at the question.

"Not that I ever met." All families have their secrets, and Garland had shared this one with her daughter shortly after her twelfth birthday during a talk about the birds and the bees. Ezekiel, Garland said, believed he was too busy to marry, but a weak moment with a teenage girl who cleaned his home produced Garland, who was named after Ezekiel's mother. Because the cleaning girl was unsuited to the social rigors of prosperous Negro circles in Philadelphia, Ezekiel paid her to disappear into the hinterlands of Virginia from where she'd come. Kendall had never been able to connect the heartlessness of this story with the loving grandfather she knew. She explained it to herself by thinking that Ezekiel had spared her mother from the truth—that the girl had wanted to leave and Ezekiel had helped her with a handout.

Kendall, heading along a graveled path shaded by banyan trees, changed the subject: "I've been thinking about taking up photography. I've got to buy a better camera than my Brownie. A Leica: Henri Cartier-Bresson does street photography in Paris with a Leica. It's small enough to carry, and I could shoot what I see instead of dreaming up a picture to put on a canvas. Derrick tells me to keep painting, but he's gaga about Cubism. I believe reality is bizarre enough without the hard lines and angles."

"True." Julian knew next to nothing about art, a state of affairs he promised himself to rectify as soon as he could get to a library or bookstore.

"Plus, so many women photographers are succeeding—Louise Dahl-Wolfe's at *Harper's Bazaar*; Margaret Bourke-White's been hired by *Life*, *and* she's done a book with the writer Erskine Caldwell; and I bet you've seen Dorothea Lange's *Migrant Mother*."

"In the papers."

Kendall stopped in midstride. "And I want to . . ."

"Aim for the highest?"

Kendall grinned, and Julian imagined leaning forward to kiss her. "I apologize for carrying on. But I've been telling Derrick: photography has room for women; painting's a man's world."

"There's Georgia O'Keeffe."

Her voice rising with surprise, Kendall asked, "You're familiar with O'Keeffe?"

"I saw her naked."

Kendall giggled. "Excuse me?"

"I'd finished up a meeting in New York, and when I came out, a crowd was next door waiting to get into a photo exhibit. I was curious and went in, and Georgia O'Keeffe was up on the wall without her clothes."

"Her husband, Alfred Stieglitz, took those."

For Julian, the exhibit was a fonder memory than the meeting, where he had to persuade a mouthy parking-lot mogul, who had survived the czar and his pogroms and concluded he was immortal, that he'd live longer with Abe Zwillman for a partner. It was the last time Julian had knocked anyone around for money, and he'd decided to quit while he was looking at the photographs. Something about the soft shades of black and white and gray and the conspicuous adoration of the photographer for his subject had convinced Julian that if he didn't quit the rackets, he'd forfeit the last shred of his humanity. One photo in particular had stayed with him. O'Keeffe was standing, arms raised as though welcoming a sunrise, her face out of view of the camera, and he remembered her full breasts, the extravagant curves of her hips, and the tantalizing nest between her legs. He was picturing Kendall in that pose when three girls, in blouses, long skirts, and saddle shoes, went by. Kendall waved to them, and they said hello to her and glanced at Julian, smiling coquettishly for an instant and then looking through him as if he were a wraith.

He said, "They think I'm here to arrest you?"

"They think you're white and therefore forbidden fruit and a mess of trouble. And you may be. I've been so busy going on about myself, I haven't asked about you. You're not a philosopher like your daddy."

"Who says?"

"Oh?" she said, not believing him for a minute. "Say something philosophical."

"There's little in life not improved by Russian dressing."

Kendall laughed. "What?"

"Russian dressing: ketchup, mayonnaise, and some pickle relish. Put it on pastrami or turkey"—and here, spotting an opportunity, Julian got bold. "When you come to New York, I'll take you to a delicatessen and you can try some."

"I'll keep it in mind."

✳

The tour lasted for one of the more disheartening hours of Julian's life, because Kendall led the way with Derrick holding her hand, while Julian lagged behind with Eddie and Otis. The campus was a collection of ivied, redbrick buildings with Doric columns and quadrangles of dormitories—a New England college blooming in the wet heat.

Eddie said to Julian, "Ya gotta listen to Jitterbug hammer the eighty-eights. My man can play."

Otis took a fast bow. "You boys wanna hear singing, take Kenni-Ann to church or pour some wine in her and she'll sing it like Bessie Smith."

Kendall smiled at Otis, and Eddie said, "No fooling, Jitterbug. Julian's got hooks into nightclubs in Newark, the Picadilly, the Alcazar—Louis Armstrong's there a lot—and if you're home and wanna make some dough playin', give us a holler."

Derrick strode over to Eddie. "My brother is getting a degree in music. He's not preparing to play for white folks who go slumming. Nor does he need any 'dough.' Our parents make certain of that."

"Bro," Otis said, "will ya back off, please?"

Derrick, in his straw boater, blue blazer, and white bucks, stood up as straight as a headmaster scolding a student, and said to Eddie, "And why do you insist on referring to my brother as 'Jitterbug'? Why not 'Tar Baby'?"

Eddie frowned like a cranky leprechaun, and Julian questioned why any sane person would mess with him. Not that Julian would've cared if Eddie downgraded Derrick's looks, though he suspected that Kendall wouldn't approve, so he said, "Let's relax."

Eddie said to Derrick, "I *refer* to your brother as 'Jitterbug' 'cause to me he looks like music in motion, and old enough, if it bothers him, to tell me himself. Whatta ya say, JB?"

"JB?" Otis said, sticking out his right palm. "I like that too."

Eddie slid his right palm across Otis's outstretched hand.

"It's hot as a stripper's fanny out here," Otis said. "Let's go to the ocean."

"We can't—" Kendall said.

Otis was already walking away, and Eddie caught up with him.

"Is the beach a problem?" Julian asked, but Derrick had taken Kendall's hand and gone after Otis and Eddie.

The problem was apparent when Julian reached the crest of the hill. Below, where the grassy slope met the beach, stakes at intervals of thirty feet were driven into the sand with red pennants flying from them and attached signs that declared WARNING: WHITES ONLY. The beach wasn't as jammed as the Jersey shore in July and August, but plenty of people were swimming and sunning themselves.

"I'ma sick of this horseshit," Otis said, stepping out of his tennis shoes and taking off his shirt. "Kenni-Ann's mama owns the damn beach, and God owns the ocean, and the Bible doesn't say I can't swim in it."

Kendall said, "Swimming at midnight's one thing; at noon on Sunday's another."

"Ain't nothing gonna happen," Otis said, bending to roll up his white ducks past his knees. "Not with my man Eddie for a lookout."

Eddie said, "Jitterbug—" and Derrick clamped a hand on his brother's shoulder, but Otis pulled away. Sunbathers did a double take as Otis flew by and dove into the silvery-green water.

"We better wait for him," Eddie said, lighting a Camel.

They sat on the winter grass. Eddie held out the pack to Derrick, who hesitated before taking one. Eddie flicked his lighter, and Derrick dragged on the cigarette, nodding his thanks.

"Your mom owns this beach?" Julian asked Kendall.

"It's part of the two thousand acres my grandfather bought. It used to belong to the Scales family. Jarvis Scales—he's the mayor of Lovewood—owns the land around the campus. My mother says Jarvis has been trying to buy her parcel, but my grandfather wanted a college on it."

"It's legal to keep owners off their property?" Eddie asked.

"The Jim Crow laws say it is," Derrick said.

"Jesus. How do people live like that?"

"Practice," Derrick replied.

Kendall was the first one to see them—four white men in denim overalls and T-shirts loping across the sand, two of them wading into the surf and grabbing Otis. Kendall shouted, "You leave him alone!" and took off for the beach, with Derrick, Eddie, and Julian behind her.

"We jake?" Julian asked Eddie, who answered by taking a snubbie .38 from an ankle holster and holding the pistol by his side.

A pale, gangly kid—twenty at most—with a patchy blond beard, buck teeth, and a jaw that appeared wider than the top of his head was cheering on his two friends who were dunking Otis's face up and down in the water. Kendall went toward him and snapped, "Hurleigh Scales, you tell them to quit!"

"Quit," Hurleigh whispered.

The older, husky guy behind Hurleigh had a pushed-in face the color of a boiled lobster, and Julian waited until Eddie had circled closer to the sun-fried goon before stepping in front of Kendall and extending his hand. "I'm Julian Rose." The kid scowled at Julian as if he were offering him a dead rat. "Hurleigh Scales, you're the mayor's—"

"Younger brother. Why, y'all know Jarvis?"

"Haven't had the pleasure." Julian removed a gold money clip from his pocket and held up a hundred-dollar bill for Hurleigh to see. Well versed in the art of pressuring unwilling sellers, Julian pondered why Hurleigh—who, with that fish-belly-white complexion, was no sun worshiper—was at the beach, a stone's throw from the campus.

Tucking the bill into the bib of Hurleigh's overalls, he said, "Why don'tcha let the kid up and buy your pals a beer?"

Hurleigh's expression made him look like death sucking a lemon. "I might could do that, 'cept niggers ain't s'pose to be heah. That's why there's signs." He glared at Derrick. "Y'all *can* read?"

"Yes," Derrick said.

"This boy can read," Hurleigh called out. "Well, slap my head and call me silly."

Which is precisely what Derrick did, slapping Hurleigh with such force that Derrick's straw boater fell off. Hurleigh stumbled back onto the sand as Derrick, with the measured tone of a judge announcing a verdict, said, "Silly."

No one moved, and Julian felt as though he were at the movies and the projector had gone on the fritz, leaving the actors frozen on the screen. Then Hurleigh sprang toward Derrick. Julian, who had three inches and thirty pounds on Hurleigh, got one hand on this throat and the other on his overalls and lifted him off the sand, while he saw the goon collapse as Eddie smacked his skull twice with the butt of his .38.

Julian said, "Let that kid out of the ocean."

"Why should I?"

"One, if you don't, my associate will shoot your pals. And two"—Julian dug his thumb into Hurleigh's Adam's apple—"it's gonna get difficult for you to swallow."

He heard Hurleigh choking and drew back his thumb.

Hurleigh croaked, "Let the coon go!"

Otis came up from the sea, spitting out water and grit, and Julian released Hurleigh, who said, "I be waitin' on that nig-nog, and when I's finished, he gon' feel like a alligator done chewed up his ass and shit him down a swamp hole."

"That's not very neighborly, is it?"

Hurleigh appeared confused, as if Julian were asking him a trick question. "Y'all can jist fuck yoah—" Hurleigh spat, but he was unable to complete the sentence because Julian clutched the straps of his overalls and brought his knee up into Hurleigh's groin, hearing him yelp with pain and letting him fall onto the beach, where he lay on his back, groaning.

Julian turned. Kendall was gaping at him, her eyes shining with anger and fear.

"I guess the tour's over," he said.

# Chapter 6

An hour later, Eddie was packed and waiting outside the college gate for a taxi to Miami Beach. "We should both take off. Suppose the Lovewood cops pinch you?"

"I'll call Abe," Julian replied. "He has a piece of a gambling joint in Hallandale and told me the Broward County judges and the sheriff are on the payroll. You check into the Arlington. I'll be there tomorrow, and we can go shopping."

"Shopping?" Eddie's eyebrows arched so high they almost got lost in his hairline.

"Give your eyebrows a rest. I gotta come here to see my mother and—"

"And you need to own a hotel so you have somewhere to stay?"

"A little hotel."

"Only a little hotel?"

"The bums running Miami Beach won't let Jews buy a big one."

"You don't a need a hotel, you need your friggin' head examined. Did Kendall strike you as overly friendly when we got done beating on those boys?" Kendall hadn't spoken, even after Otis had apologized to Eddie and Julian, and Derrick had berated his brother for causing the trouble.

"She'll get over it," Julian said.

Eddie saw the cab coming down US 1. "Remember I once told you I was your friend because you're as crazy as I am?"

"Yeah."

"I was wrong: you're crazier."

✳

The wind blowing through the palms was rattling the coconuts when Julian returned to the cottage. Kendall was sitting in one of the plank chairs and reading the *New Yorker*.

"Good article?" he asked, and sat in the other chair.

"It's about Thomas Hart Benton."

"He was on the cover of *Time*." Julian was pleased that he'd heard of the guy.

"He was." Kendall placed the magazine on the arm of her chair. "Julian, what do you do?"

"I used to be in the hospitality business."

"And Eddie? He's a headwaiter?"

"You'll have to ask him. Me, I see things."

Kendall grinned; flexing her beauty muscles was how Julian saw it. "You hallucinate? Like you're insane?" Kendall may have been joking, but she was also studying him as intensely as her mother had done at dinner.

Julian said, "I see a space and imagine what can go there. Then I pay people to fill in the space."

He thought his reply had a nice artistic ring to it, and sounded better than the humdrum truth, that he conjured up a project—an apartment building, houses, or stores—purchased the land, hired an architect and general contractor, and when they were done, he either sold or rented and managed the properties. It wasn't as glamorous as bootlegging or owning nightclubs and gambling joints, but he made boatloads of cash and it was unlikely that anyone would shoot him.

Kendall seemed to be contemplating his answer, and she stopped studying him. "Did you eat lunch? I can take you to the cafeteria."

"Your mother sent over sandwiches, and I'm having supper with my parents—if I can find their place."

She nodded toward the blacktopped road. "They're not far—at one-eleven Frederick Douglass Lane. All the professors here, except your father, are Negro. If it weren't for the faculty housing my mother put up, they would've had to live in Coontown—the Negro section of Lovewood. My mother thinks it's disgraceful for anyone to live in a place with that name."

"She's got a point."

"My mother usually does. Once, she was walking through the student center and heard *Amos 'n' Andy* and shut off the radio and gave the boys listening to it a lecture: 'If two white men choose to act like fools so America can hear them, they don't have to pretend they're Negroes. White men are foolish enough on their own.'"

As if it had just dawned on Kendall that Julian might be insulted by her comment, she glanced at her lap and nervously threaded her fingers together. Julian wanted to reassure her that he wasn't offended by taking her hands in his. Yet he no more would've done this than he would've touched her breasts. And his restraint bothered him, since he was uncertain why he felt it. Because Kendall had class and she was dating a law student, and Julian was afraid of being rejected? Or because Julian was unwilling to violate some invisible barrier of the racial divide?

Kendall looked up. "I'm sorry about the beach."

"It wasn't your doing."

"Otis was showing off for Eddie, and Derrick was . . ."

"Showing off for me?"

Kendall hunched and unhunched her shoulders, a gesture with more ire in it than resignation. "Derrick wouldn't have done it unless you were there."

"The man's not dumb. He would've been outnumbered." Julian wasn't eager to defend Derrick, though he had no intention of taking the rap for his slapping the mayor's brother.

"Sometimes people . . . need to stand on their own. To prove they can find their own way. Can . . . can rely on themselves to— Is this making any sense?"

"Depends. On whether you're talking about Derrick. Or . . ." He hesitated, doubtful that his most effective strategy was to bend their conversation in too personal a direction. "Or you."

Smiling wistfully, Kendall said, "Could be . . . both of us?"

That she was perplexed by the mystery of herself appealed to

Julian: here, at a Negro college in the middle of nowhere, he'd stumbled upon a kindred spirit. It made him want to buy fate a case of champagne.

Glancing at her watch, which Julian noticed was a man's rectangular Hamilton on a black leather band, Kendall stood and took her *New Yorker*. "You're leaving?"

"In the morning."

She held his eyes with a gaze as intimate as a kiss. "Safe travels."

"You too."

"I'm not going anywhere."

※

Julian spent the afternoon in the college library. A librarian peered suspiciously over her wire rims when he requested directions to the fine-art books, and behind him, as he went by the tables where students were studying, some wiseass remarked, "He probably lost his map," and the ripples of tittering that followed embarrassed him. Julian selected the fattest volume on the shelf: *Art Through the Ages* by Helen Gardner, an encyclopedic survey from cave paintings until the modern era, and to escape the stares of the students, he went to the basement and hid in a carrel, reading through the Renaissance before he had to leave.

The faculty resided in rows of stucco bungalows that had been painted in pastels of pink, yellow, and blue. As Julian searched for Frederick Douglass Lane, he heard mothers summoning their children to supper and snatches of conversations and radio programs—Billie Holiday singing "What a Little Moonlight Can Do" and Bob Hope cracking jokes—filtering out through screen doors, a Sunday-evening symphony that left Julian wishing for a family of his own.

His parents' bungalow was redolent with Elana's pot roast, a double-edged memory for Julian, his joy and sorrow fighting to a draw as he sat at the kitchen table.

"Are you settling in?" Julian asked.

Theodor said, "I've never been warm in December before, and I've been preparing my lectures in English. It has been years since I have lectured in that language. I was lecturing in English when I met your mother. Remember, Elana?"

"Yes, Theodor."

They ate in silence. Any visitor uninitiated into their traditions would have been uncomfortable, but Julian took solace in the absence of conversation, for their meals in Berlin had frequently ended with a tongue-lashing from Theodor. It hadn't always been that way. Julian could remember the woodsy scent of his father's pipe tobacco and sitting with him in an armchair while Theodor read Greek myths to him in German, and in the summers, holding his hand as they walked from their rented villa through the crowd on the shore of the Greater Wannsee and out into the lake, where Theodor taught his son to swim, and Julian recalled thinking that the water dripping off his father's broad shoulders and beard made him look as powerful as Poseidon. Things began to go bad the summer Julian was twelve. One afternoon, when he and his father returned from the lake, they found Elana on the terrace mumbling to herself and sprawled on a chaise with a bottle of *Kirschwasser*, a glass, and a vial of Veronal by her chair. As Theodor pulled his wife to her feet, shouting, "Elana, Elana, what have you done!" Julian ran to their neighbor's villa, where a neurologist from the Charité university hospital was vacationing with his family, and he told the doctor that his mother had swallowed her sleeping pills with cherry brandy. The doctor came, and Elana recovered, but once the Roses were back home, they barely spoke to each other, and Julian was soon infuriating his father by exploring the neon-lit debauchery of Berlin.

"President Wakefield told me the Committee for Scholars in Exile is attempting to bring more professors to Negro colleges," Theodor said, wiping his mouth with a napkin. "But the State Department is—*stingy* is the word she used—with visas. She said Lovewood was fortunate."

The committee had also been fortunate. Julian had mailed a check for ten grand to its office in Manhattan, a donation that insured his father would be on top of the committee's list.

"Well," Theodor announced. "I must get back to my manuscript."

When he was gone, Julian said, "How are you, Mama?"

"Getting along. President Wakefield says they have tenant farmers, and some of them and their children could use a nurse. It'll keep me busy."

Julian gave her an envelope. "Here's two thousand dollars. If you need more—"

"I don't need this."

"Take it. And if there's anything else—"

"You've done enough. We're safe now. With the trouble Hitler's making, there's going to be a war, isn't there? Your father says no, that mankind will come to its senses."

In Julian's experience, people rarely came to their senses unless they were threatened, but why burden his mother with his opinion? "I hope he's right. Listen, I have business in Miami. I'll be back next month and—"

"She is beautiful, Julian."

His first line of defense was to play dumb. "Beautiful?"

That didn't do the trick. "Kendall is beautiful, but it's not so easy with the way things are. Love is worth it, though. Always."

Julian was stunned. Given her marriage, he hadn't the slightest notion of how she had come to that conclusion. Julian looked at his mother. Elana was in her forties yet there was still something girlish about her: her unlined face, her pinned-up blond hair, her bright blue eyes and faint smile; and Julian realized, with a disconcerting clarity and sadness, that despite her struggles, his mother—perhaps back when she first sat across the table from Theodor in a Romanian restaurant—had once nurtured dreams of her own.

Julian started clearing the table.

"Leave the dishes," Elana said.

He kissed her forehead and took a long, slow walk back to the cottage.

# *Chapter 7*

By morning, no one had come to arrest Julian for roughing up Hurleigh, and he decided that it wouldn't hurt his cause with Kendall and her mother if he found out whether Mayor Scales was using his brother to pressure Garland into a land deal. He took a taxi to Lovewood and had the cabbie wait for him outside Scales Antiques.

As Julian entered the store, a bell tinkled over the door.

"Can I he'p you?" a man called out from a seat behind the counter. He was wearing a short-sleeved white shirt and red shoestring tie with a rhinestone clasp and puffing on a roll-your-own. Julian zigzagged between barrels of stuffed baby alligators and seashell necklaces, display cases of salt-and-pepper shakers in the form of Negro mammies, and glassware imprinted with the Confederate flag.

Julian said, "Mayor Scales?"

"'Round heah, I'm Jarvis." His face was all sharp edges—pointy chin, thin lips, a tiny nose as hooked as an eagle's beak, even his bristly flattop, which was receding into the shape of an arrowhead.

Julian introduced himself, and Jarvis snickered. "You the one gave my baby brother a bellyache?" Julian responded with a slight nod, and Jarvis reached back to open a cooler. "Lemme get you a drink. That Hurleigh be like a palmetto bug in my shorts."

He took out a Dr Pepper, popped off the cap on the lip of the counter, and handed the soda to Julian. "I done told Hurleigh to keep away from the college and the beach—even if them colored kids take a dip. I ain't got nothin' to do with my brother's foolishness, but it ain't no secret I'll pay Miz Wakefield 'bout any price she name for her property."

Julian couldn't tell if Jarvis was being straight. He'd helped Abe buy politicians by the bushel and knew that if one of those greedy equivocators swore it was daytime, you better peek through the blinds to check. So he opted to push the mayor and see what happened. "Oceanfront property's not cheap," he said with a faint bite of sarcasm. "You must be selling stuffed alligators by the ton."

"You think I don't know what you is—some northern boy in a fancy suit, silk tie, and fourteen-karat collar pin? A boy with a friend that pistol-whip one of them pissants Hurleigh hang 'round with? We southern and talk more natural poetry than most, but we ain't nohow dumb. I'll wager the Lord was as gen-rous to me as He was to you during Prohibition."

"We didn't dump sugar into vats of cat shit and turpentine."

Julian had meant to insult Jarvis, to irritate him enough that he'd let something slip, but Jarvis wasn't easy to insult. He chuckled, a gruff rumbling in his chest, the way Satan would chortle if he chain-smoked. "Didn't use no cat ingredients, but I'll allow we mighta put in a dash a rattlesnake piss for flavor."

Jarvis shot out a salvo of smoke rings. "Boy, you funny as a nine-legged dog, lookin' down your nose at me, believin' I ride 'round with the Ku Kluxers. Like up north all y'all love Negroes. Few years ago, me and the wife went to New York. Checked into the Plaza Hotel. We been to Radio City. Ate veal Oscar at the Waldorf. And the only colored we seen was carryin' luggage, operatin' elevators, and shinin' shoes. Yet y'all of the opinion you cut from a finer cloth than us. Shoot, me and Miz Wakefield ain't no white–colored folderol. She educated and smart, and that don't always go together, do it?"

Julian didn't reply, and Jarvis said, "Miz Wakefield told me 'bout her grandmother bein' sold by my grandfather. That's plumb ugly history, 'cept what it got to do with me? My father didn't own no slaves. He had colored men workin' our farm, and whatever they do, he do. And Daddy kept them men on when they so old they couldn't do doodly-squat. Hurleigh ain't but a boy and ask, 'Daddy, why don't you let them shiftless niggers go?' and Daddy done took a switch to Hurleigh till his legs bloody as a cut pig and say, "Cause they decent, God-fearin' men, and if'n I evah heah that ugliness from your mouth agin, I'll beat the blond out your hair.'"

"That's a heartwarming tale."

As Julian had intended, Jarvis began to fume, standing and stamping out his cigarette on the floor. "My father nevah harmed nobody or nothin'. The day the bank took his farm, he go to the barn, mix some pesticide in a dipper of milk, and drinks it down. I'm the one found him, every inch of his sufferin' still on his face. My mama was nevah the same. Died six months later. And Ezekiel Kendall bought that land from the bank for a song so cheap no self-respectin' mockingbird would sing it. So till I'm dead, I'ma try and buy my daddy's land back. Y'all unnerstan' now?"

Julian, in as affable a tone as he could muster, said, "Please send Hurleigh my regards."

In the taxi, he wondered why Jarvis hadn't mentioned Hurleigh getting slapped by Derrick. That should've been major news. Maybe Hurleigh had been too humiliated to tell his older brother. Or maybe not. At least Julian had something to think about—other than Kendall—on his trip to Miami.

# Chapter 8

Holding the handles of a shopping bag, Julian paced back and forth under the fierce gaze of Kendall's grandfather. The students going to and from classes paid no more attention to him than to the statue, but Julian felt out of place until he spotted Kendall coming toward him with a khaki satchel slung over her shoulder. Julian slipped on the Ray-Bans he'd bought yesterday on Lincoln Road. The aviators were stylish, and with the green lenses he could stare at Kendall without her teasing him.

"You're staring," Kendall said.

"How can you tell?"

"Educated guess."

Julian took a package out of the bag. The wrapping paper featured snowmen in Santa outfits.

Kendall said, "Aren't you Jewish?"

"I am, but God lets us buy presents for the other team."

She laughed and carefully removed the paper. "A Leica! Julian, this is the Three-B! I just read about it in *Popular Photography*."

"Saw it in a store, and you told me you needed a better camera."

Her eyes opened wide as though it had suddenly occurred to her that he might have an ulterior motive for buying her the Leica.

"It's a gift, Kendall. No strings."

"Thank you."

"Try it out." Julian took a box of film from the bag and began to open it.

Kendall clamped a hand over his. "I'll have to cut off the end of the film to load the camera. There's a darkroom. Want to come?"

Julian would have preferred to stand there with her hand on his, but he returned the film and camera to the bag, and they went up a path behind the chapel.

Kendall asked, "Do they have girls up North?"

"They do." And with little effort, Julian had collected his share. Showgirls and pretty girls who wanted to be showgirls; nice girls who were tired of being nice; and practical girls who'd had it up to here with bad news and breadlines and would've married a fire hydrant if it paid the mortgage.

"Then why'd you come back to see me?"

Julian had never felt this drawn to a girl. Behind the sublime mask of her face, he saw a hardness equal to his and a loneliness as deep as his own. "Because you're as tough as I am."

"Who told you that?"

"Otis."

"The ass-kicking contest? Otis say that to any boy get near me. Even his brother."

"How come you only sound southern sometimes?"

"You heard that, did you?" she said with a quick laugh. "I went to a private Quaker school in Philadelphia, but when I was thirteen my mother started overseeing the construction of the college, and I spent the summers here. My mother didn't want me to be spoiled, so she had me working six days a week with the farmers. Their talk stuck in my head, probably because they sounded like my grandfather: he was from Lovewood and had himself a South mouth. I used to help the children with their reading and writing, and I picked oranges, fed chickens, mucked out barns, and learned how to sew dresses from flour sacks. I made this one."

"It's lovely," Julian said, and it was, the mustard-colored cloth sprinkled with miniature bunches of purple grapes and drawn in to her tiny waist.

"You know we're different colors?"

Ahead, beyond the sand dunes, Julian saw a sparkling patch of ocean. "I don't care."

Kendall stopped. "How do you do that? Not care?"

He wanted to tell Kendall that it helped to have a mother and father who knew nothing of how he felt and demanded more from him than they offered in return. Yet confessing these facts to himself shamed Julian, because he considered himself culpable, as though he would've had better parents if he'd been a better son. "Could be that I grew up Jewish in Germany. Or that I left home at fifteen."

Kendall, eyeing him as if sensing that his explanation was incomplete, said, "I wish I felt easier about that."

"Not caring what people think?"

"My mother, for one. And even myself. So I could go off and be an artist and not second-guess my choices—make myself up as I go along and be content with what I become."

"I could help you with that."

"I reckon you could." Nothing in her tone indicated that she was going to give Julian the chance, and she cut over to a whitewashed shed near a cluster of slender palms with scarlet fruit under the fronds. "Simon, a friend of mine, built the darkroom here because he liked photographing the dunes. He graduated two years ago and left some equipment for the students. Simon's a reporter at the *Pittsburgh Courier* now."

Surmising that Kendall and Simon had been an item, a pang of jealousy shot through Julian. "That's understandable. Not much sand in Pittsburgh."

Kendall ignored his sarcasm and unlatched the door. The shed was hot and permeated with a sour chemical smell. She rummaged around on a cluttered table, then switched on a flashlight with a red lens, took the bag from Julian, and gave him her satchel. "My sketchbook's in here. I wanted to show you what I drew today. Wait out where it's cool."

Five minutes later, as Julian looked at nude charcoal sketches of a regal Negro lady with lively eyes and hair as short as a man's, he heard a click and glanced up to see Kendall snapping his picture.

Julian said, "These sketches are terrific. Who is it?"

"Hazee Thomas. She owns the local juke joint."

"Didn't your mother say no nude drawing?"

"Hazee's doing it for free. She was a stripper in Memphis and says if my mother climbs up her back about it, she'll be explaining to her there's uglier ways to spend an hour than posing in the altogether. Even my mother won't mess with Hazee. Can you stand against that palm?"

Julian stood, and Kendall, looking through the viewfinder and fiddling with a front dial, moved toward him, snapping pictures. Then, lowering the camera, she tugged on his polo shirt. "Can I take a picture of your chest?"

Julian assumed she was kidding, but she held out her hand, and Julian gave her the polo. After folding it in quarters, she set the shirt on the ground. "Rest your head on it."

Julian lay down, and Kendall stood over him, taking photographs.

Kendal said, "Clasp your hands behind your head."

Julian complied, though he disliked being ordered around like a trained dog. "If I take off my pants will you talk to me?"

He was only trying to get her attention, so he was astounded when Kendall replied, "Would you?"

Julian kicked off his Weejuns, shucked off his seersucker slacks, and felt ridiculous. Yet soon he was spellbound by Kendall and her photographer's minuet, stepping left and right, leaning one way, then the other, bending down, standing up, all the while aiming the Leica at him. And now that Julian was relaxed with a silken breeze caressing him, he was self-conscious about being in his boxer shorts in front of Kendall. Despite focusing on his favorite moments in his third-base seats at Yankee Stadium, he grew excited and was certain his boxers looked like a white cotton tepee. He worried that his excitement would embarrass Kendall, but she reacted with a kittenish grin, and Julian wasn't sure how he felt about that.

"Roll's finished," she said.

Julian wriggled into his slacks, and Kendall sat beside him, angling her legs to the side. This close to her it seemed that her skin had been storing up the sunlight and was now releasing its heat into the air. Sitting up, Julian put on his polo and slipped into his loafers.

Kendall said, "Derrick will be here tomorrow morning."

Julian's heart sank to his toes. "Isn't he at law school?"

"I've spoken to him long-distance eight times, but he wants to speak to me in person. He doesn't have classes on Fridays, so he's driving down."

"What's the emergency?"

"I told Derrick I didn't want to marry any boy. Not now."

Julian's heart, now back where it belonged, was hammering away like a Gene Krupa drum solo. He could wait for her.

"Jesus, God, Derrick called my mother last night. She came to my dorm room, yelling that young men like Derrick—Negro lawyers who are going to take over the family firm—don't grow on trees, and I ought to quit acting like I was born foolish and grew up ignorant. I tried to tell her why, but you can't tell my mother anything."

"You can tell me."

"Did—did you ever feel as if there's something wonderful waiting for you, somewhere, in the future? You're not sure what it is, only that you're sure it's out there?"

Julian looked straight at her, thinking that he'd found what had been waiting for him.

"Last semester I read Emily Dickinson's 'Hope Is the Thing with Feathers.' The poem's beautiful, but for me hope's a thing with plain old feet; hope puts one foot in front of the other; hope is New York and Paris and believing that searching for something wonderful—whether you find it or not—makes life worthwhile. Derrick says he wants his future settled. I asked him why. To get tomorrow over with before you wake up in the morning?"

Kendall looked toward the dunes, then back at Julian. "You're not like that, are you?"

"I'm more day-to-day." Julian was almost sure that this was true.

"I thought so," she said, and kissed him. Her hair and skin smelled of lemons, and his right hand roamed past the ridge of her bra, down the rough cotton of her dress.

Kendall drew back. "You're the first white person I've ever touched."

"You mean kissed?"

"Touched—except for first grade and holding hands playing ring around the rosy. Sometimes I drive along the coast and stop to paint landscapes and mostly sell them to white folks. If I charge two fifty or three fifty and they don't have any silver, nearly every one tells me to keep the change."

"Maybe they're generous."

"Maybe, but I swear they don't want to touch a colored gal."

"That's not a problem I have."

She laughed. "No, you want to touch me too much." Kendall stowed the camera in her satchel. "I have to study tonight. Will you be here tomorrow?"

"My parents have a spare bedroom. I'll be there or in the basement of the library."

"I'll find you when I'm done talking with Derrick. But we have to be careful. I'll go back to campus by myself."

Kendall was past the darkroom when she turned with a smile that she hadn't shown him before—a hopeful, buoyant smile. "Don't worry none about what Otis says. It's my mother that'll shoot you."

# Chapter 9

The next afternoon, as Julian sat in the basement of the library reading *Art Through the Ages*, Otis Larkin showed up. "Kenni-Ann's gone bughouse. Derrick telephoned her from Jacksonville last night, and she says he shoulda been here hours ago. She wants me and Mrs. Wakefield to look for him. Man, I told the girl: my big bro get lost in Harlem. Or maybe he pull over to knock a nod. But Kenni-Ann lay her doom and gloom on Mrs. Wakefield till she agrees to go, and Kenni-Ann says you'll help."

"My car's at my parents'."

"Sweet, let's get the gas buggy and I'll give you directions. Sorry, Jules. This ain't nothin', except Kenni-Ann—"

"No big deal," Julian said, but he was afraid of what they'd find. He doubted that Mayor Scales had any intention of reining in his brother, and Hurleigh had struck Julian as a vindictive son of a bitch.

Julian, putting the top down on his Cadillac, felt safer knowing that he had a .32-caliber Beretta in the glove box.

❋

The day was hot and still as Julian drove along a dirt road.

"Spoke to Eddie last week," Julian said. "He told me when you were home, you came over to Newark and sat in at the Alcazar."

"The band was cookin'. And Eddie and me got boiled as owls."

The road went by orange and lemon groves, the fruit jewel bright against the dark leaves, then curved around pastures with cows sleeping in the sunlight and fields of lettuce, sugarcane, and corn stubble.

Negro men in floppy straw hats and women in bonnets were working the fields. Newark had no shortage of poverty—Julian's early days in the city had been spent in a cold-water tenement that smelled of coal smoke and backed-up toilets—but he could hardly bear to look at the shacks of the tenant farmers. To earn a few extra pennies, the farmers allowed the sides of their shacks to be plastered with handbills advertising tobacco and patent medicines; the steeply pitched roofs were patched with tarpaper; and the sagging porches were packed with young and old seeking shelter from the sun.

"If Derrick's car broke down near here, he'd go to Hazee's." Otis said.

Hazee's was a clapboard-sided, tin-roofed juke with a sign over the door advertising Jax beer. Garland was sitting in her wood-bodied Ford station wagon in the dusty parking lot, and Julian pulled up alongside her.

"Hazee says Derrick hasn't been by," Garland said. "Keep straight, and I'll come around the opposite way."

Four miles from Hazee's, Otis said, "Over there, Jules. On the other side of the road. That's Derr's Chevy. Daddy bought it for him as a graduation gift."

Julian and Otis inspected the eggnog-colored car. The rear left tire was flat, and so was the spare, which was on the back seat.

"Hot dog! I bet big bro's just down a ways."

They drove for fifteen minutes without spotting Derrick. A breeze, offering no relief from the heat, was blowing, and Otis said, "Damn, you smell that? Nasty, ain't it?"

Julian had helped clean up some of the messes Looney and Gooney had made, so he was familiar with the stench of seared flesh. Gently, Julian said, "Otis, you gotta prepare—" but he didn't finish his warning because up ahead he saw Garland in a clearing and heard Kendall scream. She and her mother were ten yards from an oak tree. Most of its branches were bare and as crooked as the fingers of a crone, but swaying like a grisly pendulum from the oak's thickest limb was Derrick, his head thrown back with the coils of a noose up against his chin and his blind eyes raised heavenward as if searching the clouds for mercy.

"Jules?" Otis said, his voice cracking.

Kendall stopped screaming as Julian and Otis rushed into the clearing, trampling the remnants of a celebration—empty bottles of soda and beer, cigarette butts, peanut shells, and lollipop sticks. Derrick's feet were charred, the gasoline can dumped behind the tree with the overturned barrel on which Derrick must have been forced to stand. His right hand, the hand he'd used to slap Hurleigh Scales, had been hacked off at the wrist, and blood dripped along the bark of the tree like sap. The buttons from his vest and suit coat were missing, most likely snagged by souvenir hunters, who had also taken his shoes, belt, tie, and wristwatch.

"You two did this!" Kendall shouted, her eyes luminescent with rage. "Both of you!"

Catching his breath between sobs, Otis stammered, "Ken-Kenni-Ann, I—" but she spun away from him, taking out her Leica and flinging her satchel to the ground.

Julian was neither hurt nor perplexed by her explosion: it had to be less agonizing for Kendall to hurl accusations than to remind herself that Derrick wouldn't have been driving to Florida had she agreed to marry him. As Otis sank to his knees, wailing, "Derr, I'm sorry, Derr," and Julian crouched to comfort him, he thought that parceling out responsibility based on contingencies was futile. Because of the violence Julian had committed in pursuit of Abe's approval and worldly success, he fluctuated between belief and disbelief in God, but he was convinced that if the Arch-Mathematician of the Universe existed, He was the only one who could tally the numbers.

"This isn't on you, Otis," Julian murmured as he watched Kendall get down to business with her camera. The balletic grace of yesterday was gone, and she circled the clearing with the predatory strides of a carnivore hunting prey.

Garland, her eyes wide, watched her daughter, then said to Julian, "Take him down."

※

On the ride back to campus, Otis said, "I'ma gonna kill the mother-fuckers."

"You'll wind up on the same tree as Derrick. And what about your mother and father? It's only you and Derrick, right?"

"So nobody pays for Derrick?"

"Somebody pays. I promise." Julian had maintained his composure in the clearing. He had backed up the Cadillac to the tree, gotten up on the hood, uncoiled the rope from Derrick, then put him in the back of the station wagon. Otis and Kendall stood there, crying. Garland had stopped at Hazee's to phone the Broward County Sheriff and the Negro undertaker in Fort Lauderdale. Julian had waited in the parking lot, listening to Otis repeat that the lynching was his fault and watching Kendall in her mother's car with her head in her hands. An icy fury made Julian's palms sweat. He thought about Derrick's terror as they dragged him to the tree, and how his death was eating up Otis and Kendall, and what it would mean for him with Derrick gone. Live competition was one thing; competition with a ghost was another, and Julian was disgusted with himself for allowing his thoughts to drag him in that direction.

At the Wakefield house, a van from the Benton Funeral Home was in the circular drive, and two Negro men in suits were loading Derrick into it.

"Swear to me," Otis said. "Somebody pays for my brother."

"Somebody pays. And you want me at the funeral with Eddie, you got his number, give us a ring. Anything you need, ask."

Garland came over to Otis. "We'll call your parents from the house. I'll be along shortly."

Julian extended his hand to Otis, who gave him a clumsy hug instead before walking up the driveway.

Garland said, "Hurleigh killed that child, and the sheriff tells me the Lovewood police will handle the investigation."

"Lovewood's got police?"

"Two of them. And Jarvis Scales is in charge of the department. I called the mayor and gave him holy hell. He said his store's open late, and he'll be by in the morning."

"Kendall okay?"

Garland looked at him as if his question had proved his ignorance—and by extension the ignorance of his race—beyond all doubt. "She's a mess. Went to her dorm."

There was nothing he could do here. Not now, maybe never. "I'm going back to Miami Beach."

Garland glared at him. "Good."

※

The lights were on in Scales Antiques. Jarvis was alone inspecting his display cases and making notations on a clipboard. Outside, Julian stood with his body hidden by the building and peeked through the window. The bell over the door would ring when he went in, so he held off until the mayor was facing away from him, and then he slipped into the store. Turning, Jarvis said, "Can—" but he shut up and dropped his clipboard because Julian, towering over the mayor, was pressing the Beretta against his forehead and walking him into a back room, where he pushed the mayor into a desk chair.

Julian said, "You seen Hurleigh?"

"I ain't, but when I do he'll answer if'n he had a thing to do with that boy gettin' hung. But Hurleigh gone. Look out the window."

In the fading light Julian saw a two-story, wood-frame building with double doors.

"I own that garage, and Hurleigh stay in the apartment above it. Him and his car's gone. I wager he went to see our cousins in Mississippi."

"It's good you got a big family."

"What you— Why?"

"Because if I find Hurleigh, you won't miss him at Christmas. Now lie on the floor. Facedown."

Jarvis did as he was told. "Lookit, heah. I been fair with the colored in Lovewood. Ask any of 'em."

Jarvis rambled on, telling the ash-gray linoleum that every fool involved in the lynching would be arrested, but before he completed his speech, the bell jingled as Julian walked out of the store.

# Chapter 10

## HARLEM, NEW YORK

On a raw, blustery Monday morning, Julian waited with Eddie in the shadow of the Abyssinian Baptist Church. Derrick's lynching had made the New York dailies, accompanied by Kendall's photograph of him dangling from the tree, which somehow she'd gotten to the Associated Press. Thousands of people were lined up along 138th Street, and the police were everywhere, on foot and horseback, and the Negroes eyeballed the white cops as if they were Visigoths come to sack Rome.

Julian said, "Otis isn't talking about acing anyone?"

Eddie replied, "When he called, he said we're gonna do that. Are we?"

"After I flew home, I sent the Goldstein twins down."

Eddie and Julian passed a flask of Jameson's back and forth until Julian's face was as numb as his toes. Eddie said, "Kendall's here."

"I would've asked if I wanted to know."

"Who you kidding? Look around: a nice guy from Harlem got strung up because some white people hate coloreds, so why shouldn't the coloreds hate 'em right back? You get in the middle of that because of Kendall and you expect it to be smooth sailing? You're the smartest moron I ever met."

＊

As the pews and balcony filled up with a dark sea of somberly dressed men and women, Otis stood beside Derrick's casket, which was adorned with lilies and rested on a bench below the marble pulpit.

"Thanks for being here," Otis said, wiping his swollen eyes with a hankie, then shaking hands with Eddie and Julian. "Come meet my folks."

The Larkins, a stately couple, sat in the front pew. Julian had never witnessed a mother and father burying a child, but while Otis introduced him and Eddie, and they offered their condolences, Julian thought the Larkins looked as though their insides had been scooped out. When Julian turned so Otis could point out their seats, Mr. Larkin tugged on the sleeve of Julian's Chesterfield and leveled his forefinger at the casket. "It should be me in there."

Again, Julian said, "I'm sorry for your loss," but Mr. Larkin appeared not to hear him.

Otis had reserved spots for Eddie and Julian five rows back on the far left side of the sanctuary. Trailing Eddie to the pew, Julian nearly ran over Garland, who was standing by her aisle seat. Kendall was facing away from him, sitting and talking to an elderly fellow next to her. Julian said, "Hello, Mrs. Wakefield."

Giving him the once-over as if she expected him to rip the strand of pearls off her neck, Garland hissed, "You've been drinking."

Julian moved on, thinking that, in all probability, the favor he was doing her with Hurleigh Scales wouldn't improve her opinion of him. He was about to take a seat when he heard Kendall call his name. He stepped out of the pew, and Kendall, in a black velvet cloche and black silk dress, came to meet him. Her hair, flowing from under her cloche, cascaded over her shoulders in shining brown waves. He wanted to tell her that she looked beautiful, but knew he shouldn't say that. "I saw your photo in the *Herald Tribune*."

"I sent it to my friend, Simon, at the *Pittsburgh Courier*. It made me feel less helpless. Simon got it to the AP."

"Derrick would've approved."

"He would've."

They were silent. Then Kendall said, "Can you forgive me? For blaming you."

"It's okay."

"I felt—I feel so—so responsible."

"You're not."

Her face was melting toward tears. Julian wanted to hold her, wanted to leave the church and take her to Café Society to hear Big Joe Turner, to the Carnegie for pastrami with Russian dressing—anything to chase her sadness away. He touched her arm, and it stirred him when she covered his hand with hers. Despite her dressy clothes, the man's rectangular Hamilton with the cracked leather band was on her wrist.

Kendall saw him looking at it. "My grandfather left me his watch."

The choir, in scarlet robes, filled the balcony behind the pulpit.

"It's about to start," Kendall said, and returned to her seat.

⁂

As the choir sang and the minister preached, Julian was preoccupied with thoughts of Kendall and only heard snatches of the service. "The Nazis ain't got nothin' on Jim Crow," the preacher thundered. "Our brave son of Harlem, Derrick Larkin, was neither afraid nor dismayed. Not even a hanging tree could separate him from the love of Jesus. . . ."

After two hours Julian decided that it was crazy for him to pursue Kendall. White and colored, it wouldn't work. And she had dreams. Julian would be in her way. He should find a white woman with a yen for a mansion in the Jersey suburbs. That idea infuriated him, since she wouldn't be Kendall, but he meant to stick to his plan—at least until the preacher announced that Derrick's brother and his dearest friend from college were going to perform a song.

Eddie had told Julian that Otis could tickle the hell out of the ivories, but Julian was unprepared for the music he heard as Otis played that baby grand. Julian recalled hearing the Utica Jubilee Quartet perform the spiritual on WJZ, but Otis was jazzing it up and that pounding music in a minor chord rose to the vaulted ceiling, asking, *LordLordLord, why, oh why did You let my good brother die?*

Then Kendall, standing alone in the center of the pulpit, sang:

*I am a poor wayfaring stranger,*
*Travelin' through this world of woe . . .*

Her voice was darker than Julian had ever heard it, and the loneliness that he'd seen behind her radiant facade was on display for all
to hear.

*I want to see my good Lord's glory*
*I want to walk His Promised Land*
*I'll tell Him our long, sad story*
*He'll heal all hatred with His loving hand . . .*

Light slanting through the stained glass windows behind Kendall
enveloped her in a red, yellow, and blue mist. Otis went somewhere
else on the piano, somewhere beyond this broken world where the
sky is saturated with sound instead of light. And Kendall, a songbird
in velvet and silk, went with him, head thrown back and clapping her
hands. The church followed her, this girl blown by a gale of her own
making, and the clapping reverberated across the sanctuary like stone
being hammered to dust.

*I'm just goin' over Jordan,*
*I'm just goin' over home . . .*

As the final notes of the song faded, Julian wondered if he was really supposed to be released from this life without ever loving anyone.
In which sacred text was it written that he and Kendall were destined
to be prisoners of their skin? And here was a better question. What
color was love? Julian laughed out loud, and while Eddie glanced at
him as if a few of his screws had come loose, Julian figured that even
God would have to forgive him for backing out of his plan, because
only in Kendall's presence did his anger dissolve and make room for
hope, and no being, divine or human, could blame a man for trying
to save himself.

# Chapter 11

One evening, eight weeks after the funeral, as an ice storm was transforming New Jersey into a skating rink, Kendall called Julian at his apartment.

"How— How are you?" he asked.

"Better, thanks. I'm doing better."

Julian had been so excited to hear Kendall's voice and—because he didn't want to scare her off—so intent on hiding his excitement that the gift of speech deserted him. When he recovered it, the best he could do, much to his chagrin, was "I'm listening to *The Lone Ranger*."

"How's Tonto?"

Julian laughed, but he was still distracted, because listening to the radio was only part of what he was doing. The other part of him was studying a Baedeker's guide to Paris. On Valentine's Day, after refusing a fix-up with a friend of Fiona's, he'd bought the guide at Brentano's. Since then, he had given up seeing any of his regulars and spent his free time with his face in the guidebook, imagining visiting Paris with Kendall and impressing her with historical tidbits and by not having to stop for directions.

Kendall said, "I have to be in Miami the weekend of March eleventh. For a regional sorority meeting."

That information led to a sudden change in his plans. "Me too."

She chuckled, and Julian realized that he'd just claimed to belong to a sorority.

The operator broke in, requesting that the caller deposit another dollar. "Julian, I'm using the pay phone in my dorm, and I'm out of change. I'll be at the Mary Elizabeth Hotel. On Saturday. Is two o'clock okay?"

"Yes," he said, and was asking her to call back collect when she hung up.

＊

The Mary Elizabeth Hotel was in Overtown, a colored neighborhood in the City of Miami, and Kendall, with her khaki satchel slung over her shoulder, was standing in the entranceway, under a lime-green banner with swirly black lettering: WELCOME ALPHA KAPPA ALPHA.

"So that's your sorority?" Julian said as he held the car door for her.

"The oldest Negro sorority in the country. It was founded in nineteen-oh-eight. At Howard."

Just the mention of where Derrick had gone to school was enough to keep them quiet, and Julian wondered if it was still too soon for her.

As he drove across the causeway, Kendall said, "We get together every March to elect officers and talk about budgets. But this year we were writing letters asking people to contact Mrs. Roosevelt and see if she'll help Marian Anderson find a place to sing in Washington."

The Daughters of the American Revolution, owners of Constitution Hall, had forbidden Marian Anderson, a Negro opera singer, from performing on their stage. In response, the president's wife had resigned from the DAR and detailed the fiasco in her newspaper column. Julian had followed the story thinking that with Japan invading China and the civil war in Spain and Mussolini cozying up to Hitler, the last thing those DAR biddies should worry about was the color of a singer. Julian, having made a fortune from Prohibition, was in no position to complain about some Americans' preoccupation with bullshit. Without the tight-ass legions busting up saloons, his wallet would've been a lot thinner.

Julian parked on Ocean Drive, and they walked north.

"Would you like to get an early supper?" he asked.

"You and me? At the same table? We can't. Miami Beach's no different than Mississippi."

"Who says?"

"Jim Crow."

"And how about not caring what people think? I thought we were gonna work on that."

"We are, but it doesn't change the rules."

"Let me show you something."

Julian marched up a walkway of crushed seashells toward a hotel and stood before a sign in the bottom corner of the lobby window: NO JEWS, NO COLOREDS, NO DOGS.

"Rules are supposed to protect people," he said. "You play along, there's a payoff. But what do these rules do for me? Or for you?"

Kendall laughed. "Or for dogs?"

They started walking again. Men and women, all of them white and dressed with the fastidiousness of well-to-do tourists, streamed past, and Kendall noticed them gawking at her and Julian. From the corner of his eye Julian saw her break into a triumphant smile, as if she'd proved her point.

Julian, more accustomed to overt hostility than subtle odiousness, saw admiration in the faces of the tourists. He'd known Jewish and Italian girls as dark as Kendall and saw nothing peculiar in a white man strolling beside a woman with a light-caramel complexion. The gawkers, he thought, were responding to the loveliness of her face and how her tight ruby sweater and coral-pink skirt emphasized the curves and swells of her body.

"They're looking because you're beautiful," Julian said, and took her hand.

Kendall squeezed his fingers, then let them go.

"You don't want to hold my hand?"

"I do, but does it have to be in Florida?"

"Where else?"

"Africa?"

She was grinning. Julian said, "The rules again? Fu—"

He caught himself before he cursed, which doubled the width of Kendall's grin.

"Fuck the rules?"

"Exactly."

Kendall stood on her tiptoes and kissed him on the lips. Julian held her hand, and they strolled along Lincoln Road, window-shopping at Bonwit Teller, Saks, and Harry Winston, and then went south on Washington Avenue. They didn't say much; they didn't have to, which pleased them both, for when they reached the end of the avenue and stood outside Joe's, a restaurant with the rugged simplicity of a hacienda, something new had sprung up between them, an ease, Julian thought, that a white couple would probably have taken for granted.

Kendall said, "We can go in?"

"Why not? They let Al Capone in."

Julian wouldn't have been so confident if he hadn't stopped by yesterday to double-check his arrangements with the owner, whom he'd met last winter while eating there with Walter Winchell.

A waiter in a tuxedo uncorked a Riesling, and after they ordered the house specialty, Kendall removed a pack of Marlboros and a matchbook from her satchel. Before she could strike a match, Julian fished a gold lighter from his pocket and held it for her.

"Didn't know you smoked," he said.

"Now you know all my bad habits: I smoke and say *fuck*." Kendall smiled. "Which do you prefer?"

"Guess."

The game ended there. Julian smoked a cigarette to keep her company. Kendall said, "You never asked how I got your phone number in New Jersey."

"Didn't have to. I spoke to my mother on Thursday."

"Did she mention the fire?"

"No, she didn't."

"The building behind Mayor Scales's store burned down. Hurleigh lived in an apartment there. Rumor is that it was arson, and Hurleigh won't come near Lovewood."

"That's good, right?"

Kendall peered at him. Julian had no intention of telling her about the Goldstein twins' proficiency with gasoline and matchsticks, and he was relieved when the waiter brought their dinner: stone crabs with mustard sauce and the sides of creamed spinach and fried potatoes were renowned for keeping conversation to a minimum.

✳

They were walking up Ocean Drive when Julian suggested that they get a drink. Kendall, as if explaining the situation to one of the less astute seagulls winging above them, replied, "I have to be off Miami Beach by sundown. You have to cross the causeway to get to Overtown, the guard at the gate will ask me for my pass, and I'll get arrested. They say the police chief down here once caught a colored boy without a pass and beat him to death."

"I wouldn't let someone hurt you."

"We're in the South, and I'm not white."

"We can have a drink here," Julian said, nodding at the building behind them, a five-story, white-stucco hotel that brought to mind a steamship, with porthole windows shaded by mauve concrete eyebrows and a vertical marquee with an orange-neon sign.

"The owner's a friend of yours?"

"Your friend too. Me."

Kendall looked at the sign and laughed. "Hotel Jerusalem?"

"My little joke. The drinks are up in my suite. So's your pass. Joe's owner knows this cop, and I bought one from him."

"Why didn't you tell me?"

"I did. I said I wouldn't let anyone hurt you."

✳

Julian's suite was on the fifth floor, and after he poured two glasses of Chablis in the galley kitchen, he led Kendall out to the rooftop deck. They stood at the railing, gazing over the palm trees and traffic. The ribbon of beach glowed whitish gold, and the ocean was pale green close to shore, turning a darker, more ominous blue as the Atlantic spread out to the horizon, all of it bathed in the violet and peach light of sunset, as though flowers and fruit had burst into flame.

Kendall said, "I wish I could paint it."

"The beach?"

"No, this moment." Kendall smiled, which was when Julian realized—and this he never forgot—that Kendall had sixteen or seventeen different ways of smiling, and he didn't fully understand any of them.

Kendall sipped her wine, and Julian guzzled his like seltzer, an effort to blunt his jitters.

"I love the Florida weather," he said. "I could stay here all—"

"Will you kiss me?" Kendall asked.

Their kiss was long and slow and soft, and Julian felt a tremor of panic when she broke away.

"I have my own room at the Mary Elizabeth, so no one will know I'm gone if you take me back before breakfast."

"You planned ahead?"

"Options are a girl's best friend."

❋

When Kendall came out of the master bath with her hair brushed out and wearing the Brooks Brothers button-down she'd found on a hook behind the door, Julian was in his boxers, smelling of Pinaud-Clubman aftershave and lying under the sheets of the double bed. It seemed to take forever before she joined him and they lay facing each other in the light of the hurricane lamp on the nightstand.

"Who goes first?" Kendall asked, treating him to smile number six or seven, he couldn't be sure, and Julian answered by kissing her neck. She shifted on the sheets like a cat stretching in the sun, and he inhaled the vanilla tanginess of her perfume and unbuttoned his shirt. He caught his breath at the sight of her breasts, so round and full, her nipples unbearably sweet in his mouth. His hand went under the ivory silk of her panties and gamboled in warm damp curls, while she tugged down his boxers and her hand stroked him—slow and fast and slow again.

Julian reached over to open the drawer of the nightstand and removed a tin of Trojans.

Kendall whispered, "I haven't done this."

"You're very good at it."

"I mean I've done what we're doing but not what you're getting ready to do."

"You don't have to whisper. No one else is here."

She had a sheepish expression now. "I was taught to hang on to my virginity till a boy marries me."

"We can wait."

"I don't want to wait anymore except—does it hurt the first time?"

"We'll go slow. Gentle." He kissed her chin, then headed down past her breasts.

"Julian, where you going?"

"Sightseeing."

"Why?"

"It's Florida. Everybody goes sightseeing."

"Not down there they don't."

Thinking she'd be less shy in the dark, Julian paused to switch off the lamp.

Kendall said, "What're you—"

"A surprise."

"I don't always like surprises."

"You'll like this one. Trust me."

She allowed him to slide off her panties, but kept her legs close together, so he worked his hands under her firm buttocks, massaging her until gradually her thighs parted, and he buried his face against her, losing himself in the brazen spices of her body. Her back arched and every one of her sinews seemed as taut as piano wire as she strained against his darting tongue, moving closer and moving away, and moaning as waves of pleasure rolled through her.

❋

Julian spooned himself around Kendall, and she said, "Quite the education I'm getting. Where'd you learn—"

"The library."

"From a book?"

"A librarian."

She chuckled, and fleetingly, Julian thought back to Berlin and

Trudie. He was so young when they started, and when it was over he was never young again.

"I should send her a thank-you note," Kendall said, and pressed backward. Julian felt the full length of her nakedness against him, and he touched her shoulder so that she turned toward him. They began again, their languid rhythm broken only by his sliding on a Trojan. Then he was above Kendall and, in that velvety instant when he entered her, he nipped at one of her earlobes to distract her from any pain. She gasped and lay still, though evidently her discomfort was brief: she scissored her satiny legs around him, thrust upward, and rotated her hips with a nimble deliberateness that Julian struggled to match. For a while they could hear their murmurs and the thrumming of bedsprings, but soon enough they heard nothing at all, and in that astonishing silence their movements seemed no more under their control than the rising and falling of the tides.

# Chapter 12

Julian awoke dreaming of Trudie and felt guilty that she'd appeared with Kendall nestled beside him. In his dream, Trudie—a pixieish blonde in a beaded black dress—had been passing through the neon green of the sign outside *Ekstase*. The proprietor of Ecstasy, known as Kaiser Wilhelm, was an ex-cop who had all his graying hair and most of his yellowed teeth. He took a liking to Julian, a rangy fourteen-year-old who was always hanging around the nightclub, and the Kaiser paid Julian to pick up cocaine for him and to carry payoffs to the police doctors who issued cards certifying that his girls were free of disease.

Trudie was the star of the Kaiser's stable, with a genius for keeping middle-aged men drinking overpriced champagne. Julian had a crush on her but was too shy to talk to her until the evening a drunk Russian nobleman tried to fuck her on a tabletop. Julian cracked a champagne bottle over the nobleman's head, and Kaiser Wilhelm emphasized his no-fucking-downstairs policy by tugging on the knob of his cane, withdrawing an eighteen-inch blade, and carving a KW on the palm of the drunk's right hand.

"You are very brave," Trudie said, her German accented with the lilt of Bavaria. Emboldened by her compliment, Julian offered to escort her home. She lived in a basement flat in one of the dreary buildings near the Alexanderplatz railway station. It was a single room, with a toilet and bath down the hall, and the sole place to sit was on the lumpy mattress of the four-poster. Trudie removed a record from the stack on the bureau and put it on the gramophone.

"What's that music?" Julian asked.

"Bessie Smith. An American blues singer. When my last boyfriend sailed off to Australia, he left me his records. I wish I understood English."

Julian liked Bessie Smith's clear, plaintive voice and that he could translate the lyrics of her songs, which he did several nights a week along with the repertoires of Ma Rainey, Big Bill Broonzy, and several other blues singers. As the music played, Trudie smoked greenish chunks of hashish in a vermilion porcelain hookah. Julian hadn't smoked before and he discovered that the hash made the blues bluer, and when he got hungry, Trudie gave him coffee and slices of pumpernickel with strawberry jam.

"You're shy," she said to him one night. "That's not unusual. But you're too sad for a boy your age."

Julian hadn't mentioned that he'd never kissed a girl and hated seeing her with the men at *Ekstase*. He said, "Why don't you get a different job?"

"I haven't decided whether to be a film star or the Queen of England."

That summer, Trudie announced she was going to cure Julian of his shyness, and for six weeks she was good to her word, teaching him to perform acts that he'd been too timid to imagine. As school started he could only see her at night, but she was in no condition for sex. She was taking pills, Eukodal—like codeine, she said—which left her flat on her bed gazing at the water-stained ceiling. And Eukodal wasn't her most dangerous problem. She was skipping work, enraging Kaiser Wilhelm, who limited his girls to six days off a month for their periods.

One evening, Julian arrived at *Ekstase* to find the bartender cleaning up shards of glass and explaining to the girls that Trudie had come in earlier and swept the liquor bottles off the shelves, hollering, "I quit!" and stumbling out. When Kaiser Wilhelm had heard about it, he'd said, "I better go talk to that lazy cow." Julian was unnerved that the Kaiser was still gone. Riding the underground, he had a sickening feeling, which didn't improve when Trudie didn't answer her door. Removing her spare key from behind the baseboard, he went in. Trudie was lying on the floor, blood spread across the front of her shirtdress. She had a jagged hole in her throat, and in a flash Julian understood what had happened. The Kaiser had spoken to her through the door as if all were forgiven, and Trudie, stupefied on Eukodal, had let him in, and the Kaiser had plunged his sword through her neck.

Bending over her, Julian pressed his lips to her bare shoulder. He felt no sadness at her death, only a glacial rage. The next afternoon, Julian went to Kaiser Wilhelm's place. He lived a block from *Ekstase*, in a stone house with crumbling scrollwork around the windows. Julian had been there to deliver the doctor's certificates. As instructed, he'd used the back door, since it was left unlocked, and he rapped on that door now. If the Kaiser appeared, Julian would ask if he had any errands for him. No one came to the door, and Julian entered the kitchen. He'd expected silence and almost fled because classical music was leaking from a stairway. Julian went up, gripping the paring knife in his coat pocket.

Down a hallway, past a half-open door, he saw Kaiser Wilhelm sitting in a claw-foot bathtub. A radio shaped like a church window was on a three-legged stool at the other end of the bathroom, and Julian stepped in, startling the Kaiser, who snapped, "You ass-fucked turd! What are you doing here?"

"I have a message for you."

"Stop standing there like a dumb cunt. Give me the message and get out."

"Trudie," Julian said, and feinted toward the radio, as if he were going to tip it into the tub, an option he'd contemplated and dismissed as an untested experiment.

The Kaiser jerked forward, which made it easy for Julian to lock his hands around his neck and force him into the hot, sudsy water. Julian heard him gurgling over the radio—a piece Julian recognized as one of his father's favorites, Strauss's *"An der schönen blauen Donau."* It seemed to Julian that the Kaiser was kicking his feet in sync with the Strauss, as if he and Julian were partners in a macabre waltz. Julian pressed harder and when, after several minutes, he let go, the Kaiser's face bobbed up with foam oozing from his nostrils.

When Julian got home, his mother was preparing dinner in the kitchen. For the last year, she had been so distraught over the battles between her son and husband that she had urged Julian to go to America. Julian had hesitated—at first, out of concern for Elana and then because of Trudie. Now, after telling his mother that he wasn't hungry, he said that he was ready to leave. Then he went to his room, having learned two new facts about himself: one, he could kill a man, and two, he could go to sleep without giving it a second thought.

Julian was startled by a car horn honking out on Ocean Drive, and Kendall murmured, "Are you all right?"

"I'm fine." Julian put an arm around her, remembering that stricken, twisted-up boy in Berlin and believing now, as Kendall shifted her head onto his chest, that he could leave that boy behind.

# Chapter 13

Walk into the administration building at Lovewood and there it was, centered on a wall, a huge photograph of Garland Wakefield in her high-necked blouse and ankle-length skirt, raising her eyes to the statue of her father.

The picture had been taken by Simon Foxe, who had dated Kendall her sophomore year. He had prevailed upon Garland—who regarded the ambitious young man as an appropriate candidate for a son-in-law—to enlarge the photo and display it as an inspiration to the students. Nevertheless, while a picture may be worth a thousand words, in this instance not one of those words was true. Staring up at her father's pitiless expression, Garland felt more resentment than awe. The seeds of her rancor had been sown when she was a girl and Ezekiel told her that he'd banished her mother—an illiterate slattern, he'd called her—back home to her snuff-dippin', tobacco-pickin' family in Virginia. Nor did Ezekiel have a higher opinion of the governesses he'd hired—and quickly fired—to care for her, teaching Garland that the one person she could rely on was her father.

That reliance had determined her choice of a career and husband and stifled her desire to search for her mother, so that by this Sunday afternoon, as Garland glanced at the statue, she wondered if Ezekiel had escaped one form of slavery only to impose another form of it on her. Lately Garland had been beset by these musings, which she blamed on her battles with Kendall over her refusal to learn the intricacies of managing wealth and operating a college; the girl insisted on spurning the achievements of her grandfather and mother for the puerile scheme of relocating to New York City to become—and this literally made Garland retch—an artist, which Garland considered a hobby for white men who'd been dead at least a century. And that was the good news, for if her daughter's aesthetic pretensions had prompted Garland to up her daily dose of Pepto-Bismol, Kendall's flirtation with Julian infuriated her to the point that at work she often had to fight off the urge to bite anyone within range of her teeth.

Garland reckoned that Kendall's eagerness to join her Alpha Kappa Alpha sisters in Miami had more to do with Julian than it did with her sorority. She intended to give her daughter a talking-to after tidying up her in-basket, and she was resigned to confronting Kendall without a shred of evidence until Professor Rose, in a bowler and three-piece suit, came striding between the banyan trees, doffing his hat at the students who greeted him with exuberant hellos. Garland reasoned that the professor would know the whereabouts of his son.

"Good afternoon, President Wakefield," Theodor said, taking off his bowler as Garland approached.

"Good afternoon. I see you have your devotees." Through the grapevine, Garland had heard that Professor Rose had become quite popular. She hadn't observed him in the classroom but knew that it was rare for Lovewood students to encounter a white authority figure who treated them with such Old World courtesy and respect for their intelligence.

"My students are splendid. And I have been meaning to thank you for helping Elana pick up nursing again. It's been a boon to her spirits."

"Professor Rose!" someone called, and Theodor and Garland spotted Otis hurrying down the library steps.

Otis arrived out of breath. "Ma'am. Professor."

"How you doing, Otis?" Garland asked. According to Kendall, for a month after Otis came back from Derrick's funeral, he'd been drinking day and night at Hazee's juke. Kendall had stepped in, making sure he completed his assignments and eating with him in the dining hall. That was her daughter, Garland thought. Compassion for everyone—except her mother.

"I'm doing this paper for Professor Rose on Descartes's *Principles of Philosophy*."

"I remember it well," Garland said. " '*Cogito ergo sum*.' "

"That's my question for Professor Rose. That whole thing—I'm not down with it. Sometimes I can think myself into believing I don't exist at all."

"Fair enough, Mr. Larkin," Theodor said. "How do you prove your existence?"

Otis recited, "*Ego can . . . Ego canentium piano ergo sum*."

"Intriguing. 'I play the piano; therefore, I am.' Plato wrote that music bequeaths a soul to the universe. Perhaps the same holds true for the individual."

"Professor Rose, I think we listen to music so we can hear our own hearts."

"Then I look forward to your defending that position in your paper. And Mr. Larkin?"

"Sir?"

"Over my many years, I have taken comfort in the idea that the mind can conquer any event that torments the spirit."

"I appreciate the advice, sir."

Theodor and Garland watched Otis go toward the library.

"Professor, I meant to ask: how is your son?"

"His mother tells me he is in Miami Beach on business."

"Business," Garland muttered, as Theodor headed into the shade of the banyan trees. "Is that what they call it now?"

※

Kendall was a resident assistant for the second floor of her dorm. The job paid thirty-five dollars a month and let her live without a roommate in a space she believed had once been a broom closet. She'd hung some of her paintings on the walls—copies of her latest obsession, cityscapes of the Ashcan painters, John Sloan and George Bellows; the revelatory light of Edward Hopper; and her favorite, the psycho-realist Dodd Brigham, who taught at the Art Students League. Their renderings of New York were as powerful and detailed as color photographs even with their wet, buttery brushwork, but they didn't make her room any bigger.

To keep her claustrophobia at bay, Kendall left her door open, which made it impossible for her to pretend she was out when Garland dropped by to enumerate her shortcomings, adding to a list that she was certain her mother had been compiling since becoming pregnant with her. "I'd like to speak with you" was the gambit Garland used after rapping on the doorframe, and this afternoon was no exception.

Kendall swiveled around in her desk chair. "How you feeling, Mama?"

"Not well." Garland set her briefcase on the floor and sat on the bed, the room so narrow that her knees nearly touched her daughter's. "Why aren't you studying?"

"Just about to." The real answer was that she'd been too busy imagining herself walking arm in arm with Julian through Greenwich Village and meeting John Sloan and Dodd Brigham.

Garland was silent, gathering herself. Then: "Do I have to explain your history to you? Our family's history."

"You've done that already. Lots of times."

Kendall's eyes wandered to her paintings, and Garland wanted to slap her, thinking that at least it would get her daughter's attention.

"Grandpa worked hard, I've worked hard, and your rejecting that to go paint—it's more than I can say grace over. How you going to support yourself? I won't give you a dime."

"I don't want your money. I've been working since I was fourteen and saved up from every job I ever had. If I'm careful in New York, I have enough for a couple of years. If I need more, I'll find work. I know Grandpa would want me to try."

"Not if he was your father, he wouldn't. And getting him to change his mind was about as easy as sticking your head up your hind parts and reciting the Gettysburg Address in pig Latin. Nohow would he put up with a daughter of his running off to New York."

"I'm not running off."

"Your grandfather used to say that a colored man has to be twice as good to go half as far. And I can tell you it's worse for a colored girl."

"Does the past have to be my future?"

"You don't change the past by taking up with a white man. Some white men would like nothing better than to take a rich, good-looking colored girl up North and pass her off as white."

Calmly, Kendall said, "I know I'm not white. And if I forget, they's lots of nearby folks to remind me."

"That's God's own truth, so I suppose I taught you a thing or two. And here's something else. White people don't have a clue what it is to be a colored. Not one damn clue."

Kendall was not as calm as she appeared. Her time with Julian *had* been wondrous. When they'd finished making love, Kendall was sore, and Julian had drawn her a bath, sprinkling in bath salts that made the water as redolent as the air after a thunderstorm. As she soaked he changed the blood-spotted sheets, then brought her a terry-cloth robe, which he'd warmed up in a tumble dryer, and when they were done drinking another glass of wine, her soreness was gone, and they got into bed, and he rubbed her with baby oil. Then he was kissing her—everywhere—until she couldn't take it anymore, and this time there was no pain, just their pushing against each other until someone who sounded exactly like Kendall started singing a scat song with the refrain, *Fjul-uck-jul-jul-ian-ian*, and she shuddered as the tension began to leave her in long, slow beats. But the next day, as Kendall ate breakfast with her sorority sisters in the hotel coffee shop, she was distressed by Julian's failure to see the people on Ocean Drive gaping at them with revulsion. And though Kendall ached to be with Julian now, that didn't mean Garland was without wisdom; one reason her mother was so vexing: she frequently knew what she was talking about.

Garland said, "Where do you come to a boy like Julian? I swear you got ahold of the only Jew who drinks."

"Mama!"

"Don't 'Mama' me. I don't have a prejudiced bone in my body. But Kendall, our family's made a name for itself, and we did it when white folks thought we should be doing for them. What's his family got?"

"His father's a professor—"

"Without a nickel to his name. The mother grew up in an or-phanage and their son ran away to become a moonshiner. Like Jarvis Scales. Not even a high-school diploma. This boy Julian's not good enough for you. He's got nothing but the ability to forget his place."

"Jesus, God, you're talkin' like one of those Main-Line white ladies Grandpa couldn't stand."

"You're not hearing me because you're like a man now—a person more interested in what's happening in his drawers than his head."

They laughed, both of them embarrassed. Save for the facts-of-life talk Garland had given Kendall years ago, it was the frankest conver-sation about sex she'd had with her daughter.

Garland wagged an index finger at Kendall. "Don't you bring me any of those zebra babies. No black-and-white stripes, you hear?"

"I hear."

Garland had calculated that by now she'd be furious. Yet her fury had deserted her, leaving her so sad she couldn't bear it. In a searing flash of memory, she recalled Ezekiel sitting in his rocker with Kendall on his lap as he read to her from an illustrated book of fairy tales, and Garland became so enraged at her father and daughter that she had to retreat from the parlor.

"I have to go," Garland said, then picked up her briefcase and walked out of the room.

# Chapter 14

On a hot May morning, a week before her daughter graduated from Lovewood, Garland stopped her station wagon outside a storage barn, and she and Elana loaded up the car with a shipment from Sears, Roebuck—towels, gauze, bars of soap, boxes of cornstarch, and bottles of calamine lotion. Elana had ordered and paid for the supplies because in March an outbreak of measles had swept through the shacks of the tenant farmers, and Elana wanted to be prepared if it happened again. Last evening, a farmer had informed Garland that some children had rashes.

When Garland learned that Elana had acquired nursing skills at the Hebrew Orphan Asylum, she asked her to help care for the farm families. There were only two Negro physicians for all of Broward County, and they drove hundreds of miles of unpaved roads to make house calls and oversaw Provident Hospital in Fort Lauderdale, the one local facility that accepted colored patients. So Elana sewed up gashes and sterilized wounds, dispensed aspirin, and assisted Hazee Thomas, who, when she wasn't at her juke, was a midwife. Owing to a lack of iodine in their diet, the elderly developed goiters, and Elana made sure they ate enough table salt. She preached that cleanliness was not just next to godliness, it could prevent family or neighbors from taking sick; and she sang the praises of Coke syrup for nausea and castor oil for almost anything else: add two tablespoons of it to a cup of warm milk to get rid of tapeworms; heat some in a saucepan and rub it into arthritic joints to alleviate pain, or below the belly of a woman cramped up with her monthly.

Garland said, "We don't pay your husband enough for you to buy supplies. Please send me the bill."

"They weren't expensive." Elana had used some of the money that Julian had given her, but she didn't want to tell Garland. From her phone conversations with her son, Elana concluded that Julian was involved with Kendall, and apparently Garland didn't approve, because she had complained to Elana that on a few occasions she hadn't been able to find her daughter on weekends.

＊

On the stream bank down from the shacks, boys and girls spotted with measles were taking turns in the metal washtubs. The water was cloudy from the cornstarch Elana poured in to relieve itching. Mothers were bathing their children, but thirty kids were milling around whining and scratching themselves, and the tubs had to be emptied and refilled after each use, so Elana pitched in. Dabbing the children's rashes with a washcloth flooded her with a joy she hadn't felt since Julian was a child, and as she rubbed a bar of Lux soap on a boy's chest, she remembered bathing her son, and a Yiddish term of endearment slipped out of her mouth.

"Is that good, *bubbeleh*?" she asked.

The boy pouted. "I ain't bubbewho's-it. I be Talbert."

"I apologize, Talbert."

Grown-ups had gathered on the bank, all of them watching Elana bathe Talbert and dry him off with one of the new towels. The dark faces watched Elana with a wariness that baffled her, and later, in the station wagon, she asked Garland if she had offended her audience.

"They were in shock. Negro women wash white children. You bathing a colored child is news. White women down here think they're above that."

"I was a week old when my mother or father left me on the steps of an orphanage in a box. Who in this world do you imagine I feel better than?"

＊

Garland brought a picnic lunch when they visited the farmers, saying that it was the least she could do, but Elana, intimately acquainted with loneliness, recognized a fellow traveler. Today they picnicked on a hilltop from where they could see the ocean beyond the campus with its palms standing like swaybacked sentinels among the brick rectangles of buildings and vibrant plantings of flowers.

Garland said, "When Daddy saw this view, he told me he was going to build the prettiest college anyone's ever seen."

"And he did."

"I did. He watched."

"Did he live to see it?"

"He only passed four years ago. Around the time Kendall started here." Ezekiel had spent his final month reading the King James Bible. Garland was astounded: save for her wedding, she'd never seen him in a church. Spotting her astonishment, Ezekiel sighed. "I been tryin' to forgive that peckerwood Scales who sold my mother. Can't forgive that man nohow." Garland said, "Don't trouble yourself about it, Daddy." Ezekiel lay back on his pillows. "Ain't rightly clear why, but it done took all the willpower God give me not to poison the highfalutin Philadelphia trash that ate my food. If I hadn't had to take care of you, I sure nuff woulda done it."

Elana said, "Did you always want to run a college?"

"Wasn't raised to want for myself."

"All the good you've done—for the students and the farm families."

"The families I do for my mother."

"You've never mentioned her."

Garland retreated into a glum silence as they ate slices of ham folded into buttered biscuits and drank sweet tea from Mason jars. Ever since she and Elana had started visiting the tenant farmers, she'd been tempted to tell her about Ezekiel and her mother, certain that an orphan would appreciate her feelings. Yet Garland had never been one to cultivate close friendships. She was mortified by her father's behavior and loath to admit her mortification to a stranger, let alone a refugee Jew who could've passed for a Protestant daughter of the Main Line and who rekindled Garland's envy of those Penn coeds in all their ethereal beauty.

Garland stretched forward and rubbed her left ankle.

"You hurt yourself," Elana said.

"Twisted it, back by the stream."

"Here, let me."

Garland hesitated, then moved her hand.

Elana, scooping some ice cubes from the cooler, folded them into a napkin and pressed it against Garland's ankle.

Garland gazed off toward the college. "My mother was a young girl—poor, illiterate—that Daddy got pregnant, and after I was born, he sent her away. I do for those farm families, it's like I'm making up for what Daddy done."

Garland turned toward Elana, expecting to see traces of pity or contempt on her face, but all she saw were blue eyes wide with curiosity and compassion. "I told Kendall, but that girl doesn't believe a thing I say. Ask her, she'd swear her granddaddy invented starlight."

Elana could feel Garland looking at her as if she were expected to tell her a secret in return. Elana didn't mind, but which one should she tell her? That after Theodor completed his yearlong tour of America and they went to Berlin with their new baby, her husband brought less ardor to their bed than he did to their Sunday strolls on Unter den Linden, leaving Elana with a throbbing in her back, a yearning for the rapture that she had once thought was every wife's reward, and a bottomless guilt about her own desires? That she became infatuated with men she didn't know—shopkeepers, trolley-car conductors, policemen, any man who even glanced at her as she passed him on the sidewalk? That in the mornings after Theodor left for the university, she daydreamed about these men and touched herself until the clenching and unclenching of her body wrung the gloominess from her and she was able to face the day? That her loneliness had once become so unendurable she had taken barbiturates with a glass of *Kirschwasser*?

The sexual content of her confession would have embarrassed Elana and, she sensed, Garland as well, so Elana said, "Six years ago, the Nazis burned twenty thousand books because the writers were declared enemies of the Reich. It was in the square by the Opera

House and the University of Berlin. The first three volumes of Theodor's work on the Enlightenment were in that bonfire, and we saw the students and the Brownshirts celebrating. Theodor cried until we got home. By that point, Julian had been in the States for several years. Theodor hadn't mentioned his name. Or shed a tear for him. He had tears for his books but none for his child. After that night, I could take care of my husband, but loving him? That was beyond me."

Garland stared at Elana, her face expressionless. Elana was growing uncomfortable with the silence when Garland surprised her by reaching over to squeeze her hand, hard, and said, in a voice tinged with sadness, "I'm sorry. I'm very sorry."

# PART III

# Chapter 15

Five days after Hitler sent his Wehrmacht to invade Poland, three days after Britain and France declared war on Germany, and one day after the United States announced that it would remain neutral was the happiest day of Julian Rose's life.

On that Wednesday afternoon, with the blare and beat of Manhattan in his ears, Julian stood outside the Greyhound terminal as Kendall, in a royal-blue dress with a ruffled lace collar and her hair knotted in an intricate bun, stepped off a bus and into his arms.

"I can't believe I'm here," she said.

Julian couldn't believe it either. She'd spent the summer keeping a promise to Garland, helping to reorganize the library, which gave her mother two more months to talk her out of going north. Since her first night with Julian in Miami Beach, Kendall had only seen him three times: a chaste Sunday in Washington, DC, bunched in with seventy thousand people—several hundred of them from Lovewood College—to hear Marian Anderson sing on the steps of the Lincoln Memorial; and two less modest Saturday visits to the Jerusalem Hotel.

As Julian put Kendall's three suitcases in the back seat of the Packard, she went to a newsstand and bought the *Herald Tribune*, *Journal-American*, the *Times*, the *World-Telegram*, and the *Sun*.

"Where do you want to live?" Julian asked, driving toward the Lincoln Tunnel.

Kendall had the *Trib* opened to the rental listings. "Greenwich Village."

Julian was considering telling her that landlords downtown weren't renowned for their desire to rent to Negroes when Kendall said, "I'm not going to Harlem. It might as well be Lovewood's Coontown. And I'm done riding in the back of the bus."

"I could help you find a place. In the Village."

She rested her hand on his leg. "I want to do it alone."

"Why?"

"I want to know I can take care of myself."

"That's overrated."

"Only if you already know it."

Julian said, "Wanna stop for something to eat?"

"You're not in a hurry to get me to your apartment?"

"Yes, but I was being a gentleman."

Kendall pressed a hand against his thigh. "That's overrated."

✳

Julian lived in a two-bedroom on the top floor of his modern, buff-brick apartment building, and Kendall hardly had a chance to notice the pearl-gray wallpaper dappled with miniature claret bouquets in the sunken living room before she was kissing him. In anticipation of Kendall's arrival, he had purchased a bed with a fawn-colored brocaded headboard and azure satin sheets from Bamberger's, the fanciest department store in Newark. The aesthetic appeal of the sheets was undeniable, yet as Kendall and Julian, naked now, enlaced themselves on the satin, they kept slipping away from each other until Julian, turning to retrieve a condom from the night table, slid off the bed, which started them both giggling.

Julian stripped back the sheets, then sat on the cotton mattress pad holding a Trojan and spotted an unfamiliar eagerness in Kendall's eyes as she lay looking up at him. Maybe it was that she no longer had to worry about exams or her mother bird-dogging her, but Kendall seemed completely at ease and surprised Julian by taking the condom from him, rolling it on, pulling him on top of her, and raising her legs to ease his way.

Neither of them questioned the change just then, nor afterward, under the steaming spray in the tiled shower stall, while Julian rubbed Kendall with a washcloth and determined, somewhere in midscrub, that her breasts needed some attention from his mouth. With her breath quickening, Kendall lathered up Julian with a bar of Palmolive, and when they finished, both of them were panting and the hot water was gone.

Temporarily satisfied, they got dressed and strolled through Meadowland Park behind the apartment house, past swans gliding across the lake, and stopped at the public library, where Julian checked out a copy of Hemingway's *To Have and Have Not*, and Kendall was delighted to find *Taos Pueblo*, a collection of photographs by Ansel Adams. Julian carried the books under his arm and held Kendall's hand as they walked by the shops on South Orange Avenue. No one gaped at them, Kendall observed, though she didn't see any Negroes other than a handful of women in maid's uniforms coming out of the grocery store or wheeling baby carriages.

"Ready to try Russian dressing?" Julian said, and opened the door of Town Hall Deli.

"If they put it on food. I'm starving."

There were no tables in the deli, just butcher-block counters and glass cases of meat, fish, and salads, and the air smelled of pickles soaking in barrels of brine. At the register, Julian paid and was presented with his order in a cardboard box, the New Jersey version of a sloppy Joe—a triple-decker sandwich on thinly sliced rye, cut into eight sections, with roast beef, pastrami, Swiss cheese, coleslaw, and Russian dressing.

They ate on the couch in Julian's living room with its sweeping views of the park and listened to Billie Holiday on the big console RCA radio. Evidently, Kendall liked the Russian because she finished two sections of the sloppy Joe before taking a sip of her beer and two more before the music gave way to Edward R. Murrow reporting the news:

"*This*—is London," Murrow announced in the dry, flat tone of the American West. "And from here I can tell you that Herr Hitler's blitzkrieg is scorching the Polish countryside. The dead compete for space in grain fields and woodlands. The *New York Times* reports that Nazi military leaders are currently devising plans to relocate Poland's three million Jews . . ."

Julian got up and turned off the radio, then sat in one of the burgundy club chairs across from the couch. Kendall went to sit on his lap.

Julian said, "It's odd thinking that being Jewish should be worth a story on the news."

"Like being colored down South. One wrong move, you're a headline in the Negro papers. You think we'll get into the war over there?"

"Roosevelt says no."

"What do you say?"

Julian tightened his arms around her. "That I'm glad you're here."

# Chapter 16

Kendall had intended to stay with Julian for a few days before beginning her search for a rental in Greenwich Village. Yet as the weeks went by and leafy canopies of red, orange, purple, and gold cast shadows across the streets, the New York newspapers she'd bought remained on the coffee table, along with her art and photography magazines and the course catalog from the Art Students League.

Her life with Julian took on the rhythm of a honeymoon. They borrowed books from the library and walked to the Cameo Theatre to see *The Wizard of Oz*. They ate double-dip ice-cream cones from Gruning's and took long walks through South Orange and into Maplewood, the next town over, until the gas lamps came on, and the smell of burning leaves permeated the tumbling darkness. They cooked together: Kendall taught him her grandfather's art of frying chicken, from the buttermilk soak to the batter mixed with cayenne pepper, paprika, and molasses, and Julian impressed her with his beef stew—his secret ingredient, generous pourings of cabernet sauvignon.

During these weeks the closest Kendall got to Greenwich Village was when she and Julian drove through Manhattan to the World's Fair in Queens. Flushing Meadows was mobbed, all those people crushed by today eager for a glimpse of tomorrow. They wandered through the planetarium and the RCA pavilion; they watched swimmers frolic like balletic porpoises in the Aquacade, inspected the paintings in the Masterpieces of Art exhibit, and drank champagne at Le Restaurant Français.

Kendall said, "I saw the Baedeker's guide to Paris on your bookshelf."

"So when we go I can show you around."

"You'd go with me to Paris?"

"Say the word."

"Why?"

"I—I love you."

He had whispered this to her in bed, but you couldn't count what a man said when his clothes were on the floor. Kendall reached across the table and toyed with his fingers, and she felt wonderful until they went to see the Westinghouse Time Capsule, a copper tube that would be opened in five thousand years and had been stocked with hundreds of items—from a tobacco pouch to a safety pin—that would give future generations a taste of the 1930s. As Kendall considered the exhibit, her mother popped into her head, denouncing her talk about becoming an artist as an excuse to loaf around and reminding her that no daughter of Garland Wakefield was brought up to be a hootchie-cootchie girl for some white man. Kendall had written her mother once, saying that she'd forward an address and phone number when she got settled, and in the event of emergency she should contact Julian. Kendall could imagine the steam shooting out of Garland's ears when she read that information. But what gnawed at Kendall was that she agreed with her mother, and Garland's critique, combined with too much champagne and the pencil-thin white lady who was glowering at them, soured her mood.

"We should climb into the capsule," Kendall said. "And when they dig us up maybe it'll be normal for whites and Negroes to traipse around holding hands."

The spiky edges were plain in her voice, and in the car, with that same tone, she said, "You know that you and my mother are the only ones who don't call me Kenni-Ann?"

"Why doesn't your mother?"

"Because she's always mad at me."

"I'm not mad at you," Julian said, believing that Kendall was just blowing off steam because of the nasty look that old dame had given them.

"So why don't you?" she asked.

"Kenni-Ann's too cute."

"I'm not cute?"

"You're too beautiful to be cute."

From her sullen expression Julian could see that the compliment hadn't mollified her, but fortunately it did bring their conversation to a close—at least until they entered the lobby of his apartment house, and she said, "That time capsule was pure arrogance. Who'll care about us in fifty centuries?"

In an effort to dodge an emotional slugfest, Julian gave her the keys. "I'm going to Gruning's to get some dessert. I'll meet you upstairs."

When Julian returned with a quart of ice cream, Kendall was on the sofa with her legs drawn up under her skirt and the twilight coming through the windows cocooning her in a violet glow. As Julian dropped his hat and coat on a chair, he saw something beyond the melancholy that occasionally seeped into Kendall's eyes—he saw an unbridgeable separateness, a confinement behind invisible walls that Kendall herself had built. Perhaps it was an unavoidable consequence of being a smart, talented Negro in a society that expected you to scrape and bow, or of being a woman whose supreme goal wasn't a husband, or of her yearning, over the objections of her mother, to be an artist.

Julian respected her self-containment: it was a quality he valued in himself. All the same, as he sat on the couch and Kendall smiled ruefully at him through a lilac cloud of light, he had to admit that those walls around her were frighteningly high and he might not be able to scale them. He was willing to risk it, though, believing that if he cherished her enough, opened himself up enough, if he just flat out loved her enough, they wouldn't end up like the couple on the cover of the avant-garde art journal Kendall had left on his coffee table—a woodcut done by some dotty Norwegian artist whose name was Much or Muck. In the picture, a young woman with flowing hair stood on a beach, facing away from a man standing behind her and staring at the moon above the water. They were several steps apart, but the feeling of the distance between them was so profound that they might as well have been on different planets.

Kendall said, "I thought you weren't coming back."

Her eyes were puffy from crying.

"Where would I go?"

"I don't know. . . . I shouldn't have barked at you."

Julian hugged her, and Kendall trembled against him. "I'm sorry. I hate when I bark like that. I sound like my mother."

"Only younger," Julian said, and laughed.

Kendall laughed too. "Am I really going to wind up like her?"

"Not if you don't want to." Julian let her go. "Feeling better?"

She grinned. "Depends on the flavor ice cream you bought."

"Your favorite." Julian reached over to the oblong glass coffee table and removed the carton from the bag. "Butter pecan."

Kendall used her forefinger to sample the ice cream, then pushed Julian back, kissing him deeply, taking off his tie, unbuttoning his shirt, and rubbing him, his stomach as flat and smooth as ivory and the hardness under the flannel of his trousers giving her ideas, none of which, she was certain, her mother would approve of.

Julian's hand crept under her sweater, and she pulled away, sitting astride him, dipping two fingers into the butter pecan and slathering his nipples with ice cream.

He shivered.

Kendall asked, "You think what's good for the goose is good for the gander?"

Julian smiled to indicate that he was interested in finding out, and as Kendall cleaned off the butter pecan by nibbling at him with her lips, they determined that the cliché contained more than a grain of truth. Julian would've been content to continue their inquiry, but Kendall sat up, tugged off her sweater, and undid her bra.

"These?" she said.

"Those." As fond as Julian was of the high, round firmness of her breasts, it was the creaminess of her skin that left him breathless, and her coloring, as though someone had mixed honey and cinnamon and sunlight in a jar.

"You sure?" she asked.

Julian lifted his head toward her, but she was gone, kneeling on the floor and ridding him of his loafers, socks, trousers, and boxers, then coating his cock with butter pecan, the ice cream melted now and as slick as oil. Julian felt her tongue licking him, circling him, and then her mouth covering him, up and down, tentatively at first, her movements accelerating until all Julian was aware of was the rising and falling of his hips.

Kendall hadn't done this before. For the last several days, she'd wanted to try it yet was scared that she'd choke to death, which, she told herself, wouldn't lead to the most flattering obituary. Now, with her mouth bobbing on Julian, a peacefulness flooded through her, and she reveled at arriving in this place beyond the clutches of self-doubt. Pausing for an instant, she admired the divine agony on Julian's face and felt so pleased by her sense of power and the tingling between her legs. It was a revelation to her, this getting by giving. Necking and petting had always felt to Kendall as though she were guarding a prize that boys were attempting to steal from her. Even with her serious college romances—first Simon, then Derrick—all she'd received in the exchange was a pleasant tepidness instead of the devouring heat she'd expected, and stroking them until her hand was sticky was a relief, because—for that evening—they stopped trying to coax her into surrendering a gift she preferred not to give them.

Kendall was disappointed by her response to these encounters. Sometimes she believed that her desire to live in Paris had less to do with art than with her wish to shuck off the straitjacket her upbringing had fashioned for her, as if by breathing the voluptuous air of that sublime city, scented as it was with the sexual mists of centuries, she might become as daring as the most ambitious coquette at the court of Louis XV, a seductress out of the paintings of François Boucher, lush and wanton, a stranger to shame.

Julian was groaning louder, and Kendall wondered why her erotic metamorphosis had occurred with a white, Jewish ex-bootlegger who'd grown up in Germany. She loved looking at Julian: his broad shoulders, wavy hair, and cleft chin; his smile that was two parts irony and one part joy; and his blue eyes that seemed to change color, like the ocean depending on the height of the sun. He was curious and listened to her as if she were the one person on earth with something to say, and he knew his business in bed. Yet none of this explained why her pleasure with him possessed the intensity of a glorious tantrum. She liked that he could protect her, that he hadn't thought twice about manhandling Hurleigh Scales, and he'd probably been responsible for somebody's burning down the garage apartment where the mayor's brother lived. Ever since meeting him, she had envied his independence and contempt for rules, and wished that those two qualities would rub off on her. Both mattered to her, though ultimately, Kendall decided, as she stood up and Julian watched her unhook her skirt, unsnap her garters, then peel off her stockings and panties, her reason for letting herself go with Julian was that she trusted him. Positioning herself above Julian on her hands and knees, Kendall let her breasts brush his face, and he went at them like an infant with an unquenchable thirst. She murmured a string of nonsensical syllables, thinking that she trusted Julian because of her perception that, like her, he viewed himself as flawed in an unfixable way, a flaw that marked him as a permanent outsider, lonely beyond redemption. They were kindred spirits. In his arms, her loneliness was finally assuaged; she never heard Garland's harangues; and it was Kendall's fear of feeling so hopelessly alone again, with just her mother's razor-sharp voice for company, that had kept her in South Orange longer than she'd planned.

"I love you," Kendall said. It was the first time she'd told him that, and she rocked backward until he started to enter her.

"A Troj—"

"It's safe. My period's tomorrow."

She let him in deeper. He stopped talking.

After a minute, she asked, "Do you love me?"

"You know I do."

"I do?" She grinned, rocking forward so Julian wasn't inside her.

"I love you."

She allowed him to slide into her again. "You like this?"

Julian nodded.

"This?" she asked, speeding up.

He didn't answer. The cords of his throat looked tight enough to snap.

"Do you?"

His eyes were slits.

"Should I stop?"

"Don't."

"Do-o-o-on't?" she moaned, throwing her head back.

"Stop."

"Stop?" She was moving faster.

"Ever."

"Everrrrrrr?"

"Don't ever stop," he said.

# Chapter 17

Julian had ordered a vanity table with a clamshell mirror for Kendall, and he loved to lie in bed and watch her there on the padded stool, brushing her hair while the light, coming through the windows, sparkled on the glass skyline of Shalimar, Chanel No. 5, and Lancôme Tendre Nuit. Below the perfume bottles, like the sprawl of a mythic, feminine metropolis, were cartons of Madame C. J. Walker's Vegetable Shampoo; white jars of Queen Helene cocoa butter; tiny bottles of clear and strawberry-colored nail polish; tubes of Max Factor lipstick; a shocking-pink, circular powder-puff box, three hairbrushes, and a big-toothed, wood-handled metal comb.

Now, on this Saturday, they had agreed to have dinner at the Tavern with Fiona and Eddie, and Kendall sat before the mirror in her bra, panties, and garter belt. Usually this sight entertained Julian to no end, but he was distracted by a flash of clarity: he would've preferred to stay home and keep Kendall to himself, a result of wanting her more than he'd ever wanted anyone. He loathed his desperation. Sure, he was thrilled that he'd finally found a woman to adore, but it made him feel like a ninety-pound weakling and filled him with dread for the day that Kendall would move to New York.

She said, "I'm not that pretty, you know."

"Yes, you are."

"Only because you can't see inside me."

Julian wasn't sure what she meant. Perhaps it explained those walls she lived behind. The walls didn't bother him, but what might lie behind them made him nervous. "If you want to show me, I'll take a look."

Kendall walked over to the bed and kissed him. "We'll be late."

✳

The Tavern featured first-rate food and formally dressed waiters who expected you to tip them enough to make doctors or lawyers out of their sons. On Saturday nights the line ran out through the vestibule and up Elizabeth Avenue, but Eddie and Fiona were already seated in a private corner, one of the privileges of being associated with Longy or Julian.

"You're famous," Kendall said, as they veered between the tables and the diners glanced at them.

Julian was used to being looked at in Newark, but he suspected that the people were giving Kendall the once-over to figure out if she were a high-yellow bimbo or just a tan showgirl. Julian didn't care what people around town thought of her. Kendall could go anywhere in Newark and, if they knew she was with him, she'd be safe. New York was a whole other ball of wax. Julian was pals with some illustrious troublemakers and bent cops across the Hudson, but he couldn't protect Kendall there, and the city was rough on the ambitious. You could ask Mad Dog Coll or Dutch Schultz if they weren't deader than yesterday. Or Jean Harlow. Abe had fallen in love with her and helped make her a movie star, and by twenty-six the poor girl was on the unlucky side of the grass at Forest Lawn. Realistically, what kind of shot did any single girl have in New York? Especially a colored girl who thought she'd left Jim Crow in Florida. That was why Julian had offered to help Kendall rent an apartment. When she refused, he didn't want to insult her by mentioning it again. However, Fiona, who was on her second gin rickey, brought it up the instant Kendall sipped her pinot noir and started talking about her plans.

Fiona said, "You better get yourself some comfy shoes because you'll be walking awhile if you're gonna try'n rent from one of those hateful shitheels in Greenwich Village. Most of them'll get a gander at you and offer you a nickel to clean their toilets."

Eddie took a slug of Jameson's. "Why don't ya mind your own business?"

"Edward doesn't like me to drink," Fiona said. "He says it makes me too quiet."

"Yeah," Eddie said. "It works wonders."

When Kendall first saw Fiona, with her ginger-colored hair pinned back from the elegant angles of her face, she hoped that she wasn't one of those prissy Irish bitches she'd known at school in Philadelphia. Then Kendall noticed the eerie, bluish-green fire in Fiona's eyes, and she concluded that whatever Fiona was thinking would, in short order, come out of her mouth—a crassness that Garland would've abhorred and that Kendall decided, on the spot, was an admirable quality.

"Toots," Fiona said to her, "don't take any lip off a landlord. They're all Satan's spawn. If he gives ya any shit, tell 'im you're Black Irish and your old man walks a beat. If that don't work, send one of these lugs here to beat him senseless."

Dinner was the Tavern classic: aged prime rib, baked potato, and string beans. As they ate, Fiona asked Kendall her opinion of Paul Henry.

"Who?" Eddie asked.

"The painter," Fiona said. "Does landscapes of west Ireland."

"Never heard of him," Eddie said.

"I read about him in a book."

Eddie said, "You're not supposed to be smarter than me."

"Too late," Fiona said. "Now let Kendall talk."

Julian swelled up with pride as Kendall said, "Henry was influenced by Vincent van Gogh and his painting *Starry Night*. It was how he learned to capture landscapes and people as they were—stripped of the usual Irish romanticism."

Despite his pride, the excitement in her voice saddened Julian, that she was so enchanted by a world he knew almost nothing about, and he despaired of ever catching up with her regardless of how many art books he read.

For dessert, they had coconut cream pie, which had achieved some nationwide fame because of the radio and newspapers. The pie was deemed so fundamental to the restaurant's success that the recipe was stored in a safety deposit box at the National Newark and Essex.

"Could either of you ladies learn to bake this?" Eddie asked.

Fiona and Kendall looked at each other.

Eddie said, "I hear the way to a man's heart is through his stomach."

Fiona and Kendall began laughing and, nearly in unison, answered, "A little lower."

❋

Later, in bed, Julian reached for Kendall, and she gave him a fast hug and sat up, lighting a cigarette and dropping the match in the yellow, butterfly-shaped glass ashtray on the night table. She exhaled a curl of smoke. "Do you think I can be an artist?"

"Isn't it more important what you think?"

"Probably, but I want your opinion."

"I'm not an art critic."

"I'm not asking for a review."

Julian held out his hand for the cigarette. She gave it to him. He took a drag. "I think you can be anything you want. And I—"

"You?"

Julian stubbed out the cigarette in the ashtray, and he heard the forlorn notes of a lost child in his voice when he said, "And I hope some of what you want is me."

"Just hold me."

"Not in the mood?"

She didn't answer and lay with her head on his shoulder and his arm around her. A few minutes later, Kendall said, "I'm going to start looking for a place on Monday."

"Okay," he said, and wanted it to be, but it wasn't, and he'd look back at this moment, this beat of fleeting time, and wonder if this was the night he began to lose her.

# Chapter 18

Kendall was grateful to Fiona for recommending that she wear comfortable shoes, because after two weeks in Greenwich Village she felt as if she were trying to rent in the whites-only section of Lovewood. At an apartment hotel on Grove Street, where a sign above the entrance claimed Suites/Apts Avail, she asked the goggle-eyed man at the desk in the lobby if he could show her a rental, and he said, "I can't. My foot hurts."

"Will it be better soon?"

"Maybe in twenty, thirty years."

And Fiona was right about the toilets. At a townhouse on West Fourth, where a studio in back off the garden had been listed for rent in the *Herald Tribune*, she rapped on the door with the brass knocker, and an old man in a black silk dressing gown came to greet her and exclaimed, "Bella, the new maid's here!"

Only one person demonstrated any kindness. When she inquired about an apartment above a candy store on Bleecker, the paunchy, middle-aged soda jerk replied, "I apologize, my sister just rented it."

As Kendall started to leave, the soda jerk said, "Ya know the bandleader Noble Sissle?"

Hoping the fellow might have reconsidered, Kendall smiled at him. "I don't."

"Noble got a singer looks like you. Lena Horne. A real doll."

"You think Lena Horne knows where I can get an apartment?"

Before he could understand that there was more irony in her question than curiosity, Kendall was gone.

With minor variations, these scenes reoccurred day after disheart-
ening day, and yet, after she rode the train back to Penn Station and
Julian picked her up and asked, "How'd it go?" she always answered,
"Didn't see anything worth a damn."

In part, she lied because she knew he'd offer to solve her problem,
which Kendall didn't want him to do. Her other motive for lying was
less virtuous: Kendall resented the white people who rejected her,
and she found herself, against her will, resenting Julian right along
with them. Unfair, yes, but true, and she castigated herself for her
ugly secret.

Her frustration didn't dampen her enthusiasm for the eccentric
cosmos of the Village. A wispy man, bearded like Father Time, walking a quartet of calico cats on leashes down Perry Street and stopping
people to ask for donations so he could finish composing the greatest
history ever written—*An Oral History of the Universe*. In Washington
Square Park, a group of short-haired white women in camisoles,
dancing in a circle in the fountain while a Negro man watched from
a bench, playing a guitar and singing the blues. In the Life Cafeteria
on Sheridan Square, where Kendall regularly stopped for an egg-salad
sandwich and carton of milk, she encountered bohemia in its full
odoriferous flower: prostitutes, women and men, decked out for a
party by lunchtime; assorted cranks and philosophers arguing; writers
and painters scribbling in notebooks or drawing in sketchpads on their
knees, all of them engaged in the hallowed task of translating their
ephemeral misery into deathless art.

Now, late on this windy October afternoon, Kendall was hurrying
along Seventh Avenue. She had just overheard two sailors at the cafeteria talking about rentals on Washington Square South. The door
was answered by a heavyset guy with bear tracks of coffee stains decorating his undershirt. He looked Kendall up and down as if trying to
determine whether she met some preconceived specifications.

"I'm Herm," he said, leading her down the steps of the brownstone. "The building's been converted into apartments, so if the
basement ain't to your liking, I got one on the third floor after New
Year's. Rent for either's a hundred a month."

That was fifty dollars less than Kendall had budgeted, and her heart almost leapt out of her chest. As a painter, she was concerned about the presence of natural light, but up a few stairs off the kitchen was a solarium that led to a walled, flagstone patio.

"It's perfect," Kendall said when they were back outside.

"Swell. So all's you gotta know is my end's a third of your take."

"Take?"

"You're a working girl, yeah?"

"I'm going to the Art Students League."

"That'll bring in a classier trade. And I get a ride a week—on the house. I wouldn't ask, but the wife died in July."

Kendall backed away, unsure what had her more worked up: Herm assuming she was a prostitute or imagining her mother lambasting her with an I-told-you-so.

Herm interpreted her reaction as an objection to his terms and, like a carny barker attempting to drum up an audience for a freak show, said, "You'll make good money. And the last girl in the basement met a peach of a fella. They got hitched, and I hear he got elected to Congress."

She wasn't able to stop herself from crying until Julian met her train in Newark. He put an arm around her and gave her a hankie. She dried her eyes and, after telling him the story, said, "Am I ever going to find a place?"

"Absolutely," Julian said.

# Chapter 19

Orchard Hill Township was in the northeastern border of Essex County, five square miles of dairy farms and apple orchards that, acre by acre, were being acquired by Julian with an eye toward putting up housing developments. The county population was over eight hundred thousand, with fifty-two percent of it jam-packed into Newark, and Julian was betting that sooner or later people would trade the city for the suburbs.

The three men in charge of the local government—Chairman Warren Willingham and the two other members of the Township Committee who elected him—were weasels of the highest order. They had appointed their wives as the sole agents for every land sale in Orchard Hill, and not only were they pocketing a six percent commission, they goosed up the asking price on the parcels. Julian accepted this as an inconvenience of the real-estate game. But when he asked Willingham to rezone a portion of his acreage from residential to commercial so one day he could put up an outdoor mall with all the stores that families would need, Willingham said the rezone would cost Julian twelve grand—four for each member of the committee.

Julian wasn't inclined to pony up; the committee was already screwing him. But he calculated that his investment in Orchard Hill would earn a fortune, so he forked over the bribe. Except Willingham wasn't done. Yesterday, he'd phoned and demanded another nine grand to modify the zoning, which was why Julian was more than slightly pissed off when he entered the Township Committee meeting room with Eddie carrying a new leather briefcase in each hand and another tucked under his arm.

Willingham was at one end of a polished walnut table, his two lackeys at the other, and a mural covered the wall behind them—a bunch of Puritan assholes swindling some Indians out of their land by trading them axes and kegs of rum.

"Mr. Rose," he said. "Good of you to stop by."

In Julian's experience elected officials came in two basic flavors: hard guys like Mayor Scales in Lovewood with his folksy gab and unabashed belligerence, and the oilier version embodied by Warren Willingham with his salt-and-pepper-haired, craggy-faced earnestness, and bogus rectitude oozing from every pore. Scales annoyed Julian, but Willingham reminded him of a venerable parson who in his off-hours was humping every girl in Sunday school, and Julian had to stifle a desire to break his jaw.

"I bribe a guy," Julian said, "he's supposed to stay bribed. I don't like chiselers."

"I would guess chiseling was a modus operandi with your people."

"My people?" Julian said, aiming his icy blues at Willingham.

"Bootleggers, Mr. Rose."

"Alleged ex-bootlegger," Julian said, knowing that Willingham had meant gangster *and* Jew. "Where's the rezone paperwork?"

One of the lackeys held up a sheet of official township stationery. "Here. The chairman has to sign it."

Eddie set a briefcase before each of the two men, then brought Julian the other one and the piece of paper, and returned to watch the lackeys. After reading the rezone order, Julian stood over Willingham, putting the case, paper, and an uncapped fountain pen in front of him. Willingham flicked up the brass clasp and peered inside the case. "Empty. I'm disappointed."

Julian withdrew a penny from the case and held it up with the thumb and index finger of his left hand.

"Not empty," Willingham said. "Let's say the pot's light."

With stripes of red, white, and blue, the mayor's tie resembled a barber pole, and Julian took the tie in his right hand and read the label.

"Ohrbach's?" Julian said. "You shake me down for twelve grand, and you shop at Ohrbach's? You're a chintzy prick."

Letting go of the tie, Julian plucked the fuchsia paisley pocket square from Willingham's suit coat and, like a magician about to perform a trick, began rolling up the penny in it.

"I'm not so easily entertained," Willingham said.

"That kinda talk frightens the secretaries, does it?"

"Don't be foolish. The township has a police force."

"You figure they get here before the ambulance?"

Willingham sprang to his feet. He was almost as tall as Julian, but older and not as strong or quick, so beyond flailing his arms there was nothing he could do when Julian grabbed the lapels of his suit coat, slammed him onto the table, and, with his thumb, started shoving the pocket square with the penny in it into one of his nostrils.

"This is all you get from me," Julian said, pressing with such force a nasal bone cracked, all the while wishing that he could do the same thing to those SOBs who refused to rent Kendall an apartment.

"Stop!" Willingham yowled. "Stop!"

Julian released the mayor, who eased himself into his chair, using the paisley silk to blot at the blood trickling from his nose.

Julian held out the fountain pen. "Give me back my twelve grand or change the zoning."

Willingham's right cheek was puffing up. He took the pen and signed.

"Enjoy the briefcases, boys," Julian said, taking his pen and the paper and walking out with Eddie.

# Chapter 20

You sure you don't want any help?" Julian asked, pouring pancake batter onto a griddle. Kendall still hadn't found a place, and she'd become so remote that he was worried about her.

"I appreciate the offer, but no."

"I've got business in the city today," Julian said. "I could drop you off."

Kendall nodded. "I have to register for a class at the Art Students League before I . . ."

She went to get dressed without finishing her sentence. Nor did she perk up in the car, but at least she was talking. Julian couldn't bear her silence. It reminded him of living with his mother in Berlin.

"What business do you have in the city?" she asked.

"Going over some numbers for a guy."

"For your friend Abe?"

"Siano Abruzzi."

"I read about him in the *Star-Ledger*. He's a mobster. The head of his own gang. Didn't he almost kill Abe?"

"They had a disagreement. A long time ago."

Kendall looked at him, but Julian couldn't tell if she was curious about his meeting Siano or suspicious. She was so perceptive that Julian would have to watch his mouth, especially now. The disagreement between Siano and Abe had escalated into a war. The Abruzzis had tried to horn in on bars supplied by Abe, and Julian and Eddie beat one of their salesman senseless. Siano sent a pair of his goons to shoot Abe, and Julian and Eddie buried them in the Dumpster behind Giordano's Bakery. Then Abe cut a deal with Siano. War over.

"I'm gonna be working till the afternoon," Julian said, as he let her out at the arched doorway of the Art Students League. "I can come get you. We could get a bite or see a movie."

"There's a luncheonette next to the Loews on Seventh Avenue and Twelfth. I'll meet you there at four."

Julian tuned in WNEW and whistled along with one of his favorites, Benny Goodman and his band doing "Sing, Sing, Sing."

Things were looking up.

※

The luncheonette was empty, and Kendall sat in a booth by a window with gingham curtains. A waitress in a white-trimmed black uniform came through swinging, saloon-style doors and set a pie plate on the counter.

"Pardon me," Kendall called. "May I have a cup of tea?"

The waitress glanced at Kendall. Her gray hair was wound so tightly in curlers that her eyes appeared half shut. "We're out," she said.

"Coffee then?"

"The urn's getting scrubbed."

"A Coke?"

"Syrup's gone but we maybe got some bottles in back."

The waitress barged back through the louvered doors as Julian came in, removing his hat and sitting in the booth.

"Drink up," the waitress said, putting a glass of Coke on the table.

Julian said, "I'd like a Coke too, please."

"How nice," the waitress said, and disappeared.

Kendall sipped the soda, then spit it out into the glass. "Jesus, God, there's vinegar in it."

Kendall looked mad enough to skin the waitress. Julian helped her on with her coat and put on his hat. The waitress was standing behind the counter next to a man in a grease-stained shirt and pants. He had a handlebar mustache and was as squat as a circus strongman.

Kendall walked over, Julian beside her. "Was that vinegar?"

The waitress said, "You don't like our soda, go somewhere else."

Kendall pointed her index finger at her. "You redneck bitch—"

"Watch your mouth," the man said, coming around the counter. "That's my wife."

Julian stepped toward the man. "How much for the pie?"

"The lemon meringue?" the man replied. "It ain't for sale."

"I'll take it to go."

"I says that pie ain't for sale. Beat it."

Julian tossed a fiver on the counter next to the pie and, when the man looked down at the bill, Julian slipped his hand under the plate and smashed the lemon meringue in his face, then shoved him backward so that he stumbled against the sink.

When Julian turned around, Kendall was gone.

＊

Julian had found a space less than a block from the movie theater, and Kendall was in the passenger seat. As he got into the Packard, she said, "What the fuck's wrong with white people?"

"You mean the Ku Klux waitress and her husband? Or you mean all white people?"

"Do we have to talk about this?"

"You brought it up."

"I mentioned it."

"Isn't that the same thing?"

"I wasn't inviting you to a debate."

Once, when Eddie was yammering on about Fiona arguing with him until he felt as if she were sticking one of her knitting needles in his eye, Julian told him that any guy dumb enough to argue with a dame deserved his fate. Now, instead of heeding his own advice, he pressed on: "You were simply stating the facts."

"I was stating the facts as I've experienced them."

"And you're including me in this?"

Of course she didn't mean him, but she was too enraged to concede the point. "You think a pie in the face fixes anything?"

"Shooting both of them would've been better. But you get the electric chair for that."

"That stop you before?"

"You wanna talk about that now?"

"Do you have any idea how it feels? That people'll pour vinegar in a Coke to keep you out of their luncheonette?"

"Yeah. Some idea."

Kendall clutched her bag against her chest. "The hell you do. So quit talking about it."

They didn't speak for the rest of the evening, but the next morning, a Saturday, Julian opened his eyes and saw Kendall sitting beside him on the bed.

"I'm sorry about yesterday," she said, rubbing his back. "I know you want to help. I'm going into the city. Landlords might be friendlier on the weekend."

"I'll take you to the train."

"You get some rest. I can take a bus."

Kendall kissed him, and Julian tried to go back to sleep, but his mind was racing and he got up and dialed Siano Abruzzi. The two of them had some details to iron out.

# Chapter 21

That Saturday, as a church bell rang in the golden air, Kendall's luck didn't improve, and by noon she was walking by tour buses of suburbanites who roamed the Village as if they were on safari, hoping to spot wild bohemians in their natural habitat.

At the Caffe Reggio, where the waiters couldn't have cared less about your race, Kendall drank a cappuccino. An older couple was at the next table. The man, in a butter-yellow suit without a shirt, had long white hair and the white chin whiskers of a billy goat; the woman, with a fuzzy cap of gray hair sprinkled with reddish brown and the face of a wise and mischievous angel, was draped in an olive poncho made from a blanket. Neither of them spoke, but they didn't seem unhappy—more like sculpture designed to provide the out-of-towners, chatting over coffee and pastry, with a glimpse of bohemia.

Kendall didn't spot the tether until the man stood to pay the bill. He was holding one end of a fat-looped chain; the other end was clipped to a bracelet on the woman's right wrist; and she shuffled behind him, chanting, "Here we go round the mulberry bush, the mulberry bush . . ."

Horrified and fascinated, Kendall dropped a dollar on the table, took the Leica from her satchel, and followed them up MacDougal Street, listening to the droning nursery rhyme and the jingle-jangle of the chain hitting the sidewalk. As the man reached Washington Square, he turned, saying, "Come along, Christina," and by the time she caught up with him, Kendall had clicked a fast five pictures of their backs as they disappeared into the crowd around the fountain.

On Monday, as Kendall rode the train into Manhattan to begin her painting from life class, she wished she'd been able to photograph the couple's faces and wondered if she'd see them again. All she had to do was wait the eighteen minutes it took her to walk from Penn Station to the Art Students League, because in a studio on the fourth floor, the man in his linen suit was poised beside an easel, staring at the dozen or so students on the folding chairs, and Christina, in her poncho, was sitting cross-legged on the floor, the chain running from one of her ankles to one of his.

Kendall was ecstatic. The man was Dodd Brigham—*the* reason she'd enrolled at the League. She hadn't recognized him in Caffe Reggio because in the photographs she'd seen of him, he was young, with a crew cut and clean-shaven.

"I cannot teach you to paint," he said. "I can help you learn to see. Like the cubists, futurists, and surrealists, you may be tempted to twist form like a cruller or merge the realistic and fantastic to arrive at the essence of truth . . . I say there is paradox aplenty around you, and if you can render a paradox truthfully, then you will be an artist. So before you play with form, open your eyes. Wide. Consider my wife, Christina."

The chain rattled when Christina stood and removed her poncho. A few students reacted with awkward laughter. Christina was naked, and she rotated in a full circle.

Kendall was astounded that she hadn't seen it immediately. Christina had to be in her midfifties. Her forehead, cheeks, and neck were lined, and her pubic patch was white. Yet her skin was taut, unmarred by sags or stretch marks, and she had the sleek curves, pert breasts, and beautifully shaped legs of a college girl. It was as though her face and hair had aged while her body had been exempted from the wages of time.

"A paradox, isn't it?" Brigham asked. "Its cause? A hiccup of nature? Exercise? Prayer? Who cares? Your task is to see it, then paint it."

❋

That evening, after Kendall told Julian about her experience in class, he said, "Let me get this straight. His wife's body looked younger than her face, and that's a paradox?"

"Over thirty years younger."

"Nothing strange about them being chained to each other."

"To me it was, but he didn't mention it."

"And you paid for this?"

Kendall performed her shoulder trick, hunching and unhunching them, a gesture that appeared to express resignation but, Julian knew, was designed to dismiss his criticism. "Do you mind if I set up my easel and paint in the spare bedroom?"

"No problem. We could stop at a hardware store and get a chain."

Kendall laughed, reluctantly, it seemed to Julian, as if she really didn't think it was funny.

# Chapter 22

After four days, the painting was done. On the top half of the canvas was a young Negro woman in a lavender swimsuit standing in the sea, her eyes on the dawn coming over the horizon. Below her was a snowy sidewalk at dusk and a man in a fedora and overcoat walking with his head lowered. Julian could see the left side of his face. The man was white.

"It's great," Julian said, not feeling as chipper as he sounded, because the painting made him nervous. "Don't I know those people?"

"They're not us. They're a paradox. They're together and they're in different places."

"Where are they together?"

"Uh, in the painting?"

Intending to reassure her, Julian said, "Now I get it," though the symbolism hadn't been apparent to him.

"Knew you would," but Julian heard the doubt in her voice.

*

Perhaps it was painting again, but when Kendall went into New York on Monday, she was optimistic about her future. Not even the terse letter her mother had mailed to Julian's, demanding to know when she was going to move, or her discovery that the basement apartment next door to the Cherry Lane Theatre was no longer for rent could dampen her spirits. At the corner of Commerce Street and Bedford, Kendall bent to retie her Keds and noticed a man in a blue work shirt and dungarees watching her through a courtyard gate. When she stood up, she saw that it was Dodd Brigham. He called out to her, "You are in my class, are you not?"

"Yes, sir," she answered, and introduced herself.

Opening the gate, he let her into the courtyard and said to his wife, "Christina, my student Kendall Wakefield is here."

Christina was seated on a redwood settee in a black velvet smoking jacket and squinting against the sun. Again, Kendall was amazed by the contrast between the age lines creasing her face and the youthfulness of her legs. Like her husband, Christina was barefoot, but both had a metal cuff on their right ankles and were connected by the chain.

When Kendall said hello, Christina chanted, "Humpty Dumpty had a great fall."

"My wife's displeased with one of my paintings. Why don't you give them a look?"

Six paintings, magnificent additions to his series *The Rooftops of New York*, were on a bench and tilted back against a wall of a townhouse. Brigham's technique was borrowed from the Ashcan School, but the critics referred to him as a "psycho-realist," for his sole focus was the stormy internal weather of women, and though Kendall believed that her race had made her life more difficult than her sex ever did, two of the paintings disturbed her.

The first was of a rooftop wedding on an overcast afternoon, the groom slipping the ring on his bride's finger as the minister and guests watched. The only person not paying attention was the bride. Her left hand was extended to receive the ring, but her right hand was pressed against the pregnancy swelling her gown, and with eyes as desolate as the clouds, she gazed out at the surrounding rooftops, where women were hanging laundry on the lines.

The second was the painting that Kendall guessed Christina had objected to. On a twilit roof, Brigham, in a tuxedo, sat at a cocktail table. Across from him the chair was empty, and on the table was a candelabra and two flutes of champagne. Behind Brigham, a violinist in top hat and tails played. Cupping a hand to his mouth, Brigham called through the shadows to a woman. She was naked and, with her cropped hair, resembled Christina. Yet only her back was visible, because she had jumped from the ledge and was suspended in midair, the lights of the city glittering on her pale skin.

"They're extraordinary," Kendall said.

Brigham was perched on a stool, so shameless in his admiration of Kendall's chest that she thought it was a miracle his eyeballs didn't shoot out of his head. Just then, Christina yanked on the chain, the links rattling, and Brigham flew off the stool, exclaiming, "Good grief!" Kendall managed not to laugh. Brigham said to her, "Excuse our contretemps," and once on his feet, asked Christina, "What would you like, my dear?"

"Jack Sprat could eat no fat, his wife could eat no lean."

"Yes, the pharmacy. The key, please."

She gave a key to Brigham, who unlocked the cuff from his ankle, put the key on the arm of the settee, and stepped into a pair of moccasins. Brigham was gone before Kendall could conjure up an excuse to leave. Wary, she looked at Christina, who erupted in laughter. Kendall had expected a mad cackling, but her laugh was warm and whimsical, like a smile set to music.

"Take a load off," Christina said. "What brings you to the Village?"

"Trying to rent an apartment."

"That must be a hoot and a holler. Negroes used to live in Little Africa, over on Minetta Lane and Minetta Street, before the Italians chased them uptown."

Kendall knew it was rude to stare, but she couldn't stop staring at the chain, which was coiled on the grass. Christina said, removing the cuff from her ankle, "I'm sorry if the chain upset you."

"It made me think of my grandfather."

Christina flung the cuff onto the grass. "He was a slave?"

"He was. And his mother was sold to another plantation when he was a child."

"I told Brig it was in bad taste, but the chain's his trite notion of a metaphor for the bondage of longtime love."

"Is that how it feels? Like being in chains?"

"More or less. You feel imprisoned and safe, and after a while, you can't tell the difference. Do you have someone?"

"We're sort of starting out."

"The chains take time. I've been with Brig since high school. My father was the headmaster of Tabor Academy. That's eighty miles from Boston. He'd been roommates with Brig's father at Harvard. Brig's from Chicago, but he came east for Harvard and spent Thanksgiving with us. I showed Brig the town, and he showed me my clitoris."

Kendall blurted out, "You got the better end of that deal."

Christina laughed, and Kendall suddenly felt a rush of affection for her. "Brig and I ran off the night of my graduation. We didn't get married till years later. In the garden at Saint Luke's. It was an interesting wedding. Vincent Millay wrote a poem for us."

"You're kidding? I've heard her read her poetry on the radio. She's a friend of yours?" Kendall was excited, feeling as if she were inching closer to the carnival she'd come to find.

"Vincent lived next door, and if I didn't clock her at my wedding, she'd have diddled Brig in the rectory. My parents said I loused up the ceremony with the fight and because the guests threw marijuana seeds at us instead of rice. You ever smoke Mary Jane?"

"It's illegal, isn't it?"

"Not if you buy it from a doctor or druggist who pays the federal tax on it. Brig's getting some now. I'll give you a couple of samples and you can smoke them with your someone. And don't fret. You won't end up reciting nursery rhymes. That's a game I play with Brig. He has to figure out what I mean. How's your painting going?"

"I just finished one. I don't know if it's any good."

"No artist knows. Brig has to ask me. He hates that."

Kendall wished that Julian could critique her paintings, a wish that made her feel selfish and unappreciative. He'd been so kind to her, and art was her choice, not his. Still . . .

"And he wouldn't have started his rooftop paintings if he didn't think I was fooling around with Sloanie. You know Sloanie? The painter John Sloan?"

"I love his work. *McSorley's Bar, Six O'Clock, Winter*—"

"And *Sunday, Women Drying Their Hair*. That roof's on Cornelia Street. Brig envied Sloanie. He was making money, and we were broke and fighting, and I said I'd bet Sloanie could really pound the feathers off the duck."

"Pound the—"

"Talented in the boudoir. Brig accused me of being unfaithful. I told him I did nothing untoward, but I'd reached my conclusion by observing Sloanie's eyebrows. Ridiculous, right? But Brig believed me. For the next month, Brig starts shifting his eyebrows around like caterpillars doing the Charleston and making me watch. He drove me so batty I had to swear to him that eyebrows didn't count in bed."

Kendall was giggling, and Christina continued, "But being jealous of Sloanie, Brig began his own rooftop series. And those paintings got him where he wanted to go."

"The chain. Do—oh, never mind. I don't mean to pry."

"If you want to paint, you'd better pry. Art isn't intended to improve the social graces. You want a cup of tea? Or to use the bathroom? Or a slice of Bundt cake? Don't be shy."

"All three?"

"All three it is."

Kendall felt as if she might start crying. "Christina?"

"Yes?"

"You're the first friend I've made in New York."

# Chapter 23

Late one afternoon, Julian and Kendall drove out to the countryside in West Orange so Julian could inspect a parcel of land for sale that adjoined property he owned. As they walked through the overgrown grass and weeds, Kendall said, "What do you see?"

"Stores. Rows of stores. Room for parking. And I know the road behind us is on a bus line."

"I see old, beautiful trees and a field of wildflowers and weeds."

"That's because you're an artist, not a developer."

They drove to Pals Cabin, a hot-dog stand that had matured into a restaurant. While they ate the best mushroom soup that Kendall had ever tasted, creamy and peppery and as thick as stew, she told Julian about the Brighams. Kendall had been hesitant to mention them because she knew that Julian would've preferred her to live with him, and she worried that bringing up anything positive about the Village would make him feel bad. She was also worried that he might try to talk her out of going and, since she was crazy in love with him, she'd give in.

His response surprised her. "We should take the Brighams to dinner. It can't hurt your career to make friends with an artist, and I want to try the Minetta Tavern. I used to go when it was a speakeasy. Siano and Eddie ate there last week and they say it's a decent red-sauce joint."

"A red—"

"An Italian restaurant. Ask them, and if they can't make it, we'll go."

Kendall felt sheepish for believing that Julian would try to stand in her way. She was suddenly terrified at the thought of exchanging the comforts he provided for the solitary discipline of art and a long shot at ever winning anything more than a membership in that pathetic club of failed artists who hung on in the Village because they had nowhere else to go.

This realization made Kendall want to smoke the two reefers Christina had rolled for her, but in her health course at Lovewood her professor—a wizened doctor of divinity who lectured students about the multitudinous paths to hell in a singsong voice—had shown them the documentary *Reefer Madness*, and Kendall wondered if marijuana could really make you a criminal or lunatic.

It wasn't until Sunday night that she asked Julian for his opinion on the matter. She was sitting on the covers in one of his shirts, and he was lying beside her in pajama bottoms.

Kendall slid the reefers from a pack of Marlboros. "Christina gave me these. Did you ever smoke one?"

"Hashish. In Berlin."

"What's it do?"

"Makes your chest hairy."

Kendall chuckled. "You lyin' like a no-legged dog. I want to smoke one."

"Go on."

"I'm scared."

Taking one of the reefers from her and a matchbox from the night table, Julian lit up, inhaled, held his breath, and exhaled. He gave the reefer to Kendall. They smoked, and after Kendall took the last puff, she crushed the nub in the ashtray. Julian felt himself drift off, like on an August afternoon at Bradley Beach.

"It's not working," Kendall said. "I'm going to light the other one."

Julian heard Kendall strike a match, and her inhaling and exhaling.

"I'm thirsty," Kendall said when she had finished. "I'm going to get a drink. Do you want something?"

"Unh-unh."

According to the alarm clock, only twenty minutes had gone by when Julian went to find Kendall. She was in the kitchen, sitting with her legs splayed on the black-and-white checkerboard linoleum. Before her was a pint carton of butter pecan and a jar of hot fudge from Gruning's. She was excavating ice cream from the carton with a scooper, then sticking her fingers in the jar, decorating the lump of butter pecan with fudge, and eating her improvised sundae from the scooper.

Grinning, Kendall held up the pint carton and sang, "All gone!"

Julian put away the fudge. "How're you feeling?"

"Like I could clap my titties!"

Kendall dropped the carton in the garbage can under the sink and sat on the windowsill.

"You know what Christina told me?"

"Not a clue."

"Christina told me on their first date Brig—that's what everyone calls him—Brig showed her where her clitoris was."

"Guys can be helpful like that."

"Can you find mine?"

"If you didn't move it."

"Why would I move it? I like it right where it is."

Julian agreed that it was in an optimal location and carried her to their room. Kendall felt as serene as a sleepy child when he lowered her onto the bed. She was aware of time passing, but she didn't know whether it was a minute or an hour. When she saw Julian's dark wavy hair between her thighs, her serenity vanished, and a mobile of images spun underneath her eyelids, images of Christina and Brig in their own bed, Christina on the bottom, her face contorted as Brig hammered away at her. Kendall was light-headed, as though watching the scene from a rooftop. She was afraid of heights—*acrophobia* was the technical term, memorized from her psych textbook in the hope that knowing the scientific name would help. It didn't. Intellectualizing was overrated, she thought, and laughed out loud and didn't quit laughing until Julian was inside her.

In Kendall's mind, Christina and Brig, bound by their chain, were really going at it, and Kendall couldn't recall if the *Reefer Madness* documentary claimed marijuana would turn you into a voyeur. Kendall imagined herself sitting beside Christina and—this shocked her—moving her mouth to her friend's breasts. Her guilt gave her pause, but Christina cooed that her intimate joys were her own affair, and the longer Kendall sucked on those breasts, the harder her own nipples became.

Kendall held Julian, feeling the rippling of his muscles in his back. Christina and Brig were gone, but Kendall could hear the dizzying jangle of their chain. Realizing that she was ensnared in a bondage that was hers alone, Kendall threw herself against Julian, trying to break free, the tension inside her terrifying because she didn't know if she were seeking freedom or oblivion or, most daunting of all, whether freeing herself was only possible if she let herself go and merged into this man. Her one solace was that she didn't feel a speck of guilt, not for the wantonness of her fantasies or her reality or that, clamping her hands on Julian's buttocks, she wanted to pull him so far inside her that he too would vanish.

Yet still he was there, she could hear him calling her name, and Kendall gave up, forgetting her terror and flinging herself from a rooftop, like Christina in Brig's painting, and plunged through an unfamiliar darkness, where she screamed—oh yes, screamed herself silly—screamed until her throat burned and she heard herself, in a raspy burble, tell Julian that she loved him.

Later, Kendall awoke and unwound herself from Julian. Replaying their lovemaking, she grew excited, but remembering the rattling chains made her shudder. Kendall was staring at the ceiling when the first fires of dawn pressed against the windows.

# Chapter 24

On Tuesday, as Kendall left class, she asked Dodd Brigham if he and Christina would like to have dinner with her and Julian.

"Kind of you to invite us," he replied, "but Christina is under the weather, and I've a dinner with several of my patrons."

Then Brig took off down Fifty-Seventh Street, while Kendall went downtown. She didn't have to meet Julian at the Minetta Tavern until six, and her new plan was to comb the Village for handwritten For Rent signs, reasoning that people who could afford to advertise in the classifieds wouldn't be as desperate for a tenant as those less fortunate souls who stuck homemade placards in their windows. She started at Washington Square and trudged as far as the Jewish cemetery by West Eleventh but didn't spot any signs. Frustrated, Kendall wandered across Fifth Avenue until she decided to visit Christina. Her mother would have chided her for dropping by someone's home without an invitation. But Kendall was lonely, and Christina wasn't feeling well. No doubt Garland, who disliked guests appearing empty-handed, would have approved of her daughter's next move, going into Veniero's and emerging with a bag of freshly baked butter cookies.

"Such a lovely surprise," Christina said, when Kendall found her seated on the settee in the courtyard.

Christina, who had been reading a book Kendall had never heard of—*The Awakening* by Kate Chopin—didn't look sick. Her complexion was ruddy, and she was even wearing shoes and real clothes: beaded moccasins, beige wool slacks, and a pullover sweater the color of Chianti.

Kendall took a seat next to Christina. "I'm glad you're feeling better."

"Brig claimed I was unwell?"

Kendall explained about Julian and the dinner invitation. Christina grimaced. "Brig and I had a tiff, and he's sulking."

Kendall didn't know what to say.

"No prying, is that it?" Christina asked, smiling warmly. "You can hang on to your manners, but if you're not curious about people, how can you be curious about yourself? Curiosity is all an artist has."

Kendall felt her face flush. "What did you and Brig fight about?"

"That wasn't so hard, was it?"

"Maybe—a little."

"This morning, Brig showed me a new painting, and I told him it wasn't among his best. He got in a huff, and I say, 'Do you want the truth or not?' He says, 'Not today,' so I tell him it's marvelous. His face lights up like the Woolworth Building, and he says, 'You think so?' and I answer, 'No.' Then he shouts if I'd wear the chain more, he wouldn't be so distracted."

"Distracted?"

"Distracted. Because if I'm not chained, I could scoot on him." Christina laughed bitterly. "I am sick of his insecurities."

Kendall couldn't imagine ever speaking about Julian with such bitterness. And she'd never wear a chain. Ever. "You could come to dinner with us."

"No thank you. Then I'd have to have another fight about that with Brig when he got home."

❋

Kendall saw nothing for rent on Bleecker or MacDougal, and since it was too early to meet Julian, she turned onto Minetta Lane, which was steep and no wider than an alley. Christina must have been right about the Italians running off the Negroes, because Kendall heard opera blaring, and the music grew louder when, on her left, she came to Minetta Street. Halfway down the block, she discovered the source of the music. An old, slack-jawed man was sitting on the slate stoop of a townhouse with the first-floor window open and the horn of a gramophone aimed outside. He wore a grayish-brown striped suit with a lemon-lime necktie that was louder than the opera and a fedora with the brim flipped down like a lady's sunhat. Kendall did a double take when she saw a professionally printed For Rent sign taped to the stained glass inset of the front door. She smiled at the old man as if he were her long-lost uncle, and when the music ended, the man, who was missing most of his upper teeth, said, "*Aspetta un minuto*, you wait, *sì*?"

He shuffled inside. Kendall heard the window close and, given her dismal experience with Village landlords, she thought he'd ditched her.

The man reappeared. "You here for rent *l'appartamento* of Mr. Ciccolini?"

"Yes, sir. I am. Is Mr. Ciccolini home?"

"*Io sono*—I a Mr. Ciccolini. You come."

The ground-floor apartment was walled off from a carpeted staircase, and on the second-floor landing, Mr. Ciccolini unlocked a door and switched on a frosted glass chandelier. It was one enormous, high-ceilinged room with a knotty pine floor, pastel-blue walls with brass-and-crystal sconces, and a marbled mantelpiece around the fireplace. As Mr. Ciccolini showed her the kitchenette, the bathroom, and, pointing through the row of tall windows, the garden in back, Kendall prepared herself to hear that she was expected to be his maid or to fuck him once a week. But all Mr. Ciccolini said was "My a grandson here for college. Now he go to the Albany Law School, and I got nobody. My wife, she gone, and I like a somebody up here again. *L'appartamento*, it is very nice, *sì*?"

"Very nice," Kendall said.

※

When Julian arrived, the Minetta Tavern was noisy with the laughter of the customers at the gleaming oak bar. He slipped the maître d' ten bucks, then followed him across the sawdust floor to a table against the wall where he could watch for Kendall and the Brighams. Before the waiter had a chance to take a drink order, Kendall entered alone. As always, Julian was struck by her beauty, and so were some of the men at the bar, who admired Kendall as the maître d' brought her to the table. She smiled as Julian stood, helped her off with her coat, and held the chair for her.

The waiter came. "A vodka martini, please," Kendall said. "Straight up with olives."

Julian ordered the same—his usual drink. Kendall generally preferred wine. "A martini? That mean a good day or a bad day?"

"Good, but the Brighams couldn't make it."

"Too bad."

Kendall laughed. "Because you won't get to see their chain?"

"Guilty as charged."

Kendall spread her napkin on her lap. "I rented an apartment." She studied his face for any change in expression.

"Congratulations."

"You're not mad at me?"

"I'll miss you, but that was the plan, right?"

Kendall, the irritation plain in her voice, said, "I asked if you were mad."

"You wanna have a fight? To make it easier for you to go?"

Kendall relished that Julian knew these things—another reason she loved him—and yet, for no reason she could name, it frightened her.

Julian said, "If people don't get what they want, they're unhappy, and so are the people who love them. I don't want to be unhappy. Tell me about the place."

"The rent's just fifty dollars a month; I could've afforded more. It has lots of light, a fireplace, a backyard, and it's around the corner from here. We can go see it after we eat."

The waiter brought the martinis. They clinked glasses and drank.

"You want to hear one of the best things about the apartment?" Kendall asked, her hand going into her satchel hanging from the chair.

"I do."

Kendall plunked something down on the table and, drawing back her hand, said, "It comes with two keys."

# Chapter 25

Kendall's move from South Orange to Greenwich Village was less traumatic than either she or Julian had anticipated. Kendall was pleased to be there, and Julian spent a couple of nights a week and every weekend with her. And the move itself had its lighter moments. Julian offered to buy Kendall some furniture, but no, this was a solo project. She trolled the secondhand stores, digging up a dresser, an oak refectory table, a brass bed, two mismatched Morris chairs, and a cherrywood drop-front desk that had been left at the curb for the junk wagon. Kendall granted Julian and Eddie the privilege of toting her finds around the apartment, and on the third try with a pinkish-white damask sofa, an oak-winged Victorian that seemed as heavy as a battleship, Julian said to Kendall, "I thought you wanted to do this by yourself?"

She laughed, explaining that carrying furniture was man's work, and when Julian started to object, Fiona said, "Do your job. It's almost dinnertime, and I made reservations."

Julian finally circumvented the no-gift edict one afternoon as they wandered over to Warren Street. Kendall was gazing longingly in the windows of Haber & Fink's, a camera shop, and Julian said, "That second pantry off your kitchen, with the sink in it. Wouldn't that be good for a darkroom?"

"That doesn't mean you're supposed to buy—"

"Your birthday's on Tuesday."

"For your birthday I only bought you—"

"A diaphragm."

"That was for me."

Julian grinned. "It was?"

Kendall gave him a playful nudge. "I don't deserve so many presents."

"Don't you know how happy you make me?"

"But I don't do anything."

They settled on Julian's buying her an enlarger, while Kendall bought herself a safelight, developing tank, hard rubber trays, enamel jugs of chemicals, and other accessories. Kendall sometimes shot and developed photographs but mainly she concentrated on her painting. With a black-and-gold Chinese screen, Kendall divided a portion of her walk-up into a studio. Her goal was to capture the quirky Greenwich Village she adored, and Kendall labored at it sixty hours a week. Julian loved to watch her work. He couldn't draw a squiggle and marveled at people who could, especially if, like Kendall, they could produce an oil painting as detailed as a photograph.

On the weeknights that he slept over, Kendall cooked, and on weekends Julian took her out. They rarely ventured above Fourteenth Street, not simply because the classier nightclubs and restaurants in midtown were as segregated as a Klan rally, but because New Yorkers tended to stick to their neighborhoods. Kendall and Julian were regulars at the Minetta Tavern and Peter's Backyard over on West Tenth, the juiciest steak downtown. For a taste of Paris, they crossed Washington Square Park and ordered coq au vin in the basement café of the Brevoort Hotel, alive with debate, gossip, and well-fortified denizens reading the latest headlines—mostly about the war in Europe—from the news ticker.

What they loved most was listening to music and dancing at Café Society. Billie Holiday, Hazel Scott, and Josh White sang there, and Julian's favorite, Big Joe Turner, who with that rockslide laugh of his could make a bad day a whole lot better. The owner, Barney Josephson, was a Jewish guy from Jersey, and Barney described his joint as "the right place for the wrong people." And most of New York City agreed, because in Barney's smoky, rambunctious dungeon on Sheridan Square, white and colored made music together, drank together, and danced together, and if that twisted your knickers in a knot, tough shit.

Just how tough it could get became apparent on that Saturday night when Otis, up on semester break, joined Julian, Kendall, Eddie, and Fiona. Big Joe's piano player had a cough and a half, and Eddie assured Big Joe that Otis would spin his head sideways. Otis got behind the piano and broke out a boogie-woogie, and Big Joe shouted and moaned about this shy little gal who worked Big Joe till he was dry as July cotton.

Otis got a big hand, and he returned to the table as Barney was seating a young white couple. The man, with a shocked glance at Otis and Kendall sitting with Julian, Eddie, and Fiona, said, "We'll sit somewhere else." A white woman at the next table, ancient enough to recall when the redcoats occupied the Village, rose with the help of her cane and said, "Go fuck yourself," and before the young man could react, she brought her cane down on his head, and Barney had a bouncer hustle the couple out the door, while everyone else in the place gave the lady a standing ovation.

✳

Julian was surprised by how much he liked Greenwich Village. The curl of Minetta Street and the sun striking the Japanese maple in Kendall's backyard. Relaxing in a Morris chair in her apartment and reading before a fire in the cozy gloom of a rainy afternoon. Holding Kendall's hand and walking the curious twists and turns of the old streets. Seeing the beauty of the brownstones and townhouses with their wrought-iron railings, and the grand churches, hidden alleyways and courtyards. Reveling in the quiet during their early-morning strolls through Washington Square Park, with the white marble arch and the sculptures of George Washington reflected in the glassy surface of the fountain.

On one of these mornings, Kendall stopped and turned to Julian, resting her hands on his shoulders. "I feel like I dreamt this. Being here with you."

"That's the nicest thing anyone ever said to me," he replied, and they stood under an elm, alone in the park, streaked with the scarlet and gold of sunrise.

Julian only had one complaint about New York: Kendall insisting that he accompany her to Chumley's, a former speakeasy that was now a watering hole for the arty crowd, including Brig and Christina, who lived down the block. Julian didn't object to picking up the tab for everyone in his orbit, or mind that Brig droned on about his lofty stature among modern painters, or that he felt lost in the chatter about unfamiliar novels, poems, and paintings, or even that some people recognized him from the newspapers or his days as a regular in the city's speakeasies.

Actually, that aspect could be amusing: most of those who approached him were young women, and they stood close enough to him at the bar to catch Kendall's attention. Once, while Julian was at the tail end of his fourth martini, a curvy redhead in a sheer white peasant dress pressed one of her legs against him and said that she admired gangsters because they were the high priests of the unconventional. Yeah, Julian replied, mobsters were real artists, especially when it came to rubbing out the competition, and Kendall, observing the scene and overhearing his remark, glared at him before returning to her conversation with Christina.

Her friendship with Christina was why Kendall dragged him to Chumley's. Julian didn't care much for her or her egomaniacal husband. He wondered if he was being childish, resenting that Christina and Kendall whispered to each other like schoolgirls. But it rankled him that frequently, after an evening with Christina, Kendall would embark on a Let's Improve Julian campaign, beginning with his encouragement of boozy hussies and ending with his indifference to discussing the latest trends in art.

"You could talk to some of the men next time," she said.

"But I got to listen to them. How else am I gonna find out how important everybody is?"

"Be serious."

"Fine. I'll read *The Communist Manifesto* so I'll know what to say."

Kendall went southern on him: "Keep on joshing, boy, I like to snatch the taste out your mouth."

"Hey, I gotta read my Marx to understand why I should always pick up the check."

Despite the kidding around, Julian sensed that Christina hated him, as if he were out to destroy Kendall, but it wasn't until Christmas Eve that he ever had to deal with her hatred.

That evening, there was a party at Chumley's, though neither Julian nor Kendall was in a festive mood. Tomorrow they were flying to Florida, where Julian would bunk with his parents for a night, then go to Miami Beach to check up on his hotel, and Kendall would spend a week with Garland.

Chumley's was covered from wall to wall with rackety aesthetes. Fruitcakes shaped like Santa and his reindeer were arrayed on the bar, along with punch bowls of eggnog. To stay awake, Julian drank coffee dosed with Frangelico, and at one point there was a break in the boredom: Christmas caroling. Julian got to hear Kendall go solo on "Silent Night," and her voice was so stirring that he forgot he was at Chumley's until afterward, when he was standing with Kendall, and Christina sidled over.

She put her arm around Kendall. "We're going to Saint Paul's on Broadway to hear midnight Mass. You'll come with us, won't you?"

Kendall turned to Julian. "We have an early flight, but maybe we could go?"

With an impatient edge to her voice, Christina said to Julian, "Is it okay?"

"Doesn't matter to me. I'm Jewish."

"Then there's nowhere for you to pray tonight," Christina said with a snicker. "All the banks are closed."

Due to Brig's success, Christina was a celebrity at Chumley's, and she basked in her role as a queen bee among the up-and-comers and down-and-outers. Yet she had no experience with the likes of Julian and mistook his lack of reaction for doltishness.

Kendall looked away, as if she hadn't heard Christina's remark and, with another jovial trill, Christina said, "I was joking."

"Be better if your jokes were funny," Julian replied, and when Christina saw his hard blue stare, she took off as if she were late for an appendectomy.

Julian said, "There's never a lemon meringue pie around when you need one."

Kendall laughed, and they left Chumley's. The streets were deserted, and with the moonlight shining on the ice-crusted snow, the Village seemed draped in tinsel.

"I know Christina's your friend," Julian said.

"That doesn't excuse her stupid joke. Or that I didn't say something to her."

"Forget all that. But be careful of her."

"Why?"

Part of what attracted him to Kendall was her energy and ambition, and he suspected that those were the qualities, along with her youth, that Christina envied. "Because that joke was also aimed at you."

Kendall didn't reply, but she snuggled close to Julian and leaned her head against his shoulder.

# Chapter 26

Garland had purchased Kendall's plane ticket, which evidently granted her the right to harangue her daughter, though she did wait a full two hours, until they were seated on the veranda with tea and banana pudding cake, before asking if Kendall had sold any of her paintings.

"I'm still working on them."

"Work? Work is what you get paid for. Come home and I'll give you some work."

"I'll pass."

"Are you still gallivanting around with that white criminal?"

"Mama, quit."

"A bootlegger is a criminal, baby girl."

"Prohibition's over. Julian's a developer."

"And work's not work unless someone pays you for it."

"You have your life, I have mine."

"You do have a life, and I'm praying you aren't wasting it."

"I think I'll go for a walk."

For the next seven days, they had this same discussion in a variety of forms. Kendall had expected as much, and she wouldn't have been so annoyed if she weren't worried about her progress as a painter. Novice artists hunger for feedback, and Kendall had assumed that her class at the Art Students League would provide it. Yet whenever Brig stopped at her easel, he paid more attention to her than to her canvas, gazing at Kendall as if he were a big game hunter eager to display her head on his wall. Kendall didn't mention his behavior to

Christina, and once she flew back to New York, Kendall lied to her when she didn't reregister for Brig's class, saying that school and the traveling ate up her day. It was then that Christine volunteered to critique Kendall's paintings. Kendall was elated: even Brig relied on his wife's critical skills.

It took Kendall six months to complete a series she referred to as *Sojourn in Bohemia*, and now, on this June morning, Christina came over to Minetta Street to see the dozen paintings, which were on the floor and leaning against the wall under the windows. Kendall sat at her drop-front secretary and watched Christina inspect the canvases, her spirits soaring when Christina paused before the ones Kendall deemed her most adept work: an aging composer and his wife in turn-of-the-century formal wear walking down a slushy Jones Street with an anteater on a leash, and a fiery-eyed bard on Waverly Place nailing one of his poems onto a fence with the religious fervor of Martin Luther nailing up his *Ninety-Five Theses*.

"Your brushwork improves with each one," Christina said, scrutinizing Kendall's rendering of two men in scally caps arguing nose to nose over a longshoreman passed out under the sign of the White Horse Tavern. "And the quality of your lines is impressive. The light too—you've been paying attention to Hopper."

Christina wandered over to the cherrywood desk and looked at the framed photograph by Lyonel Feininger above it—a black-and-white double exposure of a German street packed with spectral shadows of women.

"Lyonel's a splendid painter," Christina said. "Brig's had some epic arguments with him about cubism. But I didn't think Lyonel sold his photographs."

"I found it yesterday at the Strand. Tucked in an old *Art Studies* magazine."

On the desk Christina saw a copy of Eugène Atget's book, *Photographe de Paris*, and a catalog from the Léo Sapir Gallery on the Upper East Side. Sapir, renowned for his impeccable taste and his affluent clientele, was the first American gallery owner to exhibit the photographs of Henri Cartier-Bresson: the catalog was from a 1935 show.

"Brig and I were at that Cartier-Bresson exhibit. Walker Evans was also included. Both of them pure artists. You shoot photos, don't you? I'd like to see them before we discuss your paintings."

Kendall felt her limited supply of confidence shrinking. She opened the bottom drawer of her desk. "These are my best," she said, handing Christina a black cardboard album with LOVEWOOD COLLEGE embossed on it in gold lettering.

"My goodness," Christina said, studying a shot of Derrick hanging from a limb. "Who's this?"

"My boyfriend before Julian."

Christina was shaking her head. "This calls for some wine. It's not too early, is it?"

Kendall poured the wine, and they went out the kitchen door to the garden and sat on a bench under the flushed canopy of a Japanese maple. Christina leafed through the album while Kendall sipped from her wineglass and thought about Derrick with grief and remorse rising in her. Kendall hadn't seen those photos in more than a year, but she remembered trying to capture every lurid and banal detail of the lynching—from the bloody tear in Derrick's neck to the dark, phlegmy splashes of tobacco juice staining the dust in the clearing.

Christina closed the album. "Technically, your paintings are terrific. If you showed them at the Washington Square Outdoor Exhibit, you'd sell every one to the tourists."

"That would make my mother happy."

"You'd earn a pretty penny too, but no one who knows art would mistake you for an artist. There's an element missing."

"Which is?"

"You."

Kendall was stung, yet Christina was identifying something that had gnawed at her as she worked, a feeling that she wasn't the one applying the paint to the canvas: it was her imagined self with a brush and palette—not the woman she actually was. Occasionally—and this panicked her—Kendall even felt the same way with Julian. Like a bird in the water, a fish in the sky.

"I understand this is no fun to hear," Christina said, and drank some Riesling.

"Wouldn't I improve with practice?"

"Your technique would improve. Not your paintings."

"Why not?"

"Because your paintings lack a point of view. A depth of feeling. Look, a bohemian is just someone who wants to be different like all the other bohemians. If you were painting that self-deception, that might be art. Have you considered going back to taking pictures?"

"That's more a hobby."

"Well, these," Christina said, tapping the album, "are art."

"Any fool with a camera can sicken you with a lynching."

"That photo of your boyfriend and his charred feet—it reminds me of the suffering in Velázquez's painting of the Crucifixion. And the ones of the empty soda bottles, peanut shells, and lollipop sticks around the tree—those details elucidate the horror of the event: they hung a man and acted as if they were at a child's birthday party. You saw that, and such a discriminating eye can't be taught. It's the gift that makes someone an artist."

Kendall lit a Marlboro. "You're saying I should quit painting and become a flâneur?"

"Nothing wrong with wandering the streets and taking photographs. Like Atget and Cartier-Bresson. Both of them started as painters. And Man Ray is a painter and a photographer."

Kendall sent a stream of smoke up into the reddish-purple cloud of leaves.

Christina said, "I watch Brig and wish I could paint. I read a novel and wish I could write. I see your photographs and envy your eye. I can't do much, but I can distinguish between what's art and what's not. You're a few miles from the most celebrated Negro community in the world. Why not go have a look?"

"Harlem's poverty's been done. Aaron Siskind and the others with their pictures in the *New York Times* and the *Daily Worker*. What am I going to see there?"

"It's not what you'll see, it's what you'll make other people see."

"Didn't Degas say that?"

"Even if Popeye the Sailor said it, it's still true."

"But it was Degas, wasn't it?"

Christina, hearing the nervousness in her voice, tried to reassure her, patting her hand and saying, "Don't know. I never met him."

# Chapter 27

The first thing Kendall noticed was that Harlem had been constructed on a larger scale than the Village, as if the men who had designed the boulevards, built the row houses, apartment buildings, and theaters had harbored grander dreams than their downtown cousins. And while those dreams of beauty and power, gleaned from European capitals, were gone by this Saturday morning, evaporating with the last notes of the Jazz Age and the Harlem Renaissance, some monuments survived: the Savoy Ballroom, Small's Paradise, the Apollo, the Lafayette Theatre, Connie's Inn, the gates and brownstones of Strivers Row; and after three hours, Kendall felt more like a rube sightseer than a flâneur and hadn't bothered to take her Leica out of her satchel.

At the most superficial level, Kendall felt more comfortable here than in the Village. After all, she was the granddaughter of a slave and, at Garland's insistence, no stranger to hard work. She could kill and fry a chicken, muck out a barn, and sew a dress from a flour sack, one of which she was wearing, a lavender number dotted with tiny white stars. So it was no mystery why she felt a kinship to the women shopping in the grocery stores while their children played leapfrog and hopscotch on the sidewalk. Except what did Kendall know of the poverty she saw? The tenements like rows of unfortunate teeth; the dirty windows of the storefront churches; men sitting on crates outside barbershops or staggering out of bars; and the women leaning out of windows to hang laundry on the lines strung between the buildings.

By noon, Kendall wanted to retreat to the Village. All that stopped her was the rumbling in her empty stomach, and that at the corner of 134th and Seventh, she saw Crossroad Bar-B-Q, which Derrick and Otis had often hailed as the restaurant where God sent His angels for takeout.

They might've been right, Kendall thought, as she crossed the white-and-black hex-tiled floor, the air redolent with wood smoke and spices, and sat at one of the tables of varnished pine. The blues played on a jukebox back by the open kitchen, where a man in a puffy white chef's hat was laboring over a grill. A woman with short, iron-gray hair and a face as round and sweet as a pecan pie was darting among the tables in a full-length baby-blue apron, and she brought Kendall a glass of ice water.

"What can I get you, child?" she asked, looking at Kendall as if she recognized her.

"My friends told me to have the short ribs."

"You got yourself some smart friends. What they names?"

"Otis Larkin and—"

"Lord, I knew it. I never forget faces. You that beautiful child that sang at Derrick's funeral, ain't you?"

"Yes, ma'am. My name's Kendall Wakefield."

"We be knowing the Larkin family forever. A sin how them ofay fools done that boy." The woman turned and shouted, "Papa B, come out here with a order a ribs."

Papa B was the man in the chef's hat. His face, behind a stubbly gray beard, was as kindly as a country doctor's, and his white apron was splattered with sauce. In under a minute, he brought Kendall a plate with a rack of ribs, an ear of corn, black-eyed peas, and a basket of biscuits. "Mama B," he said, setting the food on the table, "what you hollering for?"

"This here's Kendall Wakefield. The child we heard sing for Derrick."

Papa B sat across from Kendall. "You one a the prettiest girls I ever seen, with one a the prettiest voices I ever heard. And we got us two boys—"

Mama B said, "Do she look like she need your help finding herself a man?"

Papa B chuckled. "All y'all need help. I had to help you find me. Like I's saying. Our older boy's in the Army in Virginia, his younger brother's in the Navy in Hawaii."

Mama B said to Kendall, "Sugar, you eat, and I'ma bring you some peach cobbler." She pinched her husband's cheek. "And you leave this child be."

Kendall was glad to have company. Her tour had been as disturbing as her conversation with Christina. After months of slaving over *Sojourn in Bohemia*, making detailed sketches in pencil before applying a brushstroke, dismounting every flawed start from the wooden stretchers and cutting up the canvas, it had been difficult enough to hear from Christina that her paintings weren't art. Yet Kendall felt even more dejected that afternoon when she looked at the series again and saw them as nothing more than the exertions of a dilettante. And now, she was unable to spot a picture worth taking in Harlem. If she couldn't be a serious painter or photographer, what would she do? Illustrate Valentine's Day cards for Hallmark? Shoot passport photos? No way. Not this girl. She'd almost rather go work for her mother.

Papa B asked, "You living up here?"

"Downtown. I came to take pictures."

"James Van Der Zee eat here twice a week. His studio on Lenox near a Hundred and Twenty-Fourth. He do portraits. Marcus Garvey, Bojangles Robinson, Countee Cullen, and me and Mama B. He do this funny work slapping pictures together."

"Double exposures." The food was as tasty as her grandfather's; he had occasionally chased his cook out of the kitchen and prepared Kendall some down-home fare.

"Whatever they is, they's something to see. What sorta pictures you make?"

"Street scenes."

"I hope not like them white boys come around and put they mess in the papers. Always showing how poor we all is. Hell, them boys is poor. The guvment paying 'em to take pictures, so why don't they stick to they own neighborhoods? We got poor up here, we do, but they's lots of everyday folks with everyday problems. Same as white people."

Mama B came with the cobbler. "Papa B, this child like to be deaf with all your noise."

"She told me this the finest lunch of her young life. Ain't that so, Miss Kendall?"

"Near about," Kendall said, and Mama and Papa B laughed and told her they hoped to see her again soon.

Reinvigorated by her meal, Kendall decided to stay uptown and hone her mechanics with the Leica, convinced that she'd better resign herself to photographing in New York, since with the Nazis rolling over Belgium and the Netherlands, driving French, Polish, Dutch, and British troops from Dunkirk, and marching through France, it was unlikely she'd get to Paris anytime soon. After exploring the green highlands of Mount Morris Park, Kendall exited onto Lenox Avenue and lost herself in the cranky bustle, doubting that she'd taken any pictures worth developing and feeling so clumsy and hopeless about her skills with the Leica that she wanted to cry.

Then, on 125th Street, Kendall saw her in front of a five-and-dime. A little girl with pigtails and a dress faded from too many washings. She was standing as still as a brown flower that had sprung up between the cracks in the sidewalk and looking through the window at a display of dolls from *The Wizard of Oz*: Dorothy holding her dog, Toto, with Scarecrow, Tin Woodman, and the Cowardly Lion behind her, all of them under a papier-mâché rainbow that arched across the plate glass.

Overcome by a pang of sorrow, Kendall backed away from the girl, thinking that she wanted to buy her every doll in the store and checking her new Weston light meter on the lanyard around her neck. She raised the Leica, her elbows tucked in close to her body, her fingers lowering the shutter speed and adjusting the lens to let in more light as she looked through the range finder and focused the camera. Finally, staring at the child through the viewfinder, Kendall pressed the shutter-release button, and she had her picture.

Kendall could never explain to herself what happened next, why she made the choice that would be so crucial to her career. Maybe it had been hearing about James Van Der Zee or the Lyonel Feininger photograph over her desk, but as the girl turned away from the five-and-dime, Kendall—who had read about double exposures in a Leica instruction booklet—slid the rewind lever to the left and, holding the film rewind knob, cocked the shutter with the film-advance knob, then pressed the shutter release, and in an instant she had two images of the girl in one photo.

Eager to see the result, Kendall rewound the film and removed the cassette from her camera on the subway. In her darkroom, she took the film from the cassette, winding it onto a metal reel and sealing it in the metal developing tank, which resembled a squat cocktail shaker with two apertures on either side of the top. Kendall yanked on the cord for the overhead light and poured developing solution from a jug through the apertures, shaking the tank for several seconds. Using her grandfather's Hamilton as a timer, she waited eight minutes before draining out the solution in the sink and adding the stop bath, primarily a solution of vinegar and water that halted the developing process. She counted to fifteen, dumped out the stop bath, and poured in the fixer to set the images on the film.

Kendall was rinsing the open tank under running water when she heard Julian enter her apartment and go into the kitchen. Careful not to let the film bend in on itself, she clipped it with clothespins to a line she'd strung over the sink and left the darkroom.

"How was Harlem?" Julian asked. He was making a martini.

Kendall kissed him. "I'll know when I see my pictures."

He gave her a glass of chardonnay. "How long before the photos are developed?"

"Two hours for the film to dry and about another two for the prints to be done."

"Wanna get some dinner?"

"I'm not hungry. I had a huge lunch. At Crossroad Bar-B-Q."

"That joint's famous. I've been there with Eddie. He loves it. And the couple that own it, the Bares."

"Mama B and Papa B."

"Like from Goldilocks except spelled different. We could eat there some night."

Kendall felt ashamed of herself because as soon as Julian suggested it, she realized that she didn't want to go to Crossroad—or anywhere else in Harlem—with him. Yet this realization came along with a fierce desire to have Julian inside her. Tracing a fingertip across his cheek, Kendall said, "We have an hour and fifty minutes. Any ideas?"

Indeed, he did. Afterward, with Julian dozing, Kendall put on a robe and returned to the darkroom, switching on an amber safelight. She slid the negative of the little girl into a film carrier, then placed it in the enlarger, which had its own light that illuminated the image on the easel of the baseboard. Kendall rotated the focus knob so she could study the negative. She was still studying it when Julian knocked on the door.

# Chapter 28

That July and August even the sun seemed testy at having to work so hard. Subway riders baked like muffins in a tin, while above ground people peeled off their sodden work clothes and clustered on fire escapes in search of a breeze. With the windows open Kendall could hear radios everywhere—fans roaring at baseball games; Billie Holiday, in a voice as languorous as the heat, asking God to bless a child; and word of the Nazis' massive invasion of the Soviet Union.

On weekends, Kendall escaped with Julian to the Jersey shore, staying at the cottage he and Eddie had rented in Spring Lake.

"You ain't yourself," Fiona said to Kendall one evening while Eddie and Julian were grilling steaks and they were rocking on a porch swing drinking gin and tonics.

"Working too hard."

That was true: Monday through Thursday, Kendall mined the nooks and crannies of Harlem with her Leica. Fridays she reserved for the darkroom. Shooting double exposures is a hit-and-miss proposition; some of her shots were so muzzy they were indecipherable, and most of them fell short of her standards or intentions. Strangely enough, the more time she spent in Harlem discovering her facility with a camera, the more withdrawn she became. Kendall wished that she could discuss her shift in mood with Christina, but she and Brig were summering in Provincetown and wouldn't be back until after Labor Day.

Fiona said, "You got balls, Kendall."

Kendall giggled. "Balls? Uh-oh."

"I like working in a bar. I get to be a cross between a nurse and a lion tamer. But you want to be someone grand. I'm proud you're my friend. I'd hate not to see you."

For a disquieting instant, Kendall wondered if Fiona saw something that she herself preferred not to see. "Same here, but I'm not going anywhere."

"If you say so, darlin'. Just remember, our Lord's generous, but don't go dancing in a canoe."

Kendall didn't join the conversation at dinner and went upstairs after the dishes were done. A while later, when Julian got into bed, she was admiring photos in *Life* of Rita Hayworth pedaling a bicycle.

"Are you tired of me?" Julian asked, sounding baffled and hurt.

Kendall knew she was responsible for his wounded feelings but felt powerless to help him. She dropped the magazine on the floor and smiled. "You tired me out this morning."

"C'mon, I'm being serious."

Kendall, after reaching over to kill the light, lay back and put an arm around him so that his head rested against her breast. "I love you, Julian. I do."

She stroked his hair, waiting for him to kiss her, but he turned over and fell asleep.

Kendall was not as fortunate. Ever since developing the picture of that little girl, sleep had been a reluctant visitor, and even in the darkness that photograph glowed in her mind like a black-and-white jewel. It was a dual image of a girl destined for a double life, a girl burdened by her humanity *and* the history of skin, a history that she was condemned to bear yet didn't fully comprehend. The rainbow in the window jumped out in the photo like a headline, and the sight of a little girl gazing up at it on a deserted sidewalk was stirring; so was the spectral image of the child floating away from the glass with an expression of unendurable yearning, as if one tangible object or sublime moment or perfect companion would grant her every reward beyond the rainbow. But the knockout blow was that the expression wasn't one of unsullied innocence. If you looked at the girl long enough, her ghostly face seemed like that of a woman, parched with a bitter wisdom, as though she already knew that a trip to the rainbow was a journey without end, because there was nothing beyond those misty colors but rainwashed sky and more unsated desire.

In fact, in many ways it wasn't a photograph of that little girl. It was a self-portrait of Kendall.

Now Kendall couldn't wait to get to Harlem, which she saw as a Byzantine musical production, with actors and actresses parading across the stage, delivering their lines, laughing, shouting, and cursing under the unforgiving sun, audacious and unconquerable, the grown-ups cooling themselves with beers and sodas as children frolicked in the swimming holes created by uncapping fire hydrants. Every time Kendall pressed the shutter release of the Leica, she was convinced that she was capturing some aspect of her own double life—as a pebble bobbing in an ocean of foam, as a woman shouldering her way through a man's world. Beyond these dualities Kendall was attempting to record her own mysterious yearning, mysterious because she wasn't sure where it came from or how to describe it—that is, until one morning on the subway, when she recalled lines from a poem by Oliver Wendell Holmes that she'd read in high school: "Alas for those that never sing, But die with all their music in them!"

Her worst fear had always been that she'd live out her days without leaving a trace, so with her camera Kendall attempted to portray this fear in others: a steel-haired woman in a maid's uniform waiting for a bus on Eighth Avenue, her spectral double spiraling upward like a ballerina with wings, a reminder that no woman is born hoping to iron another family's clothes and raise children who are not her own; in the courtyard of PS 186, a pair of coltish young girls and their shadows on roller skates, going round and round as if rehearsing for lives of futility; in Mount Morris Park, four women in do-rags, slumped with exhaustion and trudging up a hill, their wraithlike selves trailing them like memories of slaves returning from the fields.

By mid-August, Kendall had accumulated twenty double exposures that she judged acceptable to show Christina, and she was so anxious to hear her opinion that she made new eight-by-tens from the negatives and mailed them to Provincetown. As she came into her apartment from the post office, her phone was ringing. She dashed over to her desk and was out of breath when she said hello.

"Kenni-Ann? It's Simon."

"Simon, how are you?"

"Happy to hear your voice."

That was a typical reply from Simon, a real charmer. "I've been reading your column in the *Courier*," Kendall said. "Those stories on the colored troops at Fort Devens were great." Kendall didn't have to ask how he'd gotten her number. Simon would've contacted her mother, and Garland, whose phone calls with Kendall had been as frosty as their exchanges in Florida, would've gladly given it to him. In college, while Kendall had been dating Simon, Garland had declared him an appropriate choice for a husband, a judgment based as much on Simon Foxe's parents as on Simon. His father was a physician in Homestead, a suburb of Pittsburgh, and his mother, a board member of the NAACP and a founder of the National Council of Negro Women, was the daughter of Cato Gapps, a coal baron who, like Ezekiel Kendall, had been a self-made multimillionaire.

"Are you in the city?" Kendall asked.

"Yes, the editor in Pittsburgh assigned me here. Circulation's up to nearly two hundred thousand, and the New York office needs help."

"That's on a Hundred and Twenty-Fifth and Seventh. Across from the Hotel Theresa."

"I'm staying at the Theresa."

"Aren't you fancy," she said, teasing him. Simon liked going first-class, and owing to the generosity and estate planning of his grandfather, he could afford to. The Theresa, with its ornate white terra-cotta façade, was known as the Waldorf of Harlem, and though it had been around for over a quarter century, Negroes hadn't been permitted to check in until last year.

"The hotel has a penthouse dining room. You can see Long Island Sound and the Palisades. Would you like to have dinner?"

Joining an ex-beau for dinner at a hotel felt like crossing a line that she and Julian, without ever saying it aloud, had pledged not to cross. Kendall said, "How's lunch tomorrow?"

"When and where?"

"One o'clock. At Crossroad Bar-B-Q. If you're going to report from Harlem, it'll be helpful to know it. Juiciest ribs and gossip uptown."

Kendall gave Simon directions, and they said good-bye. Julian was sleeping in South Orange that evening, and when he phoned, Kendall said nothing about her lunch plans. The omission left her feeling guilty, and the next day her guilt spread through her like the chills while she changed her outfit three times.

"Ain't you a sight," Papa B said, putting an arm around her shoulders. Sometimes Kendall imagined that her father had been like Papa B, with the same twinkling eyes and hearty smile.

Kendall said, "A friend of mine's coming for lunch."

"He already here," Papa B replied, placing a hand under Kendall's elbow and turning her toward a table by the jukebox, where Simon was chatting with Mama B. "Introduced hisself. Friendly, fine-lookin' fella." Papa B chuckled. "Be careful, missy."

It was good advice. At college, the girls had gone gaga over Simon with his liquid eyes, smooth teak complexion, dimples, and rakish, Errol Flynn mustache.

"Child," Mama B said, as Kendall approached the table, "don't you look beautiful."

"Doesn't she," Simon said, standing up.

Kendall repaid their compliments with a droll curtsy, and when Simon bussed her cheek, she smelled the clean scent of his Aqua Velva and the Reed's cinnamon candies he constantly popped in his mouth, and she remembered their feverish evenings behind the dunes.

Mama B brought them a pitcher of lemonade and took their order. Kendall said, "You excited about working in New York?"

He gave her one of his crooked, world-weary smiles. "I am. And excited about seeing you."

Simon appeared to be in a perpetual state of amusement, yet behind that smile, Kendall knew, was an agile mind and a brimming storehouse of anger at the treatment of Negroes—an imbecility that Simon, an aristocrat by birth, viewed as the abominable pursuit of lowborn fools. Kendall had adored him: she had met him in an art class, and he had taught her how to develop film in the darkroom he'd built near campus. They had broken up when Simon had gone to the *Pittsburgh Courier*, but their romance would've ended even if he hadn't graduated. Simon, unlike Derrick, hadn't wanted to marry her. He did want to sleep with her, though, and their final months together were an incessant debate over her virginity, which Simon accused her of guarding like the Holy Grail. Now, after two years of letting herself go with Julian in ways that would've horrified her as a college sophomore, those debates seemed infantile.

"What I really want to do," Simon said, "is sail to Europe and cover the war."

"And write that novel you talked about?"

"We've got a white Hemingway, why not a Negro one? And we're going to be in that war sooner or later. With Japan too, now that they're threatening the Philippines." He drank some lemonade. "Your mother told me you're taking photographs. The *Courier* could use freelancers up here. Interested?"

"I am. But I'm more interested in what else my mother told you."

Simon laughed and performed a fair impression of Garland, " 'That daughter of mine is mixed up with someone entirely inappropriate for her.' I figure she meant a white guy."

"Correct."

"Not surprising for Miss Coconut Patty."

That was what Simon used to call her when he thought she was acting overly prim and proper. It had bothered her then, but she'd been too intimidated by the handsome upperclassman to answer him.

"Simon, you called me that because I wouldn't let you fuck me."

He winced at the word *fuck*. To irk him—and repay him for teasing her in college—Kendall astonished herself by saying, "And if you keep calling me that, you never will."

That comment made her feel unfaithful to Julian, but it also got rid of Simon's smile.

"Hope y'all hungry," Mama B said, putting the plates of ribs on the table.

"Starving," Kendall said, and she was gratified that Simon said nothing at all.

# Chapter 29

Christina and Kendall couldn't walk a straight line. And neither of them cared.

"Told you," Christina said, tittering drunkenly.

"You sure nuff did," Kendall replied.

It was three weeks past Labor Day, and they had come from the café in the Brevoort Hotel, where they had celebrated with two bottles of pinot noir, and were staggering through Washington Square. Old men in bulky sweaters were playing dominoes under the autumn-tinted trees, and Kendall saw her landlord, Mr. Ciccolini, in his grayish-brown suit and fedora, sitting on a bench, reading *L'Espresso* while the young man beside him, in a peacoat and watch cap, was riffling through that new left-wing daily, *PM*.

Christina said, "When your photos arrived in Provincetown, I started shouting. I knew you'd be good. But this good? Who could predict that? Léo was with us for dinner, and Léo became so excited when I gave them to him, he began speaking French. I go, 'In English, Léo, in English,' and Léo says, 'Whoever this is must be in my gallery.'"

This was the twelfth retelling of the story since Christina had returned from Cape Cod, but Kendall was no more tired of hearing it than Christina was of repeating it. Léo Sapir was the proprietor of the toniest avant-garde art gallery in the city, and even though Kendall had spoken to him on the phone and had an appointment with him on Friday, she couldn't get used to the news that he wanted to exhibit her photographs.

"This feels too fast. I'm not ready for my own show."

"Léo likes the art he likes, and he could care less if you or anyone else thinks you're ready. Léo's a romantic. And a tenacious French Jew who has nothing against money. Wait till you hear him talk to the critics and his rich customers. The tale he'll tell of his discovery. 'Here is my Negress with the unfailing eye. She is as gorgeous as her photographs.'"

"Christina, I don't know how to thank you."

"Thank me? I should thank you."

"Why?"

"Because Léo was so captivated by your photos, he forgot to extol the greatness of Brig's paintings. With no one paying attention to him, Brig goes berserk and starts up about our chain. I told him I was done with that stinking thing, and if he didn't like it, he could tie that chain around his you-know-what and give it a yank. I haven't had it on since."

✳

Compared to the Village, the Upper East Side was as staid as a bank, which was logical to Kendall as she came up Fifth Avenue and cut over to Madison, because it was here that New York displayed its wealth—in luxurious rows of apartment buildings and mansions of rusticated limestone shaded by the glory of Central Park. The Léo Sapir Gallery was in a townhouse on East Seventy-Ninth, beside the New York Society Library. A limousine was in front, with a liveried chauffeur standing by. Kendall went through the leaded glass doors and saw the paintings and photographs on the walls—Picasso, Duchamp, Cartier-Bresson, and Evans—and when it occurred to her that her work would be hanging with such august company, she felt like a fraud.

A man in an indigo suit and turtleneck was escorting a silver-haired woman in a chinchilla wrap to the entrance. "Mrs. Johnson," he said, "the Dalí will be reframed and at your home by five."

"See that it is, Léo. My guests will be there by eight."

He held the door for her and, after she walked out, said, "You must be my next discovery." He kissed Kendall's hand. *"Enchanté de faire votre connaissance, Mademoiselle Wakefield."*

*"Je suis ensorcelée, Monsieur Sapir."*

Up close, he resembled the portraits of Shakespeare—balding with long, wavy brown hair in back and a short boxed beard. "Come," he said. "I have a sweet tooth and a scrumptious crème de cacao. And you will call me Léo."

The sitting room had a stained glass octagonal window and a circular table with four Chippendale chairs. Léo poured the chocolate liqueur from a bottle into shot glasses and passed one to Kendall.

*"À votre santé,"* he said, toasting her health.

*"Et à la vôtre."*

Léo dug through the mail, catalogs, and photographs on the table until he found a desk calendar. "For the opening of your exhibit, I think a Friday evening, November twenty-eighth. *C'est bon?"*

*"C'est bon."* That was all the conversation Kendall could manage. She was in a mild state of shock, unable to accept that she was preparing for a show at the Léo Sapir Gallery. Kendall watched him sifting through her photographs. "Monsieur—Léo, you really like these pictures?"

He laughed, a deep, operatic sound. *"Ma chère,* they are *magnifique.* Photographers endeavor to freeze an instant for eternity. But you, you in a single glance lay bare the past, present, and future of your subjects. That little girl and the rainbow. I see her life for as long as she is alive. And these two, *mon Dieu."*

He put them on the table facing Kendall. In one, a leggy teenage beauty in a halter top and short shorts strolls past a young man in a sleeveless T-shirt, who stands outside the Lenox Lounge and eyes her as if she were a glimpse of the Promised Land, while the teenager's phantom twin hurries ahead as if fleeing from the burden his love would bring. In the other, a prostitute in a camisole, the depredations of time and boredom on her face, leans out the turreted window of a row house on St. Nicholas Avenue, her apparition beside her, both of them with eyes as hard as asphalt and watching the men filing up the stoop.

Léo said, "For now, I call them, *Love One* and *Love Two.* Your photographs must have titles—for the catalog and the exhibit. We can address that together. Monday at nine, if that's acceptable. The gallery will keep forty percent of each sale. I will sell these for three hundred dollars."

"A—a picture?"

"*Bien sûr*. My clientele can afford it and you deserve it. And as an aside, Christina told me you don't have an agent."

"Do I need one?"

"To collect a proper wage from magazines, yes. I'm starting an agency, frankly, because so many art directors and editors ask that I recommend photographers, and why should I speak to them for free? The *Picture Post*—it's the British *Life*—wants photos of the ambassador to Washington. *Look* wants children at play in New York. *Coronet* wants Judith Anderson—she will be playing Lady Macbeth on Broadway. *Glamour* calls for movie stars who want a touch of *je ne sais quoi* in their portraits. *Life* has Margaret Bourke-White, so it will be difficult for you to break in there, but perhaps they will take on a Negro. We shall see. In these other magazines, I can get you from two to four hundred dollars plus expenses, and you'll have a lab to develop your film and make prints. I earn twenty-five percent."

Kendall gulped down the rest of her liqueur. "I don't have the technical ability or the experience for—"

"You will learn, and if you don't, no one will hire you again. I say you will. I have regretted disregarding my instincts, but never heeding them. You will make a name for yourself, Mademoiselle Wakefield. And I will help you. Because I want to. And because I can. Are the terms acceptable?"

"Do we shake hands or something?"

"*Oui*," Léo said, and held out his hand.

❋

Kendall walked out of the gallery, telling herself that she wasn't dreaming. If she didn't have to meet Simon at the Museum of Modern Art, she might have spent the rest of the day wandering Central Park. So far, Kendall had done two assignments for the *Courier*, photographing the author Richard Wright, in his Brooklyn apartment, and A. Philip Randolph, president of the Brotherhood of Sleeping Car Porters, at his office near the Apollo. The photos accompanied the columns Simon was writing on the transformation of Wright's novel *Native Son* into a play, and on Randolph's persuading President Roosevelt, by threatening to lead a march on Washington, to sign an executive order prohibiting discrimination in hiring at defense plants. Kendall had earned fifty dollars, fair money for her effort, she'd thought, until talking to Léo. After each interview, Simon had invited her for a drink. She'd made up excuses, which, from his look of bemused condemnation, he wasn't buying. He'd phoned her about visiting the museum for a piece he was writing on the exhibit of sub-missions for the National Defense Poster Competition. She agreed because she could justify it to herself as helping a colleague, though she suspected that Simon had chosen the poster exhibit because he knew she couldn't resist an art museum.

Simon was waiting for her in the entranceway. "Hey there, Kenni-Ann."

"Simon, you won't believe it. I have an agent."

"Way to go, girl. Tell me about it."

As they went through the labyrinth of rooms with knots of peo-ple gathered before the bursts of colors on the walls, Kendall quietly recounted her discussion with Léo, omitting the plans for her show. Simon would want to attend and that could get complicated with Julian there.

"If you're too famous for the *Courier*, I'll miss seeing you."

Kendall grinned. "Not too famous—yet."

They came to the posters, which extolled the mundane sweetness of American life that boys, if summoned to war across the seas, would willingly die to defend: a small-town July Fourth parade; children sleigh-riding down a hill; a collie herding cows into a pasture.

Simon let out a low, harsh laugh. "How come there're no colored folks picking cotton? Or riding in the back of a bus?"

They were standing side by side, Kendall's shoulder touching his arm.

"Kenni-Ann, these posters remind me of Benton. They've got the same exaggerated realism, don't they?"

"Those three do."

"Benton must have been a fan of cartoons."

"He used to be a cartoonist." Kendall liked that Simon had seen that, liked it enough that she was uncomfortable again, as if she had betrayed Julian.

After twenty minutes, they went outside and started walking, neither of them speaking until they reached the corner of Fifty-Third and Fifth, where Simon turned to her, his eyes full of the same hunger that Kendall often saw in Julian's gaze.

"Drink?" he asked.

"Simon, I'm involved with someone."

"The more the merrier."

"I'm a one-at-a-time girl."

"Suppose I'll have to wait for you to write me in on your dance card." He tipped his newsboy cap. "See you around."

Simon strolled up through the shoppers. Kendall admired his languorous stride and imagined wrapping herself around him as he moved inside her, and the image, so sudden and shocking, left her breathless.

※

When Kendall got off the subway at West Fourth, the image was still flashing behind her eyes—disconcerting, to be sure, but suffusing her with warmth. During her drunken conversation with Christina at the Brevoort, Kendall had mentioned that she felt distant from Julian, and Christina had commented that Julian was too prosaic a partner for an artist. Kendall had dismissed her observation. She was the one who was changing. Maybe it was spending those months in Harlem and feeling comfortable in her skin for the first time in her life. Or maybe it was her growing confidence as a photographer and that, contrary to her mother's prediction, she realized that she could carve out a career for herself. Yet even though Kendall resented that Julian wasn't more like Simon, imagining living without him was unbearable and another cause of her resentment, as if Julian had trapped her by entwining himself around her heart like Brig and Christina's chain.

The Friday evening crowd was out on MacDougal, and as Kendall went past the Minetta Tavern, the image of her and Simon was gone, but the warmth had become a tension at the center of her, and upon entering her apartment and taking off her coat, she was glad Julian was on the sofa reading the *Sun*.

"How was the gallery?" he asked.

"Wonderful." She bent to kiss him and went into the bathroom.

Julian was folding up the newspaper when Kendall appeared in just her pear-colored cashmere sweater.

"You can't get into a restaurant without shoes," he said with a straight face.

Kendall chuckled, but in short order she had tugged off his trousers and boxers, and pushed him back, touching him, straddling him, guiding him into her, closing her eyes, and moving, wanting the tension to go away, if only the tension would go away, move move move, chasing oblivion, the serenity of oblivion, the tension winding her up, tight, tighter, tighter still, and Kendall came with such a loud, piercing cry that she scared herself.

*La petite mort*, the French call it, the little death, and the only trouble was that when Kendall opened her eyes, nothing had changed.

# Chapter 30

At lunchtime, 21 was as jammed and noisy as a ball game. Wild Bill Donovan, his gray-flannel-covered elbows on the table, said, "Longy says you're the guy that can buy and sell foreign currency and then make it disappear and appear again."

Julian chewed an olive from his martini. Donovan was in his late fifties, a burly corporate lawyer with distinguished white hair and jowls.

"Longy forgot to mention you're a mute."

Not that Julian didn't trust Donovan, but during Prohibition he'd been a US attorney chasing bootleggers. He'd come out of World War I with the Medal of Honor, and last year Hollywood had made him extra famous with a movie about his unit, *The Fighting 69th*, with James Cagney as a coward punk who becomes a hero, Pat O'Brien as the wise chaplain, and George Brent as Wild Bill himself. Abe knew Donovan from the city and, since it couldn't hurt having friends in high places, had shoveled some cash at him when Wild Bill had run for governor of New York. Donovan had lost the election, but lately he'd been working for FDR, speaking on the radio about the necessity of the country's readying itself for war. Abe said that the president had knighted Donovan the Coordinator of Information, an Ivy League euphemism for chief spy, and Donovan had asked Abe to recommend someone for "a project."

Donovan said, "I'm not J. Edgar Hoover, you got it?"

"I've done some banking abroad." Julian finished his martini. Donovan could've been Eddie's older, better-educated brother—a tough

Irish prick with a law degree. "Hedinger and Company. It's off the beaten path—in Lucerne, not Geneva. Money goes in with them, it can pop out anywhere you want."

"I hear your German's fluent."

"This a job interview?"

"It's not like I can have you fill out an application. If you sign on, I'll give you the oath myself. How's your French?"

"Nobody's gonna confuse me with Maurice Chevalier."

Donovan rattled the ice cubes in his tumbler of Scotch. "Mr. and Mrs. America might be acting like Hitler gobbling up Europe has nothing to do with them, but we're gonna get in this fight. And once we are, you can be drafted or volunteer. Why not do something important? We'll need somebody in Switzerland to funnel funds and weapons to partisans. Could you think about being that guy?"

"I could." Julian didn't consider himself a cloak-and-dagger type, but he was able to keep a secret and, despite the feds poring over his tax returns, they had failed to sniff out the bulk of his fortune, which was resting comfortably in bank vaults and safety-deposit boxes in Florida, the Bahamas, Canada, Ireland, and Switzerland.

Donovan gave Julian his card. "You need motivation, I'll tell you the same I told Longy. Those Nazi shitbirds are shooting every Jew they get their hands on."

*

With his Borsalino low on his head and the collar of his polo coat shielding his neck from the wind, Julian stood outside the granite edifice of Tiffany & Co. and looked at the engagement rings in a window. Donovan was right. War was coming, and Julian wanted to do his share, but it hurt when he thought about leaving Kendall, and he was determined to marry her before shipping out. That way, if he came home in a casket, she could inherit his legitimate dough and assets.

Except he couldn't say whether she'd marry him.

Not that anything was exactly wrong, but Kendall still kept him at a barely perceptible distance, drawing a line that she wouldn't allow him to cross, as if declaring that he was her companion and lover, but this was as far as they would go.

Maybe he was misreading her. Sure, that was probably it. He'd talk to her about it, straighten things out. Then he would buy her the ring.

# Chapter 31

You like it?" Kendall asked, pirouetting before the full-length mirror on her closet door.

"I do." Julian was on the bed with dresses scattered around him. It was the evening before her exhibit, and this was the ninth dress she had previewed.

"You don't like it."

"Yeah, I do."

"No, you don't." Reaching onto a shelf in the closet, she retrieved a cardboard box from Wanamaker's department store and set it on the bed.

Julian asked, "Is that new?"

"Hardly. My grandfather bought it for me my senior year of high school. He was on a civic committee with some of the Wanamakers. They were helpful to Negroes in Philadelphia, and they must've been friendly with Ezekiel, because he was able to take me shopping at the store in the morning before it opened."

"Your mother didn't take you shopping?"

"She was about as interested in my clothing as she is in my photography. I mailed her a catalog of the exhibit two weeks ago, and when I called to see if she got it, she thanked me for sending it and said she was too busy with *work* to make the opening."

Kendall slipped into the dress and inspected herself in the mirror. To Julian, the sheath of shimmering black velvet was as exquisite in its simplicity and lushness as her photographs. And suddenly, he was choked up, recalling his conversation with Donovan and looking at

Kendall with her hair back in waves of thick, dark silk and her skin the color of honey and her hazel eyes more green than brown in the light from the brass and crystal sconces. Julian tried to fix a snapshot of her in his memory and wondered how, when war came, he'd ever muster the strength to leave her.

"Something wrong?" Kendall asked. "Can I fix you a martini?"

"No thanks." He got off the bed, dug into his pants pocket, and held out a rectangular Tiffany-blue box with a white satin ribbon around it. "To remember your first show."

Kendall untied the ribbon. Inside the box was a teardrop emerald pendant on a platinum chain. "Oh, Julian."

He fastened the chain around her neck. Kendall studied the pendant in the mirror, then hugged him. "This dress is the one, isn't it?"

Julian held her tighter, memorizing the tart vanilla fragrance of her perfume. "It is."

✳

Kendall wasn't scheduled to be at the gallery for her opening until six thirty. Julian had recently rented an office in South Orange and had hired a secretary and bookkeeper, and he'd gone to meet with them, promising to be back by four. So Kendall had a whole day to get through. At the Caffe Reggio, she ate her usual croissant *and* a scone with clotted cream, drank four cups of coffee, smoking a cigarette with each cup, and read the *Times* and the *New Yorker*. Then she cleaned her apartment and was thumbing through the new issue of *Look* when she heard knocking on the door, and Brig calling, "Anyone home?"

Kendall let him in. He smelled as if he'd been swimming in gin.

"I've had more openings than I can count," he proclaimed. "They always fray my nerves like cheap shoelaces."

Kendall would have concluded that Brig had dropped by out of concern if his face, with its lusty, diabolical glee, didn't remind her of a satyr in a Rubens painting. All Brig was missing was the pointy ears, and Kendall wished that Mr. Ciccolini were downstairs, but her landlord spent every Friday at his social club in Little Italy.

"Where's Christina?" she asked.

"Christina's reconstituting herself as a Harpy. Yesterday, I had paintings for her to critique, but she had to go to Bergdorf's and buy a chiffon monstrosity suitable for burying a debutante. Christina's so enthral-l-l-l-ed about your opening, you'd believe it was hers."

"Without her, I wouldn't be—"

"Poppycock. You're an artist, like me, and an artist—even those who struggle for attention, El Greco, van Gogh, Gauguin—will ultimately attract the deserved adulation. Christina is not an artist. She doesn't deserve the artist's reward."

"Brig, it was thoughtful of you to stop by. But I have things to do."

"The most reliable place to prepare for an opening is over there."

He nodded at the bed, and Kendall replied, "I'm not sleepy."

Brig chuckled, which Kendall judged to be a positive sign, until he grabbed the sleeves of her sweatshirt. "I like you."

She canted her head away from the stink of the gin. "I like you, Brig, but your wife's my closest friend. I couldn't do that to her."

"I need new ground to explore."

Acting as if this were a joke, Kendall said, "Move to Brooklyn."

Brig latched his arms around her.

"Let me go!" She attempted to wriggle free. He was too close for her to knee him in the crotch. His arms tightened. He was a strong son of a bitch. "Julian'll be here any minute."

His chortling had more derision in it than mirth. "That gangster crap they gossip about at Chumley's? Dime-novel nonsense."

His reply enlightened Kendall: a man could be an illustrious artist and an unregenerate idiot. If Julian walked in, Brig was cooked.

He lapped her neck. Kendall wanted to vomit.

*Think, girl, think . . .*

He tugged up her corduroy skirt.

"Brig, Brig, do you want to force me or—"

"Or?"

Clutching the lapels of his denim jacket and shuffling backward, Kendall said, "Or give it to me good. In bed."

His expression was skeptical, though he allowed Kendall to tow him along until her back was against the bedstead.

"Lie down," she said.

He wouldn't release her. "You'll run."

"For a second, Brig. Let me go for a second."

His grip loosened, and Kendall shed her sweatshirt and bra, tossing them behind her.

"Where am I going to run now, Brig?"

One of his arms, as deliberately as a snake uncoiling toward prey, honed in on her, and when his clammy fingers clamped onto her breast, Kendall almost screamed as if fangs had pierced her flesh. His other arm uncoiled, and Kendall, gritting her teeth, pressed a palm against the bulge in his dungarees. "Brig, lie down and take off those pants."

He stretched out on the crocheted bedspread with its pattern of seashells. Kendall slid her hand into the drawer of the maple bedside table.

Brig said impatiently, "What're you doing?"

"A rubber, Brig. You don't want a baby, do you?"

He answered her with a lecherous smile, which persisted until Kendall pulled a .32-caliber Beretta from the drawer and leveled it at his chest.

"You'd shoot me?" Brig asked, and had the gall to sound as if that possibility hurt his feelings.

"You don't go, we'll find out." Julian hadn't given Kendall any trouble about moving to Greenwich Village except for this pistol. Julian had taught her to use the Beretta on some farmland he owned in Orchard Hill and insisted that she store it by her bed.

Brig strode through the apartment, Kendall remaining far enough away from him so he couldn't spin around and grab her. In the doorway, though, he turned. "You're despicable. Your petty triumph has poisoned my wife, and you've repaid me—your teacher—with nothing."

Kendall cocked the pistol. "I could put you out of your misery."

Brig preferred to leave. Kendall had been calm throughout the ordeal, but after dead-bolting her door, she began to shake. She couldn't tell Julian about Brig: he'd kill him. She was confident that Brig wouldn't say anything to Christina, so she wouldn't lose her friend. Kendall checked her wristwatch. Julian said he'd be back by four and it was quarter of. Julian was never late. Kendall was still shaking when she got into the shower.

# Chapter 32

When Kendall and Julian arrived, Léo was standing with another couple before the wall where Kendall's photographs were arrayed on white mats and framed in black steel.

Helping Kendall off with her coat, Julian said, "Go on, I'll catch up."

As Kendall walked over, she heard the woman, as petite as a hummingbird, say, "Absolutely stunning."

"Here's the photographer," Léo said. "Kendall Wakefield, this is Ada and Aaron Robbins."

"Delighted," Kendall said, her voice reserved and professional, but she was churning with excitement. The Robbins Press was among the most prestigious publishers in New York and had discovered many of the writers in the vanguard of the Harlem Renaissance.

Ada said, "I've bought your *Little Girl and the Rainbow*. To hang over my desk in the office. I was once that little girl. So many of us were, weren't we?"

"I was," Kendall replied. "Might still be."

Aaron, who was no taller than his wife and appeared to comb his hair by sticking his finger in an electric socket, was paging through the catalog. "Listen to this, Ada: 'I came to Harlem a stranger and saw my own double life reflected in its dark faces—the life I live each day and the other life I let no one see. I never understood how two lives could belong to one person, but they can, and I'm certain of it now because I saw them both in Harlem.'"

Ada said, "So Miss Wakefield can write *and* take pictures."

Aaron said, "Two dozen more."

"Approximately," Ada said.

Ada saw Kendall give Léo a puzzled look. "Pardon us," she said. "My husband and I are debating the additional photographs you'd have to take for a book. That is, if you're interested."

Kendall restrained a desire to jump up and cheer. "Interested. And flattered."

"We should discuss it at lunch. Léo, you will join us?"

"Certainly."

"We have to get home to the children," Ada said to Kendall. "Enjoy your show."

When they were gone, Kendall said, "A book? Was she serious?"

"*Très sérieuse*," Léo said. "We'll talk about it tomorrow. Here come the people."

As waiters circulated with trays of canapés and flutes of champagne, Kendall spoke to art critics, reporters, and Léo's regular clientele, who swirled around her in somber wool and rustling silk, appraising her signed, original photographs for their aesthetic appeal and the price they could potentially fetch in the future. After an hour, Kendall broke free to introduce Julian to Léo, and to hug and kiss Fiona, Eddie, and Abe.

"You having fun, *ziskeit*?" Abe asked.

"Trying to." *Ziskeit*, which meant sweetness, was the first Yiddish word that Kendall had learned, and it was Abe who had taught it to her. He was so courtly and kind that Kendall couldn't believe the terrible stories about him in the papers.

Julian accompanied Abe, Fiona, and Eddie as they looked at the photos. Kendall scanned the gallery for Christina and Brig. She didn't spot them and started to worry that Brig had done something crazy when he'd gone home.

Léo appeared at her side. "*Ma chère*, we've already sold eleven. I should've priced them at five hundred."

Kendall let it sink in. Subtracting his commission, she had earned nineteen hundred and eighty dollars—enough to support herself for nine months. "It's more than I could've dreamed. I'm very grateful."

Léo shrugged, still disappointed with himself. "We'll recover it on the book."

A blast of cold air blew into the gallery as Simon entered with a woman on his arm. One of the waiters took his hat and coat and his companion's white fur jacket, and Simon, in black pinstriped gabardine, glanced at Kendall as if they'd bumped into each other by accident. Kendall's initial reaction to Simon's presence was dread. If Simon met Julian, he could bring up the time they'd been spending together, and Julian wouldn't appreciate her not telling him about it. Her second reaction was stronger—jealousy at the sight of Simon with a woman who bore a passing resemblance to the young Billie Holiday with that gardenia pinned in her upswept hair, chandelier earrings, and orange-red lipstick.

"Mr. Sapir," the woman said. "I'm Maxine Thorn. From the *Amsterdam News*. I received your press release, and we spoke on the phone." The *Amsterdam News*, based in Harlem, was the most influential Negro newspaper in the country.

"How good of you to join us," Léo replied.

"This is Simon Foxe. A columnist with the *Pittsburgh Courier*. He and Miss Wakefield are both graduates of Lovewood College."

Simon winked at Kendall and shook hands with Léo. Kendall felt as if she were in a sappy romantic comedy. Maxine was giving her the once-over, her lips stuck somewhere between a smile and a sneer. Kendall thought that Maxine, with the plunging neckline of her sequined dress, might as well put her titties up on a billboard, and seeing that ebony cleavage, Kendall could picture the randy doings in Simon's hotel room.

Maxine said, "Simon would like to write a column on the exhibit, and the *Amsterdam News* will reprint it."

"Excellent," Léo said. "Come, Mr. Foxe, let me explain why these photographs caught my attention."

When they were gone, Maxine said, "Girl, you a credit to your race. It's inspiring that every now and again the master be lettin' some high-yellow poon into his house."

Kendall was appalled by Maxine's vulgarity. Her inclination was to pretend that she hadn't heard her, a response to crudeness that had been ingrained in her by Garland, who had enforced etiquette as if it determined whether the Lord sent you north or south on Judgment Day. Yet on this evening, as Kendall became who she had longed to be, she felt that no-damn-body—least of all some hussy who got herself confused with Lady Day—was entitled to speak to her with such venom.

"In college," Kendall said, "Simon always had some girl he was fucking. Y'all know how a man ain't nothing but a dog needing to bury his bone. I wouldn't be that girl for him, but I reckon there's lots of girls up here who would."

Maxine gaped at Kendall, her mouth forming an O, and if she did snap back, Kendall didn't hear it because she was off to confront a potential disaster: Léo and Simon were talking to Julian. As Kendall reached his side, Julian said to her, "Your college friend, the guy who built the darkroom, right?"

His tone was even, which unnerved Kendall, because Julian was masterful at keeping his feelings to himself and because she felt dishonest hiding Simon from him.

"Right," Kendall said. "Simon Foxe."

Léo was contemplating the trio as if they were subjects in one of Kendall's double exposures, a complicated narrative hidden in the solid and wisplike figures.

Fiona came over as the gallery began to empty out. "Eddie, Abe, and I are hungry. We'll meet you two at Peter's Backyard?"

Julian said, "I'll get the coats."

Kendall smiled at him. "Be there in a minute."

Maxine, frowning, was now standing next to Simon. Kendall ignored both of them and asked Léo if she could use his phone.

"In the sitting room."

Kendall dialed Christina, but no one answered. She hung up and dialed again, pressing the receiver to her ear and listening to Christina's phone as it rang and rang.

# Chapter 33

Monday morning, after not hearing from Christina all weekend, Kendall headed to her house on Bedford Street. No one answered the doorbell, and the blinds were drawn. Christina had an ailing, octogenarian father in Boston, but even if an emergency had summoned her to see him, she was a stickler about appointments, and Kendall was convinced she'd have heard from Christina if her absence at the exhibit wasn't connected to the unpleasantness with Brig. Kendall went around the corner to Commerce to check the courtyard. During the winter, Christina enjoyed sitting on the redwood settee while an apple-wood fire blazed in an ashcan. She wasn't there, and the gate was padlocked.

Kendall caught a subway uptown. On Saturday, she'd gone to the gallery, and Léo had urged her to take more double exposures in Harlem. He had spoken to the reviewers from the *Times* and *Herald Tribune*, and their enthusiastic opinions of her work would be on the newsstands Friday morning—fortuitous timing because Ada Robbins had been in touch and had invited them to lunch on the same day.

So Kendall revived her summer routine, scouting Harlem for photographs and eating at Crossroad Bar-B-Q. On Tuesday, when Mama B brought her a wedge of sweet potato pie, she said, "That Simon been asking after you. I told him you'd be here noon on Thursday."

"I'll be here Wednesday too."

"Girl shouldn't be in that big a rush," Mama B said, chuckling.

On Thursday, Simon was at the table by the jukebox. He said, "I apologize, Kenni-Ann, okay? I wanted to see your exhibit, and the *Amsterdam News* is reprinting my column."

"Very magnanimous of them."

"Of Maxine. She's a magnanimous girl."

"I could tell from her dress."

Simon treated her to one of his dimpled smiles. "Julian's nice. So's his buddy, Longy Zwillman. Who would've guessed in college? Kenni-Ann Wakefield—gun moll."

Kendall was indignant. "I love Julian. And if you've got a hankering to smart-mouth him or Abe, go eat with Maxine. And no more horning in where you're not invited." Simon held an undeniable appeal for her: his humor, intellect, his interest in art and literature and, although she hated admitting it to herself, the fact that he was a Negro from a similar patrician background. Yet, hearing his snide comments, Kendall was unsure if Simon would be a suitable replacement for Julian, and her thinking about lovers in such pragmatic terms bothered her, because she detected Garland's stonyhearted logic in her calculations.

Simon's smile went away. "I apologized for the gallery, and I meant it. It's that—"

"That?"

"I'd like to be higher up on your dance card and—and I wish I could write a paragraph as beautifully crafted as one of your photographs."

"If I can help you, I will. I've been incredibly lucky. And I've met Ada and Aaron Robbins."

"The Robbins Press. That's top-shelf."

"I can introduce you. They're known for publishing young Negro writers."

Mama B took their orders without a glance at Simon.

"Am I in the doghouse here?" Simon asked, after she'd gone to the kitchen.

Kendall laughed. "We won't know till after lunch."

❋

December stole her daylight, and Kendall hoarded every second of it for her photographs and didn't go past Christina's again until she came back from Harlem. And today, as Kendall shouldered her way out of the subway station, she was tempted to head home. Julian had been working late at his office in South Orange since Sunday, going over the architect's renderings and cost projections for the garden-apartment complexes he wanted to put up, and Kendall missed him. He was coming tonight; she could use a shower; and she planned to cook him his favorite meal—spicy fried chicken, grilled tomatoes, and corn bread.

In the end, Kendall chose to go by Christina's. She loved the silvery dance of snowflakes in the late-afternoon blue, the shops on Bleecker with strands of bulbs as colorful as Gumballs in the windows, and the horse-drawn wagon stacked with freshly cut firs going by with bells jingling on the roan's harness. Rounding the corner onto Commerce, she smelled burning apple wood and knew Christina was home and couldn't wait to tell her about the exhibit.

"Christina?" Kendall called through the padlocked gate. "It's me."

Christina was sitting in her settee and staring at the ashcan fire.

"Please," Kendall said. "Unlock the gate."

Christina shambled toward the gate, and Kendall, watching Christina through the gauzy curtain of snowflakes, felt as if she were looking at a painting by Seurat. Only fragments of Christina were in motion, and she was no longer whole. Kendall appreciated the virtuosity of Seurat and his paint-dabbing brotherhood of pointillists, but for her, reality as an ever-shifting pattern of dots was an assault against her wish to define herself, to stand on her own two feet, on her own solid ground.

"What do you want?" Christina asked, the coldness of her tone molding the question into an expression of pique.

"You weren't at my exhibit. I—"

"Brig bought a farm. Upstate. In Copake Lake."

"I—"

"We didn't get out of bed at the farm." Christina glared through the bars with eyes like smoldering ash. "Your attempt to seduce Brig worked him up."

Kendall felt a spurt of anger, like the sudden twist of an ankle, but overriding her anger was the hurt that the closest girlfriend she'd ever had was unfairly accusing her of seducing her husband. Still, as wounded as Kendall was, she tried to avoid insulting Christina, swallowing the response on the tip of her tongue—*Seduce that disgusting letch!*—and saying, "I'd never do that. You know me."

"I do? I know I helped you because you have everything I want: youth, beauty, and talent. I know your rich Jew isn't the man for you, but I didn't know when I suggested you find an artist, you'd sniff around my husband."

"I didn't—"

"You didn't take off your bra for him? You didn't give him a rub below the belt?"

"I had to get his hands off me."

"Maybe you should've given him a gander at your feathers."

"I chased him out of my apartment with a gun. Did Brig tell you that? Did he?"

"I knew Brig loved me. But not how much until he resisted you."

Kendall's anger was back. "Resisted? If I didn't threaten to shoot him, he'd have raped me."

Christina's laughter sounded like the cackling of a drunken witch. "All you colored girls get raped. Every mulatto's a rape baby. No colored girl ever wanted a pumping from a white man. You have a baby with your Jew, will you accuse him of rape?"

Kendall saw her hand thrust through the bars to strike Christina, who stepped out of range and went back to her settee, chanting, "Tramp, tramp, tramp . . ."

All that Kendall was able to remember from her walk to Minetta Street was that whenever she saw Christmas-tree lights through the brownstone windows, she recalled her childhood in Philadelphia and became so sad she had to avert her eyes.

"Careful, don't slip."

Kendall was outside her apartment, where a young man in a pea-coat and watch cap was sprinkling rock salt on the sidewalk.

"I'm Dominick, Miss Wakefield. Mr. Ciccolini's grandson."

His smile was as friendly as his grandfather's, only Dominick had his upper teeth. Kendall remembered seeing him on a bench with her landlord in Washington Square.

"Of course, the law student in Albany."

"I'm here for a couple days. If I don't see you again, have a merry Christmas."

"Merry Christmas to you, Dominick." Kendall was at the door when it hit her, and she turned. "Dominick, what's today's date?"

"The fourth."

"Gosh, I'm so embarrassed. I've been busy, and I forgot to pay my rent. Can I give you a check to give your grandfather?"

"You could, but you're Mr. Rose's friend, aren't you?"

"I am. Why do you ask?"

"Because you can give him the check. He owns the building."

Suddenly, Kendall was dizzy and gripped the railing.

"You okay?" Dominick asked.

"Julian owns the building?"

"My grandfather sold it to his cousin over in Jersey, Siano Abruzzi. Mr. Rose bought it from him."

Kendall opened the door and climbed the stairway, steadying herself by holding on to the banister, wanting to scream and wishing she could cry.

# Chapter 34

T hat should do it," Julian said, reclining in his high-back office chair.

Abe, lighting a cigar, said, "Nothing else?"

"No. My parents get the stocks and bonds; Eddie, the apartment building, the land in West Orange, Orchard Hill, Union, and Millburn; and Kendall, the place in New York and the cash in Howard Savings and National Newark and Essex. The rest is yours."

"Nobody's dying." Abe blew a smoke ring and chuckled. "I'll take care of your stuff and won't steal every dime."

They went out into the flurrying snow. Julian's car was in the lot across from the library; Abe had parked a block away on South Orange Avenue—safer for him, leaving his car in the middle of a well-lit shopping district.

Julian said, "Donovan's gonna be at the football game Sunday. You coming?"

"Gave my ticket to Eddie O. Got no interest in freezing my keister off at the Polo Grounds. What's with you and Kendall?"

"Best thing that ever happened to me, but she's not as—as happy as I am."

Abe took the cigar out of his mouth. "Because we get a better deal than the gals."

"How's that?"

"They're everything for us. We're not the same for them. They need more, and we're not it. And I bet it ain't no picnic for Kendall being with a white lug who wants to marry her."

"I doubt she knows that."

"Big mistake—thinking a woman don't know that." Abe tossed away his cigar. "Kendall's special. You can tell when you meet her. And I ain't never seen you so happy with a girl. If you two get hitched, the way things are, it'll be rough. She worth the trouble?"

Julian removed a Tiffany ring box from his coat pocket and opened it. Abe looked at the oval-shaped diamond. "Nice, now don't be in no hurry to get in a war."

Abe kissed him on the cheek. Julian watched him walk away, a tall man with his fedora tilted just so and his charcoal topcoat tailored to perfection.

The father he never had.

※

No one approaching the Holland Tunnel considers a caravan of tractor trailers with flat tires blocking the toll booths a lucky break, though the delay did provide Julian with the opportunity to look in the rearview mirror and rehearse his marriage proposal: *I love you, Kendall. Love you more than anyone I've ever known.* That's how he'd start. He had to be careful. Tell her the truth but not scare her off. *And I want to marry you.* He'd take the ring out of his pocket. *I'm not looking to plan your future. I'll go wherever you want. All I know is whatever's waiting for me, I want to find it with you.*

Should he kiss her? No. Put the ring on finger? No again. Too pushy. More talk? Hell no. He'd shut his mouth and wait. Wait for Kendall. That would be his best shot for a yes.

After finally driving out of the tunnel and up Sixth Avenue, Julian saw a parking space on Minetta Street, a rare find he interpreted as a good omen. Ordinarily, he didn't believe in good omens, but he brushed aside his skepticism until he let himself into the apartment, saw Kendall standing beside his two toffee leather Mark Cross suitcases, and heard her say, "Get out."

The iciness of her voice, as much as her ordering him to go, shocked him.

"Why?" he asked, taking off his hat and flipping it onto the sofa.

She grabbed his fedora and flung it at him. "Are you deaf?"

His hat sailed past him. "No."

"Take your bags and get out."

"Why? Is it Simon?"

"Simon?"

"How dumb do you think I am? Simon magically appears at your exhibit?"

As defensively as a witness tripped up in court, Kendall replied, "I didn't invite him."

"You hadn't seen him before Friday?"

Kendall glanced out the window. The snow was tapering off.

Julian bored in like a prosecutor. "You forgot to mention it?"

"What're you accusing me of?"

"Running around with an old boyfriend."

"Running— You're the only man I ever—" Her face seemed to harden into a ceramic mask of outrage. "Is that your opinion of Negro girls? Our legs are open like all-night diners?"

"Negro's got nothing to do with this. And you know it."

With a mocking, southern accent, she said, "You cain't be askin' yoah lil colored bitch to be actin' like a white girl—no suh."

"Stop it."

Julian didn't say it loudly, and his face was blank, yet Kendall was terrified. She wasn't frightened that he'd hit her: his violence had been reserved for men. But this was the first time Kendall had seen the rage beneath his calm exterior. It was a sinister emptiness, like outer space without moons, planets, or stars. And Kendall wondered if other people, those who were not blinded by love, had seen it. Perhaps Christina. Or her mother.

"You wanna take up with Simon, have the guts to tell me."

"Guts to tell *you*? You lousy hypocrite—"

"Hypocrite?"

Her scream, sharp as a gunshot, startled both of them: "You bought this place!"

The possibility of Kendall's discovering that he owned the building had occurred to him when he bought it from Siano, but he believed his motives were pure and assumed if it came up, all he'd have to do is confess. "You pay market-rate rent. What's the problem?"

"My boyfriend riding to the rescue."

"You hated South Orange. I didn't want you to be unhappy."

"I didn't hate South Orange. I wanted to live in Greenwich Village. And I wanted to find an apartment by myself."

"You'd still be looking."

"I'll never know, will I?"

"I was trying to help you," he said, his voice breaking.

"You were trying to own me."

"Own you? I was afr—"

"Afraid? Afraid I'd leave? Buying this place was like buying me."

"That's bull—"

"You can't own me. Thirteenth Amendment to the Constitution. Outlawed slavery."

"Renting you an apartment is slavery?"

Kendall began patting the pockets of her flannel shirt in search of her cigarettes.

"On the sofa," Julian said.

Kendall looked up at him. The outrage was gone. Her eyes glistened with tears.

"Why, Julian?"

"Because . . . because I always wished somebody would help me. My mother gave me a ticket for a boat—that was to make things easier for her. Abe gave me a job—that was to make money for him. I did for you what nobody did for me."

"I trusted you, Julian. You knew what I wanted. Why'd you ignore it?"

The tears streaking her face made him feel both helpless and enraged. Julian knew the smart move would've been to apologize. Except he wasn't sorry. On top of that, he resented Kendall's bohemian crap and that she was oblivious to the fact that he didn't share her romantic vision of the hard life. His life had been hard enough.

Julian, regretting each word as it came out of his mouth, said, "Maybe because I didn't grow up with a chauffeur and servants. Because no department store owner ever opened early for me. Because I don't think dead-broke drunks at Chumley's are chic."

Poets may rhapsodize about moments that last forever, but this moment couldn't end too soon for Julian. Kendall was glaring at him with loathing, and Julian was thinking that he'd never hold her again.

"Kendall," he said.

And she slapped him across the face. "Get out."

His cheek on fire, Julian left her key on the refectory table, retrieved his hat from the floor and put it on, picked up his suitcases, and went out.

*

The last time Julian cried, he was fifteen years old and crossing the Atlantic on a ship from Hamburg to New York. He was standing on deck in a moonless night with the vast, dark ocean beyond the rail, and wondering how he would survive. His loneliness had enveloped him then, a sense that he was condemned to live without connections, and he'd wept until he was exhausted enough to go below and sleep without dreams.

Now, as Julian sat in his Packard with the defroster blowing and a tightness in his chest, he recalled that rolling ship and looked through the snowmelt on the windshield. A couple walking away from his car toward Sixth Avenue paused in a pool of moonlight and turned to speak to each other, their words spirals of smoke in the ice-clear air. The girl, her hair flowing out from under a knitted slouch hat, stood on her tiptoes to kiss a boy in a duffel coat. That tearful night on the ship Julian had promised himself that he'd never cry again. For thirteen years he'd kept his promise, though watching this moonlit sculpture of lovers ratcheted up the pressure in his chest. Their kiss ended, and as they disappeared around the bend in Minetta Street, Julian rested his forehead on the steering wheel, wrapping his arms around his body, and began to weep like a lonely teenager sailing to an unknown land.

# Chapter 35

Aglacial wind sliced through the fifty-five thousand football fans in the Polo Grounds and challenged the warming capabilities of the Irish whiskey-spiked coffee that Eddie, Julian, and Donovan were drinking from paper cups. The game was meaningless: the Giants had already won their division, but whenever New York and Brooklyn squared off, the faithful packed the stadium. Donovan hadn't said much to Julian other than asking him if he'd given their conversation any thought.

"Some," Julian had replied, which was true, though most of his thinking since Thursday had been about patching up things with Kendall. He assumed that she would call, but by Friday evening he hadn't heard from her, and all through Saturday, while he did paperwork at his office and ate dinner with Fiona and Eddie at the Tavern, it required every ounce of his willpower not to pick up the phone.

Julian was gazing at the field without following the game when an announcement crackled over the public-address system: "Attention, please. Here is an urgent message: will Colonel William J. Donovan call operator nineteen in Washington."

Donovan went to find a pay phone and returned looking like a guy with terminal heartburn. "Can you give me a lift to LaGuardia?" he asked.

Eddie answered, "I'd drive ya to California to get out of this wind."

Donovan didn't say anything until he was in the back seat of Eddie's Chrysler.

"Japs bombed us in Pearl Harbor. They beat the shit out of our ships. We lost a lot of boys."

Julian said, "The Germans in on it?"

"Won't know till I get to the White House. Hitler and Mussolini signed that Tripartite Pact with the Japs, so the Germans and Italians will jump in on their side." Donovan tapped Eddie on the shoulder. "O'Rourke, what would you wanna do in a war?"

"Stay home."

Julian and Donovan chuckled.

"That won't cut it," Donovan said.

Julian had told Eddie about his lunch with Donovan at 21. Eddie said, "Can't be a spy, Wild Bill. I got red hair and I'm too good-lookin'. Nobody ever forgets my face."

"You got other skills?"

"I can drive drunk."

Julian fiddled with the radio. CBS had more details. The Japs had also bombed American bases in the Philippines, though Hawaii had taken the worst of it.

"Thanks for the lift, boys," Donovan said at the airport. "Be in touch, Julian. I'll lay two to one we'll be fighting Nazis by the end of the week."

As Eddie drove onto the Grand Central Parkway, he said, "You gonna go to work for Wild Bill?"

"Think so. Wanna come along?"

"Nah. I'll take my chances with the draft. The Army gives ya medals for shooting SOBs instead of frying ya in the chair. That ain't so bad."

Eddie was trying to amuse him. Julian wasn't listening. He said, "You mind going through the Midtown Tunnel and hanging a left on Seventh?"

"Yeah, I do. You wanna talk to Kendall—use the phone. Pretend you're normal."

"You're an expert in normal?"

"Not till I met you."

Eddie was only half kidding and, against his better judgment, did as Julian requested. On the avenue, the sidewalks were nearly deserted, as if everyone, save for a few seedy celebrants anesthetized by rotgut, was scared that the Japs were about to blow up the city.

Minetta Street was empty, and no one answered Kendall's door. Julian could've picked the locks with a penknife, but if Kendall came home and nabbed him in her place, that would be it. Out of desperation, Julian turned the doorknob. It wasn't locked. He felt guilty going in and told himself, as his hand flicked up the wall switch for the chandelier, that he was just making sure Kendall was safe.

"Kendall," he said, and his voice sounded as hollow as he felt.

The furniture was gone, and there were no pictures on the walls. He inspected the kitchen. The cabinets were bare. He checked the towel rack and medicine cabinet in the bathroom. Nothing. Then the darkroom. Empty. The silhouette of the bed was imprinted in the dust on the pine floor. In the closet, a wooden hanger from Bamberger's was on the metal rod. The hanger was Julian's. Kendall must have brought it with her from South Orange. Julian didn't take the hanger. It was the sole piece of evidence that he had once belonged here.

❋

Julian got into the Chrysler. Eddie noticed that his eyes were wet.

"She's gone," Julian said.

"Gone? Where to?"

"Don't know. Ciccolini wasn't in. She couldn't rent anything in the Village so quick. I'm guessing she's in Harlem. You hear from Otis?"

"A letter ten days ago. He won't be in from Lovewood for another week."

"There's that reporter from the exhibit, Simon Foxe. Kendall was friendly with him."

"Friendly? Or, ya saying, friendly?"

"I'll let you know."

In the morning, Julian phoned Ciccolini. Kendall had paid her rent but didn't leave a forwarding address. Julian told him to tear up the check. Then he dialed the operator and asked her to connect him to the Sapir Gallery. An answering service said that Mr. Sapir was out of town until Thursday. Julian considered his options with the radio on and FDR requesting that Congress declare war on Japan. The war felt less real to him than his heartache. Julian placed a call to the *Pittsburgh Courier* bureau in Manhattan and asked for Simon Foxe. He wasn't in.

On Tuesday, Julian went into New York by himself and asked a waiter at Caffe Reggio if Kendall had been around. No dice. Julian searched Washington Square, imagining that he saw her standing by the Garibaldi statue in a wash of diamond-blue light. At Chumley's, Julian duked the bartender a fiver and asked him if he'd seen Kendall. He hadn't. Wednesday was worse. Julian spoke to Donovan, then tried to pack, but his mind was crowded with movies of Kendall and Simon. None of them were helpful except as a motivation for Julian to surpass his previous martini record, so that when he woke up on Thursday, he felt as if Ted Williams and Hank Greenburg had been beating him over the head with their bats.

After three aspirin, a bottle of ginger ale, and a hot shower, Julian called the gallery. When Léo got on the line, he said, "Mr. Sapir, I moved into an apartment that Kendall Wakefield used to live in. There's a box of her stuff, and the landlord says I should give ya a jingle to get an address for her."

"Feel free to send it here. I'm certain Kendall will reimburse you for the postage."

"Nah, I know she's up in Harlem. I'll drop it off. All I need is an address."

Léo said, "Very thoughtful of you. She's at the Hotel Theresa. I believe it's on a Hundred and Twenty-Fourth Street."

"Thanks."

Julian phoned Eddie.

"I need a ride," he said.

"Why am I doing this?"

"So I don't shoot anybody. Including myself."

In the lobby of the hotel, none of the Negro men and women on the couches and chairs around the radio turned when Julian and Eddie crossed the green, brown, and gold Oriental rug to the front desk. The elderly clerk, with a crown of cottony hair and the dark, craggy face of a bored tribal chieftain, was leaning over the desk listening to the news. That morning, Germany and Italy had declared war on the United States and Congress was about to return the favor.

"Ain't that somethin'?" the clerk said. "All these colored boys be rushin' to die for Uncle Sammy when most of 'em can't get theyselves a sandwich at a lunch counter."

"That's something," Julian said, and slid a twenty to the clerk. "Kendall Wakefield in?"

"That pretty young thing over to the Crossroad with half a Harlem."

"What's going on?" Julian asked.

"The owners, Mama and Papa B, they youngest boy went down with the *Arizona* at Pearl, and folks be keepin' them company."

"Jesus," Eddie said.

"Thass right, young fella. And a lot more be goin' to Jesus before this mess be over."

✳

Eddie double-parked outside Crossroad Bar-B-Q. He said, "I'm supposed to ask Kendall to come out?"

"For two minutes—that's it."

"And if she doesn't want to?"

"Tell her I'll come in."

Eddie laughed. "That oughtta do it."

Julian waited on the corner and looked down toward the garbage-strewn lot on 134th Street, where maybe a dozen Negros in stingy-brim fedoras and overcoats were stamping their feet against the bite of the cold, drinking out of brown bags, and staring at Julian with the hooded-eyed rancor of men who had worked too hard for too little and didn't care for the deal. In Berlin, Julian had had his fistfights with kids who called him "Jewshit," and during Prohibition he'd earned his share of enemies who would have killed him if Abe and Eddie hadn't been around to kill them back. Being hated on sight for the color of his outer shell was a new, less-than-thrilling experience.

In just a shirt and slacks, Kendall walked out of Crossroad, her face no more animated than if Julian were a stranger hawking roasted chestnuts. Even so, just seeing her made his spirits rise.

"Kendall, I'm very sorry."

She nodded.

"I was—"

"We've been through this," Kendall said.

"I made a mistake. Can't you forgive me?"

She was shivering.

"Please, Kendall."

Her lower lip was trembling.

Julian had the Tiffany ring box in his pants pocket, and he felt ridiculous for bringing it with him. "Is this about the building? Or Simon? Or something else?"

Kendall had been asking herself the same questions. She was no longer so angry at Julian about the apartment, and her reaction seemed harsher than his crime. Yet she wanted to be free from Julian, even though she hated hurting him and her reasons hovered beyond her reach.

"I . . . I don't know," she said, her voice small, hesitant, as if she were reluctant to admit her confusion not only to Julian, but to herself.

Julian saw himself on that boat to America, his loneliness shrouding him like the fog rolling off the waves. He said, "I'm going to Lovewood to see my folks, then I'm off to Europe."

"The Army? Are you in the Army? Did you enlist?"

"Something like that."

Kendall was crying without a sound, her shoulders shaking.

"I wanted to see you before I went. And say I was sorry."

Kendall took off her grandfather's Hamilton watch and fastened it to Julian's right wrist. "Bring it back to me."

"Okay."

"Promise me, Julian."

"Promise."

She hugged him, and he pressed his face into the warm, lemony-scented hollow between her neck and shoulders. He remembered

Kendall sitting before a mirror in her bra, garter belt, and panties and brushing her hair, and how safe this intimacy made him feel, how grounded, and he wasn't sure how he would manage without it.

"Don't die," Kendall said. "Please, don't die."

She broke away and disappeared inside the restaurant. As the door closed, Julian heard the simmer of conversation and then silence. He stood there, as though Kendall would be right back, staring at the ghost-gray light, until Eddie came out and said it was time to go.

# PART IV

# Chapter 36

1944

At Lovewood College, the students and faculty followed the news on the radio and in the papers of the fighting in the Pacific, North Africa, Italy, and the landings at Normandy, but on campus little changed except that three-quarters of the classes were women and all of the men had been classified 4-F by their draft boards. When Theodor wasn't teaching, he was writing his final volume on the Enlightenment, his faith in the restorative powers of reason undiminished by the pictures of the dead and wounded in the magazines and a letter from Germany informing him that his second cousin had died at Dachau. Elana detested Theodor's blindness and envied his optimism. She considered leaving him, as she had in Berlin, but she had nowhere to go, and however desolate their marriage was, she told herself, her husband had rescued her from the orphanage, and abandoning Theodor would condemn him to the same emptiness that Elana had spent her life trying to fill.

Tending to the farm families helped her feel useful and distracted her from worrying about Julian overseas, particularly because Garland accompanied her. Garland no longer had the time for picnicking, though. Mayor Scales kept sending out surveyors to check and recheck the lines that separated his property from Garland's and inundated her with offers to buy her land; the dean of students and the chair of the Education Department had gone to fly with the Tuskegee Airmen; and Garland had to assume their workload, including teaching a course on instructional techniques. Instead of the picnics, she invited

Elana for dinner every Wednesday and Sunday. They ate in Garland's formal dining room, then had coffee and a ruby port in the parlor, where Garland, a zealous creature of habit, sat in the center of the yellow-and-white poppy-print couch and wasn't comfortable unless Elana was across from her in the cane-backed recliner.

On this Sunday, after Garland guzzled her port, she handed a book to Elana. On the dust jacket was a black-and-white photograph of a Negro man in a blood-spattered undershirt being led out of a tenement by a white policeman. The title was *City of Tears, City of Flames*, and the book traced the story of last summer's riot in Harlem. Kendall had taken the photographs; Simon Foxe had written the text.

"Are you still upset about it?" Elana asked.

Elana returned the book to Garland, who secured it between brass lion-head bookends on the wicker table next to the couch. The slender volume beside it was *Double Lives*, Kendall's first book, a long essay accompanied by photographs of girls and women in Harlem. One evening, while Elana had paged through it, Garland had commented that Kendall had made her subjects appear pathetic—"which Negroes do not need." Elana had found the pictures beautiful and haunting. But then, as Kendall had written about herself, Elana was also aware of a life that she lived each day and another subterranean life of despair that Elana let no one see.

Garland said, "I didn't raise my daughter to attend riots or run around France with Germans shooting at her."

"Kendall's very brave."

Garland treated herself and Elana to more port. "Brave? That girl has the brains of a boiled turnip." Garland emptied her glass in two gulps. "Have you heard from your son?"

"Not since he got to England. Julian told me that because he's with the Office of Strategic Services, I'd only hear about him if he died."

Elana wasn't offended that Garland never spoke of Julian in relation to Kendall. Nothing Kendall did seemed to please her mother—though Garland displayed her books prominently enough—so how could she approve of her keeping company with a white, Jewish ex-bootlegger? On his visit before going to England, Julian had struck his mother as wistful. When she'd asked him about Kendall, he'd said that she was fine, but Elana knew something was wrong.

Garland said, "You're welcome to take the leftover roast to the professor."

"Theodor can get his own dinner."

"What's he eat when you're here?"

"His dirty socks, for all I care." Elana drank the syrupy wine. "I do enough cooking and cleaning for him."

"That's how it goes with husbands. They tangle you up with everything they want and you start asking yourself what they're good for." Garland set her glass on the table. "My husband, Robert, used to like to have himself a five-course meal and climb on top of me. When he got done, I felt like I'd been spinning upside down on a Ferris wheel."

Elana giggled drunkenly. Theodor hadn't touched her in bed for three years, which was just as well, since it was a challenge for her to stay awake until he finished.

"My daddy would say, 'Baby girl, don't let no man ride you 'round the clock like no hobby horse. Waste of your time.' But Daddy, he loved his Kenni-Ann. Loved her like every girl deserve to be loved and few is. And I'll be damned if I know where Daddy thought his granddaughter came from." She laughed bitterly. "Sears, Roebuck?"

Garland rested her head on the back of the couch, and soon she was snoring. These dinners often concluded with Garland rambling about her father or daughter and drinking herself to sleep. Elana slipped off Garland's shoes, swung her legs onto the couch, and arranged a pillow under her head. The next time Elana saw her, Garland wouldn't mention dozing off. She was too proud. And sad. That was their strongest connection. Their sadness.

Elana planted a kiss on her forehead and went home.

# Chapter 37

## 1945

That autumn, with the war over, Julian made it back to South Orange right before Eddie married Fiona at Our Lady of Sorrows. Eddie had fought with the Ninety-Sixth Infantry Division at Okinawa, where so many corpses lay in the mud, it was as though a plague had swept over the island. Julian was relieved that Eddie didn't ask him about his OSS missions, and Eddie said nothing about his war until he was in church with Julian beside him as his best man and Fiona coming down the aisle in a cloud of white lace that had Julian imagining Kendall walking toward him in the same dress. Glancing back at Jesus on the cross, Eddie said, "Ya gotta love the Catholics. They don't bullshit people about what's in store for 'em."

The next day, Eddie and Fiona sailed to Ireland, and Julian ate lunch with Abe at the Weequahic Diner.

"You look good," Abe said.

Julian cut into his hot turkey sandwich. "You used to be a better liar."

Julian had lost weight and had bags under his eyes. President Truman was about to officially KO the Office of Strategic Services, so Wild Bill, now a major general and enraged at the Nazis for torturing and executing his agents, wrangled himself a position as an assistant to the chief prosecutor for the war-crimes trials in Nuremberg. The lawyers needed translators, and Wild Bill asked Julian to help with the interrogations. Julian was already in Germany assisting with the denazification program by translating official German documents, and he had accepted the assignment because he was in no shape to go home. He couldn't stop dreaming about that patrol in the Ardennes and the barn where Willy swung from the rafters like one of the Flying Wallendas and boasted that someday he'd be in the Olympics. Julian would've liked to tell Kendall about the sad-eyed faces that accused him as he struggled to sleep, but the last photographs of hers that he'd seen in *Look* were from Italy. So he moved into the Grand Hotel in Nuremberg and helped prosecutors interrogate Nazis in a monk's cell of a room in the Palace of Justice. He might have stayed in Nuremberg straight through the trials had he not been at an interview with an SS general who oversaw squads that murdered civilians and American POWs. The general denied any involvement, claiming that his name was used on the orders as a formality. Julian responded by slamming the prick's head against a wall. The concussion put the general in the hospital and earned Julian a vacation—at the insistence of Wild Bill, who said that he didn't want these shitbirds drooling on the witness stand.

"Your investments are in decent shape," Abe said. "The sale went through on Minetta Street. Siano bought the building again."

Julian dipped a wedge of turkey into the gravy and ate it. "I'm going back to Nuremberg. Could you take care of things awhile longer?"

"Yeah."

Julian put down his fork. He had no appetite.

"How your folks doing?" Abe asked.

"Good. I spoke to my mother this morning, and I'm flying down in ten days."

"Kendall?"

"No Kendall."

Outside on Elizabeth Avenue, Abe put his hands on Julian's shoulders. "It's okay by me if you flush every Nazi down the shitter. But when you're done, find a way to live, *fershtay?*"

"I understand, Abie."

"Remember—a way to live."

✳

A week later, Julian was drinking himself to sleep when the phone rang in his apartment, and the long-distance operator asked if he'd accept the charges from his father. Theodor had never called him. Julian was suddenly sober, and nervous.

Theodor said, *"Mutter ist krank."*

"How sick is she?"

*"Sehr krank."*

Very sick wasn't much of a diagnosis. "Is Mother in the hospital?"

*"Nein, sie ist mit Präsident Wakefield."*

"Has a doctor seen her?"

*"Julian, schnell kommen."*

"I'll take the first flight out."

*"Gut, gut,"* his father said.

When the taxi dropped Julian at Garland's house, he expected to find his mother dying in one of the bedrooms, but she was sitting at a cast-iron table on the veranda with her long blond hair brushed out and a shawl over her shoulders, enjoying the warm, late-morning breeze and squeezing a lemon wheel into a cup of tea. He bent and put his arms around her, and she held on to him until she began coughing. It was a deep, rasping cough, and Julian stood there, feeling helpless, until the coughing subsided. His mother took a sip of tea, and Julian sat across from her.

"Mama, are you all right?" Her hair had strands of silver in it now, and her face was paler than Julian recalled, the new lines around her eyes and across her forehead like hairline cracks in plaster.

"There was a virus going around. I was helping the farm families— five of the older folks passed away—and I must've caught it. My temperature was a hundred and four and wouldn't come down. Garland moved me to here so she and the couple who work for her could look after me. The doctor came, but there was nothing he could do. My fever broke this morning. Your father called you because I suppose he was scared."

"Sure he was scared."

Elana gazed into her cup as though some answer that had eluded her might float up to the surface of the milky tea. "His reaction was a surprise. I always thought he'd be fine without me. I once asked him if our past meant anything to him, and he said, 'A great deal. But were I enraptured by memories, I'd be a poet, not a philosopher.'"

Not the most politic reply, Julian thought, but he'd heard his father's fear on the phone.

The front door opened and Garland, in a high-necked blouse and ankle-length skirt, walked onto the veranda. Julian stood, and she gave him a terse hello.

"Nice to see you," Julian said, but he had to stop himself from laughing. Garland was the only person he'd ever met who could make a simple greeting sound as if she were asking why you weren't in jail.

She said to Elana, "You stay put until I get back. You need your rest."

"Take your time," Elana said. "I'm fine."

She began to cough, covering her mouth with her hands. When she was done, Garland said to Julian, "Your mother can have more cough syrup in an hour. And don't you tire her out none."

"Yes, ma'am."

They watched Garland walk across the road to the college.

Elana said, "Garland told me Kendall is living in Paris."

"That was her plan."

"I could get you her address. It might not be a bad idea to write her."

"Or it might be a terrible idea."

"You won't know unless you try."

"Mama, Kendall ended it with me."

Elana was twisting and untwisting the string of her tea bag around a spoon. "You know what I learned getting old?"

Julian shook his head.

Elana stared at him, her eyes shining like sunstruck turquoise. "No one gets prizes for loneliness."

# Chapter 38

## 1946

Julian hadn't finished unpacking his bags in Nuremberg when he was dispatched to Foehrenwald, a displaced-persons camp ninety miles to the south. The United States government was preparing a case against the former directors of IG Farben, a chemical conglomerate that had, among other crimes, helped produce Zyklon B, the gas used in the extermination camps. Julian spent four days interviewing Jews who had been slaves in the company's factories, then drove back past the towns with their bomb craters and mountains of debris to the Grand Hotel. He got in at midnight. The desk clerk handed him a cable and said that it had been delivered three days ago. The cable was from Theodor and written in English: *Mother died this morning. Funeral tomorrow.*

Julian's first impulse was to dash out of the lobby and hop a flight to the States, as if there was something he could do. That reaction gave way to a weary numbness, and he wrote out Theodor's phone number for the clerk and asked him to place the overseas call and direct it to his room. In the elevator, Julian thought how unusual it was for his father to write to him in English, as though by using Elana's native language he could hold on to her, and Julian remembered that winter when nine of his classmates died from the Spanish flu, and Julian asked his mother what language they spoke in heaven, and Elana assured him that language wasn't necessary in the world beyond the sky—everyone understood each other's thoughts.

He was lying on his bed when the call came through. Julian

reached over for the phone and said hello, and Theodor replied in English, "It was her fever. Her fever carried her away."

Theodor's impressive baritone was scratchy and weak and, hearing it, Julian's numbness was replaced by a medley of gloom, regret, guilt, and loneliness—the music of his childhood. He apologized for not responding to his father's cable, saying that he had been out of town.

Theodor said, "I was with her. I didn't leave her alone. . . . Your mother insisted."

All of his wretched history with Theodor compressed itself into one furious instant. Did his mother really have to insist that her husband sit by her deathbed?

"Your mother insisted. She insisted that I accept the professorship at Lovewood. I preferred not to go. If she hadn't—if she hadn't insisted . . . I would have died in the camps."

Julian's anger receded. "Do you want me to come to Florida?"

As if he hadn't heard his son, Theodor said, "I did rescue her from that orphanage. I told her if we were married, she would be a wife and a mother, and she could revise her definition. She could stop thinking of herself as an orphan."

Julian heard a simmering on the line, like the distant breaking of waves. "If you need any—"

"I'm going to be late. I have a class to teach."

"*Vater*—"

Theodor hung up. Julian put the phone in its cradle, loosened his tie, and kicked off his shoes, but he was too tired to undress. What did he expect from his father? To ask him how he was doing? That wasn't his style. A good cry? Forget it. Julian had only seen his father cry once. A gray Sunday afternoon when he was ten years old. The Roses had gone on a family outing, strolling through the Tiergarten with the dying flames of autumn in the trees. His mother had been silent on their walk, and she didn't say anything when they entered the zoo through the Elephant Gate. They toured the aquarium, Elana trailing behind her husband and son. Later, as Julian watched two lion cubs wrestling in their cage, his mother said quietly, "I can't stand it."

"What can't you stand, Elana?"

Loud enough to attract the attention of the families around them, she replied, "The cages. The animals in the cages. I can't stand it!"

Theodor placed his hand on his wife's shoulder to calm her, but she burst into tears and hurried back toward the gate. Julian looked at his father.

"Mother will be fine. She needs her nap. Let's go for Kaffee und Kuchen."

At the Romanisches Café, Theodor had coffee and a cherry streusel tart, and Julian a glass of milk and a slice of Black Forest cake. His father stared at the table as he ate and drank.

"What's wrong with Mother?" Julian asked, and it was then, as Theodor raised his head, that Julian saw the tears running down into his beard.

"I wish—" his father said. "I wish I knew."

Now, as Julian turned over on the bed and his own tears wet the pillowcase, he knew that his sorrow had another cause, perhaps a deeper one than the loss of his mother. When Julian started working for Abe as a teenager, he'd daydreamed of a better future when he would be rich and married with children of his own, and he and his parents would get together and love each other as families are supposed to. For the Roses, that future was permanently out of reach, and letting go of his daydream was as difficult for Julian as reconciling himself to the fact that his mother was gone.

"Bye, Mama," Julian said, and his voice sounded strange in the empty room.

✳

In Nuremberg, Julian attempted to put Abe's advice into practice by dating a British translator. She was pleasant company, but he hoped that Kendall would show up to photograph the trials. She never did, and the closest Julian got to her was reading her latest book, *Here & There*, which alternated between her photos of the dead and nearly dead at the Ohrdruf concentration camp, and pictures, originally published in newspapers, of lynchings across the South. The captions were the only text: the layout was the message—that is, until the final chapter, which covered the short life of Derrick Larkin along with Kendall's photos of his death.

The reviews Julian saw were terrible. The critic in the London *Observer* declared that it was manipulative of Miss Wakefield to equate the sporadic tragedies of lynching with assembly-line slaughter; and the critic in the *Herald Tribune* opined that *Here & There* was not a view of the war that Americans deserved and recommended the more rounded vision in photographer Margaret Bourke-White's *Dear Fatherland, Rest Quietly*. Julian was tempted to write Kendall that he had liked her book, but in the acknowledgments she had thanked Simon Foxe for assembling the newspaper photographs, and Julian assumed that she was involved with him.

Julian remained in Germany through the fall and a round of executions. In his dreams, the dead asked him if he hadn't earned a place on the scaffold. He refused to answer.

Returning to South Orange didn't cure Julian's insomnia, but his exhaustion churned itself into a shopping mania, which was how he became one of the largest holders of undeveloped land in New Jersey.

"You're worse than a gold digger with a charge account," Eddie said.

"I'm gonna build those garden apartments, and you're getting a piece."

"I ain't got the scratch."

"The feds'll chase Abe till he keels over or they throw him in prison. I'd like to keep you around."

"I'm grateful for you cutting me in. But boyo, are you all right?"

"No."

"Fiona's got girlfriends. You could try a date."

"I have business in Florida, and I'm going to see my father."

In Miami Beach, Julian arranged to sell his hotel. He hated being there without Kendall, and with the Beach a popular tourist destination again, he would earn a nice buck on the sale. After meeting with the Realtor, Julian called Theodor. He hadn't spoken to him since Nuremberg. They had exchanged two letters, Julian asking how his father was getting along and recounting the bizarre experience of listening to Nazi killers explain their innocence; and Theodor replying that he was adjusting to living without Elana and scrawling a quote from the writer, Mary Shelley, across the top of both letters: "No man chooses evil because it is evil; he only mistakes it for happiness."

"How are you?" Julian said, when Theodor answered.

"*Gut, danke.*" Julian thought that his father must be through the worst of his grief because he was speaking to him in German.

Julian asked if he wanted to have dinner. "*Ich bin beschäftigt,*" Theodor said, and explained that he was writing a series of lectures on Spinoza's *Theologico-Political Treatise* that he had been invited to deliver at Morehouse College in Atlanta next week.

Julian told himself that he shouldn't be surprised—or hurt—that Theodor claimed he was too busy to meet him, but he was. They said good-bye, and Julian mixed a double martini, with no olives to distract him, and halfway to the bottom of the glass, he recalled standing in the kitchen with his mother, helping her stuff a chicken with apples and walnuts, and Elana looked up from the pan and spoke to the wall over the stove: "If your father's writing and has an audience to admire him, he doesn't need me any more than my parents did," and before Julian could comfort her, Elana went back to work on the chicken.

The phone rang, and Julian hoped that his father had changed his mind, but it was his secretary. There were several messages, she said, nothing pressing. A General Donovan had called to see if Julian wanted to have lunch. Wild Bill was back at his Wall Street law firm, and Julian figured he was trolling for clients, so he asked his secretary to give him the number, his feelings of rejection mollified by the fact that somebody wanted to eat with him.

# PART V

# Chapter 39

Music was floating up from the Seine, and the afternoon light shining on the couples jitterbugging below was as thick and golden as custard. The quartet had set up on a barge moored against the quay, and from where Julian stood above the stone stairway that led down to the river, he saw Otis at the piano, hammering out "Pinetop's Boogie-Woogie," bouncing around on the bench like a puppet with a madman yanking his strings. The drummer and bassist couldn't keep up with him, and the saxophonist arched so far backward as he wailed that it seemed his spine would snap. The dancers were white and Negro: ex-GIs in their khakis and Parisian girls in their vivid scarves, all of them gyrating with the exaggerated gestures of mimes, only faster, neckties swinging, skirts flouncing up and offering glimpses of thighs and lingerie, the giddy music transforming the ancient stones of the quay into the floor of the Savoy Ballroom.

At last, Julian saw Kendall under the linden trees. He couldn't see her face because she was photographing the dancers. Her hair, still long, was tied behind her in a radiant wave. The music stopped, and the dancers clapped. Kendall lowered her camera. She was so beautiful it hurt to look at her. Going down the stairway, he concluded that showing up in Paris wasn't the wisest move he'd ever made. To suppress his nervousness, Julian gazed out at the Seine.

"Jules! My man!"

Otis had seen him on the stairs, and when Julian reached the quay,

Otis threw his arms around him. "Man," Otis said, standing back and checking out Julian's suit and wing tips. "We're gonna have to frenchify your rags. Make you *dans le vent*."

"I'm thirty-three. That's not young enough to be 'with it.'"

"It's about style, baby, not time," Otis said, patting his purple beret. "How you and Eddie makin' it?"

"We saw Art Tatum at the Downbeat and we say he's got nothing on you."

Otis chuckled. "Didn't know you boys gone deaf. What you doing in the City of Lights?"

"Yes, to what do we owe this pleasure?"

It was Kendall's voice, behind him, and to Julian it was as poignant as hearing an old love song. He turned. She was thinner, there were lines around her eyes, and the satchel she'd carried since college was on her shoulder. Julian hadn't seen her since December 11, 1941, yet now, with her close enough to touch, he froze, and Kendall appeared equally flustered.

"Kiss already," Otis said. "My break's about done."

They kissed on the lips. Julian would've been happy to let it go on for an hour or two, but Kendall pulled away, saying, "I have to get over to Deux Magots."

Julian couldn't tell whether Kendall was announcing that she had a date or suggesting that he come along. Otis settled it: "Go with her, Jules. I'll catch up later."

Kendall said, "You hate the Magots."

"Yeah, but I love you two."

As they climbed the stairway, Julian heard the quartet break into "Someone to Watch Over Me," and he imagined dancing with Kendall, holding her hand, feeling her against him.

She said, "Mama wrote me about your mother. She was really broken up about losing her. I'm so sorry, Julian."

"Thanks." Across the Seine Julian could see the Louvre, a dull gold in the shadows. He said, "Why does Otis hate that café?"

"It's a hangout for Sartre and *les existentialists*, and Otis says they'll talk you stupid and don't care none for the Lord."

On the ship over to France, Julian had slogged through Jean-Paul Sartre's *Being and Nothingness*. It was fatter than the French-English dictionary he had to consult so frequently that a steward, a kindly older fellow from Avignon, offered to help translate. Julian tipped him for the offer and plodded on by himself, deciding that because the book was written in Nazi-occupied Paris, it was understandable that Sartre had declared man useless and existence nauseating. Still, his views struck Julian as nothing but nihilism spiffed up for a night on the town. Not that Julian believed God would get him out of any fix he was dumb enough to get himself into. Yet he was a great believer in being angry at God. For the war, the dead women and children especially, and for every horror he had to remember.

Kendall said, "You didn't tell Otis why you're here."

"To open a *boîte de nuit*."

"A nightclub?" she replied, as if he were joking. "Like Bogart in *Casablanca*?"

"Bogie's was for gambling. Mine's for music."

"And that's why you're in Paris? For this nightclub?"

"And for this." Julian took her grandfather's Hamilton wristwatch from his pants pocket. "You told me to bring it back it you. When we were outside Crossroad Bar-B-Q."

Kendall glanced down at the watch and sighed, a sound with more confusion in it than resignation. "I've been thinking about Grandpa Ezekiel lately."

Julian wanted her to say that she had been thinking about him, which seemed so childish, he was chagrined that the thought had popped into his head.

"The crystal broke," he said. "I had to replace it."

Kendall ran a finger over the crystal and looked at Julian, studying him as if she were about to snap his picture, trying to discern the meaning embedded in the image.

Then she fastened the watch to her wrist and pecked Julian on the cheek.

# Chapter 40

*S*alut, *Kendall! Rejoignez-nous."*

The man who stood on the terrace of Les Deux Magots beckoning Kendall to join him and his companions had thinning blond hair and a cockeyed stare behind horn-rimmed glasses. He had spotted Kendall as she and Julian had come up Rue Bonaparte, then passed the people milling around the cobbled plaza of the Church of Saint-Germain-des-Prés, among the few sights that Julian remembered from his year in Paris as a child. He'd gone by the church with his father, who commented that the bones of the philosopher René Descartes were entombed inside while his skull was interred elsewhere, an illustration, Theodor said, of Descartes's belief in the separation of mind and body. It was the one time that Julian could recall his father laughing.

"That's Sartre," Kendall said. "The woman next to him is his soul mate, Simone de Beauvoir."

Kendall had to bend so Sartre could do the cheek-to-cheek kiss with her, but as he altered the Gallic ritual, copping a cheap feel by rubbing his hands along the sides of her black silk jacket, Julian noticed Simone, in a white shirt and a tie the same riveting sapphire as her eyes, glowering at Sartre.

Kendall introduced Julian to everyone as *mon cher ami*—my dear friend. That was a start, Julian thought. To demonstrate that he wasn't a boorish American, Julian bowed slightly and, with his best French accent that still mangled the nasal vowels even though he'd spent eighteen months in France during the war, Julian said, *"Bonsoir, je suis très heureux de faire votre connaissance*." Despite his saying good evening and that he was very happy to make their acquaintance, no one—not the publisher, Christian; nor the poet, Jacques; nor the novelist, essayist, and playwright, Samuel; nor Sarte nor Beauvoir appeared pleased to meet him. The first three men were too deep in conversation, and the two soul mates were glaring at each other.

Julian and Kendall sat, but before he could order, a waiter brought Kendall a bottle of muscadet and two glasses, and poured the wine for her to taste, and when she nodded her approval, he filled her glass and one for Julian.

"*Merci*, Albert," she said to the waiter.

"You're a regular?" Julian said.

"Sort of. I'm usually at La Palette. I'll take you there"—she laughed, clearly skeptical—"if you're not too busy with your *boîte de nuit*." She raised her glass. "To your nightclub."

The wine was cold and crisp and dry. Christian, the publisher, asked Kendall about some of her photographs, and they began to talk, and then she entered the conversation with the others, except for Beauvoir, who was in a tête-à-tête with a slender, sloe-eyed beauty. The table was like a stage in a theater-in-the-round, and men and women, most of them in their twenties, sat or stood close by their older heroes, drinking wine and smoking sharp-smelling Gauloises, the men in dark berets and sport coats that hadn't been new before the war, the women in snug sweaters, short skirts, and colorful scarves.

Julian felt ignored by Kendall and thought that the chatter at the café would be as tedious as the babbling of the bohemians in the Village. He did find it comical that he kept hearing the term *absurd* spoken with the utmost solemnity—why be so solemn if everything was pointless? Yet he admired the young Parisians. They had either scrambled to survive the Occupation or fought with the Résistance against the Nazis and the Milice—the brutal French militia created by the Vichy government, the official French government established after Hitler had conquered France in 1940. Julian could only guess at the suffering these young men and women had endured, the loved ones who had been shot in the streets or tortured in the internment camps or sent to Auschwitz. And now, on top of that suffering, were the shortages. Fuel was scarce: on the Boulevard Saint-Germain, Julian saw more bicycles than cars. Bread was rationed—a calamity, because the crusty baguettes were central to life in France—black-market prices for food were astronomical, and jobs were impossible to find.

Nonetheless, here they were, these spiffy Parisians, discussing philosophy, literature, art, and politics as if words could cure grief and quiet growling stomachs. Julian listened, not for meaning but for the delight of hearing native French speakers, which for him was like listening to Dizzy Gillespie and his bent trumpet brightening the air with starbursts of bebop.

The waiter replenished Kendall's wine: it was her third glass.

Julian was hungry, and he ordered twenty-five grilled ham-and-cheese sandwiches and a dozen bottles of wine. Albert, eyes bugging, said, *"Pardon, monsieur?"*

Albert's hearing improved when Julian handed him a couple of hundred-dollar bills—almost twenty-four thousand francs, with France devaluing its postwar currency. Smirking, Kendall said, "The rich Americans take Paris."

"I hate to eat alone. Besides, these kids won't be insulted. From what they're saying, they're all Communists."

The Communists had fought the Nazis, and these efforts, along with the shortages and their support for the beleaguered workers of France, had made the Parti Communiste Français a power in politics.

Kendall smiled at Julian with some of the warmth that he remembered. When the sandwiches and wine were brought, the young people hesitated, their expressions stuck between suspicious and resentful. Julian did a quick-and-dirty translation of Karl Marx into French and more or less proclaimed, "'From each according to his ability, to each according to his need.'"

That did the trick. They started to eat and drink. So did Sartre and his pals, save for Beauvoir, who was whispering with the girl, who seemed more beautiful the longer you looked at her, and Kendall, who was talking to the publisher again. On the boulevard, couples strolled in the spring evening, and the lights were on in the cafés with the red geraniums in the window boxes above the terraces.

"Café life's the nuts, ain't it?" Otis had come up behind Julian and sat next to him.

"Not bad," Julian said, pouring Otis some wine. "And it's good to see you recovered. Eddie says you wrote him you were wounded."

"Burns on my legs. When Patton sent us to Vic-sur-Seille. Now I can do two things. Play the piano and drive a tank while folks try to blow me up." Otis sipped the muscadet. "Surprised to see you, Jules."

"I'm opening a jazz club."

Otis grinned. "In Paris?"

"That funny?"

"No, baby. Paris swings."

"Then why you grinning?"

"You're here for Kenni-Ann."

"Who says?"

"Anybody not blind. But it's cool. The girl could use some sobering up."

They could hear Kendall talking: her speech was slurred. Julian said, "I need a house band. You think your quartet would be interested? I'll pay decent."

"The money'll be gravy. The GI Bill pays us seventy-five a month—twice the scratch most French families got."

Across the boulevard a Negro man was entering Lipp's with a flaxen-haired mademoiselle on his arm. He stopped to speak to another Negro who was exiting the brasserie, and that man, carrying an overnight bag and wearing a tan suit, walked toward the café. Julian recognized him from the Léo Sapir Gallery. "That's Simon Foxe, isn't it?"

"Unfortunately."

"Why unfortunately?"

Otis glanced into his wineglass. "Him and . . ."

"Him and Kendall have a thing?"

"Had. Simon's been reporting for the Negro wire service. He covered the cats fighting in Italy, Holland, France, and Germany. He was with us at Vic-sur-Seille. Before Kenni-Ann got there, and he bent my ear in three about her telling him to hit the road. Now he's reporting on Negro soldiers in Europe and dating this white girl—Thayer Claypoole. Kenni-Ann knows Thayer from that Quaker school in Philly. She's taking classes at the Sorbonne, and Kenni-Ann don't care about her and Simon, but he's still mad, and he sees Kenni-Ann, the shit get stirred."

The stirring began as soon as Simon got to Deux Magots. Kendall was laughing like an inebriated duck, and Simon gave her a cutting look and said to Otis, "Our girlie isn't herself unless she's lit up and got her legs wrapped around somebody."

Kendall overheard him and, standing up and holding on to the table to support herself, replied in English, "Don't 'girlie' me, you smug sonovabitch."

Simon noticed Julian, who was standing and offering him his hand. "Julian Rose. Met you years ago at Kendall's opening."

They shook, and Julian said, "Read your book on the Harlem riot. Enjoyed it."

"Thank you." Simon glanced at Kendall, as if he wanted to answer her, and then looked at Julian. He said, "Otis, I have to catch a train to Bonn. I called Thayer, but she's not in. She's supposed to be here in fifteen minutes. Will you tell her I'll give her a ring tomorrow?"

"Will do, man."

Simon got into one of the taxis outside the church. Kendall was standing with Beauvoir, Sartre, and the young beauty that Beauvoir had engaged in a tête-à-tête. Now Beauvoir whispered to Kendall, who erupted in a fit of laughter. Evidently, Beauvoir knew English, because Kendall said to her, "Don't go inviting people to a party at my pussy without asking me."

Beauvoir spoke to Sartre, probably translating Kendall's response. He puffed on his pipe and grimaced. The young beauty's face was as animated as a slab of marble.

Otis said, "You should get Kenni-Ann to her hotel. She's at the Trianon. On the Rue de Vaugirard. Where you staying?"

"At the Voltaire. Give me a call and leave your number. I'll track you down."

Julian went and took Kendall's arm. "Let me take you home."

"You want to take little ole me home?"

"Little ole you."

"Take me home and then?"

"Let's get a cab."

"Don't you wanna and-then me?"

Her expression was loopy, but underneath it she seemed to smolder. Not with lust, though. With anger.

It was a five-minute ride to the hotel. They took the elevator, a wire cage, to the eighth floor. Julian dug through her satchel for the key. A lamp was on in the sitting room. Kendall put her arms around Julian's neck, pressing against him.

"Remember how you used to fuck me?" She grabbed his lapels and tugged him into the dark bedroom. She let go and fell back on the bed.

Julian slipped off her espadrilles.

She kicked a foot at him. "Forget the shoes. Fuck me."

The windows were open, and the room was chilly. There was a cotton blanket folded at the end of the bed, and Julian drew it up over Kendall.

"Boy," she cracked, switching to her southern drawl, "when I tell y'all the blueberries is ripe, you best bring me the durn bucket."

Julian sat on the bed. "Go to sleep now."

"You don't want to fuck me?"

"Not tonight."

"Why not? Why not tonight?"

"Get some rest."

"Fuck you."

She flopped over on her stomach. He looked down at her under the blanket with her hands laced together under her chin as if she were praying, and waited until he could hear the even breathing of sleep.

"What happened to you?" he murmured, then quietly walked out of the suite.

# Chapter 41

If, as *les existentialists* claimed, existence was meaningless, then it made sense to begin each day with dessert, a plan that Julian put into action by devouring a *pain au chocolat* at one of the busy cafés in the square outside the Sorbonne. Kendall's hotel was just across the Boulevard Saint-Michel, and Julian was tempted to check on her. Her behavior had disturbed him, but he doubted that crowding her would work out well for either of them.

He finished reading *L'Humanité*, the Communist daily, then glanced at his map and the address typed on an index card, and went up the Boul'Mich with the sun already warm and the light filtering through the treetops. At Rue Soufflot, he could see the portico of columns of the Panthéon as he climbed the slope of Montagne Sainte-Geneviève, past a newspaper kiosk that resembled a small, dark-green church with its cupola, and the students going to class, and turned into the beguiling heart of the Latin Quarter. The smell of fresh-baked bread from the *boulangeries* hung over the narrow cobblestone streets, and it was quieter here and there was the soothing hiss of the espresso machines in the cafés for background music. The old houses of limestone or stucco were three or four stories high, some of them with sunny courtyards and gates glorious enough for a palace and elegantly carved wooden doors painted electric blue or bottle green or the reddish orange of persimmons. He found the bistro he was looking for on Rue Blainville. Dust coated the zinc bar and mosaic floor—so much dust that the light slanting through the windows and across the dark-haired *patronne* sitting behind the cash register at the end of the bar seemed grayish brown.

"Madame Isabella Lefevre?" Julian said.

"*Oui.*" Her face, with its high cheekbones and full lips, had been pretty once, but it was cobwebbed with wrinkles now, and her eyes were dark and vacant—the eyes of someone who had forgotten how to hope.

"*Je suis* Julian Rose."

"*L'américain?*"

Julian gave her a friendly smile. "How could you tell?"

"Because I've been waiting for you, and you speak French like you're reading from a Berlitz phrase book." She gestured behind the bar. There were no liquor bottles on the shelves, and the beer taps needed polishing. "You are here to perform miracles with your *boîte de nuit*? To make the people return?"

"You will perform the miracle. Hire the plumbers, electricians, carpenters, and painters. Restock the bar, get a bartender and cook. Whatever it costs, I'll pay for it. You have a cellar with enough space for a bandstand and dance floor?"

"I do. And this *boîte* of yours—it has a name?"

Julian had come up with one at breakfast, and he was proud of it. "Club Dans le Vent."

A one-armed man with a black beret and raggedy white beard, seated at a table on the other side of the bistro, said, "Monsieur Rose, you cannot be in fashion unless Madame takes down her picture. Go see her picture."

"And you are?"

"*Marcel le Magnifique.*"

Julian walked over. Marcel the Magnificent was ripe enough with body odor to make his nostrils flare. "It is a pleasure to make your acquaintance."

With his one hand, Marcel thumbed tobacco out of a pouch into a cigarette paper and rolled up a smoke. "A privilege. It is a privilege to make my acquaintance."

"How so?"

"Because you have never seen a one-armed man roll a cigarette."

Julian laughed and took a lighter out of his pocket and flicked it. Marcel lit up. "You want a job?"

"What else can a one-armed man do besides roll cigarettes?"

"Stand outside a nightclub and open the door."

Marcel smoked and thought this over. "I would need new clothes."

Julian placed twelve thousand francs on the table.

"All for me?" Marcel asked.

"All for you. Now where's that picture?"

Isabella, getting off the stool, said, "Come."

The bistro doglegged to the right. On the cracked plaster wall next to the door of the water closet was a large photograph framed in plain wood. Isabella was kneeling in the center of the photo, stripped to her chemise and surrounded by jeering men, women, and children, while a man with muscular forearms cut off her hair with scissors. Isabella's pruned skull made her look as sad and vulnerable as a corpse.

Isabella said, "You have heard of *les tondeurs* and *les tondues*?"

"I have." The shearers and the shorn were a sideshow of the *épuration sauvage*—the savage cleansing of anyone collaborating with the Nazis. It began after the Germans were chased out of France in the summer of 1944. Thousands were executed, some guilty, others for fun. The women accused of taking Nazis for lovers—for *la collaboration horizontale*—were shamed with public haircuts.

Marcel came to stand beside Isabella. "It's time to take it down."

"*Je m'en fous!*" Isabella snapped—*I don't give a fuck!*

"Please," Marcel said.

Lovingly, Isabella touched the shirtsleeve pinned to Marcel's shoulder. "I will not let those pieces of shit shame me." She spun around and said to Julian, "You do not want to do business with a collaborator?"

He suspected that her story wasn't a simple one. But out of pride, she wasn't going to tell it to him.

Isabella asked, "You are a Jew, *non*?"

"I am."

"You will have to trust me."

"Then I'll trust you," Julian said.

# Chapter 42

For three weeks, Julian didn't hear from Kendall. He reminded himself that he had no claim on her time—that part of their life was over. Nor had she promised him anything except a visit to La Palette. Yet that didn't prevent him from worrying about her or being annoyed that she hadn't called, especially after the evening he was scouring Saint-Germain hoping to spot her and bumped into Otis and his musician friends, all of them nicely pickled, stumbling out of Le Montana, and he asked Otis if he'd seen Kendall.

"No one has," Otis said. "The girl's a regular Houdini: now you see her, now you don't."

By then, Julian had become one of the nighttime ramblers who haunted the Left Bank. Electricity was rationed, so the great monuments weren't lit. Still, he could see sparks of moonlight on the Seine, and the towers and spires of Notre-Dame etched in black against the stars, and the comforting flicker of candles in the apartment houses on one side of Rue Guynemer with the locked gates of the Luxembourg Gardens on the other, and down a deserted stretch of the Boulevard Montparnasse, the light in the windows of Le Sélect, an all-night café and a haven for *les vagabonds nocturnes*. If it were windy or raining, Julian stopped for a whiskey, discovering that while some of the night wanderers were French, many of them were Americans drinking away their memories of Saint-Lô, Hürtgen Forest, and the Ardennes, all those killing grounds where, in a less illusory world, the grass would be red and the sky white with ghosts.

Julian wandered, hoping to shut down his thoughts so he could return to his room and sleep. Sometimes it worked; sometimes it had the opposite effect. If Julian saw lovers arm in arm, it made him feel so alone that he weighed the pros and cons of returning to the States for hours, and on the night he spotted a couple kissing beside Rodin's statue of Balzac, he double-timed it over to the Trianon and, against his better judgment, gave a note to the concierge asking Kendall to call him. Yet Julian knew that he couldn't go home—not yet. And as bad as these nights of loneliness were, he preferred them to the nights when he would remember the war and Willy doing his Olympian act.

Five days after the bombing of Pearl Harbor, Wild Bill had posted Julian to Switzerland. With the help of his banker in Lucerne, Julian transferred money to partisans in Norway, Holland, Poland, and France. Eventually, the Gestapo choked off the funds by arresting the bankers on the other end of the transactions. By this point, FDR had ordered the creation of the Office of Strategic Services, and Donovan transferred Julian to the special-operations branch of the OSS and sent him to England for training: weapons, explosives, radios, maps, and parachuting out of creaky Whitley bombers at the Ringway air station. Julian jumped into Brittany and later Normandy to aid the Résistance, arranging airdrops of munitions, sabotaging rail lines and bridges, gathering intel on German troop movements, and snatching prisoners. There had been enough close calls to scare Julian, but nothing he hadn't felt dealing with Siano Abruzzi's boys in Newark. By December 1944, shortly before Christmas, Julian was in Reims, distracting himself with the local champagne and a mademoiselle eager to express her gratitude to the United States, when he was ordered to report to the Eighty-Fourth Infantry Division in the Belgian town of Marche. With all the casualties, Julian figured the Army was short of translators and he'd be interrogating prisoners. But instead a lieutenant colonel had ordered him to patrol the snowy woods outside Marche, and it was there that Julian learned with one squeeze of a trigger you can take two lives: the person you are firing at and your own.

On the nights that this memory throbbed behind his eyes like a migraine, Julian could barely sleep. By dawn he was watching the sun turn the river to emerald glass, and then he bathed and changed into fresh clothes and walked up past Rue Blainville to the Place de la Contrescarpe. The *clochards* who had slept under the trees in the square with newspapers for blankets were just waking up looking for a drink. Julian gave them a handful of francs before breakfasting on the terrace of La Contrescarpe, reading the papers as the laborers knocked back *un petit rouge* and smoked a final cigarette before hurrying off, and the university students lingered over their coffee and brioche, and girls in smocked dresses and boys in knickers tramped by on their way to school.

Club Dans le Vent, as Julian now thought of Isabella's bistro, was around the corner, and Julian went there to check on the renovations. Isabella had the workmen well in hand, shouting at them with such an inventive string of expletives that Julian marveled at her ability to modify the noun *asshole*. All Julian had to do was make a weekly phone call to his Swiss banker, who transferred funds to the Guaranty Trust in Paris, and give the money to Isabella. He also found a one-bedroom apartment with raised paneled wainscoting and parquet floors and a fireplace in the *salon*. It was near the club, on Place de l'Estrapade, an island of serenity with its trees and benches and bubbling fountain. Marcel the Magnificent owned the building, which had been in his family for generations. The roof had holes in it; the limestone exterior required cleaning and repointing; and every apartment needed painting. Most of the tenants were broke, but Marcel didn't have the heart to throw them out. Julian financed the renovations, and because his back ached from the contortions involved in using the squat toilet in his hotel—which he could swear had been invented by the Marquis de Sade—he paid a fortune for an American toilet on the black market. Marcel oversaw these workmen. His language wasn't as inventive as Isabella's, though there was less work to do to make Julian's apartment habitable.

On the morning before Julian moved in, his phone rang, and he was still groggy when he said hello, and Kendall replied, "How are you?"

"Thinking you'd never call." He admonished himself for the sharpness of his tone and sat up, reminding himself that Kendall owed him nothing.

"I meant to call sooner. I got stuck in Marseille."

Careful not to sound overly inquisitive, he asked, "What were you doing?"

"A photo shoot of Piaf and her discovery, a singer and actor, Yves Montand."

Three weeks, he thought. "Must have been a lot of pictures."

She paused. Then, "Yes, it was. Do you still want to meet me at La Palette?"

"I do."

"Forty-three Rue de Seine. Around five?"

"*À bientôt.*"

# Chapter 43

Picasso. Julian recognized him immediately from the newspapers and magazines. Short, stocky, a silver horseshoe of hair around his bald pate. The artist was standing under the teal awning of La Palette and looking up to talk to Kendall, his hands massaging the air like a potter working at his wheel. Julian was a block from the café when Kendall started to speak. Picasso canted his head toward her to listen, and Julian recalled his first walk with Kendall on the Lovewood campus—eight, nine years ago—and he felt a surge of joy and pride and a pinch of melancholy at the passing of time. Just like now, Kendall had been wearing a navy-and-white Breton-striped top, and she'd told Julian that she wanted to live in Paris and be a painter or perhaps a photographer. And here she was, in *La Ville-Lumière*, talking to the Babe Ruth of artists.

Picasso disappeared into the dim interior of La Palette as Julian reached the café, and Kendall put an arm around his neck to hug him, holding on for a beat longer than an ordinary hello. Her hair was damp from washing and smelled liked jasmine.

"Interesting friend, Picasso," Julian said, when they were seated at the outdoor tables under a canvas roof with planter boxes of bushes and hydrangeas forming a green-and-pink wall.

"I don't know him well. He said he saw *Here & There* and some of my shots of the dead prisoners at Ohrdruf reminded him of Goya's prints from *The Disasters of War*. He was right. I carried reproductions of those prints with me."

A waiter greeted Kendall with a hearty *bonjour,* and after he took

their order, Kendall said, "The critics say I was conducting a competition: lynched Negroes versus gassed Jews."

"My impression was you were saying there's no shortage of places
where people are killed for who they are."

"I was. Except that's not what the critics wanted to hear." She
opened a powder-blue pack of Gauloises and lit up. "I turned down an
assignment in Indochina. To see the French tangle with the Communist hordes. I'm sick of photographing the news. Let Maggie White
or Lee Miller go back to war."

"Giving up? Not you."

Her smile was ringed by weariness. "Léo—my agent—keeps getting calls from *Look*, *Collier's*—plenty of magazines that want pictures
of gay Paree and singers and movie stars. Pictures that make you
happy. I'll take those."

The waiter brought them a salad Palette, a basket of bread, and a
full carafe of Pouilly-Fuissé. Kendall was more interested in the wine
than the food, and she smoked like a soldier in a foxhole—deep drags,
squinting in concentration, as though focusing your attention could
calm your jitters.

She said, "I was in Lovewood in February."

"How'd it go?"

"Mama asks if I'm ready to help run the college. I tell her no, and
she says that my success hasn't made me any smarter, and if my life's
all peaches and cream, where's my husband and her grandbabies? She
was rooting for me to marry—"

Kendall caught herself, as if supplying the name would hurt
Julian.

"Simon?" he said.

She glanced at the tables around them. People were chattering in
French, drinking and laughing. Julian didn't relish her discomfort, but
it did temper his jealousy.

"Yes."

The waiter cleared their dishes and, without being asked, brought
Kendall another carafe of Pouilly-Fuissé. Julian refilled their glasses.
He wasn't in the mood for more wine, but he didn't want Kendall

getting as soused as she'd been at the Deux Magots. Julian had no idea if she even remembered the scene in her suite.

Kendall said, "Simon—that was me trying to fix my past with my present. The shy freshman landing the suave upperclassman. And pleasing her mother. It wasn't about you."

"I believe you." That wasn't entirely true: Simon was his polar opposite, and Julian appreciated his appeal to Kendall, though he didn't see an upside in debating it with her.

"Simon needs an audience, not a girlfriend. When we did the Harlem riot book together, he'd bug me to read his every sentence and sulk if I didn't say it was better than Richard Wright and Langston Hughes combined. And he wouldn't quit going on about the great American novel he was going to write. It drove me nuts."

"He's dating your school friend from Philadelphia?"

"Thayer Claypoole. Her and Simon are made for each other. If either of them farted in a closet, they'd swear they invented perfume."

"Thayer been in Paris long?"

"She shows up six months ago, enrolls at the Sorbonne—she barely speaks French—and decides she'll host the grandest cultural salon since Gertrude Stein."

"A *salonnière*, huh?"

"She has lots of parties, I'll say that." Kendall poured herself more wine. "Tell me about you. You're done with the OSS?"

"Who told you about that?"

"Fiona. We're pen pals." A sheepish expression crossed Kendall's face. "How else was I going to keep track of you?"

Julian liked that she'd done that. "Truman disbanded the OSS."

"Won't they start it again, with this Cold War?"

"To spy on all the dangerous commies? Like Picasso?"

"Most of the artists and writers here join the Communist Party like Americans joining the Rotary."

"I hope you can convince them to come to Club Dans le Vent."

"Club Dans—"

"That's the name of my nightclub."

"It's very"—Kendall laughed—"*dans le vent*. I like it."

"I'm having a bistro in the Latin Quarter renovated."

"So you weren't kidding? You'll be in Paris?"

"I'm moving into an apartment in the morning."

Kendall smiled: it was a friendly smile, no promises in it, but Julian would take it—for now. The wine was gone, and Kendall began looking for their waiter. Julian thought that she'd had enough. "I have a busy day tomorrow. Can we go?"

Before she could answer, a man with the tousled good looks of a weekend sailor and a forelock of golden-brown hair curling over his forehead sidled between the tables, saying, "*Bonsoir*, Kendall."

He bent to kiss her cheek, running his fingers down her arm. It was a proprietary gesture and, because Kendall shifted away from his touch and her face flushed with embarrassment, Julian was certain that this guy—whom he knew—was one of her lovers. He had expected that she would sleep with other men, and he could handle his jealousy, but knowing what her partners looked like was more than his imagination could bear.

Kendall said, "Arnaud Francoeur, this is Julian Rose, a friend from home. Arnaud is an editor at *L'Humanité* and a member of the Central Committee of the Parti Communiste Français."

Kendall had made the introduction in French, but Arnaud, who was quite chic for a Communist in his white tennis shirt with a green crocodile embroidered on the chest, pulled up a chair and, grinning at Julian, replied in English. "We have met."

Kendall gave Julian a quizzical look.

"The OSS," he said.

Arnaud had been a leader of the Maquis, the guerrillas fighting the Nazis, when Julian worked with him in Normandy, a brave fighter with a creative vindictive streak. Near the village of Pont-l'Évêque, they captured two prime specimens of the SS in a farmhouse guzzling Calvados, the famed brandy of the region. The SS men had shot the farmer, his wife, and four kids. They were lying in the barnyard, the parents on top of their children, trying to shield them. Julian wanted to shoot the SS bastards after he interrogated them. Arnaud had an alternate plan for *les Boches*. He had his men build crosses from boards they pried off the barn, then ordered the Germans to strip naked, and crucified them. Arnaud had been carrying nails in his rucksack for just such an occasion.

Arnaud, switching to French, said to Julian, "I hear you are opening a *boîte*."

"How did you hear?"

"Isabella, your partner, is my cousin. Quite a coincidence, no?"

Arnaud smirked, and Julian had seen that smirk before—when Arnaud's men were getting those Germans up on the crosses. "Small world," Julian said.

"Isn't it? Kendall has met Isabella. She is a proud woman, my cousin. And confused about what she owes a friend and what she owes her country."

Julian could see the sorrow on Kendall's face. With an angry flick of a match, Kendall lit a cigarette and said to Arnaud, "We were about to leave."

He responded to her with a charming bow of the head. "Perhaps another time, then. And Julian, it was good seeing you again."

On their way out, Julian paid the waiter. Along Rue de Seine, the limestone buildings, warmed all day by the sun, seemed to glow in the evening blue, and women leaned out the windows watching men walking home from work with loaves of bread under their arms and children riding their two-wheeled scooters on the sidewalks. Kendall brooded. Had they been back in Greenwich Village instead of going up Rue de Tournon with the lights of the Palais du Luxembourg in front of them, Julian would've put his arm around her. His impulse to comfort her, to protect her, hadn't diminished. Yet he was wary of the impulse, thinking that Kendall could interpret it as meddling.

She said, "Arnaud told me that Isabella was close to a Jewish couple who were rounded up and deported to Auschwitz. They hid their twelve-year-old son Manny with Isabella. A Nazi officer heard about Manny from an informer, and Isabella made a bargain with the officer. She'd sleep with him if he protected Manny from the roundups. The day the Germans left Paris, a mob cut Isabella's hair. Manny tried to stop them. They beat him to death."

Julian sensed that whatever was eating away at Kendall was contained in that story, and hidden by it, like the angulated imagery in
Picasso's *Guernica*, the agony obscured by abstractions. Julian chose
not to press her, though. Less is more—his new philosophy.

At her hotel, Kendall said, "I spoke to Otis. I'm under orders to
help you frenchify your wardrobe."

"How's tomorrow afternoon? I'll meet you here at one?"

"The day after. I have a shoot tomorrow."

They stood facing each other. Julian didn't think Kendall was
waiting for him to kiss her. He was right. She said, "I'm drinking too
much."

"I noticed."

"And I haven't made the best decisions about my—my social life."

"I noticed that too."

"I know you did. I'm going to try and do something about it. And
the drinking."

"I'm glad."

"Me too," she said, and went into the hotel.

# Chapter 44

For ten days in a row, as Kendall rediscovered Paris with Julian, she felt as euphoric as a coed with a new beau. It would have been perfect except for her recurring nightmare of Manny lying on Rue Blainville as the mob beat him with only his eyes visible beneath the pile—burning eyes that pleaded with Kendall to save him. Whenever Manny woke her, Kendall reached for her cigarettes and a bottle of wine, understanding why a faceless boy she'd never met disturbed her sleep yet refusing to think about it and cursing her memory, that merciless thief who wouldn't let her rest.

Julian knew nothing of her nightmare because they didn't sleep together, which was partially responsible for Kendall's euphoria. The men parading through her hotel suite had once made her feel rebellious and free, as if she were living out the assertion that Beauvoir repeated to her with the same devotion as Fiona reciting the Rosary: "One is not born a woman, but becomes one through her actions." Yet, after a year in Paris, the parade had a dispiriting sameness, and some mornings, as Kendall brushed her hair before the mirror, she found herself counting her partners and feeling slightly appalled, reluctantly admitting that neither Parisian insouciance about matters of the flesh nor existentialism could revise her history—that she was the daughter of a puritanical mother and the Negro upper crust who had been taught that a young lady crosses her ankles when she sits and keeps them crossed until a man of substance marries her.

Returning to the innocence of dating freed Kendall from the oppressive demands of rebellion and adhering to someone else's philosophy, and she hadn't felt so lighthearted since her freshman year at Lovewood with its merry-go-round of chaperoned mixers and dances. That first afternoon Kendall helped Julian update his style by taking him to her favorite hat shop in the Marais and buying him a black Basque beret and a white linen scarf with tiny black triangles. After they drank lemon *pressés* on the sunny terrace of Café Les Philosophes, Kendall stood behind Julian's chair to show him how to tie a French knot. She folded the scarf in half, draped it around his neck, and when she leaned over him to tug the ends through the loop, his head brushed against her breasts. She liked the feel of him against her, but it frightened her, and as Julian glanced over his shoulder and saw her fear, she felt herself blush.

She was almost as flustered the evening they went to the Cinéma du Panthéon and saw the Yves Montand movie. Julian had brought a bag of gumdrops, and they were eating them when he whispered, "Can I have some more?" and Kendall realized that her hand was in the bag and holding on to his fingers. She had been distracted by the bittersweet song "Les Feuilles Mortes," which compared the sorrows of separated lovers to piles of dead leaves, and she was still humming it two evenings later when they went with Otis to listen to jazz at Tabou, the most popular *cave* in Saint-Germain.

Mostly, though, they walked, and Kendall noticed that Julian was quiet and studied every sight: the statue of the archangel Michael on the Boul'Mich; the sidewalk stalls of purple carnations, white and lavender roses, pink and yellow tulips, and red peonies; the bicyclists circling the Luxor Obelisk in the Place de la Concorde; the boxes of fruits and vegetables and iced fish on Rue Mouffetard; the fountains and statues in the Luxembourg Gardens and the Tuileries; the paintings in the Louvre and the Jeu de Paume. In New York, Kendall had taken Julian to the Museum of Modern Art to see *Guernica*, and he'd been blasé about the masterpiece, but now Julian peppered her with questions and listened carefully to her answers.

Kendall was curious about his new interest and brought it up on the afternoon they visited Sacré-Cœur. In the rainy light the houses below the top of Montmartre were gray and brown with orange chimney pots, and after Julian commented that it looked exactly like the print of the van Gogh painting that Kendall had hung in her Greenwich Village apartment, it began to rain harder, and they ducked into a café for coffee and *macarons*.

"You're becoming an art connoisseur," Kendall said.

She had intended it as casual observation, but he didn't react that way. Julian glanced into his *café crème*, and when he looked up, his eyes were as impenetrable to her as the darkest spaces in her dreams.

"All the slaughter in the war," he said. "And people here still believe beauty is important. That it has meaning."

He appeared confused, and Kendall didn't know how to answer him.

Julian forced a smile. "It makes a cynic feel like he's not as smart as he thinks he is."

Something changed then for Kendall; she was less euphoric and, strangely, both hopeful and melancholy, the feelings filling her like a cistern overflowing a sun shower. All at once, Kendall saw herself in the past and present, a dewy-eyed girl in the Village and the wised-up woman in Paris. Had she attempted to explain her feelings to Julian, the words would have sounded like sentimental piffle, sadness on the cheap. But that wasn't true. Her feelings were a tangle of joy and longing, because Julian was right there, in the pearly light of a café with the door open and the murmur of raindrops dripping from the trees, and they hadn't run out of time.

"Thayer's having a gathering Saturday," Kendall said. "Would you like to go?"

"I would."

By late Saturday afternoon, as Kendall bathed, then washed and dried her hair and deliberated on which dress to wear, she knew, in a barely perceived part of herself, that whatever innocence and distance she had maintained with Julian was vanishing like fog off the Seine. She settled on an A-line frock the color of strawberry ice cream, a black-and-white sash belt that accentuated her figure, and leather, spaghetti-strap sandals. She dabbed a drop of Shalimar on the back of her neck, her throat, her inner wrists, and as an afterthought, between her breasts and the inside of her thighs.

Her afterthought was not an admission that she wanted to sleep with Julian but an application of her long-held conviction that options were a girl's best friend.

This, at least, was the story Kendall was telling herself when Julian called her from the house phone and she rode the elevator to the lobby.

# Chapter 45

Thayer's family owns one of the largest insurance companies in Pennsylvania," Kendall said, as she and Julian went up a graveled path in the Luxembourg Gardens. "At our final high-school assembly, we had to get onstage and announce where we were going to college and our goals. Thayer says she'll be attending Smith, then throws up her arms like she's belting out 'Yankee Doodle Dandy' and says, 'My greatest ambition is to reduce my father's net worth.'"

If Julian was any judge of real estate, Thayer had made significant progress toward her goal by leasing the top floor of a majestic apartment building on the corner of Rue Auguste Comte and Avenue de l'Observatoire. It seemed as if every café denizen of Saint-Germain was drinking, smoking, talking, and laughing under the high, coffered ceilings—from the down-and-outers in their threadbare clothing, who collected cigarette butts from the cobbles, to the better-situated Americans and French in their stylish duds, puffing on Lucky Strikes and Gauloises, and the reek of smoke and unwashed bodies was sweetened by perfume that smelled like liquefied money. There was chintz wallpaper with a cabbage rose motif and Oriental carpets throughout the rooms, and windows with heavy drapes the exact shade of rosé, and Julian saw Arnaud Francoeur sitting with some men on balloon-backed, crimson-velvet chairs that looked as if they had been swiped from under the pointy nose of Louis Quatorze. A bar had been set up on the wrought-iron balcony, and at this golden-blue hour, as Julian got two glasses of chardonnay, he could see over the Gardens to the dark satin ribbon of the Seine.

People were lined up to greet the hostess in the master bedroom with its canopied bed spacious enough for a royal couple and a troupe of their most acrobatic paramours. To the right of the bed Julian saw four rows of four masks—two rows in porcelain, one in plaster, and the other in wood—mounted on the wall. Each mask was of the same demure young woman with short hair parted in the middle. Her eyes were shut as if she were sleeping, and below her cute, pug nose, her lips curved upward in a beatific smile.

Kendall said, "*L'Inconnue de la Seine.*"

"The Unknown Woman of the Seine?"

"In the late nineteenth century, a brokenhearted girl drowned herself in the river. Someone at the morgue was so infatuated by her face he made a cast of it, and pretty soon reproductions of the mask were selling like hotcakes. Thayer collects them. She thinks she looks like the girl."

"Does she?"

"That's her standing in front of the low table."

Thayer did bear a vague resemblance to the mask—honey-blond hair cut even with her ears, a button of a nose, and sensuous lips. That was it, though. Her smile was the opposite of demure; it was sexy bordering on lewd and matched her outfit—snug, flesh-colored turtleneck and slacks that emphasized all of the exuberant dips and swells of her body.

The line surged forward, and after Thayer swapped double kisses with Kendall, she said, "I'm so happy you could make it. Simon was supposed to be here, but I can't keep that man in town more than three days in a row. How'd you do it, Kenni-Ann?"

Kendall grimaced, obviously preferring not to rehash her romance with Simon. "I told him I liked his writing."

Julian couldn't tell if Thayer was picking at Kendall or if she were seeking advice, though he was disinclined to give Thayer the benefit of the doubt. Her eyes were as disconcerting as the eyes of a *tricoteuse*, one of those ladies who celebrated the French Revolution by knitting and watching the guillotine go chop-chop in the Place de la Concorde.

"This is Julian," Kendall said.

Thayer was shorter than Kendall and stood on her tiptoes to offer Julian her cheeks, and when he bent to kiss her, she rubbed her palms across his chest.

"Arnaud's told me about you," Thayer said. "You were an interrogator at Nuremberg?"

Julian hadn't discussed Nuremberg with Arnaud Francoeur, but while in Germany he had mingled with Soviet intelligence officers and investigators. He assumed Moscow had a file on him and that Arnaud had read it.

"I was," Julian said.

"You Jews deserved to get your pound of flesh on that one. Did you have to go to school to learn interrogation?"

Kendall answered her: "Pontius Pilate University."

Julian swallowed a laugh and recalled how Kendall had stood silently by in the Village when Christina had made some crack about Jews. He liked this better, her speaking up.

Thayer had no reaction, and Julian wasn't sure she had understood the sarcasm. "There's Arnaud," she said. "Arnaud, we're over here."

Julian surmised that if Arnaud had mentioned him to Thayer, she also knew of Kendall and Arnaud's affair, which probably accounted for her cunning, raunchy smile. Kendall wanted no part of Thayer's *petit drame*. As Arnaud Francoeur approached—suntanned and in a white linen shirt and trousers so he looked as if he'd just docked at Newport—Kendall turned away and began speaking French to someone behind Julian.

"*Bonsoir*," Arnaud said, and kissed Thayer's mouth. Julian noticed one of her hands touching the top of his leg and concluded that, whether Simon knew it or not, he was sharing Thayer with Arnaud.

Thayer said, "We were talking about Nuremberg."

Primarily in English, because Thayer didn't know much French, Arnaud said, "Ah, *les Américains* and their legal finery. Even Churchill wanted to shoot *les Boches*."

"You had a better idea?" Julian asked.

"*Absolument.* We should have fried the Nazis' innards in butter and served them with a cheerful, semisweet red from Premier Stalin's native Georgia."

"Stalin likes eating people?" Julian said.

"Premier Stalin likes hungry people to be able to eat."

"Maybe he shouldn't have murdered millions of his farmers."

"Boys," Thayer scolded them. "No fighting. Arnaud, I need to speak with you later, but I have to show Julian something."

"No fight," Arnaud said. "Only debate. *Salut, mes amis.*"

Julian watched Arnaud wend back between clusters of men and women.

"Come see these, Julian."

Thayer stood aside so Julian could step closer to a low, round mahogany table covered with perfume boxes in a variety of exotic shapes and sizes with perforated tops. Some of the boxes were lustrous wood; some were pewter with figurines of goddesses, mermaids, and even Joan of Arc perched on the lids; and some were lazuline, morganite, emerald, ruby, and topaz glass and crowned in gold.

"*Cassolettes,*" Thayer said.

"Very nice."

"I like that word, *cassolette.*"

Julian drank the rest of his chardonnay. Thayer reached over and curled her fingers around his hand before taking his wineglass and putting it on the table.

"Don't you like the word *cassolette*, Julian?"

He supposed Thayer thought she was being clever. *Cassolette* was also a reference to the natural fragrance of a woman. People were clustering closer to them.

"I practice using '*cassolette*' in French class," she said. "Listen: *J'ai une cassolette agréable.*"

"Thayer," Kendall said, "what are you doing?"

"Practicing my French."

"All you need is this." Kendall then spoke so fast that Julian had difficulty translating the sentence. Or perhaps he couldn't believe that

Kendall had said it. But the clusters of men and women around them were snickering.

"What's that mean?" Thayer asked.

"Literally? 'Bend me over the nearest chair and fuck me like a greyhound bitch.'"

Thayer was agile—or nutty—enough not to be offended. "I like it," she said. "Say it slowly."

"We have to go, sweetie. We'll practice another time."

❋

With the Luxembourg Gardens closed for the night, they went down the Boul'Mich along the gates with the wind sighing through the trees and the leaves rustling like silk in the darkness.

Julian said, "So that's your friend?"

"Thayer's certifiable. I've known her forever so I'm used to it."

Julian intended to walk Kendall to her hotel, but he didn't want the evening to end. At the fountain on Place Edmond-Rostand, they crossed the boulevard. The night was cool, so he had an excuse to put his arm around her, and thankfully, she didn't object. As Kendall stepped onto the sidewalk, she tripped, and Julian's hand slid down over taut, round flesh. Once Kendall regained her balance and Julian relocated his hand, she laughed. "Was that fun?"

"It wasn't not fun."

"Did Thayer's *cassolette* routine get you going?"

"You did. When you told her I went to Pontius Pilate University."

"You were thinking about Christina? That Christmas Eve at Chumley's?"

He nodded.

Kendall stopped and turned to him. "I knew it."

Behind them candlelight shone in the windows of a bistro.

Kendall said, "I'm not that girl anymore."

"You sound like you miss her."

"Sometimes, but . . . *bof, c'est normal.*"

"So is liking the word *cassolette.*"

Kendall smiled as demurely as *L'Inconnue de la Seine.* "I like that word."

"It's a lovely word."

"You're thinking about it now—*cassolette*?"

"I am."

"What're you thinking?"

"Guess."

"That you want to think about *cassolette* somewhere else?"

"Good guess."

"At my hotel?"

He replied by kissing her, restrained at first, until her lips parted and her arms went around him and their bodies pressed together, and the sole reason they were able to stop was that even in Paris, where passion was among the loftier virtues, it would have been gauche to make love outside a bistro on the Boulevard Saint-Michel.

※

It might have been awkward, getting into bed again after so many years, trying to recall the intimate wisdom that had once belonged to them alone or, perhaps more distracting with its twinges of jealousy and loss, noticing a touch or a word that had plainly belonged to someone else, someone who came afterward and who, in the pungent reality of their flesh and bone and sweat, drove Kendall and Julian to contemplate whether what they had shared had been adorned by the deceptive whisperings of memory and wasn't truly so special after all.

Fortunately, it wasn't awkward for either of them. In the suite, they fell onto the bed half-dressed, and the brief pause for Kendall to light a candle on the nightstand and insert her diaphragm while Julian nibbled at her ears seemed to last longer than the earth revolving from winter to spring. They were desperate to be joined, as though in the splendor of that instant they would corral the past and create a future. In the dancing, yellow light of the candle, Julian, it appeared from his deep, relentless strokes, was determined to turn her to dust, then inhale her so she could never leave him. Kendall, lithe and strong, cooperated as if she knew what he wanted, her skin sliding against his like copper abrading ivory. They were silent as the bedsprings sang their two-note song and the room became as fragrant as upturned loam and clear seaside air until Julian, rising up so he could stare into her candlelit face, said, "You have to love me," and Kendall answered, "I will—I do," and then they continued on their ecstatic journey, worshipping each other with breathy devotion, and when it was over, her arms and legs were welded to him so that Julian thought he'd need a crowbar to pry her from his body.

The candle flame hissed out, and as Julian attempted to separate himself from Kendall, she held him tighter.

"Are you okay?" he asked.

She shook her head against him, and her hair tickled his cheeks.

"Can I help?"

She hunched and unhunched her shoulders.

"Do you want to talk about it?"

Again, Kendall shook her head. Julian rolled off her, but she clung to him, and he gathered her against him, and she slept with his arm around her and her head on his chest, and in the morning Kendall didn't tell him what had been bothering her or mention that it was the first night in some time that Manny hadn't barged into her dreams and begged her to save him.

# Chapter 46

Over the next few weeks, Kendall began sleeping at Julian's apartment. She had cut back on her wine, at least in front of Julian, but sometimes when she was reading a book or inspecting contact sheets through a magnifying glass, she'd glance up with her face contorted by outrage or despair, and Julian couldn't help but feel something was wrong. If he asked, she always replied, "No, nothing." And though Julian didn't believe her, he let it drop, because he'd been so happy with their new arrangement that he was contemplating moving to Paris. Abe and Eddie could handle his rental properties and, with millions of GIs coming home and Uncle Sam backing their mortgages, Julian could sell his land in New Jersey for a bundle. Behind these calculations was his desire to marry Kendall and have children, yet their history was daunting, and Julian didn't want to scare her off by bringing up the future.

Despite his happiness, Julian still had trouble sleeping and would get up to join the other *vagabonds nocturnes* wandering the Left Bank. On this night, he tossed and turned until his restlessness woke Kendall. He remained still until she fell asleep again, then quietly dressed in the dark, slipped out of his apartment, and walked over to the Sélect, where he sat on the terrace drinking a cold beer. Two hours later, when he returned to Place de l'Estrapade, the moon and stars were putting on a show, and Julian was wide awake. He made himself comfortable on a bench and listened to the gurgling fountain. In a little while, Kendall came outside.

"I thought I tuckered you out," she said, teasing him, sitting close.

"You did." He liked the feel of her next to him, the pliant solidness of her, and her sharp, sweet smell—in her thick hair, on her smooth skin, and all over him when they finished making love. "I got a cable. Marcel stuck it under the door. My father had a heart attack."

"Oh, no."

"He's in the hospital. I'll fly to New York this afternoon and then to Florida."

"You want me to come with you?"

"Don't you have to be in Arles?"

"They can dig up another photographer."

"No, no thanks, I've got some business and—"

"Julian?"

"Yeah?"

"Why do you walk every night?"

"I try not to wake you."

"It's not me I'm worried about."

Even in the darkness, he could tell Kendall was studying him as if he were an image to be interpreted. He loved that about her, the intense curiosity, but she wouldn't push him. That was another thing he loved about Kendall, her patience.

Finally, he said, "I'm not sure if it was snowing."

"Where?"

"In Belgium."

"In the Ardennes? Fiona wrote me that you were in the Ardennes."

"The Ardennes. I remember the moon was out and the snow on the hills and trees was a metallic blue. But I can't remember if it was snowing when I got there."

Julian was clearer about the Ardennes on his way out. The charred tanks, half-tracks, jeeps, trucks, and artillery pieces, the smoldering houses in the towns, the American and German dead everywhere in the snow, many of them with the horror still on their waxy faces. Julian remembered thinking about the parents who wouldn't see their sons again, and the new widows with red-rimmed eyes, and wondering whether anyone would mourn him if he died.

"I think about it when I walk," Julian said. "If it was snowing. Crazy, isn't it?"

"It isn't. Why don't you think about it now."

"Why would I—"

Kendall, placing the palm of her hand under his chin, turned his face to hers so they could see each other in the moonlight. "Because I'm here. And because, whatever happened, I want to hear about it."

※

The Ardennes was a dark, haunted forest. Julian couldn't recall if it was snowing when he got there since he was seated in the back of a two-and-a-half-ton truck with crates of ammo, medical supplies, and K-rations, and he was fixated on the towering firs, rocky hills, steep valleys, and frozen fields, the thousands of GIs going in one direction on the roads, while Belgian refugees flowed in the other, wheeling carts of their belongings. The truck stopped twice before reaching the outskirts of Marche. Four other OSS men came aboard. Julian had met one of them, Taft Mifflin, a lanky Yale grad, during jump training in England. All of them were fluent in German, and though they knew that Hitler had launched a surprise attack into the Ardennes, none of them knew their assignment. Nor was the driver able to enlighten them beyond saying that the division intelligence honcho, Lieutenant Colonel Shavers, was an ordained minister.

Fittingly enough, the command post was in a church, and the colonel looked like he belonged in the rectory: pudgy and wan with wire-rim spectacles. Yet his vocabulary was peculiar for a clergyman: "The cocksucking Krauts murdered eighty of our POWs in Malmédy. Forty miles from here. Now these miscreant motherfuckers are dressing up in our uniforms—a direct fucking violation of the Geneva Convention—and dicking with us. They speak English, shoot our sentries, switch road signs, and scare our replacements shitless. You OSS ladies are gonna fuck the Krauts in like fashion and make them reevaluate their strategy."

Shavers, who had been standing over five olive-drab footlockers, flipped up the top of one with his boot. "Kraut paratrooper uniforms and weapons. These cocksuckers didn't have any papers on them when they got caught, but we got their dog tags. Put them around your necks after checking your new names. You go tomorrow. Briefing's at 0700. Return the day after at 1500. You see Krauts, say hi, and at your convenience, blow their balls off. Questions?"

None of the OSS men spoke until Shavers was gone. Then one of them said, "FUBAR."

Julian, who had the most experience in the field and was designated at the morning briefing to lead the operation, suspected that the military acronym for Fucked Up Beyond All Recognition applied. But even though he felt creepy putting on the uniform, coal-scuttle helmet, greatcoat, and side-laced boots of Captain Dierk Schmitt, he adopted a wait-and-see attitude. It didn't last long. As the OSS men began to wander through gusting snow and sheets of ground fog, observing dead Germans and GIs lying with each other along the ridgelines like kids at a campout, Taft Mifflin commented that FUBAR was not a sufficient superlative for their mission, and Julian had to agree. The problem was that when the Germans thrust into the Ardennes, creating the bulge that would give the battle its name, the lines became jumbled and both armies were thrown together in a lethal game of tag.

At 1630, with daylight dwindling to an ominous gloom, the OSS men were going through a clearing with firs and pines on either side when Julian heard movement to his right. Something arced through the air, and as Julian realized that it was an American grenade, he flung himself into the snow. The grenade exploded, a man screamed, and Julian heard a Thompson submachine gun and a couple of Garand rifles crackling from the tree line, the muzzle flashes winking like fireflies. If the OSS men tried to run or return fire, they would be cut to ribbons, to say nothing of shooting at GIs, so Julian, in German, instructed them to stay down, then yelled out in English, " We surrender, we surrender."

Suddenly, from the other side of the clearing, came the unmistakable buzz-saw whine of a German MG 42, its fearsome rate of fire tearing up the tree line where the Americans were hiding, along with the clatter of German small arms. In memory, this was the longest stretch of time in Julian's life, though it was probably no more than two minutes before the Americans withdrew. The clearing was silent, and Germans in grayish-green helmets and coats emerged from the woods. Julian counted seven of them. Taft was checking the OSS men. FUBAR was in full poisonous flower. Three of them were dead. Julian pocketed their dog tags and looked at Taft, who shook his head. They were too outnumbered to take the Germans. The colonel hadn't ordered them to commit suicide.

"*Danke*," Julian said to the sergeant who was leading the German unit, which turned out to be the remnants of a reconnaissance company from the 688th Volksgrenadier Division. Julian had read the intel on Volksgrenadier divisions, the infantry that Hitler had cobbled together because of his staggering losses, sticking a smattering of experienced soldiers with those who, owing to age, lack of training, and physical condition, were barely fit for combat.

Julian explained that he and his men had parachuted into the Ardennes wide of their landing zone and had been evading capture ever since, then showed the sergeant two haversacks stuffed with K-rations that he and Taft—Lieutenant Walter Theiss—had been carrying, claiming that they had scavenged them from the Americans.

"You and your men are hungry?" Julian asked, knowing that the Germans—especially the Volksgrenadiers—were woefully underfed compared to the Americans.

"Very hungry, Captain," the sergeant said.

"You are operating alone?" Julian wanted to avoid the more professional Wehrmacht and Waffen-SS units. An officer might get on a field phone to confirm his story.

"Our company was ambushed by the Americans. We are at a farm. A kilometer north of here. Waiting to join a larger force when we find one."

"Let's go."

The farmhouse had been flattened by artillery, but the stone barn had survived. The Germans—the sergeant, four men on the cusp of middle age, another in his twenties with his arm in a sling, and a teenager—ate as if they were starving, devouring ham and eggs, crackers with cheese, sausage, meat loaf, instant coffee with sugar, malted-milk bars, and squares of chocolate. Afterward, all of them except the teenager started chain-smoking the Chesterfields that were boxed with the K-rations.

"No cigarette for you?" Julian asked the teenager.

The sergeant chuckled. "That's Willy Müller. Future Olympic champion."

The man with the sling added, "Future sheepherder from Diepholz."

Willy, who could have been featured on a Hitler Youth poster if he hadn't been so slight and cross-eyed, scaled the ladder to the hayloft, grabbed ahold of a rafter and hoisted himself up, then swung round and round and round.

"My father is a sheepherder," Willy said, after he'd come down. "I am going to be an Olympic gymnast. When we have won the war and the Führer decides where the games will be."

None of the Germans responded to the prediction of winning the war. They smoked instead. Two of them had gone up into the loft and were staring out a window.

The sergeant saw Julian gazing up at the soldiers. "We keep two men there on three-hour shifts."

Julian said, "Lieutenant Theiss and I will do our share. We could use some rest, so we will take the last shift before dawn."

"Yes, sir," the sergeant said. "There is dry hay in the stalls at the rear of the barn."

Julian told the sergeant that he and his men should help themselves to the rations and cigarettes, then he and Taft went to the stalls.

"The guard will wake you first," Julian said in German. "You be behind him when he wakes me."

Julian, bundled up in his coat and a blanket, thought that it would be difficult to sleep, but he drifted off immediately, and the next thing he remembered was being shaken by a German soldier bending over him and holding a rectangular flashlight with a red filter dimming the bulb.

As the soldier backed up to give Julian room to stand, Taft got an arm around his throat. Julian took the flashlight from the soldier before he dropped it and heard Taft snap his neck. They lowered him onto the hay and pulled back the cocking handles of their *Maschinenpistoles*. Julian swept the red light across the barn and counted five sleeping soldiers. He jabbed his thumb upward. Taft went up the ladder. The burst from his submachine gun roused the soldiers. They were shouting as Julian emptied his magazine into them. He shone the flashlight on their bodies. Willy wasn't dead. He was crawling toward the barn doors. Julian stood over him with a Luger in his hand, shining the red light on his bleeding legs.

"Why are you doing this?" Willy asked, more hurt than frightened. "Why?"

※

"He was a boy," Julian said, rocking forward and back on the bench.

"A boy in the German Army," Kendall said.

"A boy playing soldier."

"A boy who would've shot anyone he was told to."

"What did I do?"

"You went to a war."

Julian rocked faster. "What did I do? I squeezed that trigger and felt part of myself die. And I'm going to be punished for it. I feel that dread every day."

"Give it time."

"He was a boy, Kendall. God forgive me, he was a boy."

Kendall had never heard Julian cry. The depth of his sorrow surprised her, and she chided herself for never having seen that his calm exterior, with the toughness and anger underneath it, could mask a sadness as deep as her own. She put her arms around him to stop his rocking and kissed his face. "I love you."

Julian was still. He had killed before but had been able to justify the killings to himself: the Kaiser was a murdering pimp; the four hoods in Newark were no-good pricks trying to shoot him and Abe; and the SS soldiers he'd helped to get rid of in Normandy were maniacal butchers. Yet now, when he thought about these men, guilt triumphed over his rationalizations. Maybe it was the beauty of Paris, a beauty that had the power to bequeath meaning to a stroll down the street. Or maybe it was being with Kendall again, which underscored how much you lose when you leave this world. Whatever the cause, lately Julian had been asking himself who appointed him to be anyone's executioner. In part, this question accounted for his insomnia. And Willy. He couldn't forget Willy. Julian should've patched him up and left him in the barn. But he didn't, and now he held on to Kendall, hearing Willy, in his wounded voice, ask him why, and believing that there was no forgiveness for him anywhere, not on earth or in heaven, just love—that was it, love—love was the best that he would ever do.

# Chapter 47

How's your old man doing?" Wild Bill asked.

"He had another heart attack in the hospital."

Julian was in the library of Donovan's Sutton Place apartment: leather club chairs and a ladder leading up to disorderly shelves of novels, histories, and biographies.

"Us old bastards can last longer than the docs tell ya." Wild Bill wasn't aging as well as his Scotch. His head resembled a beach ball with thinning, pomaded hair, and his memory was fuzzy. "Did I say Marcel speaks English?"

"You did, but he hasn't—not to me."

"Marcel's crafty, and he's got balls. I saw his arm get blown off, and all he said was 'Good thing I use my other hand to scratch my ass.'"

Julian had three hours until his flight to Miami, thankfully not enough time to hear the stories again about Wild Bill and Marcel and the First World War. They had been in touch sporadically between the wars, and after setting up the OSS, Donovan had an operative recruit Marcel to collect intelligence. After Germany surrendered, it was Marcel who had informed Donovan of Isabella's connection to the Commie big shot Arnaud Francoeur and of her bistro going belly-up, and Arnaud's running around with Kendall. Wild Bill knew about Julian and Kendall from a drunken evening during the Nuremberg trials, and that Julian had fought alongside Arnaud. Wild Bill was notorious for his harebrained schemes, and he dreamed up this one because Truman, he said, was too wet behind the ears to realize we needed spies to counter the Soviet Union and that power-mad fuck

Stalin. Some buddies in Congress got Donovan an off-book budget, and he pitched his plan to Julian, who agreed to sign on—or so he told himself—because Kendall could be in danger. That sounded more noble than the fact that he wanted another chance with her.

Wild Bill said, "My people tell me Francoeur was in Moscow talking to Soviet military intelligence. And we hear somebody in Paris is buying up surplus weapons and storing them to support the Red Army if it invades Western Europe."

"I haven't heard anything about that."

"Maybe you'll hear something once your nightclub's going, or maybe Marcel will. He's got his own network of spies. But we gotta work fast. Scuttlebutt is that Truman's gonna have an official intelligence agency operating no later than next year. We can't be doing this by then. It's probably illegal now, so let's you and me use Marcel as a go-between. You see anything, tell him. I hear something, I'll get word to him."

"So far, I found out Arnaud was screwing my old girlfriend, and Marcel can roll a cigarette with one arm. I wouldn't get my hopes up."

"Fuck hope. All you do is what you can."

It was the best advice Julian had heard in a long time.

✳

As a teenager, Julian had been enraged by his father, scoffing at his demands and exploring the sordid byways of Berlin. As a young man, with Hitler beginning his assault on the Jews, Julian had felt responsible for saving Theodor from his optimism. Yet Julian had never been surprised by his father. Not until now—in the sweltering hallway outside Theodor's room in Provident Hospital, the Negro hospital, in Fort Lauderdale.

Garland Wakefield said, "He demanded to be brought where his colleagues or students would have to go."

Julian glanced through the doorway. Students ringed Theodor's bed, and Julian could hear them: they were discussing Spinoza.

"If it hadn't been just summer-school students," Garland said, "they wouldn't have fit in the room."

"I spoke to Dr. Franklin on the way in. He said my father should take it easy and—"

"The rest is up to the Lord."

Julian could see the sadness on Garland's face, and it reminded him of Kendall, which was odd, because Kendall, tall with hazel eyes and honey skin, looked almost nothing like her shorter, darker mother. But that sad expression was identical to her daughter's, mixed with the same ire, the same rebellion against bad news.

"I appreciate you phoning," Julian said.

"Your father took sick while we were having our weekly dinner at my house. He didn't want me to call, but it was only proper. Your office told me you were in Paris."

She was eyeing Julian like a cop with a hangover.

"Kendall and I aren't—"

Garland glanced into the room, then clapped her hands and called, "Let's allow Professor Rose to visit with his son."

The students filed out, saying hello to Julian. Garland gave him a slip of paper. "Here's my home number—if you or your father need anything."

Julian said thank you, but Garland was already following the students down the hall.

His father was thinner than he remembered, and as stiff and wrinkled as laundry dried too long on a clothesline.

"*Hallo, Vater*," Julian said.

Theodor gazed up at him from the pillows. His hair and beard were as white as the top sheet. Julian wasn't sure his father recognized him until Theodor said, "You were in Paris?"

It was strange hearing his father speak English to him instead of German. Julian sat in the bedside chair. "I was."

Theodor said, "My books and money should be donated to the college."

"You're still alive."

"That's not a permanent condition. I prefer to be buried in the cemetery on campus. Next to your mother. It has no white section— President Wakefield received some threatening letters after Mother was buried there—so I instructed her to cremate my remains. Then I will be gray."

His father chuckled and began to cough. Julian held up a paper cup of water. "Take a drink, Dad."

Julian stunned himself, referring to Theodor as "Dad." He had never used it before. Kendall used it, though, and perhaps he had picked it up from her. Or perhaps he wanted to say it once before Theodor died.

Theodor waved the cup away. "I was thinking that your mother deserved to find happiness."

Julian almost replied that it was a little late for his father to reach that conclusion but decided to say nothing. What was the point?

Theodor said, "She liked nursing. Whether it made her happy . . ."

Out past the screened window, car horns honked and a fiery sunset reflected on the traffic, the shiny emblems of postwar American prosperity.

Julian said, "Did you? Did you find happiness?"

"With my writing, with my students."

"Your family?"

"I have begun to believe I may not have been designed for marriage."

Or for fatherhood, Julian thought.

Theodor cleared his throat. "Your mother used to tell me I didn't love her the way in which she wanted to be loved."

"Did you?"

"I was her husband, not her reflection."

Julian felt his anger rising.

Theodor said, "I was aware that I wasn't the husband she hoped for. Or the father you wanted."

Julian unstuck himself from the back of the chair. With the heat, he had sweated through his shirt.

"Love is a bargain, then?" Theodor asked, as if he were posing a question to a class. "You love if you receive what you want?"

Julian was in no mood for Socratic double-talk.

Theodor looked at him with a slight arch to his bushy white eyebrows. "You were the son I wanted? Studious? Obedient?"

Julian shook his head. Theodor smiled and clamped a hand on his son's forearm, holding on and not letting go until he fell asleep. Julian watched over him, gulping at the humid air, until he dozed off. The window was dark when he heard Theodor call his name.

"Dad? Dad?"

Julian switched on the overhead light. Theodor was staring at the ceiling. Julian sat beside him on the bed, pondering whether you could grieve for what you never had or, more accurately, never believed you were entitled to—your father's love.

Yes, he decided, taking Theodor's warm hand in his. You could.

# Chapter 48

On opening night, with a cool September breeze blowing off the Seine and sweeping away the mugginess of summer, Club Dans le Vent was jumping. The smell of wood smoke and Isabella's artistry in the kitchen blew across Rue Blainville, where people were waiting to get in, and inside you had to turn sideways to navigate through the crowd upstairs, which seemed sandwiched between the cream-colored tin ceiling and the oak floor inlaid with red-and-blue roadways of tile. Julian hadn't seen anything like it since the speakeasies, only now the liquor and wine and beer were legal, though Marcel had purchased most of their stock on the black market. Thirsty customers were five deep at the zinc bar, and the cash register was ringing as if Isabella were accompanying the Otis Larkin Quartet in the cellar, where Otis was pounding out "Let the Good Times Roll," remolding the slow bluesy number into a cross between the boogie-woogie and one of those gospel hymns that delivered you straight to heaven.

The turnout was due to several factors: with the US Treasury underwriting the club, Julian could keep the prices low; Otis had his fans; and Kendall had spread the word in Saint-Germain. The intellectual gang, including Sartre, was supposedly downstairs, though Kendall had heard that Beauvoir couldn't come because she was with her lover in America, and there was a mob of students decked out in black as if staging a wake for the world. Isabella and Marcel had let it be known that an ex-GI was a part owner, which attracted veterans in droves, who, in their telltale khakis, had bumped into their share of resentment in Paris, understandably because they were flush with cash while most locals scraped to get by. The sportier ex-GIs had traded their boots for penny loafers and wore tweed sport coats, and they chased the chic French girls in their felt hats and brightly colored scarves with an impressive inventiveness.

As Julian and Kendall were waiting for a drink, an ex-GI ahead of them was with a dark-eyed looker, who was saying, "Ze professor *de psychologie*, he assign us a paper on *Psychopathia Sexualis*. Why we must study *les perversions sexuelles*, I do not *comprends*. Do ever you hear of zis book?"

"Hear of it? Baby, I'm in it. Dance with me, and later on we'll blow this joint, and I'll help you with that paper."

After they had gone, Kendall giggled. "Fast thinker."

Julian sent a waiter to tell Otis he had a surprise for him, and when Otis came up between sets, he saw Eddie and Fiona standing with Julian and Kendall.

"Jitterbug!" Eddie shouted.

Otis introduced Eddie to the double-barreled Gallic smooch, which would require some practice on Eddie's part. Fiona caught on fine.

"Girl," Otis said, grinning. "You ain't shot this man yet."

"I have to wait till Christmas. He promised to buy me a shotgun."

"C'mon down," Otis said. "Jules got seats by the bandstand, and I'll play you some Mr. Thelonious Monk. That cat's a hummer."

A tobacco haze hung over the dim cellar. The walls were blond wood with engraved mirrors, and the tables were jammed. During the set, most of the audience dug the music and snapped their fingers between songs. The exception was at a table in back, where Arnaud Francoeur was sitting and whispering with Thayer and Simon. When the quartet took their next break, Kendall and Fiona headed upstairs to the WC, and Thayer followed them. Simon stayed in his chair, and Arnaud came over and said *bonsoir* to Julian.

"This is my friend Eddie."

"Hello, Eddie," Arnaud said.

Eddie, studying Arnaud as if he were a hissing snake, made a pistol with the thumb and forefinger of his right hand and fired at him. This was not his chummiest greeting.

"A *fantastique* debut," Arnaud said, nodding at a corner table across the cellar. "But you don't want a reputation as a rendezvous for *les tapettes*."

Julian and Eddie looked toward the corner, where Otis was gabbing with some young men bunched around a table. Otis had one arm draped affectionately over the thin blonde next to him, and across from them a bony-faced teenager was kissing a man with a white, rhinestone-studded Stetson on his head.

Arnaud laughed, a blunt sound brimming with scorn. "We don't need more Americans turning Frenchmen into cowboys or faggots."

"Which one are you?" Eddie asked.

From the furrows in his forehead, Arnaud appeared to be cooking up a comeback. Ultimately, he chose not to reply, a wise choice.

"*À la prochaine*," Arnaud said, and returned to his seat.

"What'd he say?" Eddie asked.

"Until next time."

"If that jerk-off likes his teeth, there better be no next time."

❋

Fiona and Eddie were in Paris for a week, and they had checked into the Trianon, so Julian packed a bag and stayed with Kendall in her suite. Eddie was a reluctant tourist, but Fiona assured him that his nights would be merrier if he did as he was told during the day. The four of them strolled up the Champs-Élysées, saw the Arc de Triomphe and the Tomb of the Unknown Soldier, the Eiffel Tower and Place de la Concorde; rode up and down the Seine on a Bateau-Mouche and explored the Luxembourg Gardens, the Tuileries, the Bois de Boulogne, the Île Saint-Louis, and the Île de la Cité. They ate dinners at Dans le Vent except for the evening they went to Chez Dumonet–Josephine for the *boeuf bourguignon* and *Grand Marnier soufflé*, and Eddie triple-tipped the waiter because he'd never gotten drunk on a dessert before.

On Sunday, with church bells ringing in the crystal air, they attended Mass at Notre-Dame. Fiona complained there were chairs instead of pews, and Eddie wondered aloud where the hunchback was hiding. By the next afternoon, Fiona got it in her head that she wanted to light a candle in every church in the city, but she gave Eddie a pass on that mission and went with Kendall.

"My wife's a firebug," Eddie said, trying—and failing—to sound as if he were joking.

"What's wrong?"

"We can't get pregnant. Docs say she's got bad ovaries."

"That's a shame."

"Whatta ya gonna do?" Eddie spotted a bunch of kids staring in the window of Foucher, a chocolate shop.

Julian chuckled. "I bet you got a plan."

"Go talk French."

Within minutes, the displays in the Foucher window were bare, and children were parading down Rue du Bac with chocolate-smeared faces.

When Eddie and Julian got back to the hotel, Fiona and Kendall were still out, so they had a beer on the terrace of a café outside the Sorbonne.

"It's lonely without you at home," Eddie said.

"Isn't it fun for you and Abe to steal my money?"

"There's that." Eddie lit a cigarette. "You ever coming back?"

"I don't know."

"It's better you're here than being a miserable fuck in New Jersey."

"I wasn't a miserable fuck."

"Yeah, you were."

"I wasn't."

"Monsieur I-Wasn't-a-Miserable-Fuck, would ya ask the waiter for another beer?"

＊

On Fiona and Eddie's last day in Paris, they ate lunch with Kendall and Julian at La Palette. They had planned to go to the Louvre when they were done, but they hadn't factored in Eddie eating a *croque-monsieur* and discovering that champagne was such a dandy complement to hot ham and cheese that he handled two bottles by himself and announced that he preferred napping to art.

"Don't you want to learn anything?" Fiona asked.

"I like to keep it simple."

Fiona snorted. "You're a master at keeping yourself simple."

"Secret of my success."

Julian told Kendall and Fiona to go ahead; he'd take Eddie to the hotel.

The women walked down to Quai Malaquais. The city was dissolving from the rousing green of summer to the softer hues of fall, and in the drowsy light, lovers and parents with children in tow stopped at the bookstalls and kiosks on the quay or watched painters try to capture the burnished magic of the Seine.

Fiona said, "That man does things to me."

Kendall laughed. "He's your husband; he's supposed to."

"Not just those things. He makes me feel safe when he comes home and worries me when he's late. Makes me believe I'd hate my life without him. Even when he acts like a feckin eejit."

Kendall suddenly felt sad, thinking about not having Julian. "That's 'fucking idiot' in Irish?"

Now it was Fiona's turn to laugh. "And my Edward's middle name."

As they went over to the Right Bank on the Pont du Carrousel, Kendall said, "Can I ask you a question?"

"Go on, darlin'."

"Do you tell Eddie everything?"

"About old flames?"

"No, things that happen, things—"

"Bad things?"

In a voice softer than a sigh, Kendall said, "Things like that."

Fiona took her arm. "You tell him because that's what a husband's for. He knows sometimes you don't want to wash your hair and you can yell at him for nothing if you're in a mood and you got sin in you to spare, and he loves you anyway. You tell him because you'll hate yourself for not telling him, and the trouble with that kind of hatred is you get used to it."

Just over the bridge, families were gathered around a young fellow, skinny as a pipe cleaner, holding out his right arm so red-faced gold-finches could land there while he fed seeds to them.

"It has a way of working out," Fiona said, and after she deposited five hundred francs in the basket by the man's bare feet, she and Kendall walked on to the museum.

# Chapter 49

Kendall's war. Her memories of the war. They were all hers, and her photographs were just part of the story. And not the most agonizing part, the part that Kendall kept to herself. After settling in Paris she thought her memories would fade. No luck. The images became more detailed, and excruciating to recall. She told herself that she wanted to tell someone. Not someone—Julian. Except he wasn't in Paris then, and once he showed up, Kendall was hesitant to put her experience into words, as if by telling her story it would become impossible to revise or forget.

What changed her mind? Fiona's advice was some of it. But mainly it was the evening Kendall was waiting for Julian to arrive and sifting through a box of her photographs, and it occurred to her that sometimes images weren't enough. Sometimes you needed words.

＊

The Negro soldiers of the 614th Tank Destroyer Battalion called her Angel, as in "Hey, Angel, you make us famous yet?" That was Kendall's assignment, she supposed, making them famous. Officers pissing in General Eisenhower's ear doubted that colored troops had the brains or courage to fight, though without them Kendall would have missed the war. Léo Sapir had peddled her photographs of Londoners living and dying in the rubble left behind by German bombs to *Look* and the *Picture Post*, but American military commanders balked at putting women correspondents in harm's way, and Kendall, a Negro who wasn't employed by a publication, was at the back of the line. In

October 1944, four months after D-Day, as the 614th was preparing to ship out for France, Kendall finally received her press credentials. Léo had cut a deal for her with the National Negro Publishers Association, which supplied stories and photos to Negro papers across the United States.

The soldiers started calling her Angel because even in her helmet, with a hole cut in back for her ponytail, you could see Kendall's face, as pretty as a cameo carved in amber. By November, they had another reason. Kendall was photographing the crew of a self-propelled cannon when the Germans let loose with their *Nebelwerfers*, which sent rockets screeching through the sky like vengeful phantoms. A soldier yelled, "Incoming!" and Kendall and the crew hit the dirt. Rockets exploded around them, yet except for the ringing in their ears, no one was injured. Now it was "Angel" because her presence explained a miracle: *Damn, Angel, you really is a angel. . . .*

Kendall became the Angel of Climbach in December. Climbach was a French town close to the German border, and as the Americans approached, the Nazis attacked. Kendall wasn't afraid. Not of the cough of mortars or the thump of the cannons or the trees bursting or the bullets whizzing overhead or the screams of the wounded or the silence of the dead. She wasn't afraid, not as long as she witnessed the fighting through a viewfinder and pressed the shutter-release button of her Leica—either the one Julian had given her or the newer model, the IIIc, she'd bought herself before going to London. Most of her photographs had their usual concision and, over the years, one of them earned a measure of fame by appearing in photography and history books: a Negro soldier lying on his back, dead and alone in a field, his helmet rolled away, his face as innocent as a sleeping Renaissance cherub, his dark skin and the pure white of the freshly fallen snow its own message, a cri de coeur—*Pay attention, America, I died for you.*

The Germans retreated from Climbach. In town, a medic asked her, "Will ya talk to these boys till we get they asses on the meat wagons?"

Kendall shared cigarettes with the wounded and listened to their morphine-induced rambling. It was a pleasant distraction. After they had been loaded into ambulances, the medic led Kendall over to a soldier lying under an olive-drab blanket on a stretcher. "This here's Pete," he said, and went to treat another batch of wounded.

Kendall knelt beside the stretcher. Pete said, "My wife, Mary, she a beauty like you."

"Where you from, Pete?"

"Omaha. Mary and me, we got a daughter, Sarah. Her third birthday was yesterday."

"You must miss them."

"I'm gon' see 'em soon."

A bare foot was sticking out from under the blanket. Kendall covered it.

"My foot freezin'," Pete said.

Kendall rubbed it between her hands. The skin was ashy and cold.

Pete sighed with pleasure. "Let's don't go tellin' Mary. She jealous as a house cat."

"We won't tell."

Pete's breathing was shallow. "You the girl they call Angel?"

Kendall's throat closed up. She swallowed. "That's me."

Pete propped himself up on his elbows. His breathing was faster, and he was gazing across the street at the church. The bell tower had been sheared off by the shelling to prevent a German sniper or spotter from hiding there.

"You—you the Angel of Climbach," Pete said, lying down.

Soon, his chest stopped rising and falling. Kendall drew the blanket up over his head. Numb, she went behind the stretcher, kneeling and taking pictures of Pete with the church in the background.

The Angel of Climbach never sold those photographs. When the contact sheets came back from the lab, she couldn't bring herself to look at them.

※

In late January 1945, Kendall took a break from the war. For a woman who had dreamt of visiting Paris since high school, Kendall's first sight of the city failed to excite her. She lived at the Hôtel Saint-Germain-des-Prés but frequented the hangout for journalists in the basement of the Hôtel Scribe, where she drank wine by the bottle and slept with men who evaporated from her memory as quickly as they filled her bed. She did meet Arnaud Francoeur, who lasted longer than the others, because he was a Parisian and took her on a tour of the Left Bank. The high point of her month was eating dinner with the photographer Henri Cartier-Bresson—in her opinion, the greatest flâneur of the century. Léo Sapir had mailed him Kendall's book *Double Lives*, and Cartier-Bresson flattered her silly by saying how grand it was. He also had some advice for her:

"To crop a photograph is a rejection of reality. You must see everything as it is. You must see the picture whole. In your art *and* your life."

Kendall kept his advice in mind on her next assignment, following the 761st Tank Battalion. Otis was with the Black Panthers—the nickname of the 761st. It was wonderful meeting up with him, but she didn't stay long. With so many GIs dead and wounded, combat units were undermanned, and the ability to fight trumped race. Thousands of Negroes volunteered to be replacements, and Kendall tagged along with a replacement platoon that entered Germany behind the Fourth Armored Division. That was how she got to the Ohrdruf concentration camp.

Kendall attempted to see things as they were, yet the emaciated dead lying outside the barracks in their striped prisoner garb, the naked corpses stacked in a shed, the mass graves with hands and feet poking up through the dirt like withered plants, and the bones resembling blackened twigs in a fire pit with the stench of death, burned flesh, and hair in her nostrils defied comprehension and made Kendall think that, through some malevolent alchemy, she'd been brushstroked into the gruesome Bruegel painting *The Triumph of Death*. Steeling herself against her disgust and a desire to throw away her Leica and weep, Kendall shot fourteen rolls of film from a variety of distances and angles of view with 35 mm, 50 mm, and 135 mm lenses. The soldiers carrying jaundiced, skeletal survivors like brides across a threshold momentarily revived her faith in humanity, but by her second afternoon Kendall couldn't shake her sense that the camp was the figment of a ghoulish imagination.

She was anxious to photograph any totem of normalcy, so when a chaplain said that he'd heard some families lived a mile through the forest, Kendall went for a walk, and she was delighted by what she saw at the end of a hard-packed trail—a gingerbread cottage nestled among beech trees with a vegetable garden on one side and a stream behind it. No one was in the garden or on the porch. Kendall shot half a roll of film, then headed for the stream. A high-pitched voice cried out in German as Kendall stepped past the cottage. An American soldier, a white soldier in muddy fatigues, had a girl on the ground and was lifting her dirndl.

"Stop it!" Kendall shouted, but not until she glimpsed two haversacks, two helmets, a carbine, and a Garand in the grass by the cottage, and an arm encircled her neck, did it occur to her that the soldier might have a buddy with him, and by then she was pinned on her back.

Her fear and her fury debated whether she should lie still and hope to survive or risk being killed to free herself. Her fury won, and Kendall clawed at the man's face, an unshaven white man with fierce eyes and hot breath stale with cigarettes and fatigues reeking of sweat and a faint stink of death. He held her wrists above her head with one hand while undoing her belt with the other, then ripped the buttons off her fly as he stripped down her khakis. Kendall squirmed and bucked, but she couldn't throw him off, and as he parted her legs with his knees and tore off her panties, the words erupting from her were as incomprehensible as the terrified burbling of the German girl.

Kendall wished that Julian's pistol weren't in a trunk at her mother's in Lovewood or that Julian would magically appear and kill this son of a bitch. Julian. She remembered the day of her gallery opening when she was waiting for Julian and Brig came over squiffy on gin and tried to fuck her. What did she do? She used her head. And got the Beretta. There was that carbine by the cottage. Garands were too heavy. Tankers were issued carbines. Kendall had photographed them, and Otis had let her fire his. She was reminding herself that the safety was a button by the trigger guard when the solider jabbed at her with his hard-on, and the girl screamed like a speared animal. Kendall pictured the other soldier and wanted to vomit hearing him say, "Nice, ain't it, baby?" He had a scabbard strapped to his right calf. Not an uncommon way for soldiers to carry knives. Kendall had noticed the scabbard when she'd shouted at him.

The man rammed his cock inside her. Her skin tore and burned as the soldier began to thrust. Gritting her teeth, Kendall murmured, "Not that fast," and smiled up at him, moving her hips sweet and slow. "Let go of my hands; we both might as well enjoy it."

He released her, and Kendall was astounded he'd think she was aroused. Of course, you didn't have to ace the Army intelligence test to be a rapist. Locking her legs behind his, Kendall strained upward. He interpreted this as her approval of his technique and stuck his tongue in her ear. She thanked God for her long arms and the soldier's short legs, and drew him to her, stroking his back, his buttocks. "Good, good," he grunted as her left hand slid to his hip, then lower, her fingers unsnapping the loop securing the grooved hilt of a knife. As he slobbered on her neck, Kendall plunged the blade into a cheek of his ass. He yowled, and she stabbed him in the side of his leg and shoved at him with her forearm. He rolled off, screaming, "Fuckin' swamp whore!" and Kendall scrambled to her feet. Her hand clutching the knife was slick with blood and, hobbling toward the cottage, she tugged up her pants and clipped her belt closed while the soldier shouted, "Ronald, help! I'm bleedin' to death."

Ronald was too distracted to help. His head was raised, his eyes were shut, and his body was jerking with his grand finale inside the girl, who was whimpering, *"Nein nein nein nein . . ."*

Kendall dropped the knife and grabbed a carbine, pressing in the safety and remembering how Otis had retracted the operating slide. The soldier was standing in his boxers, but his pants were around his ankles, and his leg was bleeding.

In a voice full of scorn and incredulity, he said, "You're gonna shoot me, are ya?"

Her desire to kill him scared her. A colored girl, even a photographer, would get tossed in prison or executed for killing a soldier. Rape would be no defense. Who would believe her and who would care about the German girl? Yet with the stinging between her legs, and her thighs sticky with her own blood, Kendall didn't give a shit, and the carbine jolted against her shoulder. The shot went over his head. Her lousy marksmanship annoyed her, but firing the carbine paid off. Her target spun around, yanked up his pants, and fled, limping toward the woods; Ronald was now paying attention, sitting beside the girl, shimmying into his boxers, and warily eyeing Kendall. The girl was on her back, one arm over her eyes, moaning.

"I ain't done nothing to you," he said. "And that guy ain't no pal of mine. We was takin' a walk."

"Leave your gear and go."

"I'll get reamed out by my lieutenant if I leave my gear."

Kendall urged him to reconsider by firing a shot into the grass a foot in front of him. She was thrilled, not only because it sent him on his way, but because she'd been aiming at that spot. The girl sat up. Her hair was braided into a gold crown. Kendall slung the Garand over her shoulder in case the soldiers returned, and rummaged through their haversacks and found a bar of soap in a paper wrapper and two undershirts she could use as washcloths. Up close, the girl looked no more than thirteen or fourteen. Her face was grimy with tears, and blood had soaked through the skirt of her dirndl. Kendall held out her hand. The girl stared at it.

"*Es ist* okay," Kendall said, using up most of her German.

The girl clasped her fingers. Kendall helped her up and, holding hands, they walked to the stream.

※

When Kendall finished telling Julian her story, she was standing at the open window in her suite at the Trianon. Julian got off the couch and came up behind her. He wanted to hold her, but she heard him approaching, her body stiffened, and he didn't touch her.

Kendall said, "I should've killed them both."

"And give yourself something else to regret forever?"

She looked across the tin rooftops with the terra-cotta chimney pots to the domes of the Sorbonne and Panthéon, both of them glorious against the wash of red and violet twilight.

"I didn't see them at Ohrdruf. The camp was a mob scene. Everyone wanted a peek. To prove we were fighting the right war. Soldiers and reporters were in and out. Eisenhower stopped by with Patton and Bradley . . ."

Kendall turned. "You would've shot them. I wished you were there to shoot them."

Julian would gladly shoot them now, but that information wouldn't help Kendall, who was resting her head on his chest. Gingerly, Julian put his arms around her.

"I felt like it was my fault," Kendall said.

"It wasn't."

"And I felt worthless."

"You're not."

Kendall was trembling, controlling herself, trying not to cry.

Julian embraced her. Raising his voice, he said, "You're not worthless."

Kendall held her breath, then exhaled slowly. Her trembling stopped.

Julian whispered, "Marry me?"

Kendall didn't respond immediately. Then her head nodded up and down against him. Julian knew they would have to talk about it later, but for now he was happy to take it for a yes.

# Chapter 50

I'm sure Thayer's fine," Kendall was saying into the telephone as Julian entered his bedroom with a towel around his waist. "Her roommate from Smith was in town, wasn't she? They could've gone off somewhere. I'll go by Thayer's, speak to her concierge, and ask around. When's your train get in? We'll be here at nine. Call."

Kendall hung up. "That was Simon. He's in Heidelberg and hasn't been able to get in touch with Thayer for three days. He got your number from Otis."

Julian began to dress. Sounding defensive, Kendall said, "Simon and I, we're not—"

"I know." Julian didn't suspect her of cheating on him, but Thayer's disappearing and Simon's going to Heidelberg got his attention. Heidelberg was the headquarters of the US military in Europe; Thayer had been awfully chummy with Arnaud Francoeur at her party, and though Julian had assumed her interest in him was carnal, not political, now he wondered if Simon, Thayer, and Francoeur could be up to something. Unlikely that it was warehousing small arms in Paris, as Wild Bill had suggested in July. Julian doubted that Stalin would order the Red Army to invade Western Europe, because the Soviet leader wouldn't want an atom bomb dropped on the Kremlin. Yet who would've predicted that the Germans, the intellectual, artistic, and scientific lodestars of the West, would annihilate millions in the camps?

Outside it was one of those sun-blessed October days with the leaves, like miniature kites, drifting through a polished-blue sky, and on Place de la Contrescarpe, the *clochards* were collecting donations from the shoppers streaming down Rue Mouffetard. Julian and Kendall sat on the terrace of La Contrescarpe.

"Don't you get bored with *pain au chocolat* every morning?" she said.

"Nope. And I don't get bored with making love to you."

"You will when we're old."

"Then I'll still have chocolate."

"Hah! Small compensation."

Julian grinned and, after another bite of his pastry, changed the subject. "We didn't finish our conversation last evening." They had gone to Tour d'Argent, and with a view of the Seine and Notre-Dame and eating duck and drinking pinot noir, they had discussed marriage. Kendall was warming to the idea, but the conversation ended when they got back to Julian's.

Kendall's smile lit up her eyes. "It's not my fault. Who told you to kiss me?"

"I thought that up on my own."

"You were saying it would be easier to get married in the States, and I said it would be illegal in Florida."

"New Jersey then."

Kendall drank her *café crème*. "But we'd live in Paris?"

"I'd have to be in Jersey now and again, but I'd live here. Marcel's finishing renovating a three-bedroom upstairs. The rent's a hundred and fifty dollars a month."

"And we could split it." She wasn't asking a question.

"Or you could pay it and I'd be a kept man."

"I like that. What would you do in Paris?"

"Compose an epic poem. *La Chanson de Julian*."

There went her smile again. Beautiful. "Like *La Chanson de Roland* only about you?"

"Exactly. I'd write in between real-estate deals."

Kendall put her hand on his. "Are you unhappy with the way we are now?"

"I want children. You said you did too."

"At some point. But I'll still have to travel for work."

"I'll be around, and we can hire a *femme de ménage*. I want a family. I want you to be my family."

"I—I already feel like I am."

Julian squeezed her hand and wished that Kendall had sounded less—less reluctant? Less afraid? He finished his *café crème* and let the matter drop. "You have a shoot today?"

"For *Ebony*. Negro expatriates in Paris. I'll be at the Café Tournon between eleven and three. First, I've got to take some film to the lab. And I told Simon I'd go by Thayer's. I'll do that, and then I'll make some calls. Otis might have seen her."

"I'll be at the club. I can swing by your place at four and we can figure out dinner."

"*Parfait*," she said, and laced her fingers through his.

※

Julian had been sitting at the bar for two hours going over the accounting ledger with Isabella when she said, "We're making a profit and you're not taking your share."

"That makes me a good partner, no?"

"A confusing one. You're supposed to take your money."

"You keep it. I got plenty."

"My cousin Arnaud wants to be our partner as well."

"What?"

"He was here last night. We were busy, and Arnaud says I am doing so well, didn't I want to contribute to *le Parti Communiste Français*? The Communists could make sure nothing happens to my bistro."

Apparently, a Commie protection racket was no different from the capitalist variety.

Isabella said, "That leprous asshole was there when *les tondeurs* shaved my head. My cousin, whom I cared for as a baby—dried his tears and changed his diapers—did nothing to stop them. Manny, my friend's son, tried to help, and the mob beat him to death." Isabella closed the ledger, then stared at Julian. "And Arnaud thinks I'll give him money so he can keep sitting in the Café de Flore acting like the king of France. I would sooner suck his puny cock."

Her eyes shone with anger, which Julian preferred to the hopeless-ness that he'd seen when they met. And since Francoeur had been one of Kendall's lovers, he didn't object to hearing that he was hung like a mouse. "Don't pay Arnaud. I'll talk to him."

"*Bonjour*," Marcel said, as he walked into the club.

Isabella was suddenly grinning like a young coquette. "Julian, did you know the girls flirt with my doorman?"

"Because you tell them I can do more with one arm than any man with two." Marcel bussed her on one cheek, then the other. "I have to show Julian the new apartment. Will you excuse us?"

"*Bien sûr*. Be here by five. So I can feed you. You are still too thin."

As Marcel and Julian headed up Rue Blainville, Marcel, speaking English to Julian for the first time, said, "I've heard from an associate. We need a taxi, and you will need to spend some of your cash."

"For?"

"To go to Pigalle and pay *une fille de joie*."

❋

The Moulin Rouge, the cabaret famous for its cancan dancers and the red windmill on its roof, was still in Pigalle, and so were the prostitutes on Boulevard de Clichy. The government had outlawed the *maisons de tolérance* after the war and, with the economy a wreck and most of the GIs gone, the girls had taken to quoting prices to men going in and out of the green, cylinder-shaped pissoir that stank from a block away. Marcel turned onto a side street, and Julian saw more girls standing on Place Adolphe Max and eyeing the statue of Hector Berlioz, as if the composer, looking prosperous in his cravat and cape, were a potential client. At the corner, an old man in a pilled sweater and patched trou-sers was selling roasted chestnuts in cones of newspaper, and Marcel said to him, "*Bon travail, mon ami*," and walked past a fleabag hotel to a house with a crumbling stucco exterior. Marcel asked Julian for a fifty-dollar bill, then banged on the door. A woman answered. She had hennaed hair done up in pin curls, a peignoir that advertised her wares, and the countenance of someone who expected nothing and got even less.

"You spoke to my friend," Marcel said, holding out the fifty. "Can you repeat the story?"

She took the bill as if plucking a grape from a vine. "Four days ago a Negro in a nice suit was outside. I came downstairs and asked if he would like to come up. He said no, he was waiting for a woman. His French was shameful. He was an American."

"And the woman?"

"She arrived in a taxi with a scarf over her hair. I saw her from my window. She had a face like a doll. The Negro handed her something and went away. She stood there long enough for me to smoke a cigarette and two men came in a truck. One had light hair, the other a beret like yours. The woman unlocked the front door of my building and went in."

Julian said, "So the Negro gave her a key?"

"Perhaps. The two men carried six wooden crates into the apartment below mine. Then they left in the truck, the woman on foot."

"May we see the crates?" Julian asked.

"Do you have a key?"

"No," Julian said. "Do you?"

"I have a knife, hammer, and screwdriver."

Another fifty rented all three. Julian had no trouble with the lock. It probably hadn't been changed since the reign of Napoleon. The apartment was unfurnished and the walls were mildewed. A dirt-ringed bathtub was in the kitchen, and the crates were in the windowless bedroom. Inside the crates were M1 carbines; M3 submachine guns; military Smith & Wesson revolvers; and ammunition for all of them.

Marcel said, "The American weapons Wild Bill mentioned to you."

Nodding, Julian loaded a revolver, tucked it in the back of his waistband, and dumped some cartridges into the pocket of his sport coat. Then he hammered the crates shut. The woman was standing in the entranceway. Julian returned the knife and tools, then gave her a hundred dollars and warned her, "Talk to no one about this. You'll be safer."

They were out on the boulevard again. Marcel said, "The one

with the light hair, I would wager that's Francoeur. Do you know the others?"

"Two out of three, I think. They've been at Dans le Vent. The Negro's Simon Foxe, the woman's Thayer Claypoole. No one has seen her for a while."

Marcel let out an exasperated sigh. "She's missing? You should've told me. Wait here."

He went into a *tabac*, and from the open windows Julian could smell the aroma of potatoes frying in oil. When Marcel came out he headed straight for a cab with Julian behind him, and he gave directions to the driver as they settled into the back seat.

"What?" Julian asked.

"My younger brother was an inspector at the Brigade Criminelle. He has retired to Brittany. But he had many friends at the Brigade, and I spoke to a detective. This Thayer's college roommate—a niece of the American ambassador—has been searching for her."

"Have they located Thayer?"

"Maybe."

"Where?"

"Nowhere you would want to be."

# Chapter 51

Bicycle patrolmen weaved between the police cars parked on Quai des Tuileries. A crowd had formed along the low wall on the quay, and *les flics* in their kepis and capes were blocking the onlookers from going down the stone ramp to the Seine, where the linden trees bent toward the river as if their autumn-gold leaves were peeking over the shoulders of the police.

Marcel said, "I'll see if I know anyone."

He was gone for five minutes.

"I'll have to call the Brigade for details, but I heard reporters from *Le Parisien* and *France Soir* talking. There is a dead woman, and the cops believe she jumped from the bridge. Another lovesick young woman, and someone told the reporters she had a wooden mask on."

"Of *L'Inconnue de la Seine?*"

"How did you—"

"Thayer collected those masks."

"It will be an hour before I learn anything."

"I have to make a stop. Can your detective send the police to get those weapons?"

"He can. You are going to see Francoeur?"

"*Oui.*"

"*C'est bon ça.* Whatever the Communists think, I don't want their revolution here, and France is also my country."

※

The Café de Flore was a few doors down from Deux Magots. The terrace was full, but just a handful of customers were upstairs, and Arnaud Francoeur, in a blue blazer and white tennis shirt, was among them. He sat by himself at a marble-topped table in back eating an omelet and drinking a glass of white wine.

"*Très intéressant*," Julian said, taking the chair across from him. "An epicurean Stalinist."

Francoeur put down his fork and looked at Julian like a poker player calculating whether to call or raise. "Your French accent is improving."

"It seems the police fished Thayer out of the river."

Francoeur combed his fingers through his golden-brown hair. "A rich, naïve American girl with a taste for intrigue. That's a pity."

"She died for the cause, did she?"

Francoeur wiped his mouth with his napkin. "Jealous?"

Francoeur was playing with him. Jesus, how could Kendall have fucked this jerk? "Of what?"

"Of someone with a cause? You must not be a typical American, Julian. Americans love causes, *non*? For example, your General Marshall will soon be buying entire countries in Europe."

"Feeding the hungry is preferable to some of your countrymen sticking Jews on trains to Auschwitz."

"You Americans make me laugh. You are ignorant of your history and assume everyone else is. But we are not. Had Zyklon B been available, your Indians would have died in gas chambers. And Americans will have time to murder their Jews when they are done hanging Negroes like Christmas ornaments on trees. Is that not why so many, including Kendall, are in Paris?"

Julian could have countered with Stalin and his purges, but he was allergic to philosophical masturbation. And he loathed hearing Francoeur say Kendall's name. "Isabella told me you came by."

"She is my cousin."

"Isabella is not paying any protection money."

"That is up to Isabella."

"And me. I'm her partner."

"*Quelle surprise*. My old comrade, the OSS commando, the former lover of my former lover, turns up in Paris to go into business with my cousin. How stupid do you believe I am?"

Julian pressed the table toward Francoeur, shoving him and his chair against the wall.

Francoeur smirked. "This is a schoolboy game, *non?*"

Julian got more of his weight behind his side of the table, wanting to break Francoeur's ribs, but the smirk didn't go away. While he may not have been able to write an epic poem, Julian wasn't without creativity. Leaning close to Francoeur and locking eyes with him, Julian snatched the fork off his plate and drove the tines through the top of the man's left hand. The smirk disappeared, and Francoeur sounded as if he were gagging.

"Isabella pays you nothing. *Rien.* Not a *centime.*"

Francoeur nodded, his face almost as red as the blood seeping around the tines.

"Annoy her—or Kendall—we'll get together again. And I'll bring a set of steak knives."

Julian left the fork in Francoeur's hand and departed without saying *au revoir.*

*

The sky was steely blue as Julian cut through Place Saint-Sulpice. Men and women sat on the lower lip of the fountain talking while the pigeons up on the statues of the bishops studied the people as if they were chaperoning a social. Julian entered a hotel off the square and phoned Dans le Vent from the kiosk in the lobby.

Marcel answered. "Isabella has made her cassoulet. She says you must eat at the club with Kendall."

"I'll try. Did you hear anything?"

"*Oui.* It was Thayer Claypoole. Her college roommate identified her. She was struck on the head and probably unconscious when she was thrown in the water. The detective says men from the American Embassy had been asking about Thayer for weeks. They were aware of her, Simon Foxe, and Arnaud, and the rumor about the weapons that Wild Bill heard."

"I'm guessing the weapons are why Arnaud got rid of her. Thayer liked to talk."

"She was sleeping with Arnaud and Foxe?"

"She was."

"Is it possible Foxe—"

"Possible, not probable. I'll talk to Simon. Can you fill in Wild Bill? Tell him I'm bringing Simon home, and after that, I'm retiring."

Marcel was silent. Then: "*Certainement*. What about Arnaud?"

"I'll give you my pistol, and if he bothers Isabella, you can take care of him."

"*Avec plaisir.*"

✳

Kendall was exiting a *tabac* on Rue de Vaugirard and slipping a pack of cigarettes into her shoulder bag when Julian saw her. With the air cooler than this morning, she had changed into a tight tweed jacket and tighter dungarees and knotted a purple-and-orange scarf around her neck. He loved to watch her without her seeing him; it was like looking at a painting—a riot of color and curves, and a lingering awe at the artistry of the creator.

"How'd the shoot go?" Julian asked after they'd kissed.

"It went well. But I didn't get a chance to eat. I'm famished."

"Isabella invited us for cassoulet."

"Yum."

They crossed the boulevard to Rue Cujas. The limestone buildings of the Sorbonne and the hotels and houses were close together blocking the sun, so it was chilly and students hurried by, shivering, and the light was as gray as the smoke from the braziers warming the terraces of the cafés.

"I went to Thayer's," Kendall said, taking Julian's arm. "Her concierge says she hasn't been there in days, and I spoke to Otis and he hasn't seen her."

Julian dreaded telling her; the story was more involved than Thayer's death, and he recalled how angry Kendall had been about his not mentioning that he owned the house in the Village.

As the street widened at the Place du Panthéon, Julian said, "I have some bad news."

Kendall stopped walking but still held on to his arm.

"Thayer is dead."

Kendall gasped. "Dead? Who told you that?"

"Some reporters."

"Reporters? What reporters?"

"The reporters were by the Seine. Thayer drowned in the Seine."

"The Seine? Why—what was Thayer doing in the Seine?"

"The police are working on it."

Kendall studied him, trying to discern—he thought—if she were hearing the whole truth. "Thayer wouldn't commit suicide. Jesus, God, does Simon know?"

"You—or me if you want—can tell him tonight."

Her eyes misted up. "I've known her since I was five. She was so young."

"It's terrible."

Kendall glanced up the hill at the Church of Saint-Étienne-du-Mont, a Gothic gem with a rosette window of stained glass and students lounging on the steps smoking. "Let's light a candle for her and make a donation to the poor."

"Thayer was Catholic?"

Kendall laughed sadly. "No, but Fiona got me in the habit."

They went toward the church. Julian would come clean after they ate. It would be easier on both of them if she heard the rest of the story on a full stomach.

# Chapter 52

The dining area at Dans le Vent was redolent with Isabella's cassoulet—a garlicky aroma rising from the bowls of sausage, confit of duck and pork shoulder, sweet onions, tomatoes, and plump *tarbais* beans that were slow-cooked under a crust of bread crumbs and tasted like the coziest starlit autumn night you could remember.

Isabella kept them company while they ate, a break for Julian because Kendall wouldn't question him about Thayer in front of her. They finished a bottle of heavy red wine from Cahors, and Julian hoped it would make Kendall sleepy, but she drank an espresso and smoked her Gauloises and, after Isabella went to greet customers, eyeballed Julian through the candlelight as if she were ready to give him the third degree. Just then, however, Otis came in with a waiter Julian recognized from La Contrescarpe. He had milky skin and hair the color of a new penny. Otis's quartet was playing downstairs later.

"You hear about Thayer?" Otis asked, his speech thick, his eyes half-closed. "It's all they talkin' 'bout in Saint-Germain."

"We did," Kendall said. "It's unbelievable."

"Yeah, baby, October ain't no month for a swim."

The waiter put his arm around Otis's waist, and they went to the bar.

"He's hopped up," Julian said.

"So's his new friend. I talked to Otis about it, and he told me it's none of my business. You're not going to tell me that, are you?"

"Doubt I could get away with it."

276

✳

In his apartment, Julian lit the candles in the jars on the mantelpiece, then sat at one end of the couch while Kendall sat at the other. On the walk home, Julian had resolved to give it to her straight. "Arnaud—or one of his Commie buddies—murdered Thayer."

Kendall stared at him as if Julian had merely informed her that Arnaud and Thayer were seen talking at Deux Magots. In a voice equal parts disbelief and contempt, she said, "That's absurd. You just don't like Arnaud because—we both know why."

"According to a detective, Thayer was knocked out and dumped in the river."

"And that proves Arnaud did it?"

"Or had it done. Thayer was working with him."

"Thayer never worked a day in her life."

"Arnaud was sleeping with her. Maybe that made her more industrious. I can't say."

Kendall glared at him. "And you're implying I can?"

"They were storing small arms in an apartment in Pigalle." Julian removed the Smith & Wesson from his waistband and set it between them on the couch. "This is one of the pistols."

"Why were you in Pigalle? And how do you know any of this?"

*Here we go*, Julian thought. "I came to Paris to check out Arnaud."

"To— Who sent you?"

"The same people who sent me to war."

"That Wild Bill character? And he knew I was involved with Arnaud?"

"He told me you were."

"You— This . . . this has to be a new low for jealous ex-boyfriends. Snake-belly low."

"Hanging around with Arnaud, you were in danger."

"Please. He edits a newspaper."

"I saw Arnaud order his men to crucify German prisoners. Not that they didn't deserve to die, but crucified? He watched that mob cut Isabella's hair and didn't try to help her. Now he's shaking her down."

Her arguing with him as if this were a lover's spat instead of a predicament that could get someone else killed exhausted his patience, and as Kendall started to speak, Julian cut her off. "Arnaud was in Moscow talking to Red Army intelligence, who likely paid for the weapons. That way Stalin can have some guerilla support if we get to World War Three. The Soviets aren't fucking around. And Arnaud isn't either."

The light of the candles flickered across the stony expression on her face. "Julian to my rescue—again. I can't trust you. You and your secrets."

Julian felt himself boiling over. "You don't want to get married, you've got your excuse. Race can't be it—we're in Paris."

Kendall snapped, "How about deceiving me? Is that an excuse?"

"Damnit, if I had a choice, I wouldn't have told you anything. I have to take Simon to the States. Tomorrow."

"Tomor—"

"Simon was at the apartment in Pigalle. Arnaud can't be sure what Thayer told him, and if he wanted Thayer dead, why would he leave Simon alive?"

Kendall was quiet, and Julian said, "Simon's caught in the middle. He's been writing articles about our troops in Europe, interviewing senior officers, and touring our bases. Who can say what Thayer got out of him and passed to Arnaud? People in our embassy are aware they were a couple. America's in the spy business now—we have a federal agency for it. Wild Bill has contacts who can get Simon out of this. Otherwise, he's screwed. By us or the Commies."

Julian glanced at his watch, then put on his beret and overcoat and stuck the pistol in one of the pockets. "I'll be at the Sélect. When Simon calls, send him there. If you feel up to it, tell him Thayer had an accident. But he can't go to his hotel. He's gonna have to sleep here on the couch. I'll explain it to him."

Kendall stood. Her expression had softened. "I'm sorry I was upset with you."

"It's upsetting to hear."

"Why are you doing this for Simon?"

He shrugged, not wanting to dig up ancient history.

"Tell me. You know. You always know."

"Derrick."

"Derrick wasn't your fault."

"You said it a long time ago: if Eddie and I hadn't been there, Otis wouldn't have gone in the ocean and Derrick wouldn't have slapped Hurleigh."

"I was young and scared and I was wrong to say that."

"And I could've taken care of Hurleigh permanently. I didn't realize he'd lynch Derrick over a slap. But I got Arnaud's number. He's not getting to Simon. Or Isabella or you. He knows I'll kill him. How's that for a jealous boyfriend?"

Kendall stroked his face. "Good."

❊

It was too early for *les vagabonds nocturnes*, but the Sélect was hopping, and Julian nursed a Scotch at a small round table beside a brazier on the terrace and watched the evening traffic on Boulevard Montparnasse. When Simon emerged from a taxi in a trench coat and holding a valise, Julian waved him over.

"How does a grown woman drown in the Seine by accident?" Simon asked after ordering a drink from a waiter. "Kenni-Ann didn't answer that one."

Julian waited until Simon had taken a swallow of his brandy and soda before telling him the story. When he was done, Simon had a hand pressed to his forehead. "What'd I get myself into? I wasn't serious with Thayer. I was having fun. Does Arnaud skate on this?"

"Not forever. Why'd you go to that house in Pigalle?"

"Thayer forgot the key in my hotel room, and she called and asked me to bring it over. She said a girl she knew from the Sorbonne was moving in."

"And she didn't ask you about your work?"

"Thayer was interested in Thayer. I'm writing about Negro soldiers in Europe and Negro veterans that stayed because they hate Jim Crow. The higher-ups I interviewed talked about integrating the military. Nothing the Soviets couldn't read elsewhere."

"You'll sack out on my couch tonight."

"Thanks, but I'm at the Hôtel de l'Avenir. It's nearby."

"It's not safe. Arnaud could be watching it, or someone from our embassy. And tomorrow we'll fly home. You can talk to Bill Donovan in New York, and I'll vouch for you. You need to leave Paris and get squared away with the government before somebody in this new Central Intelligence Agency hears the story and figures to make a name for himself by treating you like a traitor. I got a guy can collect your stuff and pay your hotel bill."

"Why you doing this?"

Julian couldn't blame Simon for sounding suspicious. Between Julian being white and in love with Kendall, how could Simon not be skeptical about his motives. "For Kendall. For me. It's not important why."

Simon sat back, fiddling with the brass Double-V pin in the lapel of his trench coat. The *Pittsburgh Courier* had kicked off the Double-V campaign right after the war started: one V for victory overseas, the other for victory over prejudice at home.

Julian said, "We got the first V."

Simon stopped touching the pin. "Yeah, and I'm in no rush to get back to the fight for the second one."

"You have to go. Believe me."

"I do, but I like Europe. It gave me the chance to worry about everything except the color of my skin."

"Look on the bright side. America's got Jackie Robinson."

"That's something," Simon replied.

※

It was after eleven when Julian came into the apartment. Kendall had made up the couch, and in the bedroom Julian undressed with a sliver of moonlight, curved like a scimitar, visible in the space between the curtains.

"I'm awake," Kendall said.

She was also naked, Julian discovered, when he got under the quilt.

"Is Simon here?"

"We stopped by the club. Simon's listening to Otis play and drinking with some friends he ran into. A last-night blowout. Marcel's there, and Simon will stay downstairs with him."

"Marcel's on our side?"

"Yeah, and if Arnaud pops up while I'm gone, talk to Marcel. He'll handle him."

Her hand went inside his boxers. "Who should I talk to about this?"

"That's my department," Julian said, and then they were done talking.

✳

In the morning, Julian walked to the TWA office. It was on the Right Bank, and he paused on the Pont Neuf. A barge loaded with coal was heading up the Seine, passing the beautifully carved stone of the Pont des Arts and a boy waving from the bridge. As the barge went by the Tuileries and grew smaller in the distance, with the river as gray as the bare trees except for the trails of foam the barge cut into the water, he finally made up his mind and bought the tickets. The plane departed at six. Julian had skipped breakfast, so he found a table outside at Café de la Paix. The opera house was up the street. With its colonnades and arches and gold sculptures on the roof and greenish-blue dome, it looked as though it had been built so the angels would have a place to sing. He'd miss Paris if things didn't work out, but it was unavoidable if he was going to be happy. His *café crème* was cold, and he didn't eat his *pain au chocolat*. It was almost noon when Julian got back to Place de l'Estrapade. Kendall was on a bench in the square reading *Le Monde*.

"I was getting nervous," she said, folding up the newspaper. "Everything okay?"

He sat and handed her a TWA ticket envelope.

"I can't leave today."

"It's for a month from today. It'll give you a chance to get organized."

"Aren't you coming back?"

"If you'll marry me."

Julian was amazed how surprise, hurt, and anger all filled her hazel eyes at once.

"I have an engagement ring I bought at Tiffany's for you years ago. Fly to the States, I'll give it to you, and we can have Thanksgiving with your mother or with Fiona and Eddie. Then you can choose a date, we'll get married wherever you say, and come back here."

"Julian, why are you pressuring me?"

"I can't live in limbo anymore. I never had much of a family and didn't want one until I met you. Not seeing you would be painful—not having a family with you is worse."

"I'm not trying to hurt you."

"I know. I just made a choice for me. You make a choice for you."

"It's not that simple."

"I know that too. But for me it's necessary."

Her tone irritated and amused, Kendall said, "All this choice jazz. You sound like the existentialists. Where'd you pick that up?"

Julian, wanting to end the discussion, kissed her and quipped, "In a café."

# Chapter 53

A week after Julian and Simon boarded their flight at Le Bourget, Kendall gave up her suite at the Trianon and rented the newly renovated three-bedroom that she planned to share as Julian's wife. The rooms were flooded with light from the windows facing Place de l'Estrapade on one side and Rue Lhomond on the other. Marcel had the workmen bring up the couch, bed, and armoire that Julian had given her when he cleared out his things downstairs, and in the *salon* there was a window seat, which a minute after Kendall unpacked was her favorite spot in the apartment. Autumn was flirting with winter, but Kendall raised the window because the air—cold and bright and blue—was seasoned with the aromas of the *spécialités de la maison* cooking in the bistros.

"Wife," Kendall said.

The word had an unpleasant ring to it. Exhausted, frustrated, someone destined to nag her husband and children. Kendall preferred the French word *femme*, which meant "woman" but was also used for "wife." So there was no change. You're a woman, then you're a wife, and nothing's different. Kendall laughed and uncorked a bottle of Beaujolais. *Merde*. A crock of *merde*. A large crock, maybe the largest crock of shit ever invented. It changes everything. Rearranges who you are and who you will be.

Yet Kendall intended to marry Julian. She loved him. Since he'd been gone, she ached for him and thought about all his qualities that she adored, cycling through handsome, smart, generous, protective, and that she couldn't get enough of him in bed. This last one was tricky. With other men it was easy; afterward, a tension was gone, and if her partners had any complaints, they could go elsewhere. With Julian, though, she wanted to please him, wanted to obliterate every strip of flesh that separated him from her, wanted to drag him with her into that shimmering, tranquil, bottomless darkness, and when they were done she felt as though a star had burned out in the sky.

That was her thinking as she drank her glass of wine. She would change the departure date on her ticket to the day after tomorrow and surprise Julian by taking a cab from the airport to South Orange. She could picture his expression when he saw her, that curious pairing of manly calm and boyish glee, and how happiness seemed to deepen the blue of his eyes. They would make love and walk to Gruning's for ice cream and make love again, and the next evening they could go out with Fiona and Eddie, draft them as their matron of honor and best man over prime rib at the Tavern, and finalize the details of their wedding.

Kendall poured herself a second glass of Beaujolais, but after a sip she set it on the floor. She had started wondering if Julian would keep his promise to live in Paris if she married him. Why wouldn't he? Lots of reasons, beginning with New Jersey was his natural habitat and after a while in Paris he'd end up as miserable as a lion in a zoo. That wasn't what scared her, though: it was that if he chose to go home, would she be able to live without him? Or would she miss him with the same dull, joy-sapping ache as she felt missing him now?

Perhaps she was being silly. She got up and dug through one of her boxes and retrieved a copy of her first book, *Double Lives*. She flipped through the pages, remembering her days shooting in Harlem; her desperation to make a name for herself as an artist and her shock when Léo Sapir offered her a show at his gallery. She recalled how the publishers, Ada and Aaron Robbins, came, and Ada bought her *Little Girl & the Rainbow* for her office wall, telling her that she had once been that girl, and at lunch a week later they'd offered her a contract for a book. It had all happened so fast, and so long ago.

Back then, Kendall had considered the double exposure a self-portrait, and now she looked at the photograph in her book with the same sense of recognition—the window of the five-and-dime, and the little girl with pigtails and the faded dress gazing at the dolls from *The Wizard of Oz* under the papier-mâché rainbow. It wasn't the image of a child wishing to own a doll that caught Kendall's attention. It was the other image, the ghostly image in which the girl appears far older, with that bitter look of disappointment on her face because she understands that cuddling a doll in her arms or traveling over the rainbow will not satisfy her—that this longing beyond longing was the essence of who she was and to renounce it was to become someone she didn't want to be.

This, Kendall realized, was her dilemma—her fear that the yearning at the center of her, a yearning that had been with her forever, would die if she married Julian, and she would cease to be an artist. Taking photographs, capturing glimpses of the life around her, was the one thing that she needed more than him, and to lose it would be to lose herself.

Kendall wanted to cry, but she couldn't, so there was no relief from her sadness, just a terrible pressure behind her eyes as she took a pad and fountain pen from her satchel:

> *My Dearest Julian: I think I have loved you ever since I saw you at my mother's dinner party so many years ago. I'm sitting here wishing that I was someone else, someone who would not have to write this note. I'm honored beyond words that you want to marry me. But I can't marry anyone and remain who I am. I can love you, though, love you always, love you for the rest of a life that I can scarcely imagine without you.*

That was all she had the strength to write. Maybe she would add more in the morning, an apology, a clearer explanation. Then she would seal the letter in an envelope with her plane ticket and mail it to Julian.

The air was too cold now to keep the window open, and Kendall closed it and gazed down at the square, where the benches were empty and leaves floated on the dark water of the fountain.

# Part VI

# Chapter 54

Four years. Over four years since Julian had heard from Kendall. It had been too long and, he discovered one morning, not long enough.

"Hello, Julian?"

He lay in bed with the phone in his hand and tom-toms beating queasy rhythms in his head. Last evening, he'd had dinner at the Forge with a guy raising capital to build the world's swankiest hotel on Miami Beach. The guy had a flair for ordering cognac—a blessing at night, a curse in the morning.

"Julian, it's Kendall."

He was tempted to hang up except he missed hearing her voice— the muted southern melody, the sharp edges, the intelligence, the whispers and sighs.

"Hi," he said. "Where are you?"

"Lovewood. I called Fiona. She told me you were staying at the Saxony."

"That woman runs her own CIA."

"Don't be mad."

"At Fiona or you?"

Kendall laughed, a soft, doleful sound. "I meant Fiona, but—"

"I'm not mad." That was true in Fiona's case. He had supper with her and Eddie twice a week, both of them pushing him to find a wife, but mostly Fiona, who said, "It'll be a snap. You're the most eligible yid in New Jersey and the state's got more temples than Israel." Julian dated and nothing lasted. His anger at Kendall had melted away, yet he still had difficulty thinking of her without sorrow, without asking himself if there was something he could've done to make it work out, and his inability to answer that question irked him.

"You're down here for a while?"

Julian heard it in her tone: she had a request, and he imagined replying—*You're on your own, kiddo.* Even as he formulated that petty riposte, Julian knew that the words would never come out of his mouth. Love erodes or hides or curdles to rage, but it doesn't go away. It etches itself into your heart, permeates the muscle, survives in the blood.

"Until this afternoon. My plane's at three thirty."

"Could—could you take a ride to Lovewood before the airport?"

"What's wrong?"

"Mama's sick."

"I'm—"

"She's dying."

His anger, his sorrow, an urge to see her, another urge to take an earlier flight home battled inside him. "I'll be there by eleven."

"I'll meet you by grandpa's statue. And Julian—thank you."

✳

Garland Wakefield sat on the yellow-and-white poppy-print couch in the parlor with her heart, kidneys, and eyesight failing, the result of her being too busy to watch her diet, test her blood sugar with a lancet, and inject herself with insulin. Even though Garland hadn't been to her office since she'd fainted behind her desk on Christmas Day, every morning she demanded that her nurse help her hot-comb her white hair into a bob and dress for work. Then she'd sit on the couch until the nurse helped her back upstairs for her nap.

Kendall said, "I made some tea for you."

"You can't drink tea without sugar—it'll kill you. And if you're done talking to your boyfriend, can we talk?"

"Julian's not—"

"Diabetes doesn't make you deaf. I could hear you in the kitchen."

Kendall pulled the cane-backed recliner close to the couch so her mother could see her.

Garland said, "I've hired a dean from Fisk and another from Spellman to run the college. Two men to take the job of one woman—that should about do. But you're on the board now, and you have to attend those meetings twice a year."

"I will."

"The board's got distinguished folks from Afro-American Insurance, the Negro Business League, the United Negro College Fund, the NAACP. You better read those financial statements or you won't be able to tell pig slop from pizza."

"Yes, Mama."

"If I had my way, you'd give up your hobby—"

"My hobby?" Kendall was looking at the wicker table beside the couch, where Garland had arranged her oeuvre between bookends. She even had her latest, *Paris in the Dark*, a pictorial guide to postwar nightlife.

"Don't go arguing semantics—it puts wax in my ears. All's I'm saying is you should quit scurrying around like a sprayed roach and come home like your friend Simon."

Garland had saved issues of the *Courier* for Kendall. Simon and his new wife were the toast of Negro society in Pittsburgh, and Simon had become the executive editor of the newspaper. Kendall didn't envy Simon's life, but she was stung that her mother would show her the papers, another of Garland's not-too-subtle critiques of her choices. Kendall almost retaliated by telling her about Simon and Thayer and how Julian had saved Simon. She chose not to because ever since arriving from Paris, Kendall had begun to mourn the only mother that she would ever have. One of them had to end their war and Garland didn't seem inclined to declare a truce.

"All's I mean," Garland said, "is if you were here, I could teach you about running a college."

"That would be nice."

In her more resentful and grief-laden moments, Kendall believed that she'd learned the lessons her mother had intended to teach her: trust no one; dedicate your life to your work; embrace your loneliness as a badge of honor, as unassailable evidence that you are your own woman, that you belong to no one but yourself.

"And this is important," Garland said. "My will states that you are the one person who can sell any Wakefield property. I don't want you to, but who knows what'll happen without me as president. If you have to sell some, not one acre to Jarvis Scales. You hear?"

"I hear."

"Not a blade of grass to any Scales."

Garland stared across the parlor. She didn't appear to be seeing anything. As if she were in her casket, Kendall thought, and grief tied a knot in her stomach.

"Your grandfather didn't want me to fetch and carry for white folks."

"Grandpa was born a slave. Why would he want his daughter to work for his former masters?"

"No, that wasn't it. He didn't want me doing for others because it would've interfered with my doing for him."

Garland's eyes were wet. Kendall sat next to her on the couch.

"Who told him to send my mother away?"

Kendall held one of Garland's hands in both of hers.

"You think I wanted to grow up without my mother? Or marry your father? I hardly knew the man. But Ezekiel Kendall, he say, 'Jump,' I say, 'How high, Daddy?' I did everything he ask; you do nothing I say. Don't hardly seem fair."

"I—"

"Who made you so damn free?"

"You did, Mama."

Garland rested her head on Kendall's shoulder. "Can't swear I did it on purpose."

※

Julian and the bronze likeness of Ezekiel Kendall watched the students cross the campus as if gliding on the sunlit wind, and Julian wondered if Ezekiel felt as old as he did. His surrealistic musing, so out of character for Julian, was a welcome distraction from his nervousness about seeing the statue's granddaughter walk toward them. Her curves seemed more lush, and Julian pondered how it was that Kendall could transform a plain, shell-pink cotton dress into a ball gown simply by wearing it.

"You're staring," Kendall said with a weak grin, a reference to their old game.

"Always."

They looked at each other, uncomfortably, for neither of them knew the appropriate move. Kendall solved the dilemma with French cheek kisses.

"How's your mom?"

"Napping."

"No, I—"

"Doc Franklin says a day, a week, or a month."

They strolled past the chapel, looking at the kids walking with books under their arms.

"How'd you and Abe do with the Kefauver Committee?" For over a year, Senator Estes Kefauver had investigated organized crime. The hearings were televised, and if you didn't own a TV, you could watch them for free in movie theaters. Abe had been asked about bootlegging and his reputation as the "Al Capone of New Jersey." He'd been polite and charming and lied about his current gambling interests, and after he was excused, Julian knew that the government wouldn't stop hunting Abe.

"They covered the hearings in Paris?"

"In the *Trib*."

"Jesus."

"Bad?"

"They say over thirty million people watched. My name kept coming up—if I ever have kids, my name'll be a curse to them—but the committee has nothing on me or I would've had to testify."

"Give Abe my regards."

"I will." Julian had been wondering why Kendall had phoned him.

He doubted she wanted to renew their relationship, and even if she did, he wasn't eager for her to hurt him again. Julian had come to Lovewood in a taxi, which he was paying to wait by the front gate, and if Kendall wasn't going to tell him why he was here, he was content to chitchat until he had to leave for the airport. He said, "*Paris in the Dark* was great."

"Thanks. With all the Americans coming over, it's outsold my other three books combined."

"The photos of Dans le Vent were terrific. So it worked out for Isabella?"

"It has. And Marcel. Otis plays the club once in a while, but he's a big deal now. His quartet was part of a show at the Salle Pleyel. Three thousand people were there, and after Otis did two encores, the audience shouted for more."

They were going up a path through scrub brush toward the sand dunes and the ocean. Julian felt older than he had standing with Ezekiel. Kendall had taken him up here to this private spot after he'd bought her the Leica. Before Greenwich Village and Paris. Before the war. Before everything. When Julian and Kendall were young.

"I sold some photographs to *Life*," Kendall said. "Of families around Saigon. I went to see how they're coping with the fighting."

"Congratulations." What about our family, Julian thought angrily, the family we'll never have? He became even angrier at the top of the path. Off to their right was the whitewashed shed, the darkroom that Simon had built. Julian had no interest in seeing it again and decided that he was done with chitchat. "Kendall, why'd you call me?"

She stood with her back against a palm tree, looking past him. "I told myself I wanted to say I was sorry. Except I did that already. It was selfish dragging you up here. Maybe I called because I've been disappointing my mother forever and now that I'm going to lose her, I'll never be the daughter she wanted. I've been thinking that's what I was meant to do. Disappoint people and lose them. And maybe I called because . . . I don't know why. I just needed to see you."

She met his eyes, and there was such an agonized look on her face that he was frightened for her. It was an agony beyond sadness, more terrible, like flaws in a diamond, deep and irreparable. She whispered to him, and Julian couldn't believe what he heard.

"Please," she said.

Her agony was the last thing Julian saw before she kissed him and he closed his eyes. Had either of them spoken as they sank to the sand, they would've asked themselves what the hell they were doing. But they were too eager for a reprieve from the present, too willing to believe that eros unbound was a curative for regret and loss, all the while knowing as they labored that it was a temporary journey, illogical and insufficient, which didn't stop either of them, and when Julian heard Kendall cry out, he let himself go, feeling so empty, he wondered if anything could ever fill him again.

They opened their eyes, their breathing slowed, and Julian stood and helped her up. They straightened their clothes without looking at each other. Kendall took his hand, and they walked to campus. Two students, a couple also holding hands, were startled by the sight of them and performed a comical double take.

"Hi," Kendall said, and giggled as the couple hurried on toward the library.

"They're gonna tell on us."

"We're too old to care."

They went up Garland's driveway to the steps of the wraparound porch.

"What did we do?" Kendall asked.

"Nothing smart."

"I love you and feel like I should apologize to you for that."

"Apology accepted."

"It was kind of you to come."

"You gonna be okay?"

"We both will, won't we?"

"We will."

They hugged and Julian watched her climb the steps. At the door, she smiled at him, a smile both heartrending and strangely hopeful, then she entered the house and the door closed.

※

It was dark and cold when Julian retrieved his Chrysler from the lot at Newark Airport. His visit with Kendall had kept him company on the flight, yet by the time he reached South Orange Village, Julian couldn't face being alone in his apartment and continued past his building and along Meadowland Park. In the moonlight, a skater was spinning in circles on the duck pond, and Julian turned and drove up and down the streets, enjoying the glimmer of the gas lamps on the snow and the lights glowing in the houses. He remembered his father confessing that he hadn't been designed for marriage. Perhaps this also applied to Kendall, but Julian rejected this view of himself, even though he was nearing forty and the only woman he'd ever wanted to marry didn't want to marry anyone. He pulled up to a stop sign. Through a living room window to his left was a cabinet television, and on-screen Lucille Ball was slow dancing with Desi Arnaz. A man in a shirt and tie was behind the window with a little boy in his arms. The boy was wearing Dr. Denton pajamas. The man tossed him up and caught him. They were both laughing. When they disappeared from the window, Julian promised himself that he would never be lonely again.

# Chapter 55

Julian met Clare Coddington while she was perched on a striped banquette at El Morocco, a green-eyed brunette with an aristocratic face, long, lovely legs, and an insouciant manner that had been refined over the centuries since her ancestors had sailed to the New World on the *Mayflower*. Clare, who resided with her parents in Westport, Connecticut, was in New York with two girlfriends for a night on the town. Julian bought the ladies a round of whiskey sours before inviting them to the Colony for dinner and a peek at high society, and after the soft-shell crabs, chicken hash, and pie à la mode, he took them over to Toots's saloon for a nightcap. Jackie Gleason and Frank Sinatra were drinking each other under a table in back, and they greeted Julian as if he had just come home from the war.

"Interesting friends you have there," Clare commented, with more irony than amusement.

Even in the stodgy circles of Westport, the connection between erstwhile bootleggers and entertainers was well-known, and frankly, Clare preferred the Colony with its flannel-and-taffeta covey of Biddles, Vanderbilts, and Whitneys, but she was smitten with Julian: his immaculate manners and tailoring, his blue eyes and free way with a buck. The Coddington clan, after producing generations of shipping magnates and investment bankers, had started churning out archeologists and museum docents at an alarming rate, presenting Clare with the challenge of satisfying her impeccable taste in clothing, vacations, and real estate with an anemic financial legacy.

They had been dating for months before Julian introduced her to

Fiona and Eddie at Peter Luger's in Brooklyn. The steaks were rare, the wine robust, and the most interesting interchange went as follows:

Clare said to Fiona, "Julian tells me you go to Mass every day."

"I like the exercise."

"At Mass?"

"I walk to church."

The next afternoon, when Julian went to the O'Rourkes to watch a Yankees–Indians game, Eddie commented, "Cute girl."

Fiona brought a tray of frankfurters, potato chips, and beer into the den, and Julian asked her, "Do you have an opinion?"

Eddie started laughing. "Does the pope got a rosary?"

Fiona, more noted for her unvarnished judgments than her sensitivity, outdid herself by replying, "I liked Kendall better."

So did Julian, who still pined for her in a private chamber of his heart. "But what do you think of Clare?"

"I think when a man decides to get married, the first woman who wants him, gets him."

"Worked for me," Eddie said, and to reward her husband for that revelation, Fiona gave Julian his food and beer and took Eddie's back to the kitchen.

✳

Julian married Clare on the lawn of the Coddingtons' ramshackle waterfront Victorian. The one surprise was that the ceremony was conducted by a Reform rabbi who dressed like a golf pro, Clare revealing to Julian the day before their wedding that she had studied with the rabbi for months to convert. Julian was touched by her effort and didn't tell her that he could've cared less about her religion. Her parents appeared to care, their shock visible in their tight-lipped smiles. Generations of rigorous Yankee breeding demanded that they remain silent, and for their sake Julian was glad that the rabbi kept the Hebrew to a minimum, preferring to quote most of the lyrics from the hit song "Some Enchanted Evening."

Clare and Julian honeymooned in the Cayman Islands, and the placid rhythms of that sun-soaked fortnight carried over into their

marriage. They were tender toward each other, if not passion-
ate and Clare fussed over him, making sure that he ate balanced
meals and went to bed at a decent hour. Julian appreciated her solicit-
ousness and got a kick out of watching her spend his money, which
hadn't brought him any pleasure in years. Clare would wake up in the
morning and say, "Let's get a sable coat and take it out for a walk," and
off they'd go. Her greatest joy was the construction of their home in
Newstead, and though Julian was skeptical about the frenzied architect from Harvard she'd hired, Clare assured him, "With the redwood-
and-glass walls we'll feel like we're living outdoors."

Paying over a hundred grand to go camping didn't seem worth it
to Julian. Yet Clare was ecstatic, and six weeks after they moved in,
their daughter, Holly, was born via caesarean and with the news that
Clare wouldn't be able to have more children. Their disappointment
was outweighed by their delight in Holly, who had Julian's cleft chin
and blue eyes. Every morning Julian fed and bathed his daughter and,
in the afternoons, while Clare made the rounds at Saks and Lord &
Taylor, he wheeled Holly's carriage through the village, introducing
her early and often to Gruning's ice cream. As she grew older, Julian
took her to Yankee Stadium for baseball and football games, and to
his business meetings. Holly was seated beside him in a booth at Ann's
Clam Bar when he arranged to buy a tract in Short Hills that would
become the site of an office park; she sat on his lap in the great room
while politicos begged for campaign cash; and because Holly loved
the ocean, Julian brought her when he visited Abe at his place in Deal,
which amused Clare, who joked that Holly would be the only first
grader with an FBI file.

Julian also taught Holly to play Monopoly, viewing it as a chance to
introduce her to the real-estate market. His reason for transforming a
board game into a seminar was that Julian wanted Holly to be capable
of overseeing her inheritance without relying on some schmuck of a
son-in-law he might not live to meet. So as father and daughter rolled
the dice and moved their pieces—the top hat for Julian, the Scottish
terrier for Holly—Julian held forth on the importance of harboring
your capital while understanding that you had to invest to win.

"Your real job," he said, "is to calculate risk versus reward."

"Daddy, Risk is another game. This is Monopoly."

Julian decided to try again in six months, and for now he was proud that Holly examined the deeds for the rental returns and building costs before buying a property.

In the midst of this familial comfort, Julian held on to his sadness about Kendall. It was his last remaining attachment to her, and to relinquish it would be to lose her forever, which he doubted that he could bear. Clare's kindness assuaged these feelings, but it was Holly who helped most of all by making the future more important to him than the past. Still, Julian suffered whenever he was reminded of Kendall. Her pictures in *Life* of the writer Vladimir Nabokov with his butterfly net in Italy. A new book on the counter at the South Orange Library, *All God's Children*, photographs of the tenant-farmer families of Lovewood with a dedication to the memory of her mother. A profile in the Sunday *Times* before a retrospective of her work opened at the Léo Sapir Gallery. The piece had been written by the author James Baldwin, a friend of Kendall's from Paris who was no stranger to converting racial turmoil into art. Baldwin asked her if she could identify a moment when she realized that she was destined to become an artist.

"The afternoon they lynched my boyfriend," Kendall said.

Julian wanted to drive to the gallery and talk to her. Instead, he phoned Eddie and ran the proposed trip by him.

"It'll be fun seeing Holly every other weekend, won't it?" Eddie said, which brought Julian to his senses.

From the mid-1950s on, Julian's biggest worry was Abe. His blood pressure was high, he had chest pains, and the government was hounding him about his tax returns, predictably because they were about as realistic as Holly's favorite novel, *Alice's Adventures in Wonderland*. Abe was charged with tax evasion, but the trial ended in a hung jury. One afternoon he came to Julian's office and, out of nowhere, said, "Ya know bribery's been a New Jersey tradition for almost three hundred years. Lord Cornbury, the first royal governor, muscled into land disputes so he could take bribes from both sides. There'd be a statue of Cornbury in Trenton if he hadn't been a transvestite."

Abe was a history buff, so Julian didn't give his mentioning Cornbury any thought until one evening—Wednesday, February 25, 1959, to be exact—when Abe stopped by his house and asked him to come outside, his usual request whenever he wanted to talk business, since you never knew where the FBI had installed its bugs.

"The feds think I bribed a juror or two," he said.

In the light of the pendant lamp above the door, Julian saw Abe shivering in his fedora and topcoat. Julian felt sick but tried to sound optimistic. "You'll beat it. Anything I can do?"

"So you listened to me. When I said you gotta find a way to live."

"I did."

Abe was studying Julian as if trying to memorize his face.

Julian said, "Let's go in for a drink."

"I gotta get home, boychick."

More often than not, Abe kissed him on the cheek when he said good-bye. Now he turned and walked to his car. In the morning, Eddie called. "Cop I know in West Orange got in touch. Abe hung himself."

Julian's feeling of betrayal was overpowering, and it stayed with him at Apter's funeral home in Newark and graveside at the B'nai Abraham cemetery out on Route 22. He watched Abe's wife, stepson, and daughter crying, and Julian became so furious that he imagined popping the lid on Abe's casket and shooting him.

*Why didn't you say something?*

Reporters showed up to talk off the record, asking if Longy's death had been a hit. Julian felt like coldcocking them. There was no percentage in pissing off journalists, so he politely said no, it wasn't a hit, fifty-four-year-olds sometimes get depressed. What infuriated Julian was the root of Abe's depression, which could have been avoided if he'd taken Julian's advice and renounced his underworld perquisites. But Abe liked that edge. And he was greedy: he also wanted to be admired by that faceless mass of Americans who haunt anyone pursuing, overtly or covertly, adoration, the seductive warmth of distant stars. During the Kefauver hearings, Mr. and Mrs. America met Longy Zwillman, the repentant ex-bootlegger, astute businessman, philanthropist, suburban dad, and husband. Yes, Abe was all those things, but once the government tossed him in prison for bribery, he'd be nothing but a common hood.

During that year, among the most anguished in Julian's life, he mourned for Abe and felt exposed, endangered, as if some protective shell had been peeled away from him. More than ever, he longed to talk with Kendall, to be in her presence, to feel safe again, and in retrospect the only good thing Julian could say about the year was that he remained blissfully unaware that soon enough it would all get much worse.

# Chapter 56

SOUTH ORANGE, NEW JERSEY
SEPTEMBER 7, 1964

On Labor Day, Julian made Holly and Clare pancakes and bacon for breakfast, and they swam and splashed in the pool until noon. After lunch, Julian and Holly began playing Monopoly. The game was still in progress at five o'clock when Holly asked if they could get pizza burgers and onion rings from Don's Drive-In. Julian was beat, but Don's was only a ten-minute ride. As he stood, Clare said, "You rest, sweetheart. Holly and I'll get takeout."

Before leaving, Holly looked at Julian's hotels on pricey Boardwalk and Park Place and frowned. "Daddy, you're lucky."

He knelt down to hug her, smelling the chlorine in her hair and the Coppertone suntan lotion that Clare had rubbed on her face.

"Luckiest man in the world."

Julian was napping on the couch in the great room when the doorbell woke him up. Officer Nelligan, a husky, moonfaced South Orange cop, was outside. Julian had met him once. He was Fiona's third or fourth cousin, and seeing him, Julian figured Eddie was in a jam.

"What's cooking, Nellie?"

"Hello, Mr. Rose. Your wife . . . your wife was turning on South Orange Avenue and this drunk sonovabitch, he ran the light . . ."

"And?" Julian knew the answer, but asking it provided him with a few precious seconds of hope.

"The drunk was dead at the scene. The Rescue Squad got Mrs.

Rose and your daughter into the ambulances, but . . . I'm real sorry, Mr. Rose . . . They didn't make it."

❄

Nellie drove Julian to East Orange General. In the emergency room, a nurse led Julian to an alcove, screened off from the ER by a curtain, and left him alone. Clare and Holly were on gurneys with sheets pulled up to their chins. Julian felt as if he were gazing down at them from the top of a hill. Clare must have been thrown against the windshield. Her face, bruised and caked with blood, looked as though someone had smashed her reflection in a mirror. She would have been appalled by her appearance. Julian kissed her and covered her face with the sheet.

Holly's face was unmarked, except for the purplish blotch along her eyebrows, but her head lolled to the side like one of her rag dolls. Julian was dizzy. A pink butterfly barrette held his daughter's long, brown sun-streaked hair behind her left ear. The other barrette was missing, giving her that peekaboo look from the 1940s. Holly hated her hair falling in her eyes. Julian combed his fingers through his daughter's heavy, silky hair, searching for the barrette. It was under her head. Julian slid it in place. He couldn't close the clasp under the plastic butterfly. The clasp was bent. He tried to straighten it. His hands were shaking.

Officer Nelligan drew back the curtain.

"What's wrong?" Julian asked.

"You were yelling, Mr. Rose."

Julian hadn't heard a sound. "I can't fix this thing."

The policeman unbent the clasp, gave the barrette to Julian, walked out, and closed the curtain. Julian clipped the butterfly in his daughter's hair, then pressed his face to Holly's cheek and inhaled the fragrance of pool water and suntan lotion. He was only able to leave the hospital by telling himself that he would see Clare and Holly again at the funeral home.

Nellie must have contacted Eddie and Fiona, because when he brought Julian to his house, they were waiting for him. Julian drank a fifth of Jameson with them, but the whiskey didn't numb his aston-ishment that emptiness could come packaged with such pain; or stop him from thinking that if he'd gone to Don's, his wife and daughter would be alive; or prevent him from lying on the carpeting in Holly's room and sobbing into her pillow until, toward dawn, he fell asleep.

The service at Apter's was a dim patch in Julian's memory, but he never forgot the ride to the B'nai Abraham cemetery—the two hearses getting stuck for twenty minutes on Route 22 behind a truck from Channel Lumber, and the cloudless blue sky glossy with sun-light, as if the universe was unaware that Julian was burying his wife and daughter. He had arranged for them to be buried in a granite mausoleum not far from Abe's grave. He liked that Abe was nearby to keep an eye on them, and Julian couldn't stand the notion of dropping Clare and Holly into the ground. He didn't want them to be cold in winter.

During the shiva, visitors streamed through Julian's house, offering condolences and eating and drinking. Clare's parents were gone, and her sister in Seattle, whom Julian hadn't seen since their wedding, sent flowers because she couldn't get there for the funeral. The great room smelled of smoked meats and fish and sour pickles. Julian handled the crowd well and didn't fall apart until the second evening, when Holly's friends from Newstead School brought him pictures they had done with colored pencils of themselves with his daughter. Julian smiled at the girls and complimented their drawings. Once they were gone, he locked himself in the master bath, crying and kneeling over his toilet until nothing was left in his stomach to come up.

Then Julian was alone with his guilt, and he could feel it devour-ing his heart like termites. Had someone suggested to him that the crash had been a tragic coincidence, he would have shaken his head at such stupidity and replied, "A coincidence is just a situation you don't understand yet."

Julian did understand this situation: it was punishment. He could tell himself any story he pleased about how he'd tried to talk Abe into going straight, it didn't alter the fact that the seeds of his wealth had come from the same illegal liquor as Abe's. Now God had handed him the bill for the bootlegging, the deals with crooked pols and cops, the handiwork that went with persuading uncooperative buyers and subduing competitors, and last but not least, for shooting Willy in the Ardennes.

Julian wasn't one to sit by and do nothing, yet that was his most hellish discovery about grief: it wasn't the twin of sorrow but an acidic brew of fear and helplessness. Being an organized man, he battled back by adhering to a schedule, visiting Clare and Holly in their mausoleum on weekdays and then going to Gruning's for ice cream and to watch the schoolkids and allow himself to dream that Holly was alive.

He had been at the cemetery on that snowy December afternoon he'd met Kendall's son, Bobby, outside Gruning's. Clare was interred in the top right corner, and Julian stared at the brass marker on the crypt below her.

HOLLY ALICE ROSE

ANGEL IN ETERNITY

JULY 2, 1954–SEPTEMBER 7, 1964

Glancing heavenward, Julian hoped to hear any word that would alleviate his grief or lessen his guilt, but the sky was silent, and the snowflakes melted on this face.

He returned to the cemetery less frequently once Bobby began living with him. The boy's appearance was another coincidence. Not that it healed him, but it made his days bearable again, and he remembered that wintry afternoon when it occurred to him that somehow Clare and Holly and Kendall must have interceded on his behalf, and Julian pressed his lips to the icy marker and thanked them, and God, for another chance.

# PART VII

# Chapter 57

Miss Kozlowski, the vice principal of South Orange Junior High, was a short-haired bottle blonde in her forties with all the charm of a prison guard. Bobby and Julian were seated on the other side of her desk as she scoured Bobby's records. "His birthday puts him in seventh grade. But public education in the South—we may have to start him in grammar school."

Julian, his anger bubbling up, doubted that she would've made the same observation about a white child. He said, "Isn't it best to keep Bobby with kids his own age?"

"Not if he's too far behind. Fortunately, we don't begin foreign language until eighth grade."

"Pardon me, ma'am," Bobby said. "I speak French. I can read and write it too. And I learned algebra at my last school."

Her look of skepticism deepened the meshwork of creases across her cheeks. Controlling himself, Julian said, "You got some tests you can give him?"

"I suppose. It'll take a couple hours. Leave him with me and come back."

Julian walked across South Orange Avenue to Bun 'N' Burger and called Eddie from a pay phone. Eddie was semiretired—he only undertook the occasional collection job to stay in shape—and most of his money came from his real-estate partnerships with Julian. He lived on the other side of the village, in a white-brick colonial on

Radel Terrace, a short walk from Our Lady of Sorrows, where Fiona went daily to beseech the Father, Son, and Holy Ghost to send her a husband who wasn't a goddamn lunatic.

"Wanna go to Alex Eng's at twelve thirty?" Julian asked. "You can meet my son."

"Your who?"

Julian spent a buck fifty in nickels and dimes to tell him the story.

Eddie said, "It's hard to imagine Kendall being gone. She was so . . . Jesus. And you're not sure Bobby's yours?"

"The birth certificate says Otis."

"Yeah? What're the odds on that?"

"Not good. But possible."

"Does the time fit? With you and Kendall?"

"Nine months."

"If you both had blood tests, you'd find out if you could be his dad."

"He's a real nice kid."

Eddie sighed. "You wouldn't expect nothing else. Not from the gal who raised him."

❋

Miss Kozlowski was behind her desk while Bobby spoke French with a wide-eyed young woman in an off-the-shoulder, bell-sleeved dress that appeared to have been designed to keep the boys paying attention in class. The vice principal introduced her as Miss Zellner.

"Bobby's beyond our best students here," Miss Zellner said to Julian, "but I have a seventh-grade homeroom, and if Bobby's assigned to me and you bring him early, I'll practice with him and give him books to read."

"That's kind of you," Julian said and, after she was gone, asked the vice principal how Bobby had done on the tests.

"A hundred on the math and science, and on social studies a ninety-four."

Julian said, "I guess we'll have to work on the social studies."

❋

Eddie hadn't arrived at Alex Eng's, so Bobby and Julian took a booth, drinking tea and eating crunchy noodles dipped in duck sauce.

"Why'd that lady think I'd flunk those tests?" Bobby asked. "Because I'm Negro? Mom told me about people like that. She said it can be an advantage, because anything you can do seems ten times better."

"Sounds about right."

"She told me you weren't that way."

Julian loved hearing Kendall's voice again—if only through her son.

"What're we eatin', fellas?" Eddie asked, sliding in next to Bobby. Eddie's red hair had gone gray, but the remnants of boyishness, his freckles and wise-guy grin, had survived. He extended his hand to Bobby. "Put it there."

"Yes, sir," Bobby said, shaking Eddie's hand.

"Lose the 'sir.' You don't call Julian 'sir,' do ya?"

"I call him Mr. Rose. That's what my mom said his name was."

"Okay, but I'm your uncle Eddie. Got it?"

"Yes, Uncle Eddie."

"Thatta boy. Whatta ya want for Christmas?"

Julian had seen this routine before with his daughter: Holly once mentioned that she liked the TV show *My Friend Flicka*, and Eddie would've bought her a pony if Julian hadn't stopped him. Eddie and Fiona had no children, and Julian knew that Eddie paid the tuition for some students who went to school at Our Lady of Sorrows and helped out their folks at Christmas. Maybe it was because Eddie's father had died before he was born and he grew up with a flat-broke mother. Or penance for all the guys he'd put in the ground.

Bobby said, "My mom told me Mr. Rose is Jewish, and Jews don't celebrate Christmas."

"I'm bettin' Mr. Rose's gonna make an exception for you."

※

When they left the restaurant, snow was falling, and the lights strung across South Orange Avenue shone like rainbows.

Eddie said, "Bobby, there's a store across the street. Got model cars and train sets. Go see if you like anything."

They watched Bobby cross. Eddie said, "He's built like you. Thinner, but he's gonna be tall. Otis was pocket-sized."

"I wish I knew where Otis was. Bobby says Kendall told him his father died in Korea. That's not true. Maybe Otis is alive."

Eddie said, "Not with the dope fiends he ran with. But I wish he was. He was always looking forward to something. And he could play the piano."

"His old man died not long after Derrick. It was in the papers."

"His ma could still be in Harlem. I could ask around."

"That poor woman's been through enough."

Eddie asked, "If Bobby's yours, why'd you think Kendall didn't give him your name?"

"She hated taking anything from me. And I told her that I wouldn't want a son burdened with my name. This was right after the Kefauver Hearings, and the Senate had Abe and half the Mob on TV. My name came up and reporters called me about it for years. With Holly I figured she'd get married, and her name would change. But my son—he'd be marked forever."

Tire chains clinked against the avenue, kicking up arcs of snow. "Does it matter? If Bobby's not yours?"

"Not a bit. He's a kid who needs help and—and he's all I have left of Kendall."

# Chapter 58

Julian and Bobby celebrated Christmas Eve at Fiona and Eddie's house. Fiona stuffed them with salmon, scalloped potatoes, and chocolate mint layer cake, and Eddie, who'd bought Bobby a Hot Wheels race-car set, raced Bobby for money and lost twenty bucks to him. Bobby was polite but acted as if he'd taken a vow of silence. At home, before bringing in the presents from the pool cabana, Julian checked to see if Bobby were sleeping. He wasn't. His desk lamp was on, and music played on the clock radio.

Julian sat on the bed, and Bobby said, "In Paris, on Christmas Eve, my mom used to take me caroling in the Latin Quarter with her friends. Then we'd have hot red wine and spice bread."

Julian remembered the fragrance of the *pain d'épices* that Kendall would bake in Greenwich Village, and he felt as sad as Bobby looked. After Bobby flopped over on his stomach, Julian rubbed his back before turning off the radio and the lamp.

In the morning, when Bobby came downstairs and saw his presents, he said, "Are they all for me?"

"All for you."

His haul included an Etch A Sketch, Slinky, Legos, a Nok-Hockey set, every one of the Hardy Boys books, the board games Risk, Life, Stratego, Clue, checkers, and chess; a stereo and stacks of records— alphabetically from the Beatles through the Temptations; a mountain of clothes; a three-speed Dunelt English Racer, and a Flexible Flyer sled.

"You wanna break in the sled?" Julian asked.

"Yeah. I learned how at the Parc des Buttes Chaumont."

Flood's Hill was next to South Orange Junior High. Dozens of grown-ups and children in colorful parkas and hats were sledding. As Bobby started down the slope, Julian noticed a group of teenagers with Flying Saucers. The teenagers sat on the aluminum platters and spun in circles to the bottom of the hill. Bobby was halfway down when his Flexible Flyer was broadsided by two spinning saucers that sent him rolling through the snow. When Bobby got up, two teenagers in Columbia High School football jackets were towering over him, holding their Flying Saucers and laughing. The huskier one said, "You oughtta watch where you're going."

"I was," Bobby said.

"Be careful, Hal," the other kid said. "He's a tough guy."

Behind them, Julian said, "Pardon me, fellas," and he pushed past them and snatched the Flying Saucer from Hal. "You oughtta ride this thing somewhere else."

"It's a free country," Hal replied.

"Don't believe it," Julian said, and bent the aluminum platter in half.

Hal and his friend, gaping at Julian, backed up the hill, and after flinging the Flying Saucer at them, Julian picked up the Flexible Flyer and put his arm around Bobby. As they walked, Bobby reached for the hand on his shoulder and held it.

"I'm here," Julian said.

"I know," Bobby replied.

# Chapter 59

By spring, after four months at South Orange Junior High, Bobby learned that it was no fun being the only Negro student in the most advanced section of the seventh grade. The school was ninety-five percent white, and Bobby didn't give his placement a second thought until a colored student, a ninth grader who held the record for most consecutive days in detention, saw Bobby at his gym locker and said, "Boy, you think your shit don't stink 'cause you be with those white brainiacs?"

Bobby didn't answer, but he was surprised the kid had spoken to him. The only people who appeared to know Bobby existed were his teachers, who said, "Excellent job," when they returned his homework and tests with As written across the paper.

In the cafeteria, nearly all the Negro students gathered at the same table, and no one of any color invited him to join their group. Bobby sat alone, trying—and failing—to soothe himself with memories of eating lunch with his mother at La Palette, where the waiters and the regulars knew them, and Bobby had a *croque-monsieur*—a grilled ham-and-cheese—and a cup of *chocolat chaud*, a perfect meal on those shining afternoons.

"You don't have to eat by yourself," Stevie Lerner said, sitting across from Bobby.

Stevie was in his homeroom. He was a chubby, chipmunk-cheeked boy with curly reddish-blond hair and braces, and owing to his habit of forgetting his homework and flunking tests, he was frequently summoned to the guidance office for conferences. Yet Stevie possessed an encyclopedic knowledge of sports statistics, and he was consulted by other boys to settle disputes about things like earned-run averages that Bobby had never heard of.

Stevie said, "You live near me. I saw you yesterday driving with that man who drops you off in the morning."

"Mr. Rose. He's my guardian."

Stevie nodded as if it were normal for kids in South Orange to have a guardian instead of a mom and dad. Bobby bit into the soggy bun and greasy patty that the cafeteria lady had claimed was a hamburger.

Stevie said, "You want to come over after school today? We can play stickball."

"I don't know how. I grew up in France."

"I'll teach you. And it's Friday, so you can eat dinner over."

"Okay," Bobby said, and the hamburger didn't taste so bad anymore.

❋

It was a mile-and-a-half walk uphill to Newstead. They stopped at Julian's first; Bobby wrote him a note and changed out of his school clothes into a hooded gray sweatshirt, blue jeans, and Converse high-tops. Stevie lived a few blocks away, next to a grammar school, in a ranch house with triangular glass walls. Mayella, a pear-shaped Negro woman in a white uniform, told them to sit in the kitchen, then stirred Nestlé Quik into glasses of milk and removed a tin sheet of oatmeal cookies from the oven.

As the boys ate and drank, Mayella squinted at Bobby. "Where you from?"

Stevie answered, "He's from Newstead."

Mayella said, "You is?"

"Yes, ma'am," Bobby said.

"Most the colored 'round heah, they be from Newark. Your people from Newark?"

"No, ma'am." On weekends, Bobby sometimes went to the Wee-quahic Diner in Newark with Julian and Uncle Eddie. On the ride down Lyons Avenue he'd noticed that the city had crowds of Negroes on the streets, and he wished that he could walk around there because it would be fun to visit someplace where people didn't gawk at him as if he were one of those weirdos on *The Munsters*.

※

Stevie and Bobby had been on the blacktop behind the grammar school for over an hour. Stevie was standing forty feet away pitching tennis balls toward a box chalked onto a brick wall. Bobby had been swinging away without success until Stevie said, "Move your hands up higher on the bat," and after choking up another two inches, Bobby smacked the ball over Stevie's head. Mighty pleased with himself, Bobby ran to Stevie, who held out his right hand, palm up. "Gimme five."

Bobby contemplated Stevie's palm, and Stevie lifted Bobby's right hand and brought it down on his. As they left the schoolyard, Stevie said, "Somebody in homeroom told me you're like one of the smartest kids in school."

"I don't know if I am."

"Wish I was. Or at least my parents do. You're lucky."

Bobby shrugged. He'd felt a lot luckier when his mother was alive.

※

Mrs. Lerner had reddish-blond hair done up like dandelion fluff. She was thin and drank a can of Fresca at the dining room table while everyone else ate. Mayella brought in the mashed potatoes, lima beans, and roast beef, and Mrs. Lerner urged Bobby to take more, as if he'd never sampled such exotic dishes. Mr. Lerner, who bore a striking resemblance to Fred Flintsone, said, "Bobby, you're in my son's class?"

Stevie said, "Dad, he's with the smart kids."

"You could be with the smart kids. If you put your nose in the grindstone."

Stevie stared at his plate. Mr. Lerner said, "Mayella tells me you're not from Newark?"

"Dad, he's from Paris."

Wistfully, Mrs. Lerner said, "I've always wanted to see Paris."

Mr. Lerner frowned at his wife and asked Bobby, "How'd you get to Newstead?"

Bobby answered that his parents had died, which produced a merciful gap of silence. Then he added, "My guardian's here. Julian Rose."

Bobby didn't understand why, but this information brought the interrogation to a close.

Dessert was apple pie and vanilla ice cream, and Stevie and Bobby were permitted to take their bowls to the den, where they watched *The Wild, Wild West*. When the show ended, Bobby thanked Mr. and Mrs. Lerner for dinner and walked home. He was on Glenview Road when a blue-and-white police car stopped alongside him with the driver's-side window down. The policeman behind the wheel said, "You lost, son?"

Bobby began to tremble. "No, sir."

The policeman, ordering Bobby to step back, got out of the car. "What's your name?"

"Bobby Wakefield."

"Where you going?"

Bobby recited his address. The policeman, broad-shouldered, his belly hanging over his belt buckle, peered at him. Bobby could hardly see his face under the bill of his cap, just that he was white. He remembered the Lovewood policeman, the mean one with the sunglasses, and Bobby felt like he was going to piss his pants.

"Why you shaking?" the policeman asked.

"Cold," Bobby replied. Then, recalling how Julian's name had stopped Mr. Lerner from grilling him, Bobby said, "Julian Rose is my guardian."

"No foolin', Julian Rose? You tell Mr. Rose, Officer Nelligan says hi."

Bobby sprinted home. Julian was reading a book in the great room. After telling him about the Lerners and Officer Nelligan, Bobby asked, "How come they act different when they hear your name?"

"I've been in town for thirty years."

Bobby sensed that Julian wasn't telling him the whole truth and that asking him another question wouldn't help.

In the morning, Julian told Bobby that he had business in Orchard

Hill and asked him if he wanted to come along. "I can't," Bobby said. "I'm learning to play stickball."

"That's swell. But be home by six. We'll go out to dinner."

Bobby waited until Julian was gone before putting on his jacket and walking to South Orange Village, where he caught a bus to the terminal in Irvington and read the schedule on the window of the information booth.

Nine minutes later, Bobby was on a bus to Newark.

## Chapter 60

Eddie, paying the toll at the George Washington Bridge, said, "I shouldn'ta told ya."

On Saturday night, Eddie and Fiona had gone to the Five Spot to hear Chet Baker. After his set, Eddie had asked Chet about Otis, who used to play piano for him. Chet said that in August he'd tried to visit Otis in a house on 137th Street, between Lenox and Seventh, where some nuns nursed people who didn't have families to take them in. Otis wouldn't see Chet. Julian didn't care. He wanted to talk to Otis. Eddie had tried to talk him out of it.

"You say you don't give a damn if you're Bobby's father," Eddie said, "so what is it? If he's yours, you can get mad at Kendall again for not getting in touch when he was born?"

"I hadn't thought of that."

"Then think of this. Even if Otis can give you an answer about Bobby's birth certificate, all you'll get is more questions."

✳

Two summers ago, after a Negro teenager was shot and killed by a white cop, a riot broke out in Harlem, but this street, with its run-down houses and river of trash in the gutters, couldn't have gotten any worse. On the positive side, parking wasn't a problem. At the end of the block, Julian saw a plaque above a door:

HE HEALS THE BROKENHEARTED AND
BINDS UP THEIR WOUNDS.

A nun with a pasty oval face answered the bell.

Julian said, "We're here to visit Otis Larkin."

"Mr. Larkin isn't accepting—"

Julian stepped past her. Eddie followed.

"Please, Sister. If Otis asks us to leave, we will." That was true. So was the fact that Julian was prepared to look for Otis without her permission.

The nun, after peering at Julian, led him to the rear of the first floor. The house smelled of disinfectant and urine. Otis was sleeping under a sheet in a hot, windowless room. A wooden crucifix was above the metal-frame bed. The nun departed. Eddie stood on one side of Otis, Julian on the other.

Eddie whispered, "We got no right to disturb him."

Seeing Otis's jaundiced face slick with sweat, Julian was disgusted with himself for coming, and as he turned to leave, Otis opened one eye. "You boys got older than dirt."

Eddie said, "What's shaking, Jitterbug?"

Otis opened the other eye. "Got every improvement, my man. Pneumonia, hepatitis, cirrhosis, and some other stuff they think's too scary to tell me." Otis gulped for air and winced. "How'd ya find me?"

Julian said, "Eddie bumped into Chet."

"Chet came by, but I want to remember the what-was, not the what-is."

Eddie said, "Chet knows that."

Otis sighed, and phlegm crackled in his lungs. "How's Kenni-Ann?"

Julian thought Otis was about to lose enough: he didn't need to lose Kendall as well. "She's fine."

"That boy of hers must be big."

"Bobby, he is."

The pain was clear on Otis's face. "Bobby, he's . . . I told Kenni-Ann, she got to tell you."

"Water under the bridge," said Julian.

Otis's breathing was shallow. "Kenni-Ann was in New York when Bobby was born. I'd just gotten in from L.A.—from recording *Witch*

*Doctor* with Chet. My mama was after me to get married." Otis blinked back tears. "I don't know what you knew about me."

Eddie said, "That you're one of the sweetest piano players I ever heard."

"Kenni-Ann put me on his birth certificate. Said I should show Mama, so she'd leave me alone. But Mama knew about me. Most of Harlem did. And Mama says, 'Don't you come here. I won't have that sin under my roof.' I went and got good and fucked up. Kenni-Ann jetted off to Paris with Bobby, and I didn't—"

Eddie said, "It wasn't on you to tell. Let it go."

"I wrote Mama a letter when I got here, but she hasn't . . ."

Tears began rolling from Otis's eyes. Julian dabbed at them with his hankie.

"Mama never forgave me for getting my brother lynched. And Daddy, he died from it."

Eddie said, "Derrick was murdered. And not by you."

Otis gazed at Julian, the air whistling in and out of his lungs. "If I hadn't gone swimmin'—Jesus . . . it hurts to breathe."

"You rest now," Julian said, and sat on the bed and held Otis's hand until he fell asleep. He didn't feel any better knowing that he was Bobby's father because he still didn't understand why Kendall hadn't contacted him. And he wasn't able to forgive her.

Eddie's eyes were red. He said, "See ya, Jitterbug," and left the room as the nun returned. Julian gave her his card and asked her to mail the bill for Otis's casket and cemetery plot to his office. That didn't make him feel better either, but it was all he could do.

# Chapter 61

On the Garden State, Eddie stopped to gas up, and Julian used the pay phone to check in with his office. He felt rotten about Otis, but when he got back into the Cadillac, he couldn't tamp down his panic about what his secretary had just told him: *God, You can't do this to me again. I paid already—I paid enough.*

Julian said, "Bobby took off from school after lunch. I called the house and his pal Stevie, but I can't find him. There was a fight, and Stevie's father had to go pick his boy up at the principal's office. The maid told me they're not home yet. Let's go there."

After Eddie pulled his Cadillac into the Lerners' driveway, he heard yelling on the other side of the high cedar fence.

Julian said, "That's Martin, Stevie's father. He gets kind of nervous around me. I'm guessing he was a fan of *The Untouchables*."

Stevie was on a bamboo chair by the amoeba-shaped pool, pressing a Baggie of ice to his left eye. Martin Lerner, in a sap-green cardigan and madras slacks, was standing over him. "Mr. Rose," Martin said, glancing at Eddie as if he might have a tommy gun under his mocha silk sport coat. "Stevie's being a little closemouthed."

Mayella slid back the glass patio door. "Mr. Lerner, the missus be on the phone."

"I gotta take this," Martin said, and hustled inside.

Julian sat on a bamboo ottoman. "That's quite a shiner. Who hit you?"

Stevie tossed the Baggie onto a chair. "I'm in trouble with my dad."

"I can't help you with that unless you talk to me."

"Karl Fuchs. He's a cretin."

"Did Karl do something to Bobby?"

"At lunch. Karl asks Bobby if he's going to be on our homeroom football team. For the intramural league. Bobby says he doesn't know how to play, and Karl says whoever heard of a nigger can't play football."

"What'd Bobby do?"

"He looks at me. Like I should take care of Karl. How am I supposed to do that? He's like the biggest kid in school. Bobby runs out of the cafeteria, and Karl's laughing. So I dump my tray on him. Karl's got spaghetti and tomato sauce in his hair, and he punches me. A teacher grabs us, and now I'm screwed."

Stevie stared at the slate deck as his father came out. Eddie intercepted Martin, slinging an arm over him. Martin froze, and Eddie said, "Lemme explain things to you."

"Stevie," Julian said, "where's Bobby?"

Stevie shook his head.

"You don't know or you won't say?"

Stevie's face contorted as though he were about to cry, and Julian's panic ratcheted up a notch. "Bobby's not in trouble with me. But he could be in trouble."

"Newark. A bar. Speedo's. Bobby says he goes to be around colored people. So he doesn't feel weird."

Julian, recalling his romance with the seedy nightlife of Berlin, disliked the taste of his own medicine.

Stevie said, "I asked to go with him lots of times—it's not safe there, and I'm his friend, I should go with him—but he won't let me."

Julian patted Stevie's knee. "Bobby's lucky you're his friend." Then he called out, "Eddie, we gotta take off."

As they got into the Caddy, Julian asked, "You ever hear of Speedo's?"

"In the armpit of the old Third Ward. Near Mercer and Broome. The Abruzzis used to run a book outta there till the bookie got shot."

Eddie pressed the button of the glove compartment. Inside were the tools of his trade: a Colt .45 auto pistol and studded brass knuckles. "You can't go there naked."

# Chapter 62

Doo-wop blared from the open windows of Speedo's, and the Friday revelers were on parade, the women in slinky dresses and high-heel pumps, the men in wide-brimmed hats, silk suits, and alligator shoes. To Bobby, who sat on the stoop of the boarded-up tenement next to the bar, the crowd appeared to bounce to the music as they streamed under the neon sign with a purple silhouette of a busty woman shimmying out of a glowing, green cocktail shaker.

Two young men were above Bobby on the steps, and his favorite, nicknamed Payback, lean and light-skinned and wearing a skimpy leather jacket and orange high-water pants, said, "Little brother, an ofay call you a nigger, you gotta bust that white motherfucker in his mouth."

"He's bigger than me."

"That don't mean nothin'. Educate him, Colwyn."

Colwyn was the other man on the stoop. He had the huge chest and biceps common to alumni of Rahway State Prison, and he stood scoping out the traffic with heavy-lidded eyes.

Colwyn said, "Bobby, we gots a customer."

A Negro man with a goatee was sticking two fingers out a window of a beat-up Lincoln. Payback handed Bobby two glassine packets of white powder, and Bobby went to the car and exchanged the packets for a ten-dollar bill.

Bobby knew that the powder was heroin, and he'd seen men and women, as scary as space creatures with their desperate faces bathed in neon, begging Payback for a handout, only to be chased away by

Colwyn. Bobby had read in *Life* that heroin was illegal, but the police, riding by Speedo's, didn't bother the two men on the stoop. Bobby asked Payback about that, and Payback chuckled. "'Cause a them envelopes you take to Sally's Diner." That was a job Payback had given him, delivering an envelope to a white detective with sweat stains in the armpits of his Windbreaker who was at the counter eating a chicken-salad sandwich.

Bobby had met Payback last spring when he got off the bus on Springfield Avenue. Anyone who knew about Newark would've been scared, but to Bobby the area appeared no worse than the Pigalle neighborhood of Paris. Payback had seen Bobby from the stoop and asked him if he were lost. Bobby said no, and Payback offered him a soda, and they began to talk. Bobby mentioned that his parents were gone and he lived with a guardian, but mostly he spoke about the white kids in South Orange who, except for Stevie, avoided him like he was radioactive. From then on, almost every week, Bobby returned to the stoop. He felt grown-up when Payback assigned him things to do and paid him a couple of bucks for doing them. But best of all Bobby enjoyed sitting in this raucous niche of the city, where nearly everyone's skin was a close approximation of his own, and no one ever gawked at him.

Bobby was handing a wad of bills to Payback when Colwyn said, "Man, check out that ride."

As Bobby turned toward the midnight-blue Cadillac with the Batmobile tail fins, Julian emerged from the passenger seat and Eddie from the driver's side.

"Get in the car," Julian said.

Bobby, shaking his head, sat on the lowest step. Julian got ahold of Bobby's shirt and yanked him up as if retrieving a puppy from a litter.

Payback stood. "Boy don't wanna split, he ain't gotta split. Colwyn, talk to this ofay."

Colwyn hadn't treated Bobby as a kid brother, but he wasn't fond of humanity in general, and Caucasian humanity he didn't like at all. Sneering at Julian, he came down the stoop. Julian shoved Bobby toward the Caddy, and when Colwyn had one foot on the bottom step and the other on the pavement, Julian kicked him in the shin of his lower leg. Colwyn buckled forward, and Julian, crouched low, sprang up with the brass knuckles on his right hand and threw a haymaker at Colwyn's jaw. The punch connected with a sharp crack, and Colwyn toppled backward, hitting his head on the stoop and lying there as if he were making an angel in the snow.

Payback was going for the .22 revolver in his waistband, but he was too late. Eddie was leveling the .45 at him. "That galoot ain't dead but you could be."

Payback raised his hands. Eddie dug under Payback's jacket and pocketed his Saturday-night special. Patrons from Speedo's had stepped out for a breath of fresh air, and one of them commented, "The nerve a you motherfuckers shakin' down these brothers."

Payback said to Julian, "Bobby could use hisself some contact with his own kind."

"Like you?" The hypocrisy of Julian's contempt for Payback didn't escape him.

"I gots to get outta heah someways."

That was Julian's—and Abe's—reasoning when Jews occupied these same cold-water flats. Julian didn't appreciate hearing it now. Backing up to the Cadillac with Eddie, he said, "You see your co-worker? I find Bobby here again, that's gonna look like fun."

✳

Bobby was in the passenger seat when Eddie pulled up to Julian's. He touched Eddie's leg and whispered, "Don't leave."

The fear in his voice bothered Eddie, and as Julian herded Bobby to the front door, Eddie went after them.

"You forget something?" Julian said.

"My hat. It's in your dishwasher."

Bobby opened the door and bolted upstairs, planning to lock himself in his room. Julian, with his long arms, clutched his shirt collar, then hemmed him in against the wall. With barely controlled fury, he said, "You wanna be a gangster?"

Bobby blinked against the light from the hanging bubble lamps.

"I was a gangster. Ask me if it was fun."

Bobby didn't speak.

"Ask me!"

Bobby looked at the floor.

"Ask me why?"

Bobby mumbled, "Why?"

"I didn't know any better, and I hate myself for doing it. Is that what you want?"

Bobby kept looking at the floor.

Julian shouted, "Is that what you want?" and got ahold of Bobby's shirtfront and lifted him up, all the while telling God, *You took my daughter, You can't have my son.*

Eddie, grabbing Julian from behind, hauled him away. "Fuckin' stop. He's a boy."

Julian let Bobby go and wrestled free from Eddie.

Glaring at Julian, Bobby shouted, "Why do you care what I do!"

Julian, panting, sank to his knees so that he was looking up into Bobby's eyes. "Be . . . because . . . I'm your father."

Crouching like an exhausted runner, Julian let out a spate of sobs. Eddie put his hand on his friend's shoulder, and Bobby stood there, listening to his father cry.

## Chapter 63

In New Jersey, Mischief Night is celebrated on the evening before Halloween. Adults complain it's an unmitigated pain in the ass, while teenagers swear they'd rather clean their room than skip the festivities. After all, what could be more gratifying than soaping up car windows, adorning trees with toilet paper, and for the more hostile merrymakers, ringing doorbells and hurling eggs at anyone dumb enough to open up?

That year, Mischief Night was on Sunday, and before Bobby went out with Stevie he ate with Julian at the Famous, where Julian had initiated him into the Pastrami-on-Rye-with-Russian Fan Club.

Bobby said, "You always watch me eat when we're here."

"It reminds me of introducing your mom to that sandwich. She liked it as much as you do."

Julian had told Bobby about his and Kendall's past when he'd brought him back from Newark—after apologizing for losing his temper and making him promise not to go near Speedo's. Bobby relished hearing the stories, but with a sour note in his voice he'd asked, "Why couldn't Mom tell you about me?" Julian had replied, "It was my fault," because why should a child resent a mother he'd never see again? Julian had explained Prohibition and the Third Ward Gang and his concern that the name Rose would be a burden to Bobby. "That's why it's 'Dad' at home or with Uncle Eddie and Aunt Fiona, but nowhere else."

Bobby seemed to accept Julian's answer and didn't bring up Newark again until Julian was driving him to Stevie's.

"Would Uncle Eddie have shot Payback and Colwyn?"

"To protect you or me, yes."

"And you'd do the same for Uncle Eddie and me?"

"I would."

"Then it's not wrong?" Bobby asked, and the seriousness of his tone startled Julian.

"It's wrong and it's against the law. And you're too young to worry about it."

Bobby kissed his father's cheek, a recent development that warmed Julian in a way he'd longed for since Holly's death. That was another story he'd told his son, showing him a photo of Holly. *It'd be nice to have a sister*, Bobby had said. The kisses had started after that. But when he let him out at the Lerners', Julian had the uncomfortable feeling that he was missing the reason for Bobby's questions.

✳

Stevie came out through the garage with his older brother, Alan, a taller, slimmed-down replica of Stevie. Alan was in from the University of Michigan to attend a wedding, and he wasn't returning to Ann Arbor until tomorrow. Bobby thought Alan was cool: he talked like Payback, and he'd chauffeur him and Stevie wherever they wanted to go.

"What's happenin', my man?" Alan said, and Bobby slapped him five.

Stevie shone a flashlight into the back of Alan's Mustang convertible. On the seat was a box of black berets and a stack of Mattel submachine guns.

Alan said, "You're gonna be Che and Fidel."

"Who?" Bobby asked, and Alan recited a romanticized Cliff's Notes version of the Cuban revolution as he drove the boys over to Foster Court.

"We made a list of those this afternoon," Stevie said, aiming the flashlight out at a three-foot-high lawn jockey. The jockey's face was painted a luminous black; the whites of his eyes were enormous; and his thick lips were as red as a candy apple.

Alan said, "Get to it, Stevie. Like I told you."

Stevie had Bobby help him turn the jockey toward the house. Then he put the beret on his head and wedged the toy gun inside the metal ring the jockey held in his right hand.

Stevie and Bobby worked their way down toward the village. In total, Bobby had spent fourteen months in Lovewood, so he was aware that the statues were insulting to Negroes, but he was unclear about how insulted he should be. In fact, Bobby was getting bored until Stevie said, "The last one's Karl Fuchs's house. It's at the bottom of Tillou Road. And there're two jockeys."

That piqued Bobby's interest, but the police were out to prevent the mischief from escalating into vandalism, and a patrol car began tailing the Mustang. Alan had to pass by Karl's, hang a left into the village, and park outside Reservoir Pizzeria before the patrol car sped by.

"Agenda's changed," Alan said. "If the cops bust us, they'll arrest me. So we can stop now; I can wait here while you take care of Karl; or I can leave you at Karl's, give you money, and you can walk to the village and get a taxi."

Bobby, with the delectable tingle of retribution in the pit of his stomach, said, "As long as we take care of Karl."

Stevie said, "Enough money for a taxi *and* pizza?"

"You got it," Alan said.

The lawn jockeys at Karl's were difficult to turn. The wiring of the lanterns was threaded through a cement base and buried in the ground. Stevie and Bobby, glancing nervously over their shoulders, clawed at the grass around the bases with their fingers, creating enough of a gap that the jockeys could be swiveled toward the columned portico of the house. The boys were arranging the berets and submachine guns when behind them a man said, "That you, Bobby?"

A policeman, who had been watching with the headlights off, got out of his patrol car.

"Officer Nelligan?" Bobby said, his voice trembling.

"That's me. What're you guys doing?"

"We're union organizers," Stevie replied. Alan had said that if a cop nabbed them, he'd prefer that explanation to revolutionaries.

Officer Nelligan inspected the lawn jockeys and laughed. "We got a complaint about this, so you'll have to knock it off. You're not in trouble or nothing. I'll take you to the station, and Mr. Rose can come get you."

At the station, Officer Nelligan took two Hershey bars from a plastic pumpkin on the desk and gave them to Stevie and Bobby. He asked Bobby for his phone number, and the boy answered so softly that the officer had him repeat it. Then he phoned Julian. By the time he hung up, Stevie had scarfed his chocolate, but Bobby hadn't removed the wrapper from the candy bar.

"Can we see the jail?" Stevie asked.

"Anybody in there, Sarge?"

The desk sergeant held out a key on a metal loop. Bobby wouldn't have come unglued from the bench if Stevie hadn't tugged on the sleeve of his CPO.

"Check it out!" Stevie exclaimed, running his hands along the bars of the cells.

After one glance, Bobby returned to the bench. He was reading the wanted posters on the wall when Julian showed up, smiling and saying, "I appreciate it, Nellie."

※

"Why so quiet?" Julian asked after dropping off Stevie. "I'm not mad. It's funny."

Bobby hunched and unhunched his shoulders, a mannerism of Kendall's that Julian had seen so often, she must have bequeathed it to Bobby in the womb.

It wasn't until Julian was on the couch and using the clicker to turn on *Bonanza* that Bobby, running to his father and bursting into tears, spoke: "I-I-I'm going to pr-pris-on."

Julian held him. "Why prison?"

"I shot a man. A policeman."

Julian reeled with dread. "A policeman in Newark?" That would be expensive but possible to fix in a city where everything was for sale.

"In Lovewood."

That was a problem. "Come in the kitchen."

Julian opened a Dr. Brown's Black Cherry for Bobby and sat across from him at the table. "Tell me."

"The mayor—"

"Jarvis Scales?"

"That's him. He wants to buy mom's land, and one night he came to the house. My bedroom's above the library. I could hear everything. . . ."

"Girl!" Jarvis snapped. "You got to be the stubbornest black bitch ever drew breath!"

Hurleigh was laughing. "She be nicer if 'n I tear her lil pussy up."

Kendall screamed, "Get away from me!"

Upstairs, Bobby removed the small automatic pistol from the night-table drawer beside his mother's bed. Kendall had taught him to use it weeks ago and ordered him not to touch the pistol if she weren't there—except in an emergency.

As Bobby stepped between the partially open pocket doors of the library, he saw his mother on a loveseat and Hurleigh slapping her across her face. Blood trickled from her nose.

"Stop," Bobby said, raising the pistol.

Two other men behind the loveseat retreated to where a portrait of Ezekiel Kendall, illuminated by a brass picture light, hung above the fireplace.

Mayor Scales said, "Hurleigh."

The policeman, in a hat and sunglasses, sauntered toward Bobby. "Boy, put that down."

"Hurleigh," Kendall pleaded, "don't hurt him. I'm begging you, Hurleigh, you want me, Hurleigh, don't you, Hurleigh?"

The policeman got closer. "Boy, I'll shoot yoah pickaninny ass."

Bobby stared at Ezekiel's burning eyes, and when he felt his great-grandfather staring back, he pulled-pulled-pulled-pulled the trigger.

The policeman fell. The other men dove to the floor. Kendall shouted, "Bobby, lâche ton arme! Va-t'en!"

Bobby followed her instructions, dropping the pistol and running to Lucinda's, where he stayed sometimes when Kendall traveled. Lucinda had

*some clothes for Bobby in a suitcase, and her neighbor drove them to Lucinda's*
*sister in downtown Miami. In the morning, they left for New Jersey.*

Julian felt sick: Bobby had used the Beretta he'd given Kendall
when she moved to Greenwich Village. And he was angry with himself: he should've strangled Hurleigh on the beach and then taken care
of the mayor.

"How come you've been saying your mother was dead?" Julian
asked, confused, struggling to parse the details of Bobby's story.

"Because Lucinda told me if those men didn't kill her, Mom would
come for me in a couple weeks, and that was forty-six weeks ago."

"You didn't see anyone kill her?"

"No, I didn't."

"You didn't," Julian said, but he was talking more to himself than
to Bobby.

# Chapter 64

The following afternoon Julian and Eddie flew to Miami and, after checking into a two-bedroom suite at the Eden Roc, changed into Florida wear—pastel sea cotton, pale linen, Italian calfskin. Then Julian placed a call to the Goldstein brothers. They had quit the rackets a year before the Kefauver Committee got going, and Julian hadn't seen them since Abe's funeral.

When he hung up, Eddie asked, "We squared away with Looney and Gooney?"

"We're meeting Looney."

"They quit dumping gas on people and lighting them up?"

Julian laughed. "As far as I know."

"I always figured them two firebugs would own filling stations."

"Once they moved to Miami Beach, the gun-shop opportunity fell in their laps."

Julian and Eddie were sitting in a booth at Wolfie's on Lincoln Road when Looney plowed through the crowd at the entrance like a fullback busting into the end zone. He was carrying a shopping bag from Burdine's and decked out in a Hawaiian shirt, striped Bermudas, and sandals with gray athletic socks. He waved for the waitress, a young Latin woman with a black ponytail.

"The usual," Looney said to her.

Julian asked for a brisket sandwich, Eddie for corned beef, and Looney said to the waitress, "Honey, scoop some cabbage on that corned beef, he'll sing 'Danny Boy' for ya."

The waitress tittered like a bashful schoolgirl before she went to put in the order.

Eddie said, "Looney, you must be some tipper; she likes your jokes."

"And you must still be the mick schmuck don't know my first name."

"Morris, but Looney's . . . more fitting?"

Looney, scowling at Eddie, held out his hand to Julian, and they shook.

"You look well, Morris," Julian said.

"Ain't at the shop but three days a week. Me and my brother got brand-new apartments across the street from here. Lots to do. Gin rummy, shuffleboard, adult education classes at the library. Miami Beach's changing some. With all them Puerto Ricans comin' over from Cuba."

Eddie said, "Morris, how's that geography class goin'?"

"Geography, O'Rourke? Are—"

Julian asked Looney, "You get everything?"

"The road map's marked like you wanted; I got the papers from the recorder's office to my lawyer in Fort Lauderdale—he can straighten out that Lovewood deal—and you need me and my brother, we'll help. And I got you them Nambus."

His voice low, Eddie said, "Them Jap pistols are junk."

Looney hissed, "Can't trace nothing nobody knew was here. I just got Nambus 'cause if cocksuckers try and sell me Lugers—or any Nazi peashooter—I throw 'em the fuck out."

✻

Julian drove the rented Impala along the ocean to Lovewood, the light spreading like pink-and-violet satin over the sand and water. When he saw the gates of the college he expected to tumble back into his past, but seeing the deserted campus only made him sad. Bobby had given him directions to Lucinda's, and he passed the shacks of the tenant farmers, with the handbill advertisements peeling off the exteriors like mildewed wallpaper, and parked by the streambed Bobby had mentioned. Black faces eyed them suspiciously from doorways and porches, and less than a quarter mile down a dirt road, Julian recognized Lucinda. She was rocking in a chair on a porch and smoking a corncob pipe.

She said, "Been wonderin' when I be seein' you."

Julian said, "Miss Watkins, this is my friend, Eddie."

"Sit yoahselfs down."

As Julian and Eddie sat on the edge of porch, Lucinda disappeared into the shack and brought out two Mason jars of clear liquid, handing one to Julian and the other to Eddie, then picking up the jar beside her chair and taking a seat. She drank. Julian and Eddie joined her. The liquid tasted like fruity varnish.

Lucinda said, "Now g'wan and tells me 'bout my Bobby."

"Doing well," Julian said. "Wishes his mom was with him."

"Gon' be wishin' foahevah. That Mayor Scales done kilt that girl. Or had her kilt."

Julian felt his hope draining out of him. He asked Lucinda why she was certain Kendall was dead.

"Kendall done loved that child, and if she be alive, she be comin' foah Bobby."

"Miss Watkins, could you start at the beginning?"

Lucinda struck a wooden match with a thumbnail and fired up the corncob. "The day Kendall tell me about it be so hot the trees beggin' the dogs to cool 'em off. The college broke; been borrowin' foah years; all them siddity Negroes teachin' be gone. Onliest ones feelin' good be the sharecroppers. Ain't nobody collectin' nothin' from them."

Julian said, "So no one's met the new owner?"

"No, suh. But Kendall had to sell the land to pay off the bills or she gon' go bankrupt. The mayor, his daddy owned the land, and he offer to buy it. Kendall say she can get more from men want to build a hotel and golf course. So Kendall say she gon' sell to the highest bidder. The mayor's brother, Hurleigh, come 'round—mean as a snake with piles, that boy—and let Kendall know Bobby might could have hisself a accident. The mayor, he sick with the emphysema and done made Hurleigh deputy chief of po-lice. And after Hurleigh start talkin' ugly 'bout Bobby, Kendall say I'm gon' have to bring him north."

Julian said, "And Bobby shot Hurleigh before you were ready to go?"

"The night before. And Hurleigh don't die. I seen him out to the Wakefields'. I check on it Wednesdays and Saturdays, and Hurleigh be askin' me and other folks they seen Bobby."

Julian said, "Bobby says there were two other men at the house."

"Don't know 'em."

Eddie, who had been gazing at his loafers while Lucinda spoke, looked up, and Julian saw a flicker of rage in his eyes that had nothing to do with the moonshine. "And nobody's looking for Kendall?"

"Mister, you a northern boy, and you be hearin' 'bout all them new laws they got make us equal. But whites down heah like them Scales brothers, they ain't hearin' that good. So even when a highfalutin colored girl like Kendall disappear, she stay disappeared, and if'n you colored, you best not ask nobody nothin', or you disappear too."

Julian said, "Eddie and I'll ask them."

Lucinda puffed on her corncob. "The Lord won't forgive me none foah this, but I hopes you send them crackers to hell."

# Chapter 65

In the morning, Eddie and Julian left the car by the commons in Lovewood, across from Scales Antiques, and as nonchalantly as tourists, ambled down the white-pebbled alley and cased the rear of the store. The wood-frame garage, with the apartment above where Hurleigh had lived and which Looney and Gooney had torched, had been rebuilt out of cement blocks, indicating that Jarvis wasn't impervious to the lessons of experience.

Scales Antiques wouldn't open for an hour, and they waited on a bench in the commons.

Eddie said, "Did I ever tell you about my father?"

"Only that he died before you were born."

"His name was Edward. He had a bum ticker—from rheumatic fever. Didn't have the endurance for laying track. So he worked as a handyman. For the Hooper family in West Orange. One of those palaces in Llewellyn Park."

"Thomas Edison had an estate in Llewellyn Park."

"Next to the Hoopers. An ancestor of theirs used to sell George Washington his underwear or something, and the Hoopers were famous for their July Fourth shindigs. The day before the shindig, my father's planting saplings. It's a hundred degrees out. He gets dizzy and's taking a break when Mrs. Hopper comes out and yells at him to get busy or get another job. Ma's pregnant with me, he can't lose the dough, so he goes to work. He doesn't make it home for supper. Ma ain't happy, but he had a habit of holing up at a bar in Vailsburg, except by morning he ain't home, and Ma's scared. She checks the bar.

He ain't been there. Maybe he's at the Hoopers. Three buses for her to get from Newark to Llewellyn Park. They got those gates at the entrance, and the guard doesn't let her in but calls the house. And the missus gives him a message. My father's fired. He didn't finish planting the trees."

Eddie dragged on his Camel. "Two days later, a cop comes to give Ma the news. My father was in a toolshed on the Hooper property. He went there to rest and died."

Eddie crushed his cigarette under his loafer. "I'm listening to Lucinda, all I can think about is Mrs. Hooper reaming out my father, and him dying in that shed. You wanna ask the mayor and Hurleigh about Kendall, that's jake with me. If she happens to be somewhere—"

"You don't sound too optimistic."

"Optimistic's against my religion."

"Catholics aren't optimistic?"

"Only if they behaved themselves and the undertaker's prettying them up for the dance. But if the mayor and Hurleigh got nothing to say, they're going in the ground. I ain't never been able to do a lot. But I can stop those bums from chasing Bobby, and maybe make things a little easier for Lucinda and those folks in the shacks."

A black-and-white Lovewood Police car came down Main Street and turned into the alley.

"Here's your chance," Julian said.

✳

Jarvis and Hurleigh were behind the counter and facing away from the door when Julian flipped over the Open sign to Closed. The mayor turned as Julian came toward him, and Julian saw the shock of recognition in his eyes. Most of Jarvis's flattop was gone, but his face was still all sharp edges.

"It's ready, Jarvis," Hurleigh said. He had been attaching a nasal hose to an oxygen cylinder. In his bluish-gray uniform, Hurleigh seemed paler than Julian recalled, and his blond hair and patchy beard were silvered. Hurleigh didn't recognize Julian.

"You don't know this fella?" Jarvis said, and Julian heard the wheeze of emphysema as he spoke. "The day that boy went upside your head on the beach?"

Hurleigh sneered, showing off his buck teeth. "I allow that coon learnt to be sorry for strikin' a white man."

Julian said, "His name was Derrick Larkin."

The mayor was smiling as Hurleigh, with his hand on his revolver, sauntered around the counter. "I might could make y'all sorry now."

"Remember my friend?" asked Julian. "The one with the red hair?"

The question hadn't stopped Hurleigh. It was the Nambu—which resembled a slimmer version of a Luger—that Eddie was pressing against the base of his skull.

Eddie, plucking the revolver from Hurleigh's holster, said, "That lock you got back there ain't for shit."

Hurleigh said, "Boy, you messin' with a officer of the law."

At the crack of the gunshot, the mayor and his brother flinched. Eddie had fired past Hurleigh into a barrel of stuffed baby alligators.

Eddie said, "Sit on the floor or the next shot goes in your noggin."

Hurleigh sat, and Julian said, "Where's Kendall Wakefield?"

Hurleigh said, "I tolt you, Jarvis, I—"

The mayor said, "Quiet, boy."

"Secret's out," Julian said to the mayor. "I got the record of sale from the recorder's office, and a lawyer tracking down everyone involved. Kendall's son saw you, Hurleigh, and the two others with you. I'll dig them up, and when I get done with them, somebody'll talk. You cared about your father's land, the others care about money. They won't die for money."

Hurleigh said, "If'n I catch that pissant Sambo done shot me, he dead."

Eddie smacked the side of Hurleigh's head with the butt of his revolver. Crying out, Hurleigh fell on his side, moaning. Eddie removed the cuffs from Hurleigh's duty belt and locked them on his wrists.

Julian said, "Jarvis, you're old and sick. Who you gonna leave the land to? Your wife?"

Hurleigh whined, "The bitch done lef' him. Her and them two brats in California. The land go to me, ain't that how you done, Jarvis?"

The mayor said, "Hurleigh, you dumber than a sack of rocks."

Julian nodded at Eddie, who yanked Hurleigh up to his feet and shoved him toward the back door. Julian withdrew his pistol from under his sport jacket.

Julian said, "First choice. If Kendall's alive, you live and keep some land."

"And Hurleigh?"

"Didn't think you cared."

"I don't."

"Good. He threatened Kendall's son, and I doubt Eddie cared for that."

"Second choice?"

Julian raised the Nambu and retracted the cocking knob. "Friend of mine—the one who set your garage on fire—gave me a map with some swamps marked on it."

Jarvis wheezed, "She's alive."

Julian, relief flooding through him, lowered the Nambu.

Jarvis said, "Ain't done it for money. I ain't collected a cent from the sharecroppers. But I kept seein' a glittery, whorehouse hotel where my daddy's farm used to be."

"You got the papers for the deal?"

"Back in the office."

"We'll get them on the way out."

"Wasn't intending to hurt no one. I just . . . Did you ever want somethin' so bad it take over every waking moment of your damn life?"

"Yeah. Kendall Wakefield."

# Chapter 66

Julian and Jarvis got into the back of the Impala. Eddie was at the wheel. The police car was gone. So was Hurleigh.

Heading west out of Lovewood, Eddie said, "Hurleigh gave me the lowdown. They had this Dr. Evarts, a headshrinker, declare Kendall incompetent. Then a judge, Evarts's cousin, assigned a lawyer—another Evarts cousin—to handle her affairs. The lawyer's the one sold the land to Scales. Jarvis had to pay these characters fifty grand. The doctor got twenty-five."

Jarvis was breathing heavily. "I paid that young woman fair."

Julian, going through the survey, deed, and appraisal in the envelope, said, "Except if she'd sold to developers. They'd've paid more."

"Them crooks maybe might. But Miz Wakefield done told me herself: Lovewood College had almost two million in debt, every dollar secured by Wakefield property. And with them civil rights laws and guvment loans, colored kids be enrollin' in the white schools. But she wouldn't sell. Say she felt like she was betraying her mama and granddaddy. I say, 'Miz Wakefield, the banks takin' it one way or t'other, and the only difference between a banker and a ignorant, no-account thief is a banker can write his name.'"

Eddie was driving on a paved, two-lane road through an area of the state Julian hadn't seen before—green countryside of marshes and cypress trees.

"So you helped her," Julian said, controlling his anger.

Before Jarvis could answer, Eddie said, "Then threw her in a mental hospital."

Jarvis was wheezing up a storm. "Mental hospital's a damn lie. It's Shady Isle Rest Home. Dr. Evarts has the patients exercisin' and eatin' good. It wasn't gon' be but another month. Lawyer say after a year, it harder to reverse the deal in court."

Reaching back with Hurleigh's handcuffs dangling from his fingers, Eddie said, "We gotta stop."

Julian cuffed Jarvis's hands behind him while Eddie glanced at Looney's road map and veered off through saw grass toward a pole with a triangular white sign that warned, in bold red letters, Danger: Keep Out! Below the warning was a picture of a green alligator, his jaws open wide enough to chomp on an elephant.

As Eddie killed the engine, Jarvis wheezed, "What—what y'all gon' do?"

"Stop talking," Julian said, getting out of the Impala.

Eddie unlocked the trunk. Hurleigh was lying on his side, cocooned in a paint-splattered tarp. Julian moved the tarp aside. Hurleigh had two blood-rimmed bullet holes below his police badge, and Julian unpinned the badge and stuck it in his wallet. Eddie grabbed the upper half of Hurleigh, Julian the bottom, and they carried him to the water and heaved him off the tarp, quickly backing up because fifty yards away three alligators, who had been sunning themselves on logs, slipped into the water as if someone were ringing a dinner bell.

Walking to the car, Julian asked, "How much longer till Shady Isle?"

"Five minutes tops."

Julian pulled Jarvis out of the back and pushed him into the trunk.

※

Shady Isle Rest Home, a U-shaped building of eggshell-colored stucco, was surrounded by a moat and across a bowed wooden bridge with an arm gate. A security guard, in a black uniform and billed cap that reminded Julian of the SS, asked Eddie to state his business.

Julian flashed Hurleigh's badge. "I'm here to see Dr. Evarts. Can you tell me where his office is?"

"Second floor. Center wing."

Eddie parked in the lot across from the entrance.

"Don't let that prick suffocate," Julian said.

Patients and visitors were sitting on the dowdy couches in the lobby, the patients groggy and wearing light-blue robes. Upstairs, music as triumphant as a John Philip Sousa march was blasting through the door of Dr. Evarts's office. No secretary was in the anteroom, but Julian saw a man in a seersucker suit standing in the inner office, next to a desk with a portable record player on it, and waggling a flyswatter as if conducting the Marine Band. He was short and pallid with the idiotic, gleeful countenance of someone easily amused. When he saw Julian, he put the flyswatter on the desk and lifted the needle off the record. "Yes?"

"Kendall Wakefield."

Evarts's countenance was less gleeful. "Is she a patient?"

Julian joined Evarts on the other side of the desk, and Evarts backed up against the jalousie windows. "You got some choices here, Doc. I could contact the state troopers, district attorney, and anyone else who can nail you for locking up a sane woman against her will. You could take a ride with Mayor Scales—he's handcuffed in the trunk of my car and—"

Evarts lunged for the phone on his desk, and Julian grabbed his hand, muscled him into his chair, took out the Nambu, and aimed the pistol at the doctor.

"Or," Julian said, "I could shoot you. Any of this appeal to you?"

"I can't say that it does."

"Then get on that phone and have her brought here and I'll take her with me."

The doctor dialed three numbers, then made the request, and Julian stowed the pistol in his jacket pocket. Part of him—the part he'd come to loathe—would have preferred to shoot Evarts and to feed Jarvis to the alligators. It was puzzling to Julian that after all he'd seen and done, depravity still outraged him as though he were an innocent discovering, for the first time, that people were not always well behaved, especially if some fanatically desired prize was involved. *My daddy's land . . . The Thousand-Year Reich . . .* But who was Julian to judge? He'd been more savage than most, and deep into middle age he was the same furious boy who had drowned the Kaiser and gone on to kill others for reasons he couldn't bear to recall. Yet Julian wondered: had he been a different sort of man, how many more girls would the Kaiser have murdered? Would Bobby have been lost to Payback and the same rough streets as his father? Would Kendall be freed from this prison? Julian needed to ask himself these questions: they were his home remedy for a guilty conscience.

A stooped, bald Negro in a light-blue smock rolled Kendall into the office in a wheelchair. Her outfit was familiar to Julian's—white polo shirt, dungarees, and tennis sneakers—and her khaki satchel, almost thirty years old now and patched with strips of leather, was on her lap, but Julian couldn't believe he was in her presence. Her thick, sable hair, with strands of gray in it, still flowed past her shoulders, and her beauty was intact: the age lines called attention to her high cheekbones and the hazel of her eyes.

However, as they stared at each other, Julian noticed that her eyes were glassy, and he wasn't sure she knew it was him.

Julian said to Evarts, "You kept her tranquilized so she wouldn't run away or get to a phone."

"Naturally, she was upset about being here, but—"

Kendall stuttered, "B-B-obby?"

Julian went to her. "I have him."

Despite his earlier contemplation of good and evil, nothing would've been more satisfying to Julian than killing Evarts on the spot, but he calculated that his probability of getting away with it was low and he was concerned about Kendall, so without another word he wheeled her outside.

※

She was asleep in the back seat before they were over the bridge, with Eddie's sport jacket balled up into a pillow and Julian's covering her like a blanket.

Julian said, "We'll go to her house in Lovewood and pack some of her stuff. Then swing by and give Lucinda the news."

"We should dump the hardware."

"I'll call Looney. He'll come to the Eden Roc to grab his pistols and take care of Hurleigh's thirty-eight. We'll stay tonight. I don't wanna fly until I know Kendall doesn't need a doctor."

"Wanna make a stop?"

"That'd be nice. How's Jarvis?"

"Resting uncomfortably."

Julian turned to look at Kendall. He had watched her sleep on so many nights and never tired of it, the peacefulness that came over him with her nearby.

At the marsh, Julian let Jarvis out of the trunk.

He was too cramped to stand up straight, and he was gulping for oxygen. "Miz Wakefield's fine, ain't she? Like I done told you."

Julian curled an arm around Jarvis's neck and led him toward the water. The alligators sunbathing on the logs were as hypnotic and frightening as dragons.

"Please," Jarvis begged, struggling to breathe. "Please."

Julian looked at him, but all he saw was Kendall sleeping, her face even lovelier in repose, and Bobby in the breakfast nook eating pancakes, and then a great sadness welled up in Julian, a sadness woven through with a memory of pure happiness—Holly jumping off the diving board, laughing as she sprang up into the sun-bright sky and splashed, in a spray of silver, through the turquoise surface of the backyard pool.

If any men deserved to be dinner for reptiles, Jarvis Scales was among them. Yet Julian couldn't serve him up. He brought Jarvis over to the Impala and asked Eddie to unlock his handcuffs.

Julian said, "You can walk to Shady Isle from here. Go right on the road and you'll see the sign. And you're gonna hear from a lawyer in Fort Lauderdale."

"I'll do whatever he says, I swear I will."

"You better think up a tale about Hurleigh taking off for parts unknown."

"I can do that."

"Jarvis, I'm giving you a break."

"Yes, suh, you are."

"Fuck around or try and chase me, there'll be no discussions. Get going."

Jarvis was already on the road when Julian got into the car.

# Chapter 67

All those decades melted away, and here they were, together again at Gruning's, Kendall eating butter pecan with butterscotch sauce and Julian digging into a scoop of coffee chip with hot fudge. Julian felt as if no time had gone by, as if God had hired the Three Stooges to design His kingdom, telling them, *Break their hearts, boys, but don't forget to leave 'em laughing.*

Kendall asked, "When's Bobby get out of school?"

"In an hour."

Last evening, Kendall had slept through dinner, then kept phoning Bobby, who was staying with Fiona. There was no answer. Relaxing in the living room of the suite, Julian had listened to her cry until she fell asleep again. He finally got through to Fiona. She'd taken Bobby to the movies, but he was sleeping now, and Julian said they'd meet him outside the junior high. On the plane to Newark, Kendall had stared at the clouds. Julian had driven Eddie home and retrieved Bobby's suitcase. Now, after four spoonfuls of her sundae, Kendall said, "I knew I was no college administrator. But I feel so guilty about losing that land. Mama would've had a fit."

"Divide your guilt in half."

"Why?"

Julian explained that there were two thousand and twenty-four acres. He was purchasing one thousand and twelve acres from Jarvis, and his portion included the college grounds, the fruit groves, and the beachfront. Julian was wiser now than when he'd bought the house in Greenwich Village, and he didn't expect Kendall to respond with unambivalent delight.

She didn't. "I can get magazine assignments and do more books, and I have some income from royalties, but I can't afford Florida real estate."

"Bobby can. The land's going into a trust for him."

Against her will, Kendall smiled. "You win—on a technicality."

"It's more than that. Bobby's my only heir."

"Your wife, she's—"

"She was killed in a car accident."

"Julian, I'm—"

"Our daughter, Holly, died with her."

Kendall's eyes filled.

Julian looked down at his ice cream. He didn't feel like eating it. "I still want to see Bobby. Wherever you wind up."

"Of course." Kendall poked at her butter pecan. "I was ashamed of myself for not telling you about him."

Julian was angry about it, but he saw no reason tell her. Not now, probably never.

Kendall closed and opened her eyes. "Remember Christina?"

"That artist Brigham's wife. With the chain."

She nodded. "After Bobby was born, I had meetings in the city, so I checked into the Chelsea with a nurse for Bobby. One afternoon, I'm waiting for an editor at the Caffe Reggio and thinking that I'm going to call you afterward. That I had to. And I'd missed you terribly in the hospital. The doctor's telling me to push and the overhead light's in my eyes, and I remembered being at the beach with you down the shore, and you standing over the blanket with cups of orangeade in your hands, and I'm looking up at you through overlapping circles of sunlight."

Kendall twirled her spoon in the ice cream. "Christina and Brig walk into the Reggio—without their chain. I hadn't seen them in years. Brig, he has to be past eighty, keeps his distance, but Christina comes over and we're chatting away as if she hadn't accused me of screwing her pig of a husband. She says they've been following my career, that my work's extraordinary, and carries on like she's my press agent. The editor arrives, and before Christina goes, she says, 'Your old boyfriend got married. It was in the Sunday *Times*. A real society dame. I told you—you were better off without him.'"

Julian grinned. "I never liked Christina much."

"Yes, well, when I heard that news, I could barely pay attention to the editor. I felt so—so betrayed. By you."

"Me?"

Kendall laughed, and Julian ached with loss hearing that laughter, her peculiar blend of melancholy and joy.

"Ridiculous, isn't it?" Kendall said. "And after my meeting I'm walking through Washington Square and I thought, *There's* a wedding present for your wife, her husband's black son. I'd hurt you enough, Julian. I couldn't . . . A week later, I went back to Paris."

Kendall glanced at her sundae. She had churned it to soup. "When Bobby was four, he started asking about his father. I wanted to tell him about you, but you'd said you didn't want him burdened with your last name."

"Still don't. He's Bobby Wakefield. At least until he's older."

Julian was eyeing Kendall. She glanced away.

He said, "More to the story, is there?"

"You always . . . how . . ."

"You skipped the stuff you were ashamed of."

Kendall put down her spoon. "I was always determined to live my life according to a plan. When I devised this grand plan, I can't say. In college? As a little girl—listening to my grandfather and my mother? Can't blame Ezekiel for his obsession with being free, for believing you can't rely on anyone except yourself. The same with Mama. But I didn't understand how closed off they were and how lonely they must've been. So I kept at my plan, even when it didn't make me happy, and look what I did to us."

"You were young, and I—"

"And Bobby?"

"Bobby? He's terrific. You did that."

"Did what? Without Bobby I would've been as empty as an image in a photograph. And look at the life I forced on him."

"Jarvis Scales? That's history. Both your families' history, the history of the whole country. You were born into it. It wasn't your doing."

"Not letting Bobby see his father was my fault. Not living in a family was my fault."

"If you could've—"

"But I couldn't. And I'm ashamed of that. Jesus, God, I didn't have anyone serious in—"

Kendall's eyes were the color of an evergreen on fire, but she didn't complete her sentence. "Let's go get our son," she said.

*

They were outside the junior high, and Kendall was gazing at the buff-brick apartment building on the corner where they had lived—all those years ago. She said, "I once fell in love in that building."

"So did I."

Absentmindedly, Kendall threaded her arm through his, and a moment passed before she understood why Julian was looking at her with surprise. She began to pull back, which was when the bank of doors flew open and children stampeded out, their shouts and laughter like the ringing of bells in the bright-blue afternoon.

They heard Bobby before they saw him: *"Maman, je suis là!"*

Kendall jumped up to look for him. "Bobby! Bobby!"

He ran to Kendall, holding on to her as though his body were a ballast that would make it impossible for her to disappear again. He sobbed once, twice, and Kendall murmured in French, "Don't cry, I'm here," but her eyes glistened with tears.

Standing back, Kendall said, "Look how tall. Julian, what are you feeding this child?"

Bobby laughed. "Pastrami."

The three of them squeezed into the front of the Thunderbird, Bobby in the middle, nestling between his parents and grinning as if he'd won a lifetime pass to the circus. "Dad, can Stevie sleep over on Friday? I want him to meet Mom."

"You got it."

Kendall was quiet, while Bobby told her about Stevie and his own straight-A report cards. As Julian drove into the garage, Bobby said, "Mom, you have to see my room."

Kendall said, "Go ahead. I'll be right up."

Julian was unloading the luggage from the trunk when Kendall walked behind the car and stood before him, shaking.

"Kendall?"

She was struggling not to cry. "Other men . . . when we were together . . ."

Julian waited.

"It wasn't us."

"It could be. If you stick around."

Nodding, Kendall tried to smile, but started to weep instead. Julian put his arms around her, believing that she wept in penance for her choices and in prayer for a chance to choose again; wept because she had lived according to the dictates of yesterday, guided by ghosts she barely knew existed; and because Julian was right—we are as haunted by the times we live in as by the monsters lurking in our own misshapen selves. Yet as she clung to him, Julian understood that Kendall wept for him and Bobby too—because there was no adequate payment for all that they had lost—and so Julian joined her, their sobs echoing in the garage, both of them weeping as if they wished that their tears could conquer time.

# Acknowledgments

Some books I've written had longer gestation periods than others; *Wherever There Is Light* has been the longest, and so I have an army of people to thank.

I'm grateful to my agent, Susan Golomb, for her wisdom and persistence. Susan brings along two others with no shortage of these qualities, Soumeya Bendimerad and Scott Cohen, and now that Susan has joined Writers House, I'd like to thank Maja Nikolic and Kathryn Stuart for their help.

My first editor, Greer Hendricks, has moved on to other adventures, but not before she improved my manuscript with her discerning eye, and then turned over the pages to the equally discerning assistant editor Daniella Wexler, and editorial director Peter Borland, both of whom helped to shape my novel into its final form.

At Atria Books, I'd also like to thank publisher Judith Curr; associate publisher Suzanne Donahue; publicity manager Ariele Fredman; senior marketing manager Hillary Tisman; production editor Carla Benton; art director Albert Tang; cover designer Greg Mollica; and copy editor Peg Haller. Also a tip of the cap to the Simon & Schuster social media team: executive director of content and programming Sue Fleming; director of programming and merchandising Aimee Boyer; and digital marketing manager Amy Kattan.

I discovered the sunlit corners of Miami Beach as a child, and I was blessed to have my cousins Richard Russ, Denis Russ, and Lori Mishkin as guides. Since then, my corps of South Florida cousins has increased by two—Gina Russ and Andrew Kern, both of whom continue to teach me about all things Miami. In New Jersey, two other cousins were quite helpful: Laynie Golden Gershwin, an excellent family historian, and Sam Gershwin, who answered my questions about the real-estate game. I've been hearing stories about Longy Zwillman since childhood from my grandmothers, Mae Golden and Etta Perelman, both of whom knew him and Newark when they were all young; and my later interviews about Longy with Dr. Milton Shoshkes and the late Dr. Arthur Bernstein were especially enlightening. Karen Robinson, a classmate at South Orange Junior High, spoke to me at length about the challenges faced by African Americans in our hometown during the 1960s; and for the technical knowledge of photography required to create Kendall Wakefield, I received generous amounts of help from Nicholas Argyros, the owner and executive director of the PhotoCenter of the Capital District; and from Judy Sanders, a first-rate journalist and photographer, who sadly passed away shortly before this novel was finished. Marc Douaisi improved my French—an uphill battle—but the errors that remain are mine.

Comments by early readers of the manuscript were invaluable, beginning with the incisive suggestions of Marlene Adelstein. The responses of Kimberley Cetron, Beth Brinser, Nancy Burke, Colleen Reynolds, Howard Dickson, Howard Sperber, and Kathie Bennett kept me going when I felt lost in history's maze.

Others have also been of immeasurable assistance: my brother-in-law, Eric Francis; Maria Buhl at the Guilderland Public Library; Susan Novotny, owner of the Book House of Stuyvesant Plaza and Market Block Books; my friends Tracy Richard and Bruce Davis, Carol and Joe Siracusa, Ellen and Jeff Lewis, David Saltzman, and James Howard Kunstler, who were always available to make me laugh and remind me why I'd wanted to be a writer in the first place. I'd also like to send a heartfelt thanks to all of the salespeople I met as I visited bookstores, and to Kathy L. Murphy and her Pulpwood Queens. Their love of—and dedication to—the written word remind an author that, even in the age of the nanosecond, books are important.

I've spent much of my career looking up things in grand libraries and dusty archives in the United States, Europe, and the Middle East.

I was often hunting for photographs, and now, thanks to Facebook, I do some of that hunting without leaving my office. These groups have been particularly helpful: Memories of Living in South Orange, NJ or Maplewood, NJ; Columbia High School Alumni; Gruning's Ice Cream; I Miss Don's; Vintage New Jersey; Newark, NJ Memories; Raised in Miami Beach; Old Images of New York; Paris Photo; and America in the '60's. I also owe a debt of gratitude to my Facebook friends, who have followed my postings on my research trips, and whose comments and questions frequently helped me clarify where I needed to focus my attention.

In *Wherever There Is Light* I have taken more than a few liberties with history, and the real people you meet in these pages have been transformed into fictional characters. To perform this alchemy, I am indebted to a long list of books. Here is a selection, which is by no means complete: *From Swastika to Jim Crow: Refugee Scholars at Black Colleges* by Gabrielle Simon Edgcomb; *The Reaction of Negro Publications and Organizations to German Anti-Semitism* by Lunabelle Wedlock; *Nazis in Newark* by Warren Grover; *Gangster #2: Longy Zwillman, the Man Who Invented Organized Crime* by Mark Stuart; *Swing City: Newark Nightlife, 1920-1950* by Barbara J. Kukla; *Republic of Dreams: Greenwich Village: The American Bohemia, 1910-1960* by Ross Wetzsteon; *The Village: 400 Years of Beats and Bohemians, Radicals and Rogues* by John Strausbaugh (who on page 207 cited the description of Café Society as "The Wrong Place for the Right People."); *Dorothea Lange* by Linda Gordon; *Margaret Bourke-White* by Vicki Goldberg; *Lee Miller: A Life* by Carolyn Burke; *Robert Doisneau* by Jean Claude Gautrand; *Henri Cartier-Bresson* by Clemént Chéroux; *Street Photography* by Clive Scott; *Exiled in Paris* by James Campbell; *Paris After the Liberation 1944-1949* by Anthony Beevor and Artemis Cooper; *Paris Noir* by Tyler Stovall; *A Hungry Heart* by Gordon Parks; *Paris Journal 1944-1955* by Janet Flanner; *The Secret Life of the Seine* by Mort Rosenblum; *Wild Bill Donovan* by Douglas Waller (The announcement at the Polo Grounds paging Wild Bill after the attack on Pearl Harbor was quoted from Dave Anderson, "The Day Colonel Donovan Was Paged," *New York Times*, 12/1/91.); *The Guns at Last Light* by Rick Atkinson; *Citizen Soldiers* by

Stephen E. Ambrose; *The African-American Soldier* by Lt. Col. [Ret.] Michael Lee Lanning; and *The Invisible Solder: The Experience of the Black Soldier, World War II*, compiled and edited by Mary Penick Motley.

Finally, I'd like to thank the two people who fill the center of my life: my son, Ben, who never fails to inform, impress, and cheer me; and my wife, Annis, reader, fellow adventurer, humorist, and the best friend a writer could have.